ABOUT THIS BOOK

Three steamy paranormal romance novellas (Books 4-6) in this multi-author series showcasing the darker, edgier, and sexier side of Havenwood Falls.

Stolen Wishes by Victoria Flynn

Gabriel Doyle feels drawn to his former hometown in Colorado, especially when the woman in his dreams begins to appear in real life, beckoning him. Needing a fresh start, Alina Anand takes a nanny job for a mage family in Havenwood Falls. At first, life is great, but everything changes when her employers steal her amulet—and take control of her wish-granting powers. When their destinies collide, Gabriel and Alina discover a connection that goes beyond their undeniable passion. But to save Alina, Gabriel must decide—pick up the dark life of bloodshed and revenge he'd left behind or ask for help from those who demand sacrifice.

Damned Allure by Justine Winter

My name is Shade StormIron, and I am an Angel of Death. Some damned souls escaped Hell on my last visit there, and I've gotta track and return these supernatural fugitives before they cause more carnage. I don't expect the mystical town of Havenwood Falls to lure me in with its hidden beauty. Especially the one with sinful legs and silky hair I'm desperate to bury myself into. Sadly, Death is snapping at my ass. Hell demands Nyx's soul, amongst the others, to be returned, and I *will* reap them. I am their courier to Hell.

Savage Salvation by Kristie Cook

My name is Reyna Moreno, and I'm a unicorn, more valuable than the Hope Diamond. Pops swore the SIN motorcycle club in New Orleans could protect me, but now he's dead, and his murderers are after me. So my brother hauls me off to another SIN chapter in Colorado that "takes us in." Takes me prisoner is more like it. My warden is sexy as hell, but he looks at me like he wants to own me. I'm not one to be owned. He's not one to be denied. They call him Savage for a reason. He's a hellhound and a savage beast. And he would be my undoing . . . but maybe I could be his salvation.

HAVENWOOD FALLS SIN & SILK VOLUME TWO

A HAVENWOOD FALLS SIN & SILK COLLECTION

KRISTIE COOK   VICTORIA FLYNN   JUSTINE WINTER

STOLEN WISHES

VICTORIA FLYNN

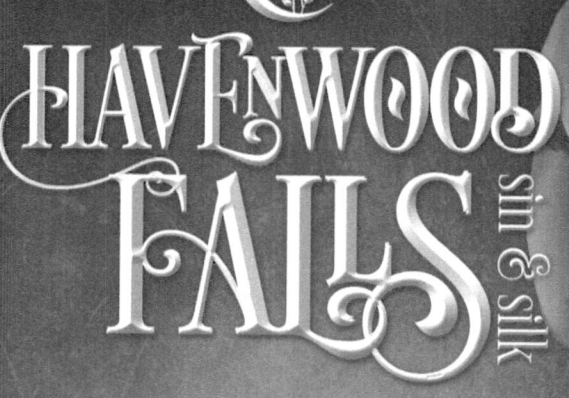

~ A Havenwood Falls Sin & Silk Novella ~

HAVENWOOD FALLS

sin & silk

Stolen Wishes

VICTORIA FLYNN

ALSO BY VICTORIA FLYNN

The Voodoo Revival Series (1–3, 4 coming soon)

Ravaged

Fly Me Home (Rescue Squad Shifters #1)

For Love and Lust. May the two forever enhance the spice of life.

PROLOGUE

GABRIEL

*H*er skin was smooth and flawless like Chinese porcelain, and the way her heart drummed excitedly in her chest when I touched her drove me wild. She was a drug I was hopelessly addicted to.

"I've missed you," she whispered, dropping the sheet she had wrapped around herself.

The scent of her arousal invaded my senses and blurred any clear thoughts. All-consuming, that was what the vixen was to me.

Tugging my shirt over my head and throwing it to the ground, I strode toward my prize. Her nipples were drawn up into tight buds as I crossed the expanse of my hotel suite to her. Oh yes, she wanted me. She rubbed her thighs together as if it could relieve the pressure of her desire.

"You're all I can think about. Even when I'm awake, I feel like I'm just passing the time until you're in my arms again," I confessed.

My nameless beauty closed the gap between us, nipping the tender flesh over my collar bone and sliding down me, sinking to her knees. Her hands worked quickly to free me from my slacks. My cock sprung free and her eyes devoured every inch. Her pink tongue swept over her lips, and her eyes dared me to deny her what she wanted.

"Hungry?" I teased, stepping out of my pants and fisting my throbbing cock.

She nodded slowly, leaning forward until her breath fanned over me, making me damn near lose control on the spot. Her fingers skimmed over my sensitive skin before wrapping around me securely. Her hand slid up and down my length lazily, and I let my eyes fall closed, relishing every second. Her hot, slick tongue traced the thick shaft from the bottom up, and her lips enveloped me as she reached the top.

"Fuck," I groaned, my hips flexing instinctively and driving me deeper into her mouth.

I could feel the muscles of her mouth stretch into a coy smile just before she set about her task, taking me in as deeply as she could. Pressure was growing low in my belly, and every nerve was firing like a Fourth of July display. Picking up the pace, her head bobbed up and down as she pushed me faster toward my peak. Her deft fingers worked furiously between her legs. It was a sight that would drive a lesser man to his knees with need, but she was mine, only mine, to savor.

She repeated the same pattern, taking me in deep and then flicking her succulent tongue over the head of my dick. The woman was driving me wild and playing me like a well-loved instrument. Her free hand snaked down, cupping my balls and dragging her nails over them, bringing me to my tipping point.

"Christ, you need to stop, or I'm going to come," I warned her, holding back and giving her plenty of time to release her hold, but she didn't.

Her devious eyes darted to my own, dancing with mirth as she sucked harder. I was a goner under her skilled touch. Not two minutes later, thick ropes of cum erupted from me, coating her throat as I roared in ecstasy. The vixen swallowed down every drop like she was starved for it, drawing it out until my last spasm faded.

She licked her lips with satisfaction, her heavy-lidded eyes betraying her arousal.

"I want more."

Drained of energy, I crossed to the bed and held my hand out to her. Just before she came close enough, the room faded to black, and she was torn away from me.

My eyes cracked open before I could reach her. The room was dark, but I could tell the sun was beginning to set. It was another dream.

Every day for months, the bronzed goddess had visited me and drawn me into her thrall. Women had thrown themselves at me, yet the nameless woman from my dreams had been all I could think about. Hell, my dick wouldn't even respond to another anymore, not of its own volition anyway. My cock was painfully hard, and my fangs dug into my lower lip with my desire, despite the exotic woman's absence.

I could still see her stunning figure standing before me as vividly as though it had just happened, begging me to come for her. Her sensuous voice called to me, telling me she was waiting for me in Havenwood Falls, and I couldn't live on dreams anymore. I had to know if she was real, no matter what.

CHAPTER 1

GABRIEL

*T*here it was again. The relentless pull to leave. This time was different, though. This time, it whispered a name I'd heard before . . . in my dreams. My recurring vision came back to me. An exotic beauty and somewhere called Havenwood Falls. The name had been repeated until it was all I could think about. When I'd done a search, nothing had shown up. I decided to make some calls. Eventually, I'd been able to narrow it down to the mountains of Colorado. No one could remember the town, nor its location, but I'd been told at least twice that I should check out the majestic mountains of the western state. With the red-eye tickets booked, I gave my thoughts back to the beauty who'd been haunting me. I could still picture her sensual form standing before me in my Paris hotel room, whispering for me to come to her in the mysterious town. She was waiting for me.

In the many nights we'd shared, never had I learned her name. It tormented me incessantly. When I ventured out into the city, it never failed that I'd catch a glimpse of a woman who shared some feature with the woman I'd come to care for—long black hair like a raven's feather, a rich tan, eyes like a smooth cognac. Those women were never her.

I pushed the thoughts away, not wanting to obsess over the identity of the mystery woman more than I already had. Swirling my whiskey around the tumbler, I stood on my suite's balcony overlooking Montmartre.

Paris had grown gray with the late autumn season. Rain drizzled down on the city, and I found I wasn't sad to be leaving. When you lived as long as I had, cities like London, Rome, Paris, and Prague lost their luster.

Home.

It was an odd thought. The closest thing I'd ever had to a home had been with my closest friend and sire, Viktor. He'd settled somewhere in Colorado and started a small empire for himself.

He was gone now, which had been a large part of why I'd stayed away from America as long as I had. Would home still be home if the person who made it special was no longer there? That was still to be seen.

"Lorenzo!" I called out, striding into the parlor and abandoning the balcony overlooking the narrow streets of France.

"What can I do for you, sir?" the small Italian man chirped, appearing almost out of nowhere.

"You may let the staff know we will be departing for America in the coming week. Have you ever been to Colorado, Enzo?" I asked, loosening my tie.

"No, sir. This will be my first trip." His thick Italian accent was barely comprehensible. "I hope you'll let me know what to expect and what I should pack for."

"It's late autumn. The Colorado mountains are cold, damp, and could be snow-covered. Layers, my friend."

"*Grazie*, sir. I will make the necessary arrangements. May I ask why the sudden change in plans? I was under the impression we'd be staying in Paris until the end of January before continuing on to Amsterdam."

Lorenzo was good people and the only person I fully trusted. He was nearly forty and had been in my service since he'd reached adulthood. As a blood servant went, he was top notch, and as a friend, he was one of my closest. His family had served me since Viktor had raised me out of the gutter and turned me into a proper gentleman over three centuries earlier. Blend in, watch, find a weakness, and exploit it—those had been my first lessons. I'd done that when I'd stumbled across Alessio De Luca, Lorenzo's seventh great grandfather. He'd been able to do something I'd thought was lost to me since becoming a vampire: he could make me laugh. Instead of killing the poor bastard, I'd offered him a job. The rest, as they say, was history.

"It's hard to explain. I've always been a nomad. However, there's something different about Colorado. It's the closest thing I've ever had to a home, even more than Ireland," I joked, letting my natural brogue slip back into my words.

"How long?" Enzo asked, concern written in the shallow creases beginning to form from age.

Despite being a few hundred years younger than me, Lorenzo looked older than my frozen twenty-eight years.

"I haven't been home in more than forty years. Not since before Viktor passed," I answered, ignoring the pangs of loss that could still send me reeling, if I let them.

"Understandable, sir. He was a father to you, and that sort of grief is felt for a lifetime," he replied.

He was right. I knew Viktor was gone, but going home without his warm welcome would be difficult. That was the thing about vampires—we'd grieve a loss for centuries, because time no longer mattered. Things were felt on a deeper level because such things are fleeting.

"I suppose you're right, but there are other matters to tackle while on this trip," I answered, and there were.

Being a vampire came with its constraints, like not being able to walk in the daylight, but it also gave those like me ample time to grow a fortune. Unlike some, I'd grown with the times, seeing no point in dwelling on the inventions and ideals of the past. When the internet had come along, I'd invested, knowing that it would somehow change the future of the modern world. Then had come the capability to conduct such investments online, and I never needed to work again. When you've been around longer than the stock market itself, you pick up a thing or two about money, stock trends, and good investments. Having spent the better part of two centuries building a fortune, I was now in a position to make moves and flex my muscles. Everyone, regardless of species, could recognize that money was power, and whoever had the most made the rules of how the rest played the game.

"I'm sorry, Gabriel. I don't follow," Enzo said.

I frowned slightly, realizing I hadn't mentioned the dreams or the side trip.

"I apologize, old friend. Things have been difficult. These dreams I've been having . . . I've never experienced anything like them. Actually, I don't believe I remember ever dreaming until a few months ago."

"Would you like me to search the archives? Perhaps there could be an answer there as to what this means?"

I nodded. "Sure. Thank you, Lorenzo. That would be helpful, though my point was that in these dreams, a voice keeps saying *Havenwood Falls*. I think it's in Colorado, near Viktor's old home. I need to know if there's something to all of this there."

"I understand. I'll make the necessary preparations. In the meantime, you haven't fed in a few days," he stated, undoing the button holding his sleeve together.

"I've already booked our flights, but other transportation will need to be arranged."

Enzo pushed his sleeve up, exposing his arm to me. He sat on the sofa, leaving room for me to join him. A pinch in my gums was all I needed to know my fangs had extended, ready to feed. The tight hold I kept on the monster inside me slipped a little, and I pounced on Lorenzo's offering. My fangs tore through his flesh like a hot knife through butter. His blood was like cinnamon and cloves, spicy and aromatic. I drank until the beast inside me was sated and released before I'd taken too much. Like the professional he was, Enzo produced a small hanky and wiped the crimson smear at the edge of my mouth before wrapping his wound tightly. He rose a little unsteadily, my only indication that I'd gotten a little carried away this time. With a quick bow, Lorenzo turned and exited the room.

Shame coursed through me.

There was a time I wouldn't have felt anything for those I'd fed from. Anyone who was unlucky enough to cross my path was lower than me on the food chain; it was natural. That's what I'd told myself for years. Hell, I'd lived for the hunt. The feeling when life finally left someone and the light faded from their eyes had been a drug to me. Viktor and I had even gone to war on several occasions, making a game of killing our foes in the most imaginative way possible. Grown men had fallen in shreds at my feet. Then one day, all of that changed.

I couldn't put a finger on what had been the turning point for me, but after almost a century of living in a constant bloodbath, I'd found myself wanting more. Viktor was calculating. One always had to be on their toes around him. He'd taught me a lot, yet there no longer seemed to be a point to life without someone to share it with, on a different level. I wanted to watch art be born from a beautiful mind and bright thinkers rise to the famed pages of history. I wanted to experience it all as a free man.

As a mortal, I'd been nothing more than a slave. Despite the practice being considered illegal, I'd been taken after the soldiers slaughtered my mother at the Siege of Galway, when King Charles II's men came to topple Catholicism in Ireland. My father had succumbed to the pox a year earlier, along with my little sister, Mary. In my twenty-eight years as a human, I'd never known what it was to do as I pleased. As a vampire, I was desperate for a taste of freedom.

My change of heart had driven a wedge between Viktor and me, but eventually, he came to understand that I needed more than he could give me. Like a baby bird, I had reached the time to leave the nest and spread my wings. So, I did.

In my arrogance and stubbornness, I'd lost almost thirty years with my sire. He'd been gone more than ten years now, lost to the insanity that came with drinking drug-tainted blood. I couldn't help feeling responsible for it. If I had been there, would things have gone differently for him? I'd spent far too long running away from my past, and it was time to go home. It was time to say my final goodbyes to Viktor Azimov, my father and sire, and it was time to look to the future and the mysteries that Havenwood Falls would offer.

CHAPTER 2

ALINA

$\mathcal{D}$addy was going to be pissed. Anands stuck together and never ventured too far from the family. Family was protection, and to Daddy, that was everything. Me getting a job hours away from home wouldn't be acceptable, but at twenty-four, it was necessary if I was to keep any of my sanity or sense of self.

I glanced at the scribbled details on the front page of my open notebook.

Havenwood Falls.

I'd never heard of it before, and no matter how many times I'd put the town into my GPS, I still came up with nothing. It was worrying. Was it so small that it didn't show up on maps?

"Do you really have to go? Things won't be the same with you gone," my younger sister, Kalene, whined from where she sat in my computer chair.

"I know, but this is something I have to do. If it doesn't work out, then fine, I can always come back home. What if it does work out though? I could have that life I've always dreamed of, a place of my own where I make my own rules, my own life. Besides, you're getting a little old to need someone to cover for your antics."

"I know, but where's the fun in that? You have to promise me that you'll still come home to visit sometimes, and after you're settled, I'll come up for a weekend. Who knows, maybe I'll fall in love with Hardwood Springs and never leave," she teased.

"Havenwood Falls. Hardwood Springs? Where did you pull that from?" I chuckled, throwing the last of my toiletries into my bag.

"Ehh, potato, potahto," she shrugged.

Kalene was only a year younger than I was, but was easily still eighteen mentally. She wasn't the type to take much seriously, but it was what I loved about her.

"All right, it's a deal. I promise to come home, and as long as it's allowed, you're welcome to come stay with me when you need to get out of here for a while."

I slid the zipper closed and moved to sit on the bed next to her. Kalene threw her arm over my shoulders and leaned in. This was going to be the last time we sat on my bed together. I'd miss her horribly, but there were absolutely zero doubts in my mind that I was doing the right thing. Space and the chance to make something for myself without my father dictating what my duties were would only ever be possible if I left.

The clock on the wall chimed. It was time to go. If I didn't get on the road, I'd miss the bus to the place where I was laying down roots —Havenwood Falls.

I bid my family who would still speak to me farewell; my father was not among them. My mother said he'd come around, and they'd come to visit me, but the rift in the family was being felt by everyone. My older brother had yet to speak to me since I'd announced I was leaving. Of my three siblings, Kalene was the only one who got it. She understood my need to leave, to be free to live my life the way I wanted to and not by what my parents told me I had to do. If they couldn't cut the cord, then I would. That's what I reminded myself of as my car pulled away from the only home I'd ever known. I was closing the door on one part of my life and turning the page to begin something new; the thrill of not knowing what lay ahead was intoxicating.

Kalene drove me to the bus station, bidding me a teary farewell and promising to come visit after Christmas. Despite the sorrow I was feeling, I couldn't hide my excitement. I was practically bouncing in my seat. When the bus finally pulled up, I almost sprinted for the open door, ready to begin this new adventure.

I climbed on board and found a seat near the back of the bus. Pulling my jacket tighter around me, I put my hood up and dug out my ear phones, flipping to my favorite radio station on my phone. Ducking my face, I tried to make myself invisible as another twenty or so people filed their way onto the bus and into seats. Luckily, no one decided to occupy the one directly next to mine.

It wasn't that I didn't like people—I did—but I'd been burned by false niceties and so-called friends too many times to go out of my way to create more relationships. So I kept to myself and liked it that way. When my cousin, Malia, sent me the job listing and it wasn't something where I'd have to put on a fake smile, I'd nearly teleported to the town on the spot. As luck would have it, the Grandvilles—a prestigious old English family familiar with the ways of magic—had hired me after only a brief telephone interview. The parameters were set in stone, and there was no doubt where I stood with these people. I'd do my job and care for their children, and they'd pay me enough to finance a life of my own. All I had to do was relax and enjoy the ride.

I closed my eyes and let the landscape pass by as the journey got underway. Soulful country ballads about love and heartbreak lulled me into a near sleep-like state, aided by the swaying motion of the bus. Somewhere along the way, not too long into the trip, I drifted off to sleep.

A cool breeze caressed my bare skin. Glancing down, I realized I was wearing a sand-colored sheer dress and not much more than that. My hair fell in curls down my back.

"I almost thought you weren't coming," a deep masculine voice said from behind me.

His words were heavy with an Irish brogue that turned my insides molten. Bright blue eyes greeted mine, crinkled with a warm smile.

"Where are we?" I asked, turning to take in the room.

A massive four-poster bed sat against the innermost wall, draped in white muslin and red silk. I squeezed my thighs together to stave off the desire that had ignited within me.

His arms circled around my waist as he pulled me back against his solid chest. My ass pressed back against the hard ridge that tented his slacks. As if by instinct, I wanted to submit and open myself up to this stranger, but was he really a stranger? The way he spoke to me and touched me made me think we'd known each other for years.

"Paris, for now," he whispered, before his lips latched onto my ear lobe.

My breath hitched, and my knees threatened to buckle under his expert touch. His ravenous lips trailed down to the junction of my neck and shoulder, placing a tender kiss there. Reaching back, my fingers threaded through his thick brown hair, tugging just enough to spur him on. Dragging me against the hard planes of his body, he lifted my skirt and his hand disappeared as he inched closer to my aching core.

The squealing of brakes jolted me out of my slumber just when things were getting good. It was another dream, and I wanted to kick myself for enjoying it as much as I had. No man had ever touched me with such passion as *he* had. He'd been working me into a frenzy several nights a week, always remaining a mystery. I'd agonized over his identity, praying he was real and would find his way to me, to no avail. I doubted a real man ever would ravage me the way I craved when I was with him. Those weren't the sort of men my father wanted for me, anyway.

Rubbing the sleep from my eyes, I glanced out the window, but couldn't get a good look at the town. The sun had long since gone down, and the moon was nearly nonexistent, making the night sky darker than I was used to in Denver. Street lights shone brightly on the little town that would be my new home.

The bus rolled to a stop. One by one, we filed down the narrow aisle and out onto the cold street. The bus driver was busy pulling suitcases from the storage compartment and piling them in a heap behind him. He didn't stick around too long. By the time I had my fingers wrapped around the handle of my bag, he had the bus doors shut and was shifting into gear.

"See ya, wouldn't wanna be ya," I murmured under my breath.

The crowd around me was quickly dispersing to their individual locations. People spread in every direction around the town square, disappearing before I could ask anyone if they knew where I was supposed to go.

The only thing I had to go on was an address. Strangely, no matter how many times I tried to pull up the map app on my phone, it couldn't or wouldn't get a read on where I was. It was useless. The only directions I had were that the home was in someplace called Creekwood, and it was off the main drag into town. When I pulled up the compass app, the needle just swung around aimlessly.

Strange.

If I could get away with it, I would use my magic to zap my butt right on over to the address on the paper, but I couldn't risk anyone seeing me. I'd never dared to use it outside the privacy of home before, and I wasn't about to start in an unfamiliar place.

"Never let anyone see your magic. It's special, my little Lina, and always keep your opal safe." My father's words replayed in my head, the same as they did every time I wanted to use my powers outside.

Too risky.

Glancing around the town square, I spied a woman closing up shop for the night. Not wasting any time, I quickly headed straight for her. Pride went right out the window when it came to being lost.

"Excuse me?" I called out, hurrying over to her.

The woman cast a quick glance over her shoulder, seeming surprised that I was addressing her.

"Yes?" she said.

"Hi! Sorry, I'm new here, just arrived actually, and I was hoping you could tell me where to find somewhere called Creekwood? Here's the address," I explained, handing over the small piece of paper with my destination scribbled on it. "Gosh, I'm sorry. Where are my manners? My name's Alina Anand."

"Hannah Pederson. Nice to meet you," she answered, extending her hand to me.

As I shook her hand, she quickly grabbed the paper and scanned over its contents. While she was reading, I looked her over a little closer. Hannah's hair was short and wild with rich fiery high- and lowlights throughout. She was petite and utterly adorable, the sort of woman that could make anyone at ease with just her presence.

"Okay, so this is just up the road that way. Right when you come into town on County Road 13, it's to the left. Look for Blackstone Road, it splits from the County Road, and Creekwood's right there, can't miss it."

"Thank you so much!" I replied, waving farewell.

Putting one foot in front of the other, I began the short walk to Creekwood. The moon was barely a sliver, casting long shadows along the valley. Mountains towered over the town, boxing it in on all sides. The night air was cold, and snow coated the ground. I pulled my coat tighter around me and kept my quick pace. Something was unsettling about my new home. The town was . . . different. Though I couldn't quite put my finger on what was off. Toeing the line between being afraid and having enough confidence in my magic to defend myself, I kept a close eye on the darkness between lampposts. It was the sort of darkness that put you on edge and made you feel like you were being watched from just beyond the borders of the lights. I may have been a Marid djinn, but I wasn't naïve enough to think I was the baddest being out there. There were things that would give even my kind nightmares.

Djinn like me had a long history of falling prey to more powerful beings. The legend was that we descended from Set, who grew jealous of Amani and Khalida, the djinn twins created by Sekhmet and Shu. He thought he could replicate them and set out to do just that. Eventually, the Marid line was born.

The wish granters.

Our power was rooted in the elements we were born from and only a fraction of the god's power, but it was enough. Each individual had his or her own strength, be it brewing up snow for a white

Christmas or conjuring a chest full of precious gems. All Marids could step between planes of existence, making travel rather convenient, as we could teleport anywhere we wanted or make a fast escape. However, there were limits. We couldn't change someone's heart or bring back the dead, much to the dismay of some.

We could make someone's dreams come true, their every desire, and that's why they wanted us so badly. If you had control of a being who could make your fantasy a reality, you'd be the most powerful person in the world. Some Marids became cocky, too loose with their magic. So we'd been cursed, each of our souls and our sources of power tied to a special object, one we must keep safe at all costs. It was a safeguard of sorts. It could be our prison or grant our freedom, because without the object, no one could force us to do anything.

My fingers went to the opal necklace set into a gold floral filigree setting hanging down between my breasts. It was still there, a stark reminder of what I had to lose. No one could know about the necklace.

When I'd first been contacted by the Grandvilles, they'd been very upfront about needing someone with certain *capabilities* to help with the children. They didn't want just any paranormal being. They wanted someone who could handle a fledgling witch. When asked what type of being I was, I had been reticent to answer truthfully, although my cousin, Malia, was known for having loose lips and had readily told the woman what I was. When Mrs. Grandville admitted to already knowing my lineage, she mentioned wanting to know how forthcoming I was with sensitive information. The family was very private, homeschooling the children and keeping to themselves as often as possible. My own family had been the same way, albeit for different reasons. My kind were fairly rare, having been hunted to the brink of extinction. That information could easily put a target on my back.

I'd left home because my father and family were stifling me, beyond overbearing. They were always reminding me how unsafe it was to live alone, out in the world, but it was all I'd ever wanted. A job to support myself, traveling the world, meeting new people—all of it had been my dream since I was small, and the reality was now within reach. If I had stayed at home, my father would have found me a suitable match and expected me to settle down and make more djinn babies, as he thought was my lot in life. He'd never really taken the opportunity to get to know me. If he had, he'd have known I'd never go along with something like that. I was headstrong, like him.

The street lamp overhead flickered. I quickened my pace, seeing the neighborhood come into view. So what if I was a magical being? The dark still creeped me out when I was alone and made me feel like a helpless child again. The only difference was now as an adult, I knew what lurked in the dark, and it was every bit as terrifying as I'd thought.

I passed into the neighborhood, eyeing the houses as best as I could. Most were lit up; it was still early, only six thirty, and families were settling down for dinner. The homes were nice—nothing too extravagant, yet clearly upscale and well maintained. Digging into my pockets, I searched for the paper with the address, realizing that I could've already passed it, as I was lost in my thoughts.

259 Flynn Court.

There was a cross street ahead, the street sign lit by the light overhead.

Flynn Court.

I was in the right place, then. I moved quickly, noting the odd numbers were on the left. Passing house after house without finding my destination, I began to worry the house didn't exist. Was it all some elaborate prank? Would some college kid jump out with a camera at any moment?

There was a single house left on the street. It had to be the one I was looking for. Shrubs grew up around the cement front porch, creating a sort of fence that obscured most of the lower level of the home. The two-story brick house sported large windows, flanked by black shutters, and mostly closed off by curtains. A mature rowan tree stood in the center of the front yard. I couldn't make out the numbers on the house from the road, so I ventured closer.

The numbers were hidden by the shrubs, however as I got closer, I could make out the 259 more clearly. I was finally in the right place. Climbing the stairs, I placed myself square with the door and hesitated before knocking. A million things that could go wrong stampeded through my thoughts.

Taking one last deep breath, I rapped my knuckles against the wooden door. I stepped back, not wanting to seem overbearing. I heard the distinct click of heels on a hard surface before a shadow appeared on the other side of the door through the frosted window. The door swung in, and a woman no more than thirty-five stood in its entrance. Her face was slim, angular, and austere, with an upturned button nose. Her light brown hair was waved to perfection. Her pouty mouth turned down in a frown as she took me in.

"Hi! My name's Alina Anand, and I believe I have the right address. Are you Mrs. Grandville?" I asked, extending my hand forth.

CHAPTER 3

ALINA

*H*er nose scrunched in disgust as she stared at my hand and then up at my face again.

"So, you're the genie," she surmised, appraising me.

Well, this is certainly not what I was expecting, I thought to myself.

"Djinn. Yes, ma'am, I am. You can just call me Alina." I tried to keep my calm as she looked down her nose at me.

"I'm Edith Grandville, but you will address me by Mrs. Grandville. Am I clear?"

I nodded quickly, not wanting to make a crap first impression. My magic prickled under my skin, being so near to another powerful being. I wondered briefly if she felt it, too, though I didn't have the courage to ask.

Is she always so formal and uptight? I wondered, despite my gut saying yes. She stepped aside, tipping her head to invite me in. I passed into her home and immediately noted the house was practically a museum. Nothing looked used or out of place, and every surface was spotless.

Mrs. Grandville moved around me and came to a stop, blocking my path farther into the house. With a flick of her hand, the door closed securely behind me. Her hand gave a sharp twist, and I could hear the metallic sound of the lock being turned. My eyes widened. I had known the Grandvilles were magical, but seeing it firsthand was a shock. I'd never seen another supernatural outside of my own family, and that was precisely the way my family had wanted it.

"You're not what I expected a witch to be like," I blurted before I could even stop myself. "I'm sorry, that was very rude of me. I just haven't been around many other people with magic."

Her eyes narrowed into slits.

"I take it manners aren't a part of your résumé? If you absolutely must know, I'm a witch, as are my children and my husband, and every member of our family dating back to the original. So please, be diligent about not using your charms around my children. They are young and impressionable, just beginning to learn about what they are and the roles they will play in this family. I don't want their heads filled with any other rubbish," she snapped, her English accent coming through thickly.

I'd apparently struck a nerve, though it was clear the woman had a great deal of pride in their lineage. It was something I could understand. Marids were a proud race, dating our lines back over a millennium. However, there were a lot of dark spots and blemishes along the way. We could be hard to control. For the most part, we didn't bring up the seedier parts of our history.

Mrs. Grandville circled around me, lips pursed, which made her almost plastic face seem even tighter. I bit my lip, trying to push away the uneasy feeling that churned in my gut. Her heels clicked against the tiled floor, echoing off the stark white walls of the foyer.

"I suppose you'll have to do. This way," she said as she turned and headed through the door and disappeared deeper into the house.

It took me a moment to gather my senses and follow my new employer. The unease hadn't lessened any, and I was beginning to regret my decision to take the job without meeting the family I'd be living with. It was clear she didn't much care for me, but I'd regret not giving this a shot. Experience was experience, even if it was bad.

At the foot of the staircase stood my new charges.

Tabitha and Cornelius, ages eleven and eight.

Luckily, I'd been sent all of the pertinent information about the children, so I wasn't walking in totally blind. The pair stood straight-backed and proper, keeping their stares downcast. Both were startlingly similar in their physical appearance to their mother, right down to the button noses. Tabitha's navy-blue skirt was complemented by a matching sweater vest and a white blouse that made her look older, more akin to a boarding school student in her uniform than an average girl her age. Cornelius was just as proper in his burgundy polo and khaki pants.

"Children, this is your new governess, Ms. Anand. You will make her feel welcome, is that clear?" she asked sternly.

"Yes, ma'am," the pair answered in unison.

"Ms. Anand, these are the children, Tabitha and Cornelius," Mrs. Grandville announced with prideful expectation.

I seized the opportunity, the need to make the best possible first impression my driving force. Placing my bag down, I extended my hand toward Tabitha first and dropped into a crouch so I was eye level with the two.

"Hi, Tabitha. You can just call me Lina if you want to. I won't mind. Same goes for you, Cornelius. I'm new at this, but I think we're going to get along pretty great. What do you think?"

The pair of them eyed my hand like they'd never seen one in their lives before casting wary sideways glances at each other. Mrs. Grandville sighed heavily, making her great disappointment known, frowning deeply.

"You're both dismissed," Mrs. Grandville barked, turning her focus to me. "Ms. Anand, I hope you understand what we're trying to do here. We are raising the next generation of Grandvilles, and such a task requires an immense amount of discipline and structure. The children don't need to be coddled; no one will do that for them in the real world. They need to know what our expectations of them are and prepare themselves accordingly. That's where you come in. You were not hired to be their friend. Have I made myself clear?" she asked icily.

My throat went dry on the spot.

I croaked, "Yes, ma'am."

My brows rose in disbelief. These were children, not soldiers. They needed fun, games, love, friends . . . but who was I to question her rules?

With a curt nod, Mrs. Grandville turned on her heel and climbed up the staircase and into a small hallway beside it. I followed close behind, but we didn't have to travel far. There was only a single door set into the hall's end wall.

"This is your room. All of your belongings are to remain in this room, and guests are not permitted. It is my understanding that you have family who would wish to visit with you, but you'll need to do any visiting in town and ensure that such visits do not interfere with your duties. Understood?" she asked.

I nodded before my mouth outpaced my good sense.

The hope that had begun to take root in my heart turned sour in the span of a moment. I had expected something entirely different than what was being presented to me. I had always enjoyed playing with my young cousins and listening to their wild, imaginative tales, which made me hope I would enjoy working with children. Upon my internet search, I'd found that most nannies became an integral part of the family, one of my many hopes when I'd taken the job. However, Mrs. Grandville was making damn sure I knew I was very clearly an outsider here.

"On the bed, you'll find a list of approved meals, emergency contacts, and schedules. Any outings you wish to take the children on must be first approved by myself or Mr. Grandville. It should also go without saying that as young and impressionable children who are new to their studies, they should not be exposed to certain types of charms," Mrs. Grandville explained.

"So no magic in front of Tabitha or Cornelius?" I clarified.

She nodded.

"All right. That's fine. I'm not really comfortable using it in front of people anyway. You never know who's watching."

"Good. I should also mention that Havenwood Falls is different than other places you may have visited. The supernatural make up a sizeable portion of the population, which, of course, requires a different set of rules. The Court of the Sun and the Moon will need you to be registered in order to stay in the town. Adelaide Beaumont will arrive shortly to begin your tattoo and registration."

"Tattoo?" I questioned.

"Yes, it's fairly simple. There are wards around the town. The tattoos are spelled to work with the wards and serve as your registration. So, get settled as best you can. Ms. Beaumont will arrive shortly."

Without another word, Mrs. Grandville turned and exited the room. As soon as she was clear of the doorway, her hand flicked overhead, and the door swung shut behind her. For someone who was so uptight, she sure flexed her magic when it suited her. The click of her heels echoed as she retreated down the hall and descended the stairs.

I had been dismissed.

Taking in the small room, I tried to remind myself that this experience was what I would make it. The room, albeit small and plain, was a blank canvas; one I could change and shape to suit my needs. And the Grandville children? Well, we'd work on it. There had to be some common ground and wiggle room to be found. That became my new mission, my purpose, and damn it if I was going to let a challenge go unanswered.

Not quite twenty minutes later, there was a knock at my door.

"Come in," I called out, putting the last of my clothes into the drawers I'd been provided.

A girl about my age with light brown hair popped her head inside the door carefully.

"Hi, are you Alina?" she asked, pushing the door open wide enough for her to slip through and shutting it quietly behind her.

"Yeah, you must be Ms. Beaumont," I said, sliding the drawer closed with my hip and extending my hand to her.

She shook my hand firmly as her eyes raked around me and over my body with a warm smile.

"You can just call me Addie. It's very nice to meet you. Has anyone explained what's going to happen or the process?" Addie asked, pulling up a chair and seating herself across from the bed.

"Briefly, but I'm still a bit confused as to why this is necessary."

"I get that all that time. So Havenwood Falls is protected by magical wards," she began, cupping her hand over several bracelets adorning her wrist.

"Yeah, Mrs. Grandville mentioned that part."

"Good. Basically, the wards ensure we don't let just anyone in this town, like those who wish to bring harm. The registry and the tattoos are linked to the wards, so we know who's in town and when someone leaves," Addie explained. "The wards extend to about twenty-five miles beyond the official city limits on all sides, so there's plenty of room to roam. But beyond that, the tattoo disappears and no longer works. As you can imagine, with a town full of supernatural beings, we need to know who's here, why, and how long they plan to stay. You know, so in case something goes bad, we know who to hunt down." She smiled before continuing. "For the most part, everyone gets along without too much trouble, but when they don't, there are consequences, just like with human laws. Number one rule—protect the secret. Do not ever let the humans see you do magic or clue them in to what their neighbors really are."

Finally, the tiny Colorado town was beginning to make sense.

"So that's why there was the in-depth background check before I was offered the position as the Grandvilles' nanny?"

Addie nodded.

"And why the town wasn't on any maps or why I couldn't find any directions to drive myself here?"

"Yep," Addie said, popping the *p* at the end. "So any ideas for a design for your tattoo?"

"Not really. I only just learned of all of this about a half hour ago. The tattoo was a bit of a shock, and I've never had one before."

"Don't worry. I promise it won't hurt. What kinds of things do you think are pretty or catch your eye? What do you like to do? Maybe something to make it easier to access your elemental magic?

I'm really flexible. I just need an idea to go on, and I can sketch something out."

"I guess if I had to choose, something feminine in black and grey, maybe on the inside of my forearm? I know that's not very helpful."

"Don't worry about it. Give me a minute to draw something up, and we can go from there. Go ahead and finish unpacking or whatever you still have to do while I'm busy."

"Great," I said weakly.

I didn't handle needles or pain well at all. There wasn't too much that needed to be put away since I'd traveled light. With only having a single bedroom, I didn't have too much space at my disposal, and I hated clutter more than anything.

Addie pulled a pad out of her bag and began to sketch. From where I stood, I couldn't tell what she was drawing, although it looked sort of like some kind of flower. Whatever it was looked intricate . . . likely requiring a whole lot of pokes to finish. Inhaling deeply, I tried not to think about the tattoo or the process and counted to three before exhaling.

"It'll be all right, I promise. I can help you relax if you want me to or even make it so you don't feel a thing." She wiggled her fingers in the air.

I shook my head. "No, thanks. It's not that I wouldn't appreciate it and it's nothing personal, but I just met you. I'm not comfortable with anything more than this right now."

"I totally get it. That's smart by the way, not trusting people too easily. That's how you survive."

"My dad always drilled into my siblings and me the importance of being cautious, especially with our magic," I explained.

"He sounds like a smart man," Addie remarked.

"More like overbearing, but yeah. If it were up to him, I'd never leave home and basically live under a rock where the world doesn't know I exist."

Addie didn't say anything right away, but she stopped what she was doing.

"I can't really blame him there. Don't get me wrong, I see your side of things and I'm the same way, but your kind aren't very common. In fact, I don't believe I've ever met a Marid djinn before. A djinn, yes, but not a Marid."

"How did you know what I was? I haven't really told anyone other than the Grandvilles."

"I have my ways," she said slyly, before flipping the notepad around to show me her completed drawing.

I'd been right when I thought it was a flower, but it was so much more. It was a mandala with eight petals and tiny scrollwork, lines, and dots dancing around its interior. It was stunning and perfect and so very me.

"Do you like it?" Addie asked when I didn't say anything right away.

"Oh yes. It's perfect." My fingers brushed over the delicate design.

Addie pulled her bag onto her lap and withdrew her kit. She unsheathed several needles and began to fill tiny cups with the ink she'd brought with her. I felt like I was watching a surgeon prepare for an open-heart surgery, though nowhere near as dangerous, even if my palms were sweating enough to give that impression.

"Excellent. Let's get started, shall we?" she suggested.

Hesitantly, I sat down across from her. My hands were shaking in spite of my attempts to calm myself.

"Is there a way for you to spell yourself into a calmer state?" she asked.

I nodded. "Yes, but this is something I should suck up and get over. I don't like using my magic as a crutch."

"Oh, well, good for you. Magic can be tempting to abuse. Just let me know if you need to stop, and I'll be happy to."

I squeezed my eyes shut and pushed my arm out toward Addie.

"Let's just do the damn thing," I muttered.

"That's the attitude I like!"

Addie applied the cool stencil to my arm and transferred the image in a bright purple ink. The buzz of the machine filled my ears, making my heart jump in my chest. I turned my face away from Addie and my arm and dug my teeth into my lip. I felt the pressure as

Addie touched the needle head to my skin and began tracing the fine lines of the mandala. There was no pain and almost no blood. Shocked at the feather light touch, I turned my face back toward her, watching Addie interestedly.

"Not as bad as you thought it would be?" she asked.

I could hear the smile in her words as she said it.

"Not at all. I'd always heard it hurt, and this is barely more than an annoyance."

"I'm decent at what I do, and these go a little differently than your average tattoo. There's magic in them, so its effect is a little different for everyone, but you're doing great, and your skin looks like it's reacting well to the ink. This should be done in no time at all. Just relax."

And I did.

Addie and I chatted while she worked, learning more about each other. She told me about the town and some of its inhabitants, like being careful about straying onto pack land or into the bears' territory, which I had zero intention of doing anytime soon. She didn't look down on me for what I was or act like she was better than me in any way, not like Mrs. Grandville had. Something told me if given the opportunity, Addie and I could be good friends in time.

I'd been in Havenwood Falls less than two hours, and I'd already found someone whom I could see being friends with. I was going to like my new home, pissy bosses or not.

CHAPTER 4

GABRIEL

*H*ow had I ever forgotten such a place existed? All those memories I'd shared with Viktor had somehow been altered to make me believe they were somewhere else entirely. The witches of Havenwood Falls were clever that way. Their magical wards guarding the town stripped memories from those who left, preventing a massive influx of humans and supernatural beings alike. Things had come back to me like a trickling stream in the spring over the week I'd been in town. Slowly, bits and pieces had been triggered by one thing or another. An image of Viktor and me sitting together, watching the sun rise over the town, came rushing back. That vision was the last time I'd seen the sun's shimmering rays and felt them warm my cool skin. I had to look at the town in an entirely new light.

Despite being absent for forty years, I was surprised to see that Havenwood Falls hadn't changed much. Sure, there were some new businesses and new neighborhoods, but its bones hadn't changed a bit. There was a ski resort—that was a newer addition—but the town still felt the same. I found myself waiting to see Viktor's imposing form walking along the town square, puffing on a cigarette with a beautiful woman on his arm. It was foolish, yet it seemed like he'd never left.

The sun had disappeared below the mountains, casting the town into darkness; however for me, it was time to make my presence known. One of the Luna Coven members would likely be making their rounds to find me. They were the instrument of the Court of the Sun and the Moon to keep track over everyone who wasn't normal or human. The whole setup rubbed me the wrong way. As much as I wanted to tell all those pompous blood bags to suck a dick with their *every supernatural being must check in*, I had to admit being able to feel the warmth of the sun's rays made possible by their damn tattoos was practically a wish come true. As soon as I'd crossed the wards, the Celtic knotted sun had reappeared on my forearm, leaving me rather confused for the next day or so until the memory came back. It was a feat which was impossible anywhere else in the world, but the people in Havenwood Falls had managed to form a mutually beneficial friendship and make such a feat possible.

Mathilde Augustine, accompanied by a much younger woman, approached me, abandoning their oversight of the year's Thanksgiving decorations.

"Gabriel Doyle. I thought that might be you. What brings you back to our town?" the old crone asked.

"Mathilde. It's been a long time. You're looking as sharp as ever," I replied, giving her my most charming smile.

"Elsmed will be wanting to see you straight away," she said, straightening up and looking down her nose at me.

"Elsmed isn't dead yet? Shame," I mused. "I was hoping this town would be rid of that old troll by now."

I harbored no ill will toward anyone in the town, to my knowledge, but that didn't mean that everyone who remembered me was fond of me either. Elsmed was an old goat who, in my honest opinion, would be best avoided whenever possible.

"Still evasive. Some things never change. Are you passing through? Or will you be staying with us a while?"

I hadn't given it much thought, though I was sure the little business I'd have to take care of would take me a few days to sort out.

"Still undecided as to the length of my stay, however I doubt my business should take more than a month, tops."

"Very well, then. *If* you are permitted to stay, it goes without saying that you should behave yourself, what with your past and all. Rumor had it you were a vicious one. I'd be careful if I were you. There are those of us who still remember the stories." Mathilde had a far-off look in her eyes. "It makes me wonder how much a man can really change."

Viktor had told his enemies tales of his bloodthirsty offspring with the hope it would make others think twice before crossing him. It was his own way of showing fatherly pride, and my youth gave way to such tales, but I was centuries apart from that young man. Time had mellowed me, and death had robbed me of my only true companion.

"Well, I hope I can satisfy your curiosity in time. It's been a pleasure as always, Mathilde," I said with a respectful bow of my head, but inside I was seething.

It never failed that when I came to town, I was always met with apprehension and leery stares, my former reputation preceding me.

Without another delay, I made my way through town to the last place I had called home. Viktor's home stood on four acres not far from Havenwood Heights, where the uppity Old Families lived, but so far as I knew, the property had never been sold. Viktor had insisted on creating a trust to keep the home in good repair on the off chance something happened to him. Little did he know he'd have to put that to good use not too long after.

The looming Italianate-styled mansion had been kept up, that much was obvious as I approached it. The front light was on, as was the dining room light to the right of the front door. However, there didn't seem to be anyone there. It was going to be an upgrade from the Whisper Falls Inn, a homecoming of sorts.

I didn't bother knocking and walked right in the front door. That was a good sign. No invitation needed meant no one lived there, or at least no one living. The wooden floors were recently polished, and the scent of fresh paint permeated the air. Lorenzo entered several moments after I did, carrying our bags. He placed them carefully at the foot of the regal staircase, which was the defining feature of the foyer. Despite not making it past the entry parlor, I could already tell it had been kept to my sire's specifications, not a thing about it changed. Not even the paint color, which was an eggshell white.

"Gabriel? Where would you like your bags?" Enzo asked, shaking me from my nostalgia.

"Oh! Right, sorry. It hadn't occurred to me that you haven't been here before. It'll be upstairs to the right. Second door. Feel free to choose any of the other rooms as your own. I don't think I'll have too much need of you during our stay, so consider this a vacation and try not to get into too much trouble."

"Won't you need to feed?"

I shook my head. "I will, but this town has provisions for that. Don't worry about me, old friend. I'll be just fine."

He bowed his head and carried the bags upstairs, disappearing around the corner. Moving to follow him, I heard steps mounting the front porch. Without so much as a knock, the door swung in, and a young woman strode in, eyes wide with shock when they met my own.

"Who are you? What are you doing here?"

I smirked and lifted a brow, leveling her with a knowing stare. The woman had Luna Coven written all over her, every luscious inch. My cock didn't even twitch, though, a sad side effect of my obsessive infatuation. However, that didn't mean I couldn't appreciate a woman's beauty. Surprisingly, she wasn't afraid of me in the least. If she was, she never let on once.

"It's very nice to meet you. My name's Gabriel Doyle, the new owner of this house," I purred.

"Tone it down, Fabio. You're not my type. As for the owner of this house? I was under the impression it had been left in trusts to manage its upkeep. Unless you're Viktor Azimov, which I'd challenge, this house isn't yours, and you're trespassing."

Clever girl, I thought appreciatively.

"You're right. I'm not Viktor, but he was my father, and this was my residence the last time I was here. If it makes no difference to you, I'd just as soon keep to what's familiar to me. This home held many memories, and I've come to pay my respects to Viktor and his legacy.

Which now begs the question, who are you and what are you doing here?"

The girl's eyes narrowed at me like she was weighing what I'd said.

"That wasn't an answer," she noted. "Either way, I'm Addie Beaumont, and I'm here to find out why you're here and keep it all by the book. Elsmed would like to see you right away to ask you some questions. We don't want any trouble here, so I'll need you to follow me. I may be giving you the benefit of the doubt, but if you prove me wrong, you'll regret the day you ever came to this town. Understood?" she announced.

I nodded. "I dare say, it's been a long while since I've been in a woman's company who could command attention the way you do. I appreciate your generosity, and I have no intention of being a nuisance. There's some business I have to attend to and then I suspect I'll be on my way once again. As for the Elsmed business, I get the feeling this isn't a request."

"You'd be correct."

Extending a hand toward the door, I said, "Well, then let's get on with it. I need to work on my tan."

The corner of her lips turned up as though she was trying to suppress a laugh.

"Sure thing, Mr. Doyle," Addie replied, turning on her heel and striding back down the steps, shaking her head as she went.

The meeting with Elsmed had been rather uneventful, a barrage of questions about some Collector, whom I knew nothing about. Though I was surprised the fae agreed to let me stay. He'd always been so open about his disdain and distrust of me. All the same, it was made clear they'd be watching me.

The next morning, I rose earlier than I had in nearly half a century. Wandering through the house, I kept finding myself standing before Viktor's closed bedroom door. Coming to grips with the reality of his loss was one of the goals of my return, and without a sign of my raven-haired beauty, I could think of nothing stopping me from accomplishing that. As I entered Viktor's room, memories flooded my mind, cutting deep, as though the loss was still fresh. I almost didn't notice the envelope sitting on the nightstand beside the bed. Crossing the room, I noted my name scrawled across the back of it in Viktor's elegant hand.

The grandfather clock downstairs chimed loudly, announcing the coming dawn. Stuffing the letter into my pocket, I turned and left the room, sure there was nothing left for me there besides secrets and heartache. Before I even knew what I was doing, I was bounding down the stairs and out the front door.

I wanted to watch the sun rise over the mountains and witness firsthand the sky changing from purple to pink and then orange, just before the sun would rise over the peak and bathe the valley in light. Taking Lorenzo's car, I made my way up Mount Sousa.

By the time I reached the top, the sky had lightened just slightly. There was no better spot to watch the sun rise than right here. I'd found it decades earlier, when the town was smaller than it was now. Finding a clear spot on the rocky ground, I settled in and got as comfortable as possible on hard stone.

As it turned out, being back in town and being given all my memories back had quieted my dreams, much to my dismay. However, being back gave voices to the past, and they'd been growing louder with each moment I stayed.

"Gabriel, one day, I won't be there to tell you what to do or how to live, not that you listen when I do. When that day comes, I want you to know that having you by my side these many years has been a privilege. We may not share blood by birth, but you are my son just the same. Know who you are and where you came from. Don't ever forget it."

Viktor clasped his hand on my shoulder and gave it a hard squeeze before he turned away and left me alone.

I'd been standing in this very place when he'd said those words to me. At the time, I thought his age was making him sentimental, but maybe he knew more than he ever let on. He always seemed to. That was the part most people never saw of him—the raw man who cared for those under his protection. The world saw him as a monster, known for his cruelty and deadly accuracy. In fact, he was all of those things, but there was something underneath all of that which was still more human than beast. That was the Viktor Azimov I'd come to know and love.

Reaching into my pocket, I pulled the envelope out and stared at it. Something told me that whatever its contents, I'd be a changed man after reading it. Sliding my finger under the seal, I pulled the letter out and set to reading.

Gabriel,

I fear my time may be limited, and I know not what tomorrow brings. My hope is that this letter reaches you when the time is right and you can find it in you to take up my reins. The Lilith Nest is dear to me, though I fear there may be a traitor among them. However, the truth is never that simple.

In the event of my demise, it is my most heartfelt wish that you succeed me as the nest leader. I know your mind is troubled and you fear the corruption that power brings, but you have a good head for justice and enough sense to know when to play your cards close to the vest or when to go all in. Be well, Gabriel, and may Lilith ever watch over you.

Viktor.

Re-reading it several more times, I couldn't shake the feeling that my sire had known what was to come. Leading had never interested me, yet Viktor's words wouldn't leave me alone. Would resurrecting the fallen nest be so bad? The Petrans held the Court seat, but they didn't understand the Gothic vampires, not with their pure blood and the knowledge that one day their lives would end—perhaps after many centuries or even millenia, but they'd still end. We faced eternity while everyone we knew and loved faded into distant memories. No, we needed a voice too. Not a Court seat, but something that would unify us and make them take notice. The revelation ignited a fire in my belly that I would no longer be able to ignore. It was time I stepped up to the responsibilities Viktor intended for me.

I stayed a while longer, contemplating what it would take to accomplish such a task. Whatever I did would have to be calculated and careful. The sun rose even higher as the morning wore on. Birds danced among the tree branches, cawing and flitting around like it was choreographed. The town had come to life below. Getting to my feet, I turned and headed back for the car. There was one thing that couldn't wait another day. I needed to pay my respects and finally say farewell to my father's ashes where he'd been laid to rest in the Havenwood Falls Cemetery.

The drive was short enough, although despite having lived in the town for a time, I'd never had need to visit the place before. Standing at the gates of the cemetery, I knew he was in there somewhere. No amount of willing myself to take a step forward would force my feet to cooperate. Pangs of the loss were gnawing at me from somewhere deep in my belly. He'd been my father for far longer than my biological human father ever had. He took a lowly slave and raised me up to a proper gentleman, taught me to survive anything. I still remembered the horror I'd felt when he'd found me on the whipping post, bleeding from the lashes across my back. Tied to the post, there wasn't anything I could do to stop him or defend myself, but that had been for the best.

I'd woken up a few days later in the nearby woods and slaughtered my master and his mistress. Vile scum, the both of them. Viktor had liked what he'd seen in me.

Then, he took me away from the Irish countryside and made me the man I was today. I'd killed my way through all of Europe over the next century or two, long ago when vampires were feared and people were afraid of the night. Times had changed, though, and now people emulated us with their plastic fangs and polyester capes.

My gaze traveled over the iron gate and down to the threshold at my feet. I stepped forward and made my way to the older section of the cemetery.

Seeing his grave marker would make his absence real. Mausoleums stood tall, casting shadows over much of the graveyard. Sunlight filtered down through the bare branches overhead. Chains and cages around tombs, runes and other magical symbols were all necessities, because sometimes the dead didn't like to stay that way. I ducked under the colored glass orbs hanging from branches.

The cemetery was like a maze, reminding me of the times I'd spent in New Orleans—times with Viktor. The Petran vault lay ahead, large and looming, stealing all my attention. I nearly missed the narrow tomb wedged in between two sister Ash trees. In shallow carved letters was Viktor Azimov's name. His birth date as well as his sire date were unknown, but his death date was clear and stark against the granite stone.

I couldn't understand where things had gone so off the rails. Viktor was careful about the people he drank from, almost to the point of being obsessive, but I couldn't deny the facts. I wasn't there for him at the end, and I didn't know the details, nor did I want to.

"Viktor, old friend. How did we get here?" I murmured.

I was met with only silence as I continued.

"Would you still be here if I'd come back to you sooner? I wonder a lot about how different things would be now. If you were here now, I know you'd tell me to quit being a sentimental sap, but I never got the chance to tell you thank you or goodbye. We were supposed to have eternity, though I suppose even an immortal isn't guaranteed tomorrow," I whispered, kneeling in front of the grave.

I dug my fingers into the cold ground at my feet. Earth. One day, we all come back to it and become one. So many things had changed since my time with Viktor Asimov. I'd lost the love of the hunt I'd once had, along with the will to keep going on. Every day was the same as the one before, only the scenery changing. Viktor had been different. He'd understood something I'd never quite figured out—the meaning of life and how to find purpose. He and I had gone our separate ways while I figured out what I wanted to do with the very long life I'd been given, but it wasn't until almost six months ago that I'd finally understood what he'd meant. The dreams that had plagued me were so real, so vivid, that I'd been convinced they were real at first. Then I'd wake and have to face a world where beauty and love were not a part of my life. That was the crux of the reason I'd come back to Havenwood Falls—something was calling me home and why not give in?

"You know, you once said to me that every dream had a meaning, and sometimes we find what we need the most when we aren't looking for it. I think you're right, you know. I've been having these dreams for months about a woman. She's never told me her name, but by God, I think she's the one, Viktor. She makes me want to live again, more than just existing, more than feeding and traveling. If you can hear me, old friend, please give me a sign. Show me what I'm supposed to do now."

I wasn't sure what I expected would happen. Perhaps I hoped he'd step out of the shadows and impart one of his gems of wisdom, but I was met with only the tinkling of wind chimes and the breeze cutting through the thin branches overhead. Thick clouds were rolling in.

"Viktor, I'm sorry I wasn't there at the end. You deserved better than the way it all ended, but I came here for a reason. That letter you left me—I got the message loud and clear. Your legacy will live on, I promise. I came to say goodbye, and I hope you have found peace at last. *Solas Mhic Dé ar a anam*," I said, letting the old Irish Gaelic roll off my tongue with ease.

Turning away from the grave, I made my way back toward the car, leaving Viktor in the past where he belonged. The future was going to be what I made it, and I wanted to start by settling some old business. My time up on the mountain had given me clarity. Viktor's nest had been decimated by the massacre, and it was high time someone stepped up and took it back. My first stop was going to be downtown —convincing the right people was going to take some strategy.

I climbed into the black Lexus and took off, checking off the names of the founding families I'd need to convince. I pulled into an open spot along Eleventh Street and climbed out, heading toward the south side of the town square. Rounding the corner, I pulled my sleeve back into place, effectively covering the sun tattoo on my arm. My eyes were adjusting slowly to the sunlight, forcing me to squint so I didn't run into anyone. The wind suddenly kicked up and shifted directions, forcing me to stop dead in my tracks.

There was a scent that had taunted me for months in my dreams. Had I fallen asleep? Was it all a dream?

I scanned the street, searching for my raven-haired goddess as I entered Town Square Park.

Then I saw her.

She was busy finding a seat at a table. Glancing at the sign, I realized it was a café. Comfortable and public, it wasn't my first choice for meeting her the first time in person, but who was I to look a gift horse in the mouth? There was a large part of me that was waiting for her lush form to evaporate before my very eyes, teasing me with what I wanted most, but never thought I could have.

Her face turned toward me, and I would've sworn that if my heart was beating, it would've been pounding its way out of my chest. It was undoubtedly her.

The woman's gaze locked with my own, and for a brief moment, the world stopped and fell away, leaving only the two of us. A smile stretched my face for the first time I could recall in what seemed like years. Our moment was over too soon as something caught her attention, and she tore her stare away from my own.

My head was spinning, and I needed a moment to regain my composure. Moving quickly, I ducked into the town square and headed for the gazebo. What the hell had just happened? Replaying everything, it dawned on me that when we had locked eyes, there was a flash of recognition. She recognized me just as I had her.

A hard knot formed in the pit of my belly. Was the woman of my dreams just a figment of my imagination? I needed to know she was real if there was ever a hope of making our dreams a reality.

CHAPTER 5

ALINA

*T*he week was going absolutely horribly. In fact, I wasn't sure the Grandvilles would keep me on much longer—if I wanted to stay on, and that was questionable. The family was difficult, but having checked my bank account, I couldn't easily walk away from that kind of money. It put me in a difficult spot.

Mrs. Grandville didn't seem to be satisfied with a damn thing I did. Every single day there was a barrage of new complaints. Tabitha and Cornelius were miserable, and I could see why. Their mother was an impossible woman, and their father was practically absent from their lives. He'd show up for dinner and eat silently before disappearing—whether to an office or somewhere else, I didn't know. I wasn't sure what he did for a living or in any other aspect of his life, and I hadn't worked up the courage to ask or speak more than a cordial greeting.

The children were too quiet, like they were afraid to interact with anyone other than each other. Being homeschooled as they were, I could understand how they'd become so withdrawn. It made me wonder what they'd been subjected to before I'd arrived. I hadn't been able to find a way to connect with them, yet. They never said much more than "yes, ma'am" or "no, ma'am." Sometimes I thought I could detect the glimmer of a protest in Cornelius—whom I'd taken to calling Neil—but he never voiced it. The day was coming when he'd rebel, and that day was going to be spectacular.

When I'd taken on the position, I'd done so with the thought that I would have some time to myself. That wasn't the case. It was all-consuming. The Grandvilles quite simply didn't have time for or interest in their children, leaving the entirety of their care to me. It was Saturday, and technically my day off, if I were to go by my contract, yet I was still scared of upsetting my employer if she had other plans for me. I'd given quitting some thought, knowing that sometimes jobs just didn't work out. However, going back to Denver wasn't an option, not when I knew my dad would hold it over my head with I-told-you-so's until I was old and gray. My thoughts returned to my current situation.

Frustration and worry were quickly becoming a constant in my life. I needed a break. Not a vacation or anything, but a couple hours to unwind among people who didn't make me feel like I was balancing on a knife's edge.

With a newly found steely resolve, I decided I was going in to town. I wanted to explore my new home and find two things. The first was where to get an excellent cup of coffee, and the second was more or less anything that would encourage something resembling a social life. The house was quiet; it was still early.

As I crept down the stairs, I stopped near the bottom when I noticed I didn't hear any noise coming from the residents. The door was in view from where I stood frozen. The familiar clinking of Mrs. Grandville's heels echoed in the hall upstairs. There was a sense of urgency in those steps, and I couldn't risk angering her further.

I bolted for the door, slipping out in near silence. Even the door was helpful as it shut silently and the hinges didn't creak or groan when jostled. Keeping my pace brisk, I turned onto the sidewalk and followed the streets toward the center of town. It was relaxed compared to the bustle of the weekends I was accustomed to in Denver, but surprisingly, I liked it. The whole town felt quaint and picturesque. If I hadn't needed to register when I'd arrived, I never would have guessed that so many different supernatural beings resided here. It made me look at every single person I passed or spied doing yard work a little differently.

The town was different than any I'd ever seen, like a floating island in the sky, unreachable from the outside. That was exactly how it felt as I gazed at the mountains surrounding the oasis. The scent of freshly roasted coffee and buttery pastries invaded my nostrils, drawing me closer to the shop. The sign for Coffee Haven was straight ahead of me.

Stop numero uno, I thought.

Something so tantalizing had to be made with magic. I'd never smelled something so wonderful in my life, and I was by no means unfamiliar with coffee shops or bakeries. Pushing open the door, I was met with the chiming of the welcome bell. There was already a short line, but it seemed to be moving quickly, so I staked my place in line and carefully contemplated the menu.

When it was my turn, I stepped up to the counter and smiled warmly at the barista who was waiting patiently with an intrigued stare. My eyes dipped to the name tag on her shirt: *Harlow*. She looked to be about the same age I was and was watching me with an amused grin.

"You're new in town, aren't you?" she asked without coming off as accusing.

"What gave me away?" I chuckled, the tips of my ears heating when I thought of being so clearly out of place.

"Small town. You get to know everyone real quick. And most people have their favorites memorized and don't usually give it much thought, unless you're a tourist, and you don't really strike me as the type," she noted, one side of her mouth lifting in a half smile.

"Nope, not a tourist, but I'll take any caffeinated drink you'd recommend and same with a pastry."

"No allergies?" she asked.

I shook my head.

"All right. Go ahead and grab a seat. I'll bring it out in just a moment."

"What do I owe you?" I asked, surprised she hadn't given me the total yet.

"Don't worry about it. This one's on me. Welcome to Havenwood Falls."

I nodded my thanks, headed to an open table near the window to put my things down, and returned to the counter, finding a sunny spot while I waited. Standing near the front window, I glanced around the café, watching the patrons as they sipped their drinks and munched on their snacks. The sensation of being watched sent shivers up my spine and gooseflesh over my body. No one in the coffee shop was paying me any attention. I cast a quick glance out the window, and that's when I saw him.

Across the street and several yards to the right stood a man in the doorway of the park's gazebo. He was tall and well dressed, like a businessman. At first, I thought maybe he was checking out the café, but that wasn't right either, because his stare was fixed on me. His build and face reminded me of the man from my dreams, but that wasn't possible. He wasn't real, though the resemblance was uncanny.

My nipples pebbled, pushing against the restraints of my bra and T-shirt as warmth flooded my core. It was the most visceral reaction I'd ever had to a man before.

I bit my lip, giving the man a coy smile. I didn't know him from Adam, and I couldn't be too careful. There was something in his stare that held me, and I couldn't tear my gaze away from him no matter how much I wanted to. He didn't move, frozen in the moment just as I was. Even though he was easily fifty feet away, I could practically feel the warmth of his breath on my skin as though he was right next to me. The blue of his eyes was bright like glacier ice, and the corner of his mouth ticked up in a smirk.

"Here we go. One café americano and a blueberry scone. Cream and sugar are over there next to the counter if you need any. Can I get you anything else?" the barista asked cheerily, breaking whatever hold the mystery man had over me.

I turned away from him, stunned into silence. I blinked a few times quickly before I could muster a response.

"No, actually. That should be it. Thank you so much."

The girl nodded and turned, disappearing behind the counter. My eyes darted back to where the man had been standing, but he was gone. I turned toward the window, searching for any sign of him along the street, but there was nothing.

Had I imagined the whole thing? Was he not really there? To be honest, I wasn't really sure. Though no one could ever be sure of anything in a town full of what should be impossible. If he was real, and that was a decidedly big *if*, then there was no doubt in my mind he was much more than human. Whatever he was, I doubted he was a djinn like me. A warlock maybe or even a shifter, if his stubbly face was a distinguishing sign.

Making my way to my table, I settled in and picked up the cup of steamy coffee, bringing it to my lips and inhaling the rich aroma. It was really strong and slightly bitter. Cream and sugar wouldn't have been a bad idea. Glancing around the room, I realized no one was paying attention to me. Getting up and leaving my purse behind, I moved to the counter, pouring a teaspoon of sugar and enough cream to fill the cup to the brim.

When I turned back, my table was no longer vacant. I froze, nearly spilling my coffee with the abrupt stop. In the seat across from my own sat the mystery man. His back was to me, but I could tell it was him. Same dark clothes, same wide shoulders and straight posture.

He is real! I thought, trying to calm my breathing and slow my pounding heart. Straightening myself out, I squared my shoulders and strode for the table as though nothing was amiss. I sat in my seat and placed the coffee on its saucer before giving the man a once-over.

His eyes were just as blue as I'd thought they were, maybe even more so, and his lashes were so long I was jealous. His nose was straight and regal, while his lips were full and luscious. I couldn't help but wonder what he tasted like. Dark hair crowned his head with one of those sexy-man haircuts, longer on top and short on the sides.

"I'm Gabriel Doyle. Have we met before?" he asked, extending his hand across the table.

I placed my hand in his. "Alina Anand. Those eyes—you remind me of someone," I said, blurting out exactly what I was thinking.

I wanted to hide as soon as my words made their way to my ears. *Could I have been any cheesier? Way to go, Alina. This is why you don't have boyfriends. Open mouth, insert foot.*

Gabriel's hand was cool to the touch as his long, slender fingers wrapped around my hand. There was a very distinct restrained power in his light touch. It was an exhilarating mix. His thumb ran over the back of my hand, sending chills shooting through the rest of my body like an electric shock.

Something about the man emboldened me, and I realized that had to be a part of the thrill. I didn't know him, and he knew nothing about me. I could be anyone I wanted to be.

"Are you new to town?" he asked, leaning forward so no one near could overhear our conversation.

I nodded.

"I used to live here myself, but admittedly, it's been a very long time since I've been home," Gabriel said, his voice smooth like rich caramel.

"How long is a long time?" I asked, noting the way he'd emphasized the *long*.

The man wasn't human; his presence was just so *extra* it didn't seem possible. That and his good looks were practically Hollywood-ready, intensified by a deadly edge.

Gabriel's eyes narrowed slightly, and the corner of his mouth ticked up in amusement. An image of the same smirk flashed through my thoughts at the same time his smile widened to show his dimples in his cheeks.

"You're an observant one, aren't you?" he noted, glancing around the café before his eyes returned to me, and he withdrew his touch. "Let's just say, my . . . family's . . . roots go back to the mid-seventeenth century."

My mouth popped open. Mid-seventeenth century? That would make him over three hundred fifty years old! I had so many questions, and it only fueled my desire to know what this man was.

I opened my mouth to say more, but Gabriel's hand brushed mine, making me pause. All my focus was on the small stretch of flesh where our bodies touched. Maybe it was the tingling of my magic under my skin in the excitement or maybe it was his. Either way, we had a chemistry that couldn't be denied, and then there was the confounding thoughts that he was too familiar to me to have never met him before.

"Why don't we get out of here and go somewhere quieter and less populated?" he suggested, eyeing the rest of the café's patrons and keeping his voice at a barely audible whisper.

I was playing with fire, and I knew it. Gabriel was a total stranger to me and could kill me without too much of an effort. Granted, I wasn't without my own charms and abilities, but I didn't think I could kill an immortal.

"Do you have any plans to kill me?" I asked, not expecting a straight answer, but braving it all the same.

Gabriel's lips pursed at my question before turning down in a frown.

"No. Although I'd be lying if I said you didn't smell wonderful or that I don't want just a taste, but I have a great deal of self-control, and one thing I can promise is you'll never have cause to fear me . . . as long as you don't try to kill me first. Then all bets are off," he said with a wink.

Vampire.

I didn't know how I hadn't seen it before. The cool skin, longevity, and his air of lethality—they were practically dead giveaways. Yet, instead of being afraid, it was exhilarating sitting across from a being so powerful I couldn't help but to be on edge.

I spied the barista in my periphery. She was watching us with interest, but her face betrayed nothing of her thoughts.

"All right. I'll do it," I answered before I could take it back.

His face morphed into a beaming smile, as though he'd just closed the biggest deal of his life, and maybe he had. Something was telling me everything I knew was about to change. What more could I do than welcome it?

Gabriel signaled for the barista's attention and got a to-go cup for my coffee and a bag for my pastry. Tracking his every movement, I couldn't help admiring the grace with which he moved. Being clumsy on my best days, it made me especially envious. Gabriel returned with everything packed up and ready to go.

"If you want to bail, now is your chance," he joked, extending his hand toward me.

Maybe it was the devil on my shoulder, or maybe just the inner me begging for adventure, but I didn't even think twice before I placed my hand in his. His slender fingers wrapped around mine firmly. As soon as his cool skin met mine, I saw a flash of the two of us on a balcony and in a bed, his lips ravaging the tender flesh just under my ear. My core heated at the image, igniting a long-buried desire that would no longer be ignored.

I blinked and was back in the café, bedrooms and sensual caresses vanished and leaving me almost panting. My face heated, and my ears felt like they were on fire with the embarrassment of being caught.

"Such a beautiful shade of pink," Gabriel remarked, lifting his hand and running an appraising finger down my cheek, following my jaw line to my chin. "On an even more beautiful woman."

Good Lord! Doesn't he know flattery will get him anything his heart desires? I thought heatedly.

"Anything? Is that so?" he teased.

"Any—" I began, then stopped as realization dawned. "Wait a second!"

Gabriel didn't utter a single word, only giving me a quick wink before extending his arm for me to take and escorting me out of the café. The man was full of surprises and could read minds, so it would seem.

We strolled at a leisurely, much slower pace than I wanted. I had too many questions, and the streets were far too crowded to ask such things without taking the risk of being overheard. Gabriel pulled me along toward a small park right across from the library.

After we'd walked for several minutes, the street cleared out a bit, and no one was close enough to overhear what I wanted to know.

"Yes, I can read minds, though I make a point to try not to. Invading your privacy is not my goal, but your particular line of thinking caught my attention, and you were practically projecting it at me. If it bothers you, all you need to do is say so, and I will endeavor to shut that down when I am around you."

I sighed. "I shouldn't be surprised, given what I've heard of this town already, but I was under the impression vampires didn't have those kinds of abilities."

"Ah, yes. But there's no other place like it. As for the mind reading itself, my kind doesn't have those extra capabilities . . . usually. I made the rather unfortunate mistake of killing the daughter of a voodoo priestess in my younger and more reckless days. She cursed me to never have a moment's silence in the hopes I'd go mad and be put down. It backfired, and while it can be annoying at times, it has its uses. I gather you don't have much experience with other species?" he asked, taking a seat on a shaded park bench near the entrance.

"No. My family likes to stay closer to our own kind."

"And what kind might that be? A siren, perhaps?" he asked, following my stare to the three-tiered bronze fountain, the crowning jewel of Cook's Corner Park. The bronze mermaid statue shone brightly in the November sunlight.

"I . . . really shouldn't. It's nothing personal, but I just met you. If anyone knows what I am, it could put me in a dangerous situation, and there are too many other people who could be put in harm's way."

"You play your cards close to the vest. I can appreciate that, and don't worry, I have nothing to gain by deceiving you or abusing your trust. In fact, I'd much prefer the opposite," Gabriel explained carefully.

I wasn't one of the lucky species who could detect lies just by hearing someone's voice. Even as a stranger, Gabriel was being bluntly honest with me, and that wasn't something I was accustomed to. In my personal experience, most people rarely told the truth even in simple, mundane situations. However, Gabriel's words rang true to me. I believed him, even if he was a vampire and the whole outrageous situation went against my better judgment.

"Do you believe in fate, Alina?" Gabriel asked, getting to his feet and plucking a dying brown leaf from a low-hanging branch overhead.

His contemplative tone shook me from my own wandering thoughts.

"I do. Three days before the Grandvilles contacted me, my father had begun putting pressure on me to find a husband and settle down. That's what women in my family do; they settle. He'd pick a man for me and expect me to go through with the whole ridiculous farce without complaint. I'd be among my own kind and safe. It would've been a great plan, if not for it being the furthest thing from what I wanted. Fate brought me that job to save me from a miserable life, and I ended up here, with you," I mused, smirking at him.

I didn't mention what I wanted to. He likely wouldn't take well my dreaming about him for months on end before ever meeting him.

"How can you be sure?" Gabriel asked, listening carefully to every word.

"Because for the first time in my life, I feel like I'm exactly where I'm supposed to be," I said, giving Gabriel's hand a sure squeeze.

He nodded like he understood. "Wise beyond your years, it would seem."

Gabriel's mouth turned down in a frown, and he leveled me with an uncertain stare before glancing away and inhaling deeply.

"There's something I must ask you, and I would like it if you could hear me out before writing this off as insane, okay?" he asked, his brows knitting together and forming a deep worry line between them.

I nodded.

"I am a dream walker, though I didn't discover this until recently . . . because of you."

"Me?" I squeaked, eyes widening at the accusation. "Why me?"

He smiled, taking my hand between his strong ones. Gabriel's thumb traced the faint blue lines of my veins on the back of my hand.

"I don't rightly know why, but—"

I sat up a little straighter, frowning in an odd mix of confusion and curiosity.

"It was all real," I murmured.

"The dreams?" he questioned.

I nodded, gulping and trying to wet my now parched mouth.

"Yes, they were as real as you and me sitting here. Though, I must confess, it's because of those dreams that I stand before you now. I've searched for you for months, hoping beyond hope that you were real, and not just a figment of a desperate imagination, but here you are. Just like you said you'd be.

"I said? I have no recollection of that, but I can't say I'm sorry for it," I said quickly, surprised at my candidness.

He lifted his hand to my cheek, his deft fingers tracing the planes from just below my ear to my chin.

"I could never be sorry for it. Thank you for giving me hope again," Gabriel admitted.

The butterflies in my belly turned into falcons, battering my insides with their tickling wings.

"I believe you. If it weren't for all these images of the two of us together, I might not, but there's no denying it now. So many nights I spent wishing for sleep just so I could dream. Now I know it was all real, well . . . mostly."

It was true. I couldn't ignore our shared history.

"We've shared more nights than I can recall and seen a dozen cities across the world. We've explored every inch of each other . . . for months. You never gave me your name, but I could never forget those big brown eyes. You, my desert rose, are what brought me back home to Havenwood Falls."

Desert rose.

Pet names had never been my cup of tea, but with Gabriel it fit. My day off was quickly becoming the strangest day I'd had in a while, in the best way possible.

I opened my mouth to say something, but I was cut off by the shrill ring of the phone buried in my purse.

"Shit! Sorry, one second," I rushed out, opening my purse and rifling through its contents to find the device.

The third ring blared loudly by the time I fished it out and caught a glimpse of the caller.

Mrs. Grandville.

"I'm so sorry. I've got to take this," I explained as I rose and strode several paces away. "Hello?"

Without so much as a greeting, Mrs. Grandville's mom-voice filled my ear. "Where are you?"

"Umm, the park?" I quipped, treading carefully.

"The park. That's just great. Where are you supposed to be?"

I didn't have an answer. It was expressly written in my terms of employment that Saturdays and Sundays were my days off.

"Getting Tabitha and Cornelius ready for piano lessons, that's where!"

"Mrs. Grandville, I think there's been a miscommunication or a misunderstanding—" I said, but before I could finish, the line went dead.

She'd hung up on me. *Fuck!*

I turned to see Gabriel watching me intently. His brows were drawn down in concern, and there was a spark of irritation in his stare.

"That was my boss. I-I have to go. I'm so sorry, but I would like to see you again, if I haven't already blown my chance."

His chin dipped once. "I understand."

I didn't know what more to say. Gabriel's words were still playing over and over in my head, and I didn't know what to make of them. Meeting him had been by chance, however seeing him again was going to be very deliberate. Taking a chance, I took a step toward him and then another, until we were only separated by a few inches.

"Gabriel? I don't know you, but I want to. Will I see you again?"

"Of course, love. It takes a lot more than a bitchy boss to scare me off. Tomorrow, by the skating rink. Two o'clock."

I frowned. "I'll probably have Tabitha and Neil with me tomorrow."

"The more, the merrier." His smile was warm and genuine.

Was this real life? Did men like him really exist? I was beginning to hope.

"Alrighty then, tomorrow at two by the skating rink it is. I'll see you then," I said, tucking my hair behind my ears.

I pulled my lip between my teeth and bit down slightly as I smiled. Biting my lip was a nervous habit I'd had since I was at least four years old. No one had been able to break me of it.

Gabriel took my hand in his and brought it to his mouth. He pressed a sensual kiss against my knuckles that threatened to make my knees buckle under me. It was my luck that he noticed the reaction and smirked, showing off his panty-melting dimples in each cheek.

Good Lord, this man is going to be the end of me!

"Until tomorrow," he whispered with a wink, before turning on his heel and striding away from me and out of the park entirely.

I'm not saying I watched him leave, at least not the whole time, but the man had a butt that could make a fine cowboy in a pair of Wranglers look like a chump. When he disappeared from view, I made my way home.

The walk back was over quicker than I was ready for. Thoughts and questions ran rampant through my mind, only begging more questions. I couldn't fathom what Mrs. Grandville had meant about needing to be there for the kids on my designated day off. Surely, she had just gotten confused about which day it was. That had to be it. Throughout the walk back, I alternated between a speed walk and a slow mosey. Mrs. Grandville seemed like the sort of woman who'd be a force to be reckoned with, and I had no interest in crossing her, but I also wasn't going to allow myself to be her doormat, at her beck and call. I had a life too, and I needed her to respect that if our arrangement was ever going to work.

I groaned as the house came into view. *Well, here goes nothing.* I marched myself right up to the house and tried to enter as quietly as I could, but as soon as I stepped through the door, Mrs. Grandville was on me.

"Where were you?" she demanded.

"Oh, um, I wanted to check out the town."

Mrs. Grandville scoffed. "I needed you here. Tabitha and Cornelius have piano lessons in an hour. What was I supposed to do if you weren't here?"

Mrs. Grandville's anger was palpable. Her words and indignant consternation were starting to piss me off. As someone who claimed to be a stickler for the contract, she sure missed the part that stated what days I had off and for myself.

Mrs. Grandville turned to leave and made it a full two steps before my mouth had a full disconnect from my brain and got squirrely.

"Um, take them yourself?" I mumbled, low enough that I was sure no one could hear me.

She froze, turning her face slightly toward me, but said nothing before continuing her exit from the room. I wanted to demand why I was still responsible for the children on the days off she had appointed herself. But I wasn't that brave. I'd have to bring it up later, when she'd had time to calm down and hopefully forget anything she may or may not have heard.

Fuck my life, that was way too close. I needed to get a damn grip on my mouth before I backtalked my way right to the unemployment line and my parents' front door. Which reminded me, I had yet to make a few calls. Pulling the phone out of my back pocket, I quickly typed out a message to my mom that I missed everyone and would call soon. I hadn't called home yet, and still wasn't sure I was ready to.

CHAPTER 6

GABRIEL

*S*itting across from the woman who had taunted me in my dreams, always staying just out of reach and without an identity, had been the true test of my resolve. It had taken everything in me not to steal her away and make her mine in every way that counted.

When I saw her—*Alina*—in the window of the coffeehouse, I almost couldn't believe it. For the first time in well over a hundred years, I felt alive again. Excitement flowed through me, where before her there was nothing. I couldn't begin to explain the depths of my feelings, and I didn't know what they meant yet. How many nights had I forced sleep just for the hope of seeing her again? How many times had I told her my darkest secrets without ever seeing her shrink away from my touch when she discovered the monster I was? No. She never needed protection from me, and if the woman turned out to be much different than the fantasy, then so be it. I'd live the rest of my life waiting for the dreams. For the time being, though, I wanted to know everything I could about Alina Anand.

When her phone had rung, it had taken all of my resolve to not steal her away for myself. I was selfish like that, and I didn't care. Her job be damned. Instead, I'd held my tongue and watched as she walked away, back to her employer. I'd followed her home, keeping my distance. There weren't any nefarious intentions behind it, merely wanting to know where she was staying. I'd overheard the way Mrs. Grandville had spoken to her, and I didn't like it. She was too controlling. Alina had been thinking rather loudly, giving me no other option than to listen to what she had to convey. I heard everything the woman had said to her since she'd been hired. Talk about a control freak.

"Gabriel?" Enzo nudged me, shaking me out of my own head.

"Hmm?"

"We're here," Enzo answered, pointing to the lettering on the building.

Bishop Enterprises, Inc.

The Bishops were a difficult bunch, to say the least. Roman Bishop was among the worst. Never doing anything without personal gain, he was exactly the sort I needed to convince. If the Lilith Nest Viktor left behind was to be resurrected, I needed as many aces up my sleeve as I could manage.

"You picked up the Cadenhead?" I asked.

Lorenzo nodded from the driver's seat, handing the bag over his shoulder.

"Excellent," I said, pushing the door open and climbing out of the back seat.

Straightening myself, I strode into the building like I owned the place. The bag was hefty in my hand. I'd remembered Roman's penchant for good whiskey, a topic I was well versed in. There was a secretary typing hurriedly on her tablet, oblivious to me.

I cleared my throat, raising a brow.

"Can I help you, sir?" she asked, not looking up from her screen.

"I'm here to see Roman Bishop. I have an appointment. The name's Gabriel Doyle."

The secretary clicked away on her computer like she hadn't heard a word I'd said. After another moment, she replied, "All right, Mr. Doyle. You can take a seat. He'll be right with you."

I nodded and walked to the sitting area where black leather sofas and chairs sat invitingly.

"No need to sit, Doyle," a deep voice said from the doorway. "Yours is a face I didn't think I'd be seeing again. What dragged you back into town?" he asked, as we passed through the door and entered his office.

Roman Bishop didn't look like he'd aged a day in the last forty years. His dark hair was slicked back, and his jaw was covered by the scruff of a few-days'-old beard. Deep blue eyes observed my every move, calculating, just as I was sizing him up. He was an imposing man, standing a few inches taller than my own six foot one frame. He was lean, but lethal.

"I brought a gift," I said, holding the bag out to him. "You preferred high quality whiskey the last I knew. I figured those tastes didn't change much. Once a whiskey man, always one."

"Cadenhead 1963, excellent cask. Impressive," he noted, examining the bottle for authenticity.

"Whiskey was one thing we Irish got right," I answered.

"No shit. So what is it I can do for you, Doyle? I don't have many visitors bringing gifts or stopping by just for shits and giggles. You came here because you want me to do something for you. What is it?"

Shrewd and to the point. I could respect that.

"Indeed. Viktor Azimov's nest, actually."

"What about it?"

"I want it resurrected. My kind need to stick together, for both our sake and the general public's. By resurrecting the nest, we'd accomplish both."

"What's wrong with the way things are now?"

"You want more power in this town. You're going to need support to get it. What better support than the vampires? You reap the benefits no matter what happens."

"How's that?"

"The vampires support you. In turn, you also get another level of security to keep the vampire population under wraps. Nest members would have to answer to the nest leader in addition to the Petran girl. We keep to ourselves, less problems for you, more autonomy for us. It's a win-win."

"You assume a lot about me."

"When you live as long as I do, you observe, watch choices over time. If I were you, I'd be less worried about me noticing your business dealings and a little more concerned about the other founders noticing," I replied, getting to my feet. "Think it over and give me a call."

I held my hand out to him, waiting for him to shake it. After a moment of contemplation, he thrust his hand into mine, squeezing it in a show of dominance.

"Thank you for the whiskey," he said.

I nodded and strode from the room. Dealing with supes was like a game of chess. The moment you blinked, your adversary could take advantage and win the game. That was precisely what I intended to do.

Checkmate, motherfucker.

When I'd first come back to town, I hadn't known why I was being pulled back. At first, I thought it was Alina, and a part of me still thought it was, but now that I was here, it had to be more than just her. Enzo had done some digging for me while I'd been finishing up some business and spending time with Alina. There hadn't been another well-organized nest since the Lilith Nest had been wiped out in 2005. The massacre had left most too scared to even think of such a thing. The town had sunk its hooks into me, and I was laying down roots. With the nest established and Alina by my side, I wouldn't need anything more.

Neither were mine yet, but things were happening, and I had a plan. I only needed to wait until she fell asleep, and then she would know exactly why she was destined to be mine.

CHAPTER 7

ALINA

$\mathcal{T}$he sun was in the final leg of its descent by the time we returned home from their piano lessons. Mrs. Grandville was nowhere to be found, but there was an empty wine glass sporting her signature mauve lipstick next to the sink.

As more evidence of their self-reliance, within thirty minutes of us arriving home, the kids had showered and gotten into pajamas before settling in to read their nightly books.

With the kids tucked in for the night, my time was now officially my own. I ventured upstairs and slunk into my room. Instantly, I could tell something was off. Things were almost where I'd left them, yet not quite. The drawer of the nightstand was slightly ajar, and my jewelry box next to the lamp sat sideways. The more I surveyed the room, the more I noticed was off. Nothing was missing, though.

Someone had rifled through my belongings, and yet, they hadn't taken a single item. Tabby and Neil had been with me, so it couldn't have been either of them, leaving their parents as the prime suspects. This sort of shit was way not cool, and there was no way I was going to put up with my privacy being invaded and not having my boundaries respected. With Mrs. Grandville nowhere to be found, I'd have to brave it and deal with Mr. Grandville.

The house was quiet as I poked my head out of my room.

Mr. Grandville was in his study, hunched over an old dusty book with a tumbler of scotch in his other hand. His face had a red flush to it that said he'd been drinking for a while. Second thoughts crept in. Drunk people were unpredictable, and this was one I didn't even know a little bit about. Remembering the disheveled bedroom, I raised my hand and knocked on the door with as much confidence as I could muster.

The man within grumbled something unintelligible before I could hear him approaching the door. I took a step back to give both of us some room before I was met with the surprised face of Alistair Grandville.

"Ms. Anand? Can I help you with something?" he asked, being more cordial than his wife had ever been.

"Actually yes. There was something I wanted to discuss with you, if you have a moment," I replied, twisting my hands together behind my back in a futile attempt to remain calm.

Confrontation was just about my biggest fear.

"Sure, come right in. I'm actually glad you stopped by. There was something I wanted to speak with you about, too," Mr. Grandville countered, holding the door open wide.

He didn't move out of the doorway, though, so I had to squeeze by him awkwardly. He smelled of a cheap cologne and heavily of his scotch. He had to have been drinking for a while, but you couldn't tell by his movements or speech. His office was about the same size as my room, with bookshelves covering two walls. Most of the titles weren't in English and looked like they'd be better locked away behind a glass case, with how aged they appeared to be. In the corner sat a small bar cart that looked well used.

"What did you wish to speak to me about?" he asked, rounding the edge of his desk and flopping down into his seat.

I took the seat across the desk and answered immediately in the most confident voice I could muster.

"Well, it appears that someone has been in my room and going through my things. While I have nothing to hide, I also won't tolerate my privacy being invaded like that. I need certain assurances that it won't happen again if I'm to continue on here. Otherwise, I'm afraid I'll need to resign."

Mr. Grandville's eyebrows rose, and his lips curled into a smile.

"Self-assured. I like that. It takes balls to stick up for yourself. As for your room, that was my fault. You see, the room used to be my den. Some of the furniture, like the small desk and the bedside table, stayed there. I was looking for a very specific object, and I had worried I may have left it in the desk. I searched for it, but alas, it wasn't there. I do apologize, and I realize I should have asked first, but I'm sure you can understand that I wouldn't be used to asking permission to look for something in my own home. It won't happen again, but this has been an adjustment for all of us. I hope it won't be a factor if you decide you have to leave us," Mr. Grandville explained remorsefully.

I nodded.

"As long as I have your guarantee that it won't happen again, I don't see why it should be an issue. I enjoy your children and would hate to leave, but I can only handle so much," I added.

Mr. Grandville stood and came around the desk until he was right beside me. He sat back against the edge of the desk and crossed his arms over his chest. His blond hair had been gelled back at some point, but it was wearing off and falling loose onto his forehead. His cheeks were flushed with intoxication, getting worse by the minute, but he didn't even act affected.

When he didn't say anything, I figured it was a great time to ask what he'd wanted to speak to me about.

"You mentioned you wanted to speak to me about something as well?" I prodded.

"Right! Erm, I apologize. How rude of me. Can I offer you a drink?" he asked, pushing himself off the desk and taking a few sure strides to where the cart stood.

My mother's voice echoed in the back of my mind: *Never accept a drink from strangers.*

"No, thank you. I'm not much of a drinker."

Nor had I been since I'd gotten drunk the first time and had promptly thrown up all over Bobby Stevens, my first real boyfriend, when I was eighteen.

Mr. Grandville nodded and refilled his own glass before resuming his spot inches away from me, perched on the edge of the desk. After a few moments of awkward silence aside from the ice tinking the side of his glass, he finally got to his point.

"So, you're a Marid djinn, is that right?" he asked.

Normally it wasn't something I went around advertising. Granting wishes came with too many strings attached, and I tried to steer clear of that at all costs. My magic was my own, and it needed to stay that way. However, there wasn't so much as an ounce of malevolence coming from the man, only genuine curiosity.

"I am," I answered.

His smile grew wider, and he leaned in closer.

"That's fascinating! I've read about your kind before, though I never thought I'd have the opportunity to meet one. I have so many questions I could ask you. I'm not sure if you're aware or not, but the history of the djinn race is amazing. Truly extraordinary that any of you survived."

The djinn weren't a species many knew much about, and that was the way we liked it. If he had a lot of information about my kind, I had to wonder why.

"What is it you do for a living, Mr. Grandville?"

"Please. Call me Alistair," he said, his English accent light, but still there. "I specialize in antiques, as those in my family had before me. It's really more of a family business."

"I'm sorry, *Alistair*. I don't know much about antiques. History was never my forte," I replied, slightly confused by what was going on.

Something didn't seem right, yet I couldn't put my finger on what.

"Would you be able to give me a small demonstration? Just to sate the curiosity of another magic wielder?" he asked, leaning forward and resting his hand on my shoulder, giving it a slight squeeze.

There it was. That's what he wanted, and I knew it. The pressure on my shoulder grew a little more, but wasn't painful or intimidating. Regardless, he'd managed to make me extremely uncomfortable.

"I'm sorry, Mr. Grandville. I'm not comfortable with that. My magic isn't for parlor tricks, and I'm not in the wish-granting business. I hope you understand," I answered, trying to stay as diplomatic as possible while still standing my ground.

There was an unmistakable flash of anger in his eyes, a slip of the mask he'd put on for me, before it disappeared, and the mask slid back into place. His hand crept down my arm until his thumb was brushing a seductive trail down the bare flesh exposed by my T-shirt. Leaning in a little, his eyes dipped to my chest. He was so close, I could smell the scotch on his breath. The man was too close for comfort, and when his eyes focused on my lips, I had no doubt what he was trying to do. I wasn't about to have any part of it.

Nope. Nopity nope.

I shot up out of the chair like a fire had been lit under my ass.

"Mr. Grandville, I'm sorry, but no. You're a married man, and I'm your employee. This is inappropriate on multiple levels, and I'm not that kind of girl."

I spun and exited the room before he could say anything more. The door shut a little harder than I intended, slamming loudly as I bolted for the safety of my room. I sped only to stop a few feet shy of the door. The sound of glass shattering sounded from Mr. Grandville's office. It would appear the man had a bit of a temper to top it all off.

When I was finally tucked safely inside the confines of my bedroom, I could finally breathe a sigh of relief to be away from that man. He was a skilled actor, which had become very clear when I'd witnessed the slip of his charming mask.

I focused on my door, half expecting the pissed warlock to come charging through it, and waved my hand in front of it. The air shimmered for a second before it settled into a secure calm. There was no way anyone was going to be coming through it without an invitation again.

Nearly twenty minutes later, the door downstairs slammed shut. Not long after, I heard Mrs. Grandville's telltale heels clicking against the hardwood floors. Curiosity was getting the better of me. My magic surged forth, allowing me to watch everything that was happening in the hallway without ever moving from my bed. No one would even know I was watching.

When I heard the door to Mr. Grandville's office open, I withdrew. Would he tell her what happened? Would he twist reality to make himself look like the victim? The man made my skin crawl, and now I knew it was for a good reason. My magic refused to be quieted, though. I reinforced the barrier around my room once again, just to be sure. I kept my ears alert, waiting for one of them to approach my door.

That night, it took me a long while to settle down enough for sleep to take me. Gabriel's words were still playing in my head over and again when I succumbed.

A WARM SUMMER breeze caressed my bare flesh. I glanced down at myself, and instead of my black pants and purple T-shirt, I was wearing a nearly skin-tight black dress that barely covered my butt. It wasn't something I would usually wear, like ever, but I had to admit I was liking what it was doing for my figure. No mirror was needed to know that I looked smoking hot.

"I'm glad you could finally join me. I was beginning to worry you wouldn't show tonight," a deep voice boomed behind me.

I turned to see Gabriel, standing with nothing on besides his low-slung black pants. The muscular V of his torso drew my eye.

"Where are we?" I asked, noting the grandeur of the bedroom surrounding us.

A large four poster bed stood against the wall with a leather chaise lounge at the foot of it. Its oxblood color drew the eye, standing in stark contrast to the white-and-gold bed with black-stained wood.

"This is my home. I hope you don't mind that I steered us here. I wanted to be somewhere a little more private and comfortable. If it bothers you, we can go somewhere else," he offered.

"No, this is fine. I was just curious. There are so many things I want to ask right now. Like, is this a dream? Is this what you were talking about when you said we'd met before?"

He nodded.

"I . . . I don't know what to say. This is so strange, but there's something about this, about you, that feels right."

He crossed to me in an instant, moving faster than humanly possible, but he wasn't a human, and all of this was real life.

"Then don't say anything. Just feel," Gabriel purred, closing the distance between us and taking me in his arms.

His lips crashed down on mine, melding together and creating something bigger than either of us. So often I was reserved and careful about my actions, but not with Gabriel. With him, I felt like I didn't have to think. I could just live and let whatever happened be.

My lips moved against his as though we'd done this dance a million times before. His tongue brushed along the seam of my mouth, begging entrance. I was helpless to do anything but surrender to him. I'd never wanted a man more than I wanted him in that moment.

In a quick swoop, Gabriel cradled me against his chest and crossed to the bed. He tossed me down into the fluffy duvet that billowed around me.

He stood at the edge of the bed with his stare fixed on the apex of my thighs. My core clenched at the thought of him touching me there. Gabriel's fingers trailed up the bare skin of my legs, peaking over my knee and skimming closer. I wiggled, trying to ease the ache of need that was driving me into a frenzy.

"I don't think I've ever seen such a beautiful sight, love. I can smell how much you want me."

His words were like throwing gasoline on an already raging inferno. I bit my lip to stop myself from trembling with need.

"Please, Gabriel," I moaned, pushing myself up.

I was about to shift around and grab for the button on his pants, but Gabriel held his hand up.

"Let me have the honors, desert rose. I want to taste you."

I shivered at his words and lay back into the cloud of a bed. He followed me, climbing over top of me and shoving my dress up to expose my throbbing bare sex.

"So wet," he groaned, gliding his finger through my soaked folds.

My legs shook and my breath came in short pants. With sure strokes, Gabriel circled my clit, never touching it directly, yet getting closer with each pass.

"Oh gods," I moaned, squirming closer.

"That's right, love. I want to hear how much you need me. Don't hold back," he said, shoving my legs wide and leaving me completely exposed.

His touch was cool, and yet he was setting me on fire everywhere he touched. Grabbing my waist, he dragged me to the edge of the bed and dropped to his knees, throwing each leg over his shoulders. The second his mouth touched my needy core, I almost detonated.

My fingers curled into his hair, tugging and twitching as he lapped up my juices like a fine wine. Pressure built inside and climbed higher and higher. Gabriel plunged his blunt finger into my molten depths, hitting that spot deep inside that made me squeeze around him tightly. I was close.

Gabe worked his fingers in and out of me at a feverish pace, while his tongue teased my swollen nub relentlessly. I was nearing my peak.

"Yes! Right there," I moaned.

It spurred Gabe on. He pushed deeper, hitting the end in a sweet mix of pleasure and pain. Then I was there, standing on the edge, and I jumped, riding the waves of my orgasm.

"Gabriel! Oh my . . . Fuck!" I cried, shattering around his thick digit.

He curled his finger, hitting it just right, and that's when I was fairly certain I saw actual stars. I squeezed my eyes shut tight, and every muscle seemed to tense up with the orgasm. He didn't stop, not until every aftershock and spasm had ceased. My heart pounded, and I let out a long languid sigh.

"Whoa."

He smirked, showing off those sexy dimples, and the tips of his fangs peeked out below his upper lip. Before he could say anything, I felt like I was falling, and then I was torn away from Gabriel and his bed and was back in my own.

My alarm blared on the side table, waking me from the most earth shatteringly delicious dream I'd had in a while. My legs still felt weak, like it had all been real, when I went to stand from the bed. I had a whole new set of questions to ask when I met Gabriel later that afternoon.

CHAPTER 8

GABRIEL

Sunlight streamed in through the window, warming my skin. I stretched out, still smelling Alina's intoxicating scent on my sheets. The dreams were getting more real all the time. God, she was stunning. I kept replaying the way she'd squirmed against me or ground herself against my mouth harder when I was doing it exactly how she wanted me to.

How was I going to be expected to behave myself after such a night? And in front of children, no less! It was going to be a challenge. I climbed out of bed and went in search of Lorenzo. He needed to know that plans had changed, because now that I'd found Alina, there was no way I was walking away from her.

My throat ached with thirst, and I knew I had to feed before I went to meet her. I'd have to make a stop at Sanguine Elixirs to quench the hunger. It wasn't anything like drinking straight from the source, but it got the job done in a pinch. I ventured downstairs to begin my day and keep busy until it was time to meet my lovely Alina.

It was becoming all too clear while I was running around taking care of the to-do list before my date with Alina that I was acting like a lovesick pup. Never in my wildest dreams did I believe I'd be *that guy*. However, the time had come, and the fact was that I no longer gave a fuck about being that guy. If I had her, nothing else mattered. All I had to do was get through the next few hours until I could see her again.

By the time two o'clock rolled around, I'd already been at the park for twenty minutes, just in case she showed up early. I'd even resorted to pacing at one point. A million scenarios played out in my head about how things would be after I made sure the memory of last night stuck with her. Every single scenario evaporated the moment I heard her voice approaching.

Alina was assuring the children they would have a good time before they rounded the corner and strode into the park.

"It'll be fine, Tabby. It's not like I'm taking you to the dentist to have your teeth pulled. It's just the park," Alina told her young charge as they made their way toward the rink.

The girl rolled her eyes at Alina, who was obliviously searching around for me. She spied me standing by the ice rink. Her cheeks instantly heated, and her luscious mouth lifted into a lazy grin.

My mouth went dry like I'd run a marathon and the butterflies felt as though they'd morphed into pterodactyls. Alina ushered the children off to the benches by the rink, keeping a close eye on them before approaching me. I closed my mind, making sure I wouldn't trespass on any private thoughts. I never wanted her to feel like she had to protect herself against me.

"Hey, um, I'll be right back. I need to help them get their skates on," she added, holding up two pairs of child-sized ice skates.

She turned and sauntered over to a bench where her young charges were busy taking their shoes off. Her perfect round ass swayed with each step. God, how I wanted to bite it and watch it turn a lovely shade of pink while her luscious lips wrapped around my cock, milking me to completion.

Apples, trees, rocks. I was thinking of anything I could to keep my thoughts from straying to the night before. The last thing I needed was to be rocking a raging boner in the middle of a semi-crowded park and watching young kids ice skating. Alina laced up their skates like she'd done it a hundred times and ushered them out onto the ice. Making her way to me, she tucked her hair behind her ears nervously.

"Hi," she said shyly, chewing on her bottom lip like she had the night before when she'd come apart under my touch.

"I want to bite that lip," I said, breaking the tension and moving in to kiss her. I couldn't help myself.

She didn't resist me in the least. Her mouth sought out mine, and her arms snaked around my neck as she tugged me closer. The kiss was quick, but full of emotions and need we were both feeling. It was everything. It was lust, excitement, uncertainty, and love, though Alina didn't need to know about that last part, at least not yet.

"This is all real, isn't it?" she whispered, pulling back a little, though staying close enough that our bodies were always touching.

"As real as it gets, love," I replied, my thumb brushing over her bottom lip.

She shivered and turned her head, watching the kids. I followed her stare and spotted the children making careful and wobbly laps around the rink. I straightened slightly, remembering we were in public. I was more than willing to give everyone a show, but Alina was mine, and I preferred her goods remained mine to be unwrapped and savored in private.

"I really should be keeping an eye on them," she mused, pulling away from me and leading the way to a bench by the rink.

I followed behind, noting the sparkle in her eye when she watched the Grandville children. It wasn't like a mother watching her young— that was too intimate for what this was. This was more like a woman respecting the great responsibility she'd been given.

"How long have you been caring for them?" I asked, breaking the charged silence that had formed.

"Not long. Only about a week. What about you? How long have you been here?"

I shrugged. "Not much longer than you. I moved away to figure out who I was away from my old life. I always felt like an outcast, searching for something more than I should be able to want. It only occurred to me a few days ago that maybe what I was looking for all along was right here. It was you."

Alina's lips parted at my unexpected confession, and I heard her heart rate kick up, but she didn't smell afraid, so I pressed my luck.

"I know you have a lot of questions. I would, too, if I were you. Last night was . . . amazing, to say the least. It's crazy and sudden, but there's a connection here I never even knew was possible. I'm not ready to give you up."

Alina had turned to face me squarely during my confession. Her face was an unreadable mask, and I wanted more than anything to know exactly what she was thinking.

"This is unlike anything I've ever experienced before. It's like my soul was calling out for something more and you answered," I added.

"I couldn't have described it better myself," she answered.

I opened my mouth to say more, but the sound of children yelling captured our attention before I could.

"Freaks!" a group of children called, cornering the Grandville children on the far side of the ice.

There looked to be five children to their two, shoving them and telling them they needed to get off their rink.

"Oh gods!" Alina exclaimed, jumping up.

"It's okay, I've got this." I stopped her and started for the ice rink.

"Are you sure?" she asked, uncertain.

I nodded and strode right for the group of bullies, carefully minding the ice. A girl with curly red hair threw a rock at the young boy, missing his face by barely an inch. Someone was going to get hurt.

"Hey!" I roared, closing the distance between the bench and where they had the children corralled. "What's going on?"

The bullies saw me and scattered like roaches before I could reach them at a human pace. Sometimes I really hated the no-humans-in-the-loop rule. It made making an example of people more difficult than it needed to be.

The girl was holding her brother's hand, and he was sniffling and trying not to cry like I knew he really wanted to.

"Are you guys okay?" I asked, dropping to my knees in front of them.

They watched me nervously, not answering me. My eyes surveyed every inch of them, searching for any sign of injury.

"It's okay, Tabby, Neil. He's my friend," Alina said from right behind me.

Alina must've been following right behind me. Tabby eyed Alina over my shoulder and wiped a tiny tear from her cheek.

"We're fine. I told you this was a bad idea," she snarled, anger warring with big fat tears that were beginning to well up in her eyes.

"Let me tell you something. I want you to remember that the problem is with them. Anyone who would single out someone else or pick on them like those kids, they're busy trying to point the finger at everyone else so no one sees how weird or broken they are. You're perfect the way you are and don't you dare listen to something those little asswipes said," I explained,

"Gabriel! Language, they're just children,"

I lifted a shoulder only half apologetically.

"How about we grab some hot cocoa? That fixes everything," I offered.

I'd never actually drunk the stuff, never having needed to. Although, as a cultural staple, who was I to tell about a billion people they were wrong?

"I want extra chocolate!" Neil yelled, wiping his nose on the arm of his jacket.

"Great choice! What about you, Tabby? What kind do you want?"

"Mother wouldn't approve."

"Well, some rules are meant to be broken," I replied with a wink.

I started for the Danzan Park concession stand and had only made it about fifteen feet when Tabby murmured, "With marshmallows."

In a few short moments, I was back with steaming cups in hand.

"Wow!" Neil exclaimed, blowing into the opening.

Alina took the spot directly next to me, across from the kids, and wrapped her arms around my shoulders.

Leaning in close, she whispered, "That was a really sweet thing you did for them. Thank you."

"If they were mine, I'd hope someone would do the same for them. It's only right."

We spent another hour chatting and making jokes. Little by little the kids came out of their shells, talking with a bit more ease and interacting more than they had when I first saw them. I could tell Alina was noticing the change too.

When the day was over, none of us wanted it to end. Reluctantly, I let my woman go, back to finish her duties with the promise she'd message me to see her later that evening. The night before, we'd shared a dream. Tonight, I was hoping to finally have a taste of the real deal. Watching her leave with Tabby and Neil, my eyes were glued to her ass as it swayed with perfect grace. It was going to be a painful wait.

With luck, I'd managed to get an audience with the local outlaw crew, Swords of the Infernal Night Motorcycle Club, or SIN, as they were more aptly called. Enzo was waiting for me in a parking spot across from the park. As soon as I climbed into the rear seat, he turned.

"They sent us a location. It's some ways out of town boundaries in an abandoned gas station. Are you sure you want to meet with them? It's not too late to back out," he pleaded.

I knew he didn't like the sort I tended to work with. Grudges lasted centuries, and having the right friends in the right places could make or break a man. I had no intention of letting them break me, so SIN was going to help me stack my deck.

CHAPTER 9

ALINA

*G*abriel wasn't at all what I'd expected. As a vampire, I'd thought he'd be dark and broody, and maybe he was sometimes, but he was also caring and compassionate. He'd been the first one to try to cheer up the kids and bring them out of themselves, more than I'd been able to accomplish in a week. I wondered what his past was like, but more than anything, I wanted time for him to volunteer everything there was to know about him.

Still on cloud nine when we arrived back home, I wasn't expecting to be ambushed as soon as I marched through the door.

"Tabitha! Cornelius! To your room now!" Mrs. Grandville roared, as soon as I shut the door behind us.

"What's going on?" I asked, wide-eyed and confused by her anger.

The kids didn't hesitate and bolted for the stairs to hide in their rooms. As soon as they disappeared from view, Mrs. Grandville rounded on me.

"What's going on is you going against my expressed wishes and cavorting with a disgusting bloodsucker in front of my children like a common whore! Who the hell are you to make such a decision? What else have you been doing in front of them or subjecting them to? Hmm?"

Red flags went up like flares from a sinking ship. I didn't know what to say, but Mrs. Grandville was only just getting started.

"Where were you?" Mrs. Grandville roared, stomping toward me from the living area.

"I went into town. Figured if I was going to be living here, I needed to know the town and meet some new people."

"And did you?"

"Yeah, the town's lovely. The rink was—"

"I'm not talking about the damn rink, you trollop! I'm talking about that disgusting bloodsucker you were seen cavorting with."

She must've seen the shock on my face.

"Yes, I know all about it. There's nothing you could do in this town that I wouldn't know about, and in this house, everything you do, even off the clock, is subject to scrutiny. If you like working here, then I would suggest choosing very carefully those you wish to associate with, not that you should have time for such a waste."

I was taken aback. The only person I'd ever had tell me who I could or could not be friends with was my father when I'd brought my first boyfriend home. It hadn't worked out well for my father, but an employer? I didn't even know what to say. I was stunned into silence. Was a job worth dealing with this sort of bullshit? My gut said hell no.

"Look, I know you're probably used to telling the children how to live, and I can appreciate the care you have to take to ensure you have people you can trust working with your children, but—"

"You are not to see him again. Ever. Have I made myself clear?" Mrs. Grandville interjected.

"No," I said simply.

"Excuse me?" she howled.

"I said no. You can tell me who the children can be around. You can tell me where they can go and what they can do. Hell, you can even tell me what I'm allowed to do when I'm on the clock. There is no fucking way you're going to tell me who I can see on my own time, which, by the way, I am taking back. Saturdays and Sundays were in my contract. If you don't like my terms, then we can end this conversation right here. I'm not your child, and you have no right to dictate my life," I forced out, my voice beginning to tremble with anger as I slammed my point home.

Her eyes narrowed. "You'd sacrifice your job for a man you just met? You really are clueless."

"I'm not clueless. I know who he is and what he is. I just won't let someone else's prejudices dictate my feelings toward a man I love."

"You think you've got what it takes to make it on your own? I can tell you from firsthand experience, you don't have what it takes. Give it time. You'll see I'm right. If I have to make my point again, you're finished," Mrs. Grandville sneered, turning and striding away from me with only the angry clicks of her heels to keep me company.

CHAPTER 10

ALINA

*L*ater that evening, my phone buzzed. Gabriel's name lit up the front of my phone. I tried to ignore the damned butterflies and giddy feelings just the mere idea of him created, but there was no use.

Meet me outside your gate at 11:30.

I replied with a smiley face and a thumbs up emoji. Glancing at the clock, I saw it was only just barely after eight in the evening. I flopped back and turned on the small TV, losing myself in old reruns of crime shows.

Grabbing a gray sweater dress from my closet, I paired it with some black tights and my knee-high boots to complete the look. It was going to be subtly sexy without being over the top and in your face. Though I was sure there was only one way tonight could go, and that wouldn't involve clothes.

The time to leave arrived, and I released the wards to my room. Creeping out, I listened carefully. All was quiet, but I wasn't taking any risks of getting caught this time. Bringing the image of the front of the Grandvilles' house to the forefront of my mind, I focused and unleashed the magic within. The sound of wind filled my ears, though I knew no one else could hear it. Closing my eyes, I snapped my fingers and let the howling wind take me. When I opened them again, I was standing outside the house on the front porch.

"I was almost worried you were going to leave me hanging," Gabriel teased from the curb.

"You think I'd do that to you?" I joked, sauntering toward him.

Gabriel's Lexus was parked on the roadside, while he held the passenger door open for me.

"I said almost, love. Now, I'm taking you somewhere special."

An excited chill ran through me.

"Where are we going?" I asked, slipping into the passenger seat and fastening the seatbelt.

"Telling you would ruin the surprise. My lips are sealed. You'll just have to wait and see," he said, shutting my door and moving around to the driver's side. He was practically vibrating with excitement.

The car was already running, and the leather seats were smooth like velvet. Without wasting another precious second, Gabriel took off, leisurely stroking my thigh as I wished it was somewhere more intimate.

I kept thinking about what Mrs. Grandville had said about Gabriel being a killer. I didn't doubt he'd killed in his long life. He was a vampire, and it sort of came with the territory. He was also from a different time, when life was snuffed out easier than it was now, with medical interventions. None of that mattered to me, though, because I knew deep down to my bones that he would never hurt me. He had his secrets, and one day, I hoped he would feel comfortable enough to share them with me, but in the meantime, I had a secret of my own that he deserved to know.

"I'm a Marid djinn," I blurted.

Gabe's head swiveled in my direction. "I know, love."

"You do?"

He nodded, tapping his temple. "You're a loud thinker sometimes. I knew you'd tell me when you were ready, and I didn't want to pry."

"Oh. I was just thinking that I didn't want there to be any more secrets between us. I don't like people knowing what I am. It can get dangerous for me, for my family, or the race as a whole."

"You're right to be afraid, but you don't ever need to fear me. Your secret is safe, but I have to ask. Is it true what they say about a Marid's power being derived from an amulet?"

I had to giggle. There were so many myths surrounding my kind that some of them were just crazy.

"Yes and no. My power comes from within myself, but it's tethered to my opal," I explained, pulling the necklace out. "If someone were ever to steal my necklace, they could force me to do anything they wished. I would no longer be in control of what I do. Worse, they could imprison me inside it for all of eternity if they wanted to."

"You'd be their slave?" he asked, his jaw flexing as he gritted his teeth angrily.

"Yes, essentially," I answered, noting the white forming on his knuckles. "You're angry. Why?"

Gabriel sighed warily.

"Once upon a time, I knew the sting of a master's whip. I bear the scars as a reminder. The practice incites me to violence, so God help the poor bastard who ever tries to take what's mine."

"Yours?" I asked, grinning like a fool, because the thought of this man being so protective and possessive of me made me want him even more.

"Yes. You've been mine since the moment you walked into my dream and showed me there was more to life than death and decay, that I no longer needed to be a shadow merely existing," he said, laying his cool hand on my thigh.

With the barest of touches, my panties were already soaked. He could surely feel the charged tension between us. It was so thick you could've cut it with a knife.

Right as I was about to throw all caution to the wind and jump on him, the car rolled to a stop in front of a grand mansion.

"We're here," Gabriel announced, giving me a devilish wink and climbing out of the car.

Moving around the vehicle, Gabriel opened the door for me and ushered me out of the car.

"Welcome to my home."

CHAPTER 11

GABRIEL

$\mathcal{A}$lina's eyes widened as she took in the estate.

"This . . . is yours?" she said, stepping into my side and wrapping her arms around my waist.

"It is now. My inheritance, if you will. It's a long story, and I don't want to bore you, so let's take this inside and get to know each other a little better. We have a private dinner waiting. What do you say? Join me?"

A bright smile graced her full lips, and she slipped her hand into mine.

"That sounds wonderful," she replied.

Stepping inside, she froze, and her eyes widened as she took in the grandeur of the foyer and the inviting marble staircase.

"This is like something out of a fairy tale," she murmured, peeking at me over her shoulder as she went.

Her eyes traveled over me hungrily, and I wanted nothing more than to throw her over my shoulder and whisk her upstairs to spend the evening with her riding my cock. She deserved better than that. Alina deserved a gentleman, though if she tested my self-control much more, I'd throw caution to the wind and do as I pleased.

"The dining room is this way," I announced, my hand settling on her lower back as I ushered her deeper into my domain.

As expected, Enzo had put together an elegant meal which was already laid out, steaming, and waiting for us. Candles were a nice touch, aided by the dim recessed lighting to set the perfect mood.

"Wow, this is . . . just wow. It smells so good," Alina remarked, taking a tentative step forward and then another.

Taking a seat, she dug right in, trying everything there was to offer. We spoke animatedly as she ate, learning more about one another. When she'd had her fill, Alina made another kind of hunger known.

Pushing myself up, I strode around the table with the grace of a cat stalking its prey. Alina's bright eyes tracked me the entire journey. The flutter of her heart picking up pace, and her pheromones flooding the air, made my dick strain almost painfully against its confines. I wanted nothing more than to lose myself in her, but all in good time.

Kneeling beside Alina, I gazed up at her, struck by her beauty that radiated from the inside out.

As I brushed the back of my fingers over her bronzed complexion, she leaned into my touch.

"Alina, I've been alive for a very long time, and never once have I faced anything as scary as the idea of letting you know the real me, letting you love me. The way I feel—it's big, and I don't know what tomorrow holds, nor can I make any promises. But what do you say, desert rose? Will you let go of everything you believe and step into the unknown with me?" I asked, pushing up to my full height and extending an inviting hand to her.

Eyeing my hand, Alina bit into her bottom lip contemplatively before reaching out and accepting my invitation.

Good girl.

With a quick yet gentle tug, I pulled her into my arms. Her lithe frame fit perfectly against my own, as though she was made just for me. Holding tightly around my neck, she lifted her cognac gaze to lock with my own. I turned, heading for the stairs, and let loose my restraint. I surpassed human capabilities as I bolted up the stairs toward my bedroom with Alina cradled carefully in my arms.

Within the span of a second, we'd entered my room, and I was laying her down on my bed. Stepping back to give her a moment to adjust, I popped the top button of my shirt free and untucked it as I got comfortable. Alina pushed up to her feet and closed the short distance between us, but unsteadily fell into me instead.

"I'm so sorry. I thought I was okay, and then the room started to spin," she said, gathering fistfuls of my shirt into her dainty hands to anchor her.

My hands came to rest on her hips, kneading the soft flesh through her top.

"There's nothing to be sorry for. The mistake was my own. It can be disorienting at first, but you should be fine. No long-term effects," I said apologetically.

As she shifted her weight, the length of her brushed over mine, and Alina's breath caught, though she wouldn't meet my gaze head on. Shaky, nimble fingers released their hold on me and moved to the buttons of my shirt. Sliding my hand up the side of her, I brought it to rest on the side of her neck, tipping her face toward me.

"Are you afraid of me?" I asked, my fangs lengthening as I inhaled her spicy, sweet scent.

Her eyes met mine and darkened with desire.

"No. I should be scared, but the only thing I feel with you is safe. I know what you are, Gabriel Doyle, and I know that you'd never hurt me. The man you were is not the man you are now, the man I fell in love with and thought for so long was just a figment of my imagination. I need to know this is real, Gabriel. Please?" she asked, her voice so raw and genuine that I had to obey.

"Your wish is my command, darling."

Gripping her tightly, I lifted her as her legs locked around my waist securely. Her lips descended on mine with a hunger that could rival a starving man's. There was no easing into it. We were both laying it all out and giving ourselves to each other completely.

Sweet and innocent was the personality she portrayed to the world, but behind a closed bedroom door, that fell away. Alina took control, tearing my shirt open and shoving it down my arms and out of her way.

Pushing her sweater up her slender torso, I tugged it over her head and tossed it to the floor. Alina gyrated her hips, bumping against my throbbing erection just right. God, I couldn't wait to be inside her. Nipping at my bottom lip, she pulled back with a sly grin. Oh, she knew exactly what she was doing to me.

With a quick snap of my fingers, her bra joined the growing pile of clothes littering my bedroom floor. As I lowered her to the bed, her hands went instantly to my belt, unfastening it and pulling it off. Popping the button on my slacks, she shoved them down, along with my briefs, freeing me to seek the warm, wet sanctuary of her waiting lips. Her hand gripped my shaft firmly, making long strokes as her cheeks hollowed and her tongue ran up and down me. Boldly, she stared up at me the whole time, watching raptly for my reaction. Every twitch and groan drove her harder. Fisting her hair, I pushed deeper, slamming into the back of her throat before pulling her free of me.

"I need to be inside of you," I growled, pulling her to her feet and capturing her lips, relishing her sweet taste with a hint of myself.

It was an aphrodisiac to know in some small way she carried my scent. In that moment, Alina decided it was time for her to seize control of the situation. I stepped out of the pants and kicked them aside before Alina planted her hand in the center of my chest, spinning me around and pushing me back toward the bed. I fell backward onto my bed while Alina slid her tights down her long legs. I sat up, reaching across the distance between us, and tore her purple lace panties from her body, leaving her bare for my eyes to feast upon.

"Patience, Gabriel. Haven't you heard good things come to those who wait?" she teased, climbing onto the bed and kneeling between my legs.

"I've been very patient, waiting as long as I have. If you tease me much more, I'm not sure I'll be able to stop myself from fucking you the way you need," I replied, my voice husky with lust.

Climbing up me, Alina nipped at my belly and chest, her legs settling on each side of me so she was straddling me. She hovered over my cock, lowering herself just enough to slicken the head.

"Is that a promise?" she asked coyly.

Narrowing my gaze at her, I grinned slyly as I gripped her hips and flexed, driving home and burying myself to the hilt in her molten pussy. She gasped, squeezing her walls around me, and let out a long moan as she adjusted. After a moment, she began to move, pushing up and sinking back down in tantalizingly slow rhythm.

Up, down, rock forward until I bottomed out.

Her pace was picking up quickly as I glided through her wet folds with ease. Alina's perfect round breasts bounced in my face mesmerizingly. They filled my palms as I brought her pinkish-brown nipple to my lips and latched on. Her head fell back as she pushed into me. Throaty cries filled my room as she began riding me harder. The thudding of her heartbeat filled my ears, and I could feel the needy ache low in my belly as she drove me closer to my end.

Alina's silky walls quivered, tightening ever so slightly, and I knew she was close to her end too. Pressure was building low in my belly with each gyration of her hips.

"Gabriel, oh yeah. Right there," she cried, impaling herself on my cock harder.

Shooting up to a sitting position, I held her tightly against me as she shattered, pushing me over the edge and igniting the spiral of my own orgasm. Pleasure jolted through me with a force that took my breath away. Thick ropes of my seed exploded from me, filling her to the brim and spilling out. Alina's nails raked down my shoulders as she pulsed around me, drawing each spasm of my orgasm out. Without thinking, I bit down, just below her collarbone. Alina's rich blood filled my mouth as my tongue lapped at the bite.

"Oh fuck. Fuck, yes. Gabriel!" she screamed in ecstasy, clutching my head to her.

I took pull after pull of the sweet liquid until I came back to myself and leaned back. I pushed my thumb onto the sharp point of my fang until it broke the surface and blood welled up. Smearing it onto the punctures, I watched the skin knit back together, staunching the bleeding.

Alina and I fell onto the bed, panting from the exertion. Her sweat-slickened body wrapped around mine.

"That was . . . wow," she murmured.

"Mmmm," I grunted, tugging her closer.

My cock twitched, hardening as the images of her riding me replayed.

"I don't think I'll ever tire of this," I confessed, rolling over her until I was seated and aligned between her legs.

She pulled my head down to hers, kissing me with renewed passion. We made love over and again, until the sun's rays began to peek over the horizon. I drove Alina back to the Grandvilles', wishing I could whisk her back to my home and keep her there forever, but she'd told me what had happened earlier. She wanted to face it head on and let the chips fall where they may. When I pulled up next to the curb, I made her promise to text or call that evening to tell me how things went. Well-fucked was a sexy look on her as she strode up the porch and slipped into the Grandvilles' home and out of sight.

Returning home, I went to open the door when the door knob turned and the door swung open before I could touch it.

I froze.

No one was there, but the door still hung open. Stepping inside, I focused on the door and just as unexpectedly, it slammed shut. Digging my keys out of my pockets, I held them in the palm of my hand and less than ten seconds later, they rose and hung themselves on the key hook in the kitchen.

Well, this is an interesting development, I thought.

Alina had shared her magic with me when I'd drunk from her. The possibilities seemed endless; however, I'd need to tell her to be more careful in the future about who she let drink from her, not that I thought I'd be letting that happen any time soon.

The rest of the day was spent testing the magic. Late in the afternoon, I braved sleep and hoped Alina was sleeping, too. Even though I'd just spent the night with her, I missed her like it had been years. Her place was by my side. Hours passed as I waited, but she never came.

Something was wrong, so very wrong.

CHAPTER 12

ALINA

*T*he house was dark by the time I returned. My cheeks were flushed with excitement. Sneaking around like what we were doing was dangerous, putting us at risk of being discovered, which gave me an adrenaline rush the likes of which I'd never known. Gabriel was addictive, and when we were together, there was an undeniable connection between the two of us.

I pushed the door open, taking each step carefully so as to not wake anyone inside. Mr. Grandville was the last person I wanted to run in to, not that dealing with Mrs. Grandville was a walk in the park. The smallest squeak from the hinges was the only disturbance.

Slipping into my room, it only took me a second to feel eyes on me and realize I wasn't alone. A dark figure was sitting on the edge of my bed. The person was large enough to be an adult, but not so big as to be a man.

Mrs. Grandville.

With a flick of my fingers, the overhead light came on. I stood there, fidgeting under her scrutinizing glare.

"Where were you?" Mrs. Grandville's calm voice broke the tense silence.

Unable to mask my confused expression, I took a moment to reply.

"I was out seeing a friend." I said simply.

"You were with the vampire again, weren't you?" she asked.

There was an accusing tone in her voice, and her displeasure was more than evident. It was the quiet before the storm. She took my silence as an admission of guilt.

"Of course you were. You smell like sex. I thought I had made myself clear that you were not to see him again?"

The way she spoke about Gabriel lit a fire inside me that couldn't be quelled with any amount of logic. She'd pushed me too far this time.

"You made it abundantly clear I was not to have Gabriel, which is his name, around the children. I have obeyed that request, but what I do in my own personal time away from Tabitha and Neil is my business. I'm sorry, Mrs. Grandville, but you're neither my mother, nor my husband, and therefore have no say in who I am friends with or associate with. Nothing about my relationship with Gabe affects my ability to do my job and keep my professional life and personal lives separate."

"That's where you're wrong. We brought you into our home, entrusted you with our children, provided you with a place to live and a reasonable wage. The way I look at it, you owe us a lot more than the disrespect you've shown time and again. This is my home, and you *will* obey my rules. Have I made myself clear?" she demanded.

Her calm demeanor was more unsettling than her words, which had downright pissed me off. By the end of her rant, I was shaking mad.

"Mrs. Grandville, I left my parents' home because I refused to live my life by someone else's rules. This is no different. I love Gabriel, and he loves me. There's nothing you can say that's going to change that. If you are that opposed to who I see when I'm off the clock that you break into my room and wait for me to come back, then I guess I'll need to find another family. Respect is a two-way street, Mrs. Grandville, and I wish it didn't have to be this way. I care about the children, but I won't give him up, and I won't tolerate anyone disrespecting my privacy."

"Oh, you're going to quit, are you? How rich. You're not going anywhere, and you won't be seeing that demon again, I promise. Recognize this?" she said, dangling my necklace from her long fingers.

The bottom dropped out of my belly, and my blood ran cold. Instantly, my hands went to my neck where my necklace had been sitting securely. My fingers brushed over the cool metal, not understanding what was going on. How did she have my necklace if it was still around my neck? As soon as I thought it, it dawned on me. Somehow, she'd swapped a fake out for my amulet. Pulling it from around my neck, I watched as the glamour wore away to reveal a simple crystal dangling from a silver chain. My blood ran like ice through my veins.

"I thought you might. See? I as good as own you. You don't like my rules or requests? That's fine. You can spend some time alone until you give some serious thought to your actions. Wishes are your specialty, no?"

My mouth went dry instantly. A million questions ran through my head, but the one that stuck out the most was *what happens next?*

The door hinges croaked behind me, and I glanced over my shoulder to spy Mr. Grandville sneaking into the room and cutting off any chance of escape.

"We have some important business to discuss, don't we, Alistair? It would be much easier for everyone if you would be reasonable and cooperative. See? We need money."

I rolled my eyes so hard I could almost see my own ass.

"The Grandvilles were a powerful family once upon a time. We served kings and queens for centuries, and yet, somehow, here we are with nothing more than debt to our names. We can thank Alistair for that."

"Edith, that's enough. You don't know what you're talking about. There were bad investments made, nothing more."

"Do you really think I'm that stupid? Come on, Alistair. You've known me almost twenty years. Have you ever known me to make false accusations? Did you think I'd never discover the *companies* you invested in were shells for escort services? Or the tens of thousands in scotch and high-stakes poker games? You're not the most discreet man."

I could feel Mr. Grandville shift uncomfortably behind me. Not that I could blame him; Edith had a glare that could make an elephant want to shrink to the size of a mouse.

"So what is it that you want from me?" I braved when neither said anything.

"I thought that would've been obvious. You're a wish granter . . . and now you belong to us. Grandvilles used to be wealthy, powerful, respected. That's what I want, what I've earned, what I was promised when I took a philanderer for a husband. Giving me Tabitha and Cornelius's birthright would be a fabulous start," Edith explained.

"And what about me? Are you planning on keeping me as your own personal slave for the rest of your lives?"

There was something in Edith's gaze that confirmed my worst fears.

"Fuck you! You're wasting your time," I spat.

Mr. Grandville's strong fingers gripped my arms. No matter how hard I struggled, he was unmoving. Panic rose within me, and I did the only thing I could think of—I tried to magic my way out of there. My body grew hot, and a scorching wind cut through the room, but I wasn't fast enough.

Mrs. Grandville's words sucked the magic right out of me. It was ancient Sanskrit, the language of the Marids: It was a language I wasn't familiar with, not firsthand anyway. I tried to pull the power up from my core, cursing myself the whole time for not practicing with it more when I'd come of age. However, when I tried to grasp onto something—anything—there was nothing there to answer.

My brain grew foggier by the second, and blackness crept in around the edges of my vision.

And then . . . there was only the empty darkness to keep me company.

CHAPTER 13

GABRIEL

The hours ticked by as I waited anxiously for Alina's call. I typed out text after text, sending them frantically as I asked where she was, what she was doing, asking her to call me, anything. I needed to do something. Crossing my bedroom to the door, I pulled it open and stuck my head out.

"Enzo!" I hollered down the hallway.

"Yes, sir?" he asked, sleepily wiping the grit from his eyes.

"Can you do something for me?" I asked.

He nodded, smoothing his wild hair down.

"I need you to drive by the Grandville residence and tell me if anything seems off. I can't reach Alina, and I'm beginning to worry something happened to her. It's really just for my peace of mind."

"Yes, sir. I'll leave right away," he answered, disappearing into his bedroom.

He emerged a moment later fully dressed and left on his task. I dialed Alina's number and held the phone to my ear, but it went straight to voicemail.

"Damn it!" I roared, chucking the phone onto the bed.

It took thirty tense and half-panicked minutes for Enzo to return.

"All of the lights were off at the house, sir. There was no sign of the girl. If you'd like, I could inquire after her to the homeowners in the morning?"

I shook my head. "No. That won't be necessary, Enzo. Thank you for trying."

He bowed and slunk into his room, shoulders slouched.

The rush of Alina's magic coursing through my veins gave me an idea, but I had to try it quickly. Alina could teleport, and if her powers could work for me, then maybe I could too. I let my eyes fall shut. Focusing on the Grandville home, I pictured myself being there, at the front door. When I opened my eyes again, I was still standing inside my bedroom at Viktor's old estate.

"Fuck!" I exclaimed, slapping my hand against the wall, hard enough to leave a crack in the boards underneath.

It wasn't going to work. A backup plan was exactly what I needed, yet I didn't have one. My thoughts were filled with the worst possible scenarios. Had they kidnapped her? Was she dead already? Had she run away? The worst was not knowing. She professed her love for me when she'd finally remembered everything we'd shared, but had it all been an act?

As soon as daylight broke, I was going to be on the Grandvilles' front steps, demanding answers and to see Alina. If she wanted nothing more to do with me, then I'd hear it from her lips and cross that bridge when we got to it. If it so happened that the Grandvilles were keeping her from me, then I'd kill every last one of them and take back what was mine. They didn't know who they were fucking with, but her disappearance had awakened the beast within, and he was hungry for their blood.

CHAPTER 14

ALINA

I'd heard rumors about my cousin's stay in her stone's prison. She'd come home, thankfully, but she was never the same. Her brother had told us she'd gone mad with the solitude of it, and now, facing it myself, I could see why.

They called this place the Mahashunya for a reason. It was the Great Emptiness. Not even my power would answer my call.

My bare feet were submerged in almost six inches of water. In every direction, for as far as the eye could see, the glassy water's surface was flat and still. The sky was gray and cloudy, yet unchanging.

"Hello?" I yelled, hoping someone else was there with me.

There was no answer. There was nothing.

A chill seeped into my bones and drained the energy from me. I didn't want to move or do anything.

"Anyone? Is there anyone out there? Somebody? Anybody?" I screamed at the top of my lungs, sending up silent prayers that someone would hear my cries.

I couldn't be the only one, I just couldn't.

Not knowing what else to do, I started walking and kept walking until my muscles ached and my feet had long since gone numb. Water had slowly climbed my dress and was weighing me down.

My teeth chattered as my knees buckled under me, sending me into a splashing heap. The tiny reasonable voice in the back of my head kept telling me to get up and keep going, don't give up, but I couldn't muster a reason to obey. What was the point? No one was there with me, and no one was coming for me. Hell, no one even knew where I was besides the Grandvilles, and they'd put me there.

I'd been so stupid. When they first started acting wrong, I should've left, quit right then and there. I'd let my pride and thirst for independence get the better of me, and look what I had gotten for it. They wanted my compliance. If I refused, there was no telling how long I'd be trapped.

Searching the sky, I tried to locate the source of the light, but there was nothing that stood out. For all I knew, I could've been walking for hours in circles. It seemed like hours, though there was no way to track the passage of time.

Exhaustion was beginning to weigh on me, but how could I sleep? One wrong turn in a deep sleep, and I was done for. I wasn't sure I could die in this prison dimension, but I sure as shit didn't want to find out.

Cupping my hands, I let the water pool in the palms of my hands and lifted it in a quick splash against my face. It was the only thing I could think of to keep myself awake. Droplets fell from the tip of my nose, and tiny rivulets spilled down my cheeks, sending ripples through the steady surface. I watched as they spread, growing larger by the second. They didn't just grow in girth, but in size too. Normally, as ripples grew larger, they began to even out and disappear, however that wasn't happening.

I scrambled to my feet, reenergized by the oddity I was witnessing.

The sickening pull I'd felt the instant I was sent into the prison returned as the world was tipped on its side and darkness swallowed me whole.

When I could finally see again, I was back in my bedroom in the Grandvilles' home. The Grandvilles stood side by side, speaking animatedly in hushed tones.

"What's going on?"

I pushed myself up to a seated position from where I was sprawled out on the bed.

"She's awake," I heard somebody whisper, although I couldn't tell who it was.

My head throbbed. In a rush, everything came back to me. They'd trapped me in the opal prison, which now hung around Mrs. Grandville's slender neck.

"Now that you've had some time to think things through, I imagine you're a little more apt to see reason. Don't you think, Edith?" Mr. Grandville said.

She nodded, lifting the necklace and rubbing the stone between her fingers. There was a steady coldness in her eyes that said she'd send me right back without a second thought the moment I chose not to cooperate. The choice was mine, not that it was even a choice —give them what they wanted or go back to the Mahashunya indefinitely.

"What do you want?" I questioned warily.

My fists knotted into my skirt, wrinkling it.

"My parents owned one of the mansions in Havenwood Heights, where we summered. All of that's gone now, and I want it back. I've earned it a hundred times over, but as you would understand, life's not fair."

"I can give you wealth, which will bring status, but there's nothing I can do to change your ways. All the wealth in the world isn't going to make you a good father for Tabitha and Cornelius, who just want your time and attention, and it's not going to stay if you spend it as irresponsibly as Mrs. Grandville suggested."

Mrs. Grandville stepped forward with fire in her eyes. Her hand whipped out, making a meaty crack as it collided with the side of my face. Hot pain exploded from my cheek, fanning the growing flames of hatred.

"You'll hold your tongue before you find you don't have one," she threatened. "You will do this."

A low creak from outside the bedroom door caught everyone's

attention. Mr. Grandville shoved the door open, hand at the ready to dispatch anyone caught eavesdropping.

"Tabitha! Cornelius! What in the devil are you doing out here? I thought you were told to stay in your rooms," he reprimanded.

"Yes, father, but we heard—" Tabitha began, but was cut off by her furious father.

"What you heard is irrelevant! You were given directions and then disobeyed me. Back to your rooms, now! Both of you. I'll be in shortly to hand down your punishment. In the meantime, give this some thought: blood is thicker than water and the world is a cold, cruel place. Especially for children," he spouted, terrorizing his kids in the process.

Fear was written on Tabby and Neil's taut faces. Mrs. Grandville's mouth turned down in a barely discernable frown. It seemed the woman wasn't as heartless as she let on, and if that was the case, there was hope for the kids after all.

"Y-yes, sir," Tabitha muttered, grabbing Cornelius by the hand and dragging him along with her to their room.

Mr. Grandville shut the door, cutting the children off from view. The thought of running was tempting, but I couldn't go anywhere without the opal. It would always pull me right back to it. Mr. Grandville stared over my shoulder at Mrs. Grandville, who stood by the wall behind me.

"What do you say? Think you can manage fifty million? Nothing too large a genie like you can't handle," he said, still not looking at me.

"All right, I'll do it!" I cried. "But I need a few things first."

"We're listening," Mrs. Grandville said behind me.

I'd never done anything on this scale before, but how hard could it be? A wish was a wish, but even then it was complicated.

"Tick, tock, Alina. Your time's about up," Mr. Grandville declared, taking an imposing step toward me.

"Wait!" I shouted, throwing my hands up to keep him at bay. "I-I need the account number where you want it transferred. Unless you want it in cash?"

Mr. Grandville scratched his chin as he contemplated his options. Coming to a decision, he reached into his back pocket and withdrew his checkbook, handing over a blank check.

"Here's the number. Be quick about it. Oh, and I'll be checking to make sure the money's there, so don't get any lofty ideas."

"Don't worry, it will be."

I plucked the check from his hands and scanned the account number, committing it to memory. Magic hummed under my skin, coming alive as I focused on the wish. Normally, I wouldn't attach any strings, but seriously—fuck them. They could keep me locked up for the rest of my life, but I could do everything within my power to make their lives the same hell they'd forced me into.

Pulling my powers to my center, I kept the wish at the front of my mind, picturing it as the transfer was made. The pair had never stipulated that the money had to be untraceable. Mr. and Mrs. Grandville were going to be in for one hell of a rude awakening when the U.S. Treasury discovered they were fifty million dollars short. I couldn't imagine it would take too long for them to trace it, especially with an electronic transfer.

"It's done," I confirmed.

"I'll be the judge of that," Mrs. Grandville voiced, flipping open a laptop that was laying at the foot of my bed.

Her fingers whirred over the keys, pulling the bank account up.

"Fifty million dollars just cleared. She did it," Mrs. Grandville confirmed.

My phone buzzed on the bedside table. Gabriel's name was clear on the screen. How many times had he called? Had he realized I was missing? Would he come looking for me? I liked to think he was my knight in shining black armor that would come to my rescue, but there was no telling. I didn't want to get my hopes up.

I took a step to grab the phone, but Mr. Grandville held a hand up to stop me.

"Not another step," he ordered.

The buzzing stopped, but only momentarily. Gabriel's name flashed across the screen again.

"Oh for fuck's sake!" Mr. Grandville roared, "*Uanescere!*"

The phone disintegrated into dust, littering the table top and carpet. That was as good as my last lifeline. Someone would come looking for me eventually, but who knew where I would be by then or what was waiting for me. My stomach was tied into knots, and I was shocked into silence.

Loud pounding shook the front door of the home. My heart jumped, and I wasn't the only one startled. Mr. Grandville was sweating like an ice-cold can of soda on a hot summer's day, and his eyes were on the verge of bugging out of his head.

"Open the door! Where is she?" Gabriel yelled through the thick wood.

Mr. Grandville shot a wary look at his wife, who appeared just as uneasy as he did. Hiding my elation was the hardest thing I'd ever done. I was giddy with hope that justice would be served.

"I thought you said he wasn't going to be a problem? He was just feeding off the girl, a meaningless tryst?" Mr. Grandville accused.

"I was obviously mistaken," Mrs. Grandville retorted, checking herself over in the oval mirror hanging beside the dresser.

A quick series of slams shook the house as though Gabriel was threatening to tear the whole thing down brick by brick.

"Take care of the girl. I'll get the door before he catches the wrong sort of attention. The last thing we need is an inquisition by the sheriff or the Court," Mrs. Grandville remarked.

Mr. Grandville nodded, holding his hand out to his wife. She took my opal necklace off and dropped the stone into his waiting hand.

I knew what was about to happen before he even began the incantation. I was watching my life happen from outside my body in slow motion. His lips moved, though I didn't hear a sound, and then the pull began. Waves of nausea rolled over me, and in a single blink, I was cast back below the waves.

Back to the Mahashunya.

CHAPTER 15

GABRIEL

*J*was seeing red as I paced frantically on the front porch of the witches' home. There was no doubt in my mind they were responsible for Alina's disappearance. She wouldn't have no-showed on me herself. That wasn't the sort of woman she was, and despite only knowing each other a short time, I knew she wasn't the type to run away from anything, especially not when she cared as much as she did about the Grandville kids.

The lady of the house opened the door with a dour expression plastered on her magically enhanced face.

"Where's Alina?"

"I'm sure I have no idea what you're talking about."

"Did you know people like me can hear lies in your voice? There's a slight waver and a wrong pitch every time you tell an untruth. I'm calling bullshit. I'm going to be reasonable and give you five seconds to divulge what you know and where she's at before I make a choker out of your entrails."

Mrs. Grandville seemed unfazed by the threat. That was her misstep; she had no idea what I was capable of.

"You think you can come to my home, in front of my family, and make idle threats like an impetuous child? Tell me, Mr. Doyle, do you enjoy being a member of the living? I can promise you, it's well within my power to change that status, should you tempt me. Now, I have no idea where your plaything is. She didn't come home yesterday, or maybe you're trying to cover your own tracks. Maybe you got a little overzealous and accidentally killed the poor woman. Think carefully about that. What story do you think the Court will believe more? That an upstanding member of this town committed an atrocious crime or that a known killer from out of town slipped back into his old ways?" she remarked coldly.

With a roar, I took a step forward, only to be pushed back by the woman's magic. Her palm was open and waiting. My pride had always told me that as a larger specimen, hitting a woman was the cowardly thing to do, but I was on the verge of throwing that sage advice out the window. My fangs were pricking at my gums, threatening to lengthen if my patience was tested any further.

"Is everything all right?" called a bloated middle-aged neighbor, who in his curiosity forgot he was wearing his bathrobe to take out his trash.

"Everything's just fine, Bill! My friend was just leaving," Mrs. Grandville answered, never breaking eye contact with me.

"All right! Just holler if you need anything," the man shouted back, worry lacing every word.

My nostrils flared as I caught a whiff of Alina's scent coming from inside the home. My cheeks stretched into a malicious grin.

"I can smell her," I said simply.

"Oh really? I'm giving the Court a call to come collect you. If you know what's good for you, you'll be gone and far from this town by the time they arrive," Mrs. Grandville spat, slamming the door in my face.

Fuck! Why in the devil would the gods be so cruel to implement the whole invitation rule for vampires? It became rather inconvenient when time was of the essence. Mrs. Grandville was right. If she made the call, knowing I was Viktor Azimov's heir, they wouldn't be lenient, and they very likely wouldn't believe me without an official questioning. By then, Alina could be gone.

Five minutes later, as if on cue, the sheriff's black pickup truck rolled up in front of the house, parking damn near on top of the curb. Sheriff Ric Kasun stepped out of the vehicle, slamming the door a little too hard behind him. He strode around the vehicle and marched right for me. I didn't miss his silver eyes constantly checking the surroundings. I guessed those wolfy instincts never really shut off. He seemed a little informal for the occasion, wearing jeans and a red flannel shirt like some damn lumberjack. The man didn't seem older than forty-five, but I knew he eclipsed that by a few centuries at least.

"Mr. Doyle," he stated, hooking his hands on his hips.

I nodded.

"Can you come over here by the car for a moment? I'd just like to get your side of things before I go talk to the caller."

I complied. If I wanted to help Alina, I needed to keep my head and stay the fuck out of jail.

"Now what can you tell me about what's going on? I received a call that you were trespassing and harassing the residents."

A chuckle escaped before I could quell it.

"I guess all of that's correct. The Grandvilles conveniently forgot to mention that my girlfriend works for them and has gone missing. I came looking for her."

"Missing? When was the last time you saw her?"

"Yesterday morning when she left the home I'm renting for the time being. I've tried to call her close to a hundred times, but there's no answer."

"Did you two have a fight? Would there be any reason you would suspect she's in danger?" he inquired.

I nodded. "She's a rare woman."

"How rare? Be straight with me. I'd prefer to know what I'm walking into and not waste the time to call the Court."

"She's a Marid djinn," I explained.

Sheriff Kasun's eyes widened in surprise. "Oh."

"So you see how this could very easily be more nefarious than a runaway girl?"

He nodded. "I do. However, that being said, it doesn't mean that these folks are keeping your girlfriend locked up. It could be a misunderstanding. Let's talk with them and see if we can get some more information from them and then go from there."

I could see the doubt in his eyes and hear it in his thoughts. He didn't think he'd find Alina inside. He wasn't overly thrilled to be dealing with my kind, but respectably, he put his job first.

"I could smell Alina inside the house. When I told her as much, she called you and slammed the door in my face. Let me be clear, I don't care if I have to bleed the answers I want out of them, but I will be getting those fucking answers."

"Do you think tough talk to the town's sheriff is a good idea? The call we got was about *you*. Not about them, not about your missing girlfriend, but you. If you can't handle yourself, I'll need to cuff you and put you in the back of the car while I go talk to them, which is probably what I should do, if I'm being honest."

Inhaling deeply, I tried to calm my frayed nerves enough to do what I had to in order to get my woman back.

"You won't have to worry about me . . . now. If they're going to jerk us around, then all bets are off."

"That's not how things work here, Doyle. This ain't the Wild West. You need to let us handle this in a way that's best for all involved, if you catch my drift," he said, side-eyeing the neighbors who were nosily creeping onto their porches at the first sight of trouble.

I nodded.

My jaw was clenched so tightly that if I was still human, my teeth would've cracked right in half. Sheriff Kasun took the lead, marching up the paved walkway to the front door. His back was straight and regal, the sort of posture that came with self-pride and only a little edge to make himself seem larger and more intimidating. I stayed behind him, reminding myself that ripping that cunt's throat out wouldn't solve any problems, only create a dozen more.

Ric banged on the door a few times and hooked his hands on his waist as he waited. It's funny how time can bend according to perception. A hundred years had passed in what had seemed like a blink of an eye because there was nothing of value or significance during that time. Alternately, the seconds that ticked by waiting for someone to answer the door stretched into what seemed like an eternity because the woman who had managed to capture my heart and soul depended on me doing right by her. My fists balled at my sides, and my nails dug harshly into the thick flesh of my palms.

Finally, I could see a shadow moving within the home. The door swung in, and to my great surprise, it was not the woman of the house who came to the door. Tabitha came to the door. Her hair was pulled back to reveal her nervous face.

"May I help you?" she asked meekly.

We shared a knowing glance.

"Hi there, I'm Sheriff Ric Kasun. Can you please get your mom for me? I have a few questions to ask her," he said smoothly, pouring on the kind of charm that could easily sway people to do as he wanted.

It was exactly that quality that made the Court appoint him as town guardian and, ultimately, sheriff. I wanted to ask her where Alina was, what had happened to her, but the fear wafting off her made me stop. Something had happened. Tabitha disappeared back inside, leaving the door open a crack.

Rage warred with fear as the seconds ticked by, while we waited for the Grandvilles to open their door. They'd taken Alina from me, and for that, I would make sure they paid dearly.

"If there's so much as a single hair on her head out of place, I swear I will rip them limb from limb and enjoy every second of it," I growled, pacing at the foot of the porch.

"Threats? Really? You're dumber than you look," Sheriff Kasun grumbled.

Quick steps caught my attention as someone rushed to the door. I clenched my fists to stop myself from doing something I'd regret. Witches or not, I knew people who made these folks look like simple card magicians. Not to mention, I could probably rip a throat or two out before they could utter any sort of incantation to stop me. That was the problem with their words—they would never be quite fast enough to stop me.

Mrs. Grandville came to the door, austere superiority written in every movement and glance.

"Sheriff Kasun." She nodded.

There was something in her voice that grated against my last nerve. My jaw clenched. I wanted to barrel through her and find Alina. Fucking curses preventing me from entering without invitation.

"Where is she?" I demanded, leveling the woman with a glare.

Her brows knit together, but otherwise, she remained unfazed.

"Back off, Doyle. Don't make me arrest you for being a nuisance," Kasun said, his eye twitching as the only indication of his apparent dislike of my kind. "Mrs. Grandville, I'm sorry to disturb you, but Mr. Doyle insists that his *friend* was staying here with you as your nanny and she has gone missing. I'm hoping you can offer some insight into the whereabouts of Ms. Anand."

The woman's expression didn't change once, seeming practiced.

"Unfortunately, Ms. Anand is no longer residing with us. She left us late last night without explanation."

"You're lying," I interjected.

"If she were lying, I'd be able to hear it in her voice. You need to calm down and go back to the car. Now. I'm not asking, either," Kasun ordered.

The carefully maintained grip on my rage was beginning to slip. If I wasn't careful, I could reveal something I shouldn't in front of a mostly human crowd, which was beginning to form, curious about the police presence.

"You know what the girl is, Kasun. You know how valuable she could be to the wrong sort of person—"

"Wrong sort? Like you?" Mrs. Grandville remarked, smugly arrogant.

"More like the sort who have no scruples about forced servitude and putting on false airs. I remember your husband's grandfather well. How does it feel to know that you almost had it all and now, you're practically peasants? That's got to rub you the wrong way. Isn't it just convenient a woman who could give you all that just so happened to fall right into your lap. I can't imagine why she'd go missing . . ." The sarcasm dripped from every word as I said it.

Kasun's brows rose at my words, before he regained his sensibilities and pointed toward the patrol car at the curb.

"Mrs. Grandville, I hope you understand that I can't simply take your word for it. Would you mind if I took a look around?"

"Is that really necessary?" she protested weakly.

"You could refuse . . . but then I'd just come back with a warrant when the girl fails to turn up anywhere," he said matter-of-factly.

Kasun was nothing if not professional, even if he was a damn wolf.

"All right then. Be my guest," Mrs. Grandville said, stepping aside and allowing the sheriff into her home.

Something about the whole situation and the family set me on edge. I'd seen people like them once upon a time—the sort who viewed everyone around them as servants to their own greater purpose. My master before I'd been turned had been such a man.

"Kasun?" I said quietly, though I knew even at this distance he could hear me. "Look for Alina's opal necklace. If she's anywhere, it could very well be there."

"Don't you think that's a little extreme?" Kasun pointed out.

"Not in the least. I've seen what humans are capable of inflicting on their own kind, and I've seen what they can do to those they see as different. We may be a different species, but some things don't change that much, no matter the kind."

He nodded, understanding, and disappeared into the house. Mrs. Grandville stood in the doorway after Kasun passed through, casting a glare the likes of which could've killed. There was a smug set to her mouth.

Creaking boards echoed as the man of the house, Mr. Grandville, came to join her at the entrance. He looked me up and down, appraising me.

"What is it you hope to gain from all this? You're making yourself look like a lunatic in front of the whole town. Do you think people will look favorably on your actions? Showing up and issuing threats to upstanding citizens about crimes with no evidence?" he sneered.

"You must be Mr. Grandville. You live up to your reputation."

"I'm sure. And what might that be?" he scoffed.

"A man with very little to offer anyone, especially a woman, but thinks it should all be handed to him on a silver platter. Tell me, Mr. Grandville, was your plan to replace the old ball and chain with the younger model when you came onto the nanny?" I could see the taut lines around Mrs. Grandville's eyes. It seemed I'd struck a nerve. "Or do you just throw it out there and pray someone will want someone as pathetic as you are? Now, let me be clear. I've had far more time on this earth to make friends in high places, much higher than your name will ever get you. All I have to do is snap my fingers, and this town, and more specifically your farce of a family, would be wiped from the pages of history. No one would ever even remember who you were. So here's a bit of advice: know who and what you're playing with before you come to the table. Otherwise, you'll lose your ass every single time until one day, you'll lose far more. And last I checked, you don't have a coven backing you if you fuck up."

"If you're finished," he replied, casting a fleeting glance over his shoulder. "You should know you've made an enemy here today. I'd consider that very carefully."

"Good, I was counting on it. I'm going to make this as clear as I can. If you have Alina, and I have no doubts that you do, I'm going to pick off every branch of your family tree. You'll get to spend the rest of your life looking over your shoulder, and then when you least expect it, I'll come for you."

"Sheriff, I hope everything was as it should be?" Mr. Grandville said loudly, ignoring my threat.

Kasun stepped forward, out of the house, peering at me with uncertainty.

"I didn't find anything to suggest she's in the home, currently," he said, eyeing the neighbors and lowering his voice. "There was a lingering scent that didn't belong to your family. It was recent enough for me to believe the girl was here more recently than you let on. Care to explain that?"

The Grandvilles didn't even flinch.

"No clue, Sheriff, but if you don't mind, we've caused enough of a scene for one day. If you have any more inquiries, I hope you return with a warrant or the Court, because this is feeling an awful lot like a witch hunt."

"Are you not concerned that your nanny is missing?" Kasun asked, scrutinizing the pair even more closely.

"Not really. Seeing what sort of company the girl keeps, it's best not to have one such person around our children. I wish you both the best in your search," Mrs. Grandville replied, stepping back and shutting the door once and for all.

"Fuck!" I roared.

"Not here. Can you follow me?" Kasun asked, his gaze pleading with me.

It was in that moment I knew he was on my side. He'd seen something inside that house that was off, enough that he was doubting what they were telling him.

Kasun turned and started for his truck, waving off the prying eyes who'd gathered.

"Show's over. Everybody can go back inside," he said with an edge.

The sheriff climbed into his truck and slammed the door a little too hard. I followed as he began to drive. He made his way back to the police station too slow for my liking. Time was of the essence.

Pulling into the station parking lot, I came to a stop and was out of the car before Ric had even gotten to his feet.

"What is it? What did you find in the house?"

"Nothing."

"Nothing?"

"Yeah, that's the troubling bit. I could smell her like she'd been there within moments of my arrival. I checked every room in that house, and there wasn't a single trace of her. No clothes, no personal belongings, no necklace, and no Alina. There should've been something, some trail she left behind, even in scent, that would give me a clue where she went, but there wasn't. I don't know what to make of it, but I'm convinced they're hiding something. "

"What's the plan, then?" I asked.

"I'll have to make a few calls. Magic isn't my specialty, and it's going to require someone who could feel something if it was unusual."

"Unusual how?"

"Magic works in mysterious ways. If Alina is a Marid like you say she is, that should leave some kind of imprint on the environment. We need someone who can feel that well enough to be able to find it. Come inside and sit down. I'll give the Luna Coven a call and see if they can be of some assistance."

"Don't involve them. The fewer people who know about what Alina is, the safer she'll be. Besides, I've got someone who I think might be able to help, but I've got to try to reach Alina first. I'll need maybe an hour tops."

CHAPTER 16

ALINA

*M*y entire body felt waterlogged. Where I used to have feet, I now had bloody, beaten remnants. Every muscle in my body hurt from the tensing and contractions as it tried to spasm and stay warm.

Hunger was my constant companion. I'd begun to talk to the growls when they happened. Sometimes it seemed like they answered me, but I knew that was stupid. More than anything, though, I just wanted to hear another person's voice, to know I wasn't alone.

Who knew how long I'd been imprisoned in the Mahashunya? There was no cycle of day to night to keep track. Gabriel's face had begun to fade from memory, too. It no longer had the sharpness of familiarity that it once had. I wondered if my mom and dad knew I was gone. If they did, had they come looking for me?

There'd been so much resentment toward my father before I'd moved, so many fights that now seemed pointless. I'd been stubborn and selfish, unwilling to listen to someone who genuinely knew more about the world and people than I did. I'd figured that one out a little too late.

"Daddy, I don't know if you can hear me, but you were right. I gave my trust to someone who wanted to use me, but you were wrong too. Love, real everlasting love, exists. I don't know if you'd like

Gabriel, but I think you'd be proud that I found someone who cares for me, flaws and all," I whispered, letting the emptiness steal my words away.

Had a Marid ever died in this place? It was a question I'd contemplated close to a thousand times. It would've been easy to end it all. Shame reared its ugly head. Giving up wasn't an option.

My eyes grew heavy, exhaustion threatening to overtake me. I lay back in the water like my dad had taught me how to do as a child when I would float. My hair floated around me like a dark halo. From limb to limb, relaxation eased me into a light sleep. With the water lapping gently at my body, I drifted deeper into the sweet bliss of sleep.

No longer was I trapped inside the Mahashunya. Instead I was standing at the edge of the pool at the base of the falls Gabriel had shown me. Of course, even in my dreams, I was bound to water. A warm breeze blew, carrying a scent I'd become so familiar with since meeting Gabriel Doyle.

I turned and spied him leaning against the trunk of a large tree. He seemed to be waiting for me.

"Alina? Is that really you?" he asked, taking an unsure step forward.

"Yeah, it's me," I croaked, my voice having grown too accustomed to remaining silent with no one to talk to.

Gabriel was to me in an instant, folding me into his arms and crushing me against his chest. He was restrained, trying to be as gentle as he could, but I could tell it was a struggle for him. I clung to him like my life depended on it. I squeezed my eyes shut tightly, relishing the feel of his solid form against my own.

"Where are you? What happened? Tell me how to get to you," he urged, burying his face into my hair and inhaling my scent deeply.

"Are you really here?" I asked, afraid to open my eyes and have him disappear.

He leaned back, taking my face between his hands. With a gentle finger, he tipped my chin up and brushed the hair away from my eyes.

"I'm here, love. I'll never leave your side again. If it means I have to stay here forever, then I'll gladly never wake up."

"This is all a dream?"

He nodded, pointing to the clear night sky where the moon seemed larger than possible.

It shed so much light on the falls and the trees around us that it made it less imposing. I wasn't afraid of being seen and could relax and enjoy the moment.

"I'm in the Mahashunya, and I can't get out. Gabriel, I don't know how much longer I have."

"What's the Mahashunya? Why can't you get out?"

"There are rules. My kind were created by Set, who had grown jealous of Amani and Khalida's power. He stole a feather from Thoth's wing and set it ablaze. He watered the ashes with the Nile River and from that, the first Marids were born. They were too powerful and too greedy to be contained, though. They ravaged the lands and the people began to starve. Set grew angry at his children and decided they could no longer be free. He bound our souls to an amulet. Should we ever grow too bold, the amulet would be our prison. I-I lost my opal, Gabriel. It's gone, and I don't know that I'll ever get it back."

I looked away, feeling the misty beginnings of tears pricking my eyes.

"Listen to me, Alina. Do you trust me?" he asked.

My chin dipped once.

"Then trust me when I say that I'm coming for you. I might not be able to go to the Mahashunya, but I'm working damn hard to bring you back to me. I won't stop until the Grandvilles pay for what they've done and you're here with me. Do you understand? You're mine. Forever and always."

His words were so sure that I wanted to believe every bit of it. I almost did, but there was still the tiny nagging voice in the back of my head that doubted I would ever be saved. I didn't even have magic here, leaving me royally screwed.

Gabriel rested his forehead against mine, rubbing my back

soothingly. I'd never grow tired of his touch. I just hoped I got the opportunity to feel it again.

The moon grew dark, and I knew my time was almost over. I was waking up.

"I don't want this moment to end. Hurry, Gabriel."

"Stay with me, love. Don't go yet."

I was torn away before I could tell him the words I'd been wanting to since the moment he'd given me every dream we'd shared: I love you.

My eyes fluttered open. The dull gray sky stared back at me. My fingers and toes were borderline numb, and my skin was so cold to the touch, but not cold enough for hypothermia to set in. As I sat up, my thick hair was weighed down, laden with water. Giving it a hard twist, I wrung it out and got to my feet. Peering out at the flat water stretching in every direction, it all came crashing right back down on me that I was truly alone. My heart sank at the thought.

I didn't know why I hadn't thought of trying to reach out to Gabriel before. The dream walking was one thing, but that he could reach beyond his realm and into a different plane entirely changed the game. There wasn't any more I could offer him. I was too far out of touch with what was going on back home. Hell, I didn't even know how long I'd been gone. Had it been a couple days? Weeks? Months? The Grandvilles could've cut and run, taking the opal along with them, although I could still remember Havenwood Falls, so I doubted I'd tripped the memory wards.

Pondering the seriousness of Gabriel's words, I began my trek. He'd said he'd never leave my side, but there I was, all alone once again. I knew it wasn't his fault. Homesickness. That was what ailed me, though not the home I'd always known with my parents. No, not there. Since moving, I'd found a new safe haven in Gabriel's arms. He was my home now, and I was more homesick than I'd ever been before.

Letting my foot fly, I kicked through the water, sending a spray of droplets and a fine mist soaring. I screamed as loud as I could, unleashing my anger and frustration. There was so much going on in my head that it was too loud to even think clearly. So much rage, sorrow, and uncertainty all rolled into a ball that had been weighing me down. I had to let it out, so I did. Tears streamed down my cheeks, and my throat was raw, mimicking the pain I felt inside. The tears came until my body just wouldn't let me weep anymore.

I was fucked, there was no other way around it. I sniffled and dragged the back of my hand across my face, smearing the wetness on my cheeks more than anything. An ache had begun to form at the base of my skull, throbbing in time with my pounding heart.

"This just keeps getting better, doesn't it?" I sighed sarcastically.

Before I could make another move or utter another word, that familiar tug came rushing back, and I was thrown into darkness as I was dragged back to the world outside of the Mahashunya.

CHAPTER 17

GABRIEL

$\mathcal{R}$oman Bishop hadn't anticipated my call coming so soon, but much to my surprise, he answered and he showed . . . twenty minutes after the decided time. Luckily, the Grandvilles hadn't decided to skip town and run for the hills since we'd visited them. Alina had looked so broken when I'd seen her by the falls in our dream walk. It was the first time I'd been able to reach her since she'd disappeared four days prior.

Stepping out of the rear of a black sedan, Roman strode right for Ric and me where we'd parked at the curb across from the Grandville residence.

"You're late," I noted.

"I'm here, aren't I? Let's get this over with. I have plans."

Bishops. Always the smug bastards of the group. That was one thing that hadn't changed since I'd first visited the town. Ric was standing back, silently watching the two of us disinterestedly.

"Tell me again why I've been summoned," Roman demanded.

Ric answered before I could even put together a response. "A Marid girl has been missing for four days now. When I checked the house, her scent lingered like she'd been there just a few moments before, but she wasn't. All personal effects were gone, and the trail is going to go cold if we don't find one specific object. We think the witches who live here might've hidden the girl in an opal necklace."

"And you need me to find this?"

I nodded. "The necklace is bound to the girl's soul. It should have a fairly high concentration of magic contained within it. We need to find her at any cost."

"You want me to find your pet for you. Do I look like a fucking bloodhound?" he asked, stretching his neck from side to side.

"Bishop, if you can't help me, I'm sure I can find someone who will," I pointed out.

"I'll find it. Just hold up your end of our deal when it's time to collect."

"If the two of you are done bickering like schoolgirls, then let's do this," Ric quipped, striding right for the front door.

Sheriff Kasun knocked and stepped back while Roman and I stayed back. Seconds ticked by without any sounds coming from inside. Just as Kasun was about to knock again, the door opened, and Mr. Grandville poked his surprised face out.

"Sheriff, can I help you?"

He didn't spare a single glance for Roman or me.

"You can, actually. Mr. Grandville, we're here to conduct a more thorough search of these premises. Both myself and Mr. Bishop are here on behalf of the Court. I'll need you to gather everyone in the house immediately."

Just as it looked like the man was about to protest, Roman spoke up.

"I'd do as he asked. There's no need to make this any harder than it needs to be," Roman remarked, his eyes narrowing on the English prick.

Mr. Grandville had to be seething internally, but no one doubted Roman would destroy him if Mr. Grandville tried anything. Knowing better than to challenge a Bishop, the lesser mage stepped aside, allowing Ric and Roman entry. I stood just the other side of the threshold, waiting for my invitation.

Mr. Grandville chuckled at my predicament.

"If you know what's good for you, I'd quit toying with me. I'll take any reason to kill you slowly like the *míolra* you are," I threatened.

"I'd listen to him if I were you. I'm not saying I'd let him kill you outright, but there's nothing I could do if he moved faster than me," Sheriff Kasun chimed in.

Mr. Grandville's jaw tightened, and the man was glowering with an intensity that had to hurt.

"Please come in," he gritted.

My lips quirked up.

Smart move, asshole, I thought.

Kasun was standing with his arms crossed, waiting expectantly. Roman stood next to him, waiting for the rest of the household to join us.

"Edith! Tabitha, Cornelius! I need you all down here," Mr. Grandville hollered up the stairs.

All three came quickly, sensing something was off.

"Al? What's going on?" Mrs. Grandville asked, eyes wide as she strode into the room.

She froze as soon as she saw us all. The surprise quickly morphed into outrage.

"What's the meaning of this? I thought we'd made ourselves clear that you were not to come back—"

"Without the Court? That's why I'm here. Roman Bishop. I don't believe we've met," Roman purred, pouring on the charm as he extended his hand to her.

"I know who you are, but what are you doing here?" she hissed, ignoring his hand.

"I'm here on behalf of the Court of the Sun and the Moon to investigate the unknown whereabouts of a Miss Alina Anand. This being her last known address and the residence she was last seen at, we thought we'd stop by. Check things out. I'm sure you understand. We all want the girl found, right?" Roman asked, listening closely for the woman's response, but staying casual, so as to not let on that he was waiting for any indication of a slip up.

Instead of answering, she crossed her arms over her chest and kept her mouth shut. The kids stood next to their mother, wide-eyed and silent. From what I knew of them, they liked Alina a lot. I couldn't fathom either of them having a thing to do with her disappearance.

With the calm of a stalking predator, Roman strode through the house, hands at the ready. There were so many things I could say about the man waiting for the object to *talk to him*. Every time I pictured Alina, I thought better of it and held my tongue. He was being generous enough to help me find her, or at least hope to.

Mr. Grandville took a step to follow him, looking to the sheriff as though asking permission. We all gave Roman room to work, staying a good way back, yet following his every move. No one wanted to miss anything.

He passed through the first floor without taking so much as a second look at anything. Then he began to climb the stairs to the second floor. He'd made it halfway up before he froze. Stepping back down one tread, Roman stomped his foot on the lower step and then the one above it.

There was a completely different tone between the two, and one was certainly hollow. Taking another step down, Roman examined the seam of the step carefully, lifting the board to reveal a hiding hole.

The Grandvilles were silent, eyeing the stash with unreadable expressions. I quietly wondered if they were contemplating how screwed they were, but my need for my woman was stronger. I had to know what was in the hole.

"Well, it's no necklace, but I think we've found the girl's personal items," Roman said, producing a sketch pad with images of my face and a tiny ceramic Ganesh statue.

"Are they hers?" Ric asked.

I nodded, smelling her scent on both.

"There's no necklace in here, and nothing is giving off enough of a signal to think it was spelled in any way," Roman mentioned as he emptied the space in the compartment under the stair and shut the lid.

"Do you have anything you want to tell us before we continue the search? Keep in mind, this is your chance to come clean before we find anything more incriminating than we already have," Ric warned.

The couple remained silent.

"I'll love every second of watching whatever punishment the Court finds appropriate for you," I quipped, passing them to follow Roman upstairs.

Roman mounted the steps and made his way down the hall, checking room by room. Still there was nothing.

"Anything?" I asked.

"I see what Kasun's saying about there being an imprint, but not having anything solid to go on. There's definitely something here, though."

Hope blossomed and began to take root.

Roman strode past me and just as I was about to turn and follow after him, something in my periphery caught my attention. Giving it a closer inspection, I saw the tiny end of a pull cord slipping out of a nearly invisible seam in the ceiling.

"Roman?"

"What?" he said, irritated.

"The ceiling. I think there's an attic up here." I pointed.

With a snap of his fingers, the panel swung down and produced a ladder to the space above.

"Now we're fucking talking," Roman said as he passed me and climbed up.

The attic was dusty and littered with boxes covered in illegible writing. As soon as I had completely entered the space, I could tell there was a very distinct shift in the air. There was something here that was lacking in the rest of the house, something begging to be discovered.

"Do you feel that?" I whispered, scanning the room.

"I do, but I didn't think your kind would," he remarked suspiciously.

"Normally, I wouldn't. I don't know how to explain it, but I can feel her close here."

Without saying another word, Roman strode forward, plowing

through stacks of boxes. Glass cracking and heavy objects smacking the wooden floor filled my ears. That was going to suck for the unlucky son of a bitch cleaning this place.

Against the back wall, farthest from the trap door, sat an old wooden chest. It wasn't anything spectacular or something that particularly stood out, but there was an energy coming from it that couldn't be denied.

"Gentlemen, I think we may have struck gold here," Roman called over his shoulder, as he latched on to the box and dragged it out from where it sat.

Fuck! Mr. Grandville's thought came loud enough to stand out to me.

"I think you could be right, Roman. This one has loud thoughts about the box," I announced.

"Is that so?" Ric asked, eyes narrowed in the Grandvilles' direction.

Roman said a few unintelligible phrases as he focused on the lock. As soon as he finished, there was a loud click, just before the lock opened and fell to the floor with a hard metallic thud. The chest was dusty, but there were marks along the edges to suggest someone had messed with it recently.

Peering inside, I saw there were old pictures and folded materials that had to have been passed down for several generations. Shoving all of that aside, Roman uncovered a felt-encased jewelry box, made specifically to house a precious necklace. Not waiting another minute, he opened it, and lo and behold, Alina's opal necklace sat pristinely inside.

"Case closed, gentlemen," Roman muttered, handing the necklace over to me.

"Will you make this as simple as possible and let her out? I'll even throw you a bone and say please. Please?" I mocked, not expecting a damn thing from any of the witches.

As expected, Mr. and Mrs. Grandville leered defiantly at me as I handed it back over to Roman.

"Can you free her?" I asked, hoping like hell he had the ability to bring her out of wherever she was.

He nodded and took the opal from my hands. As soon as Roman's fingers brushed the opal, the air zinged to life, bursting with an electricity unlike I'd ever experienced. His focus was absolute, and the hairs along my arms and neck stood on end.

With a quick flip of his wrist, a bright white light exploded forth from the opal, blinding everyone who was watching. The glass in the window panes shook, yet there was no rumble through the house to cause such an effect. Without warning, Alina appeared, her back arching off the floor like she had been lifted. An anguished scream tore from her throat, and her eyes were black as tar. She began to speak in tongues none of us could understand.

"Roman? What the hell is going on?" I yelled, unable to look away from her.

Alina's veins were sticking out, and every muscle looked like it was stuck in mid-spasm. I spied Roman, whose concentration hadn't been broken by my question. His mouth barely moved, but I could hear his words. The lights along the walls grew brighter until I was sure they would blow the circuits. Just as suddenly, the lights dimmed to barely on, casting the room in darkness, and Alina fell to the floor with a thud before I could react and catch her.

"It's done," Roman announced with finality.

Alina was barely breathing, and I could hear the faint flutters of her heartbeat, but it wasn't strong, like it should have been. Ric took a step toward her, but I held a hand up. We didn't know what we were dealing with. I approached her carefully and kneeled down beside her shivering form. Her skin was slick with sweat and was growing pale compared to its usual tanned vibrancy. There was nothing that stood out to me as being wrong. Physically, she was fine. Mentally, she was confused, but that wasn't necessarily abnormal given her situation. There was a fear in her eyes that made my stomach drop to my toes. Whatever was ailing her was serious, and the only thing I could think of was the broken bond. The Grandvilles refused to release her from her confines, and the only way for her to be free was to the break the bond between her soul and the opal. Either way, one thing was becoming clearer by the second.

I was losing her.

Without thinking, I pushed up the sleeve of my dress shirt and homed in on the stark blue lines on my wrists, where my veins were. My fangs descended, and without wasting more time, I tore into my flesh before pushing it to her mouth.

"You need to drink, love. Trust me, everything is going to be all right. I promise," I whispered, letting her dark hair run through the fingers of my free hand.

Her mouth was slack at first, but then her lips closed over my skin. I felt her tongue caress the gash as my blood flowed into her. I watched her throat bob as she swallowed pull after pull. Gently, I pulled away from her. My flesh was already knitting itself back together while I held her and prayed for the best.

We were in uncharted territory.

CHAPTER 18

ALINA

I landed on my back, but I instantly knew something was wrong. It had to be. My magic hadn't come back, and my body was weak.

I didn't want to open my eyes, but there was an earsplitting ringing in my ears forcing me to search for the source. The light was too bright when I managed to crack an eye open. The room was crowded with people, some I knew and others who were total strangers to me.

All of the words were distorted and had echoes. My lips parted to say something, but my voice refused to cooperate.

Gabriel gathered my head onto his lap and kept his touch feather light. The hard wood floor grounded me to the present. It was so hard to focus on anything, and everything was too hazy. Something was definitely wrong with me. Fear crept in.

Gabriel's lips were moving and sounds were spilling from his handsome lips, but no matter how hard I tried to concentrate on what he was saying, I couldn't understand. The harder I tried to focus and make sense of things, the slipperier they became, always staying just out of my reach. My whole body felt floaty, almost as though if it weren't for Gabriel's hands acting as an anchor to the world, I'd lazily float away. Maybe I'd go somewhere in the beyond; I wasn't sure. The coppery tang of Gabriel's blood coated my mouth. I thought I'd be sick, but the spasms never came. I would've welcomed spasms. It would've been a sign of life, something that wasn't giving up. My reality was slipping away while I was incapable of doing a damn thing to stop it. Somewhere in the back of my mind, I knew I was fading into nothing. Being afraid would've been natural, but I didn't feel anything.

Darkness began to creep in around the edges of my vision. Breathing was hard; it felt like a horse was standing on my chest. My pulse pounded in my ears, slow enough that I saw the writing on the wall. I was dying.

Just as I thought my heart would stop forever, something changed. A subtle shift in my trajectory, as Gabriel's blood mingled with mine, healing every broken bit.

My heart began to beat stronger, and each breath came a little easier. The tiny flicker where my magic had been gave a small glimmer of hope as I felt it fanned back to life.

"Gabriel?" I whispered with more strength than I'd had before.

"I'm here."

I lifted my hand so he could see what I wanted to show him. My words were failing me, but he needed to know. Lifting my palm, I felt my magic flow freer than it ever had before and fill my palm. Without so much as an active thought, a small flame burst to life.

"We're going to be all right," I whispered, low enough so it could only be heard by his ears.

I gave him a weak smile before my eyes scanned the room, growing heavier by the second. A man and the one who'd broken the bond between my soul and the opal were escorting Mr. and Mrs. Grandville out of the room in handcuffs. Their children followed after one another, fear pooled in their eyes as they clung to each other.

I drifted off into the sweet oblivion of exhaustion, wondering what was to become of us all. However, that was a question for another day.

EPILOGUE

GABRIEL

*T*he weeks following Alina's imprisonment were a whirlwind. The Court of the Sun and the Moon had convened to hand down punishment to the Grandvilles and determine the future of both myself and Alina here in Havenwood Falls.

The punishment for the Grandvilles was lacking. Alina wasn't of a similar mind on the subject. I wanted them to pay dearly, but Alina argued there were the children to take into account. Because the idea of owning Marid djinn, like her, had a long history which was deeply rooted in some, the Court found that while wrong, the Grandvilles hadn't really hurt Alina in any significant way.

They couldn't punish the *what if.*

Banishment was the final verdict. They left, the whole family, and had their memories wiped as they left the confines of the memory ward. There wasn't a day that went by that I didn't think about exacting revenge. But Alina needed me to be better than that.

Tabitha and Cornelius also had to be considered. The hatred and sense of entitlement found in their parents would likely grow to infect both of them. They weren't bad kids, and they didn't deserve the hand they'd been dealt.

Alina's father had finally called to congratulate her on making a life for herself. We managed to keep what had happened under wraps, though she did confess that she was now unemployed and depending on her boyfriend. Ignoring all the gory details, he wasn't thrilled, and he wanted to meet me right away.

Catching me staring at her from her periphery, she gave a sly smirk.

"What? Do I have something on my face?" Alina joked.

"No. Do I need a reason to admire you? To appreciate what a lucky son of a bitch I am that you chose me?" I teased, though there was nothing false in my confession.

"I suppose not, as long as you know just how lucky I am to be loved by someone like you. You never gave up on me, even when I'd just about given up on myself. You've stolen my heart and given me back my soul. Now that I know how sweet freedom truly tastes, I want to spend the rest of mine with you," she said with finality.

My hand slid from her lower back to the side of her neck, where I held her firmly. Swooping in, I stole a quick kiss. Her eyes reflected everything I was feeling.

Thanksgiving had passed, and now Christmas was coming in a few weeks, and there were some big things coming for us. In fact, we were on our way to the Court of the Sun and the Moon to petition them for my right to the vampire nest Viktor had once presided over.

With her hand wrapped securely in mine, we strolled down Eighth Street, admiring the glistening Christmas decorations the city had put up. Lighted snowflakes hung from street lamps, and the stores were beginning to put together their storefront holiday displays, making the picturesque town even more so. Almost losing Alina had put things into perspective and allowed me to appreciate the tiny in-between moments. Not just the major events, but the connecting time, when life really happened.

It had been three weeks, and I had yet to feel the urge to leave. Each day with her was a gift, one that I was beginning to see could last. I didn't even mind the stares we occasionally received. It was our own slice of normalcy, but first, we had one last hurdle.

Roman Bishop would be calling to cash in on that favor. When he would eventually call in his price, I'd pay it. I was a man of my word.

"Are you nervous?" she asked, tucking herself in closer.

"No. Nerves are for people who are unsure of themselves. I'm confident the Court will see that my claim is legitimate. I am Viktor's heir, and it's my duty to honor him as such. Besides, it's best to keep my kind on a tighter leash than most."

"I hope you're right. I love seeing you with such a purpose now. This is what you were always meant for, and I'm blessed to be by your side for this ride," she replied.

"I thank God every night for giving me the gift of dream walking. Without it, I never would've met you. I love you." I stopped and turned toward her, dipping down so I was level with her.

The ring in my pocket was heavy. When I took my place at the helm of the Lilith Nest, I'd ask her to rule by my side. It didn't matter that she was a djinn and the kindest person I'd ever met. She made me want to be better than the monster I'd been for so long.

"I love you too. Forever and always."

"Good. Now let's get to this hearing so I can get you home and out of that dress. I'm starving." I smirked.

Oh yes, it was going to be quite a night.

ABOUT THE AUTHOR

Victoria Flynn is a married mother to two daughters. She loves to travel and try new things and experiences, and spending time with friends and family. Her favorite place in the entire world is New Orleans, including everything from the mudbugs to the swamps, and yes, even a HUGE ASS BEER. When she's not writing, she can be found with her nose buried in a good book or outside enjoying the unpredictable Michigan weather. Victoria graduated from the University of Michigan with a degree in Biology and published her first novel, *A Soul's Sacrifice*, her senior year in between classes and homework. She loves the paranormal and loves to explore historical places, hopefully combining the two.

ACKNOWLEDGMENTS

First and foremost, I would like to thank Kristie Cook for being a fabulous editor and for giving me the opportunity to share a part of this world. You have pushed me to become a better writer, and I thank you for it. To Regina Wamba, your work on the cover still amazes me, and I'm honored to provide a story that showcases your work. This book wouldn't have been possible without the help of the Havenwood Falls authors, all of whom offered advice and coached me when it came to crossover characters. To my husband, Jacob, thank you for never letting me quit even when I'm crying and sure the end of my writing career is knocking on the door. You believe in me even when I don't believe in myself.

DAMNED ALLURE

JUSTINE WINTER

~ A Havenwood Falls Sin & Silk Novella ~

HAVENWOOD FALLS

sin & silk

Damned Allure

JUSTINE WINTER

ALSO BY JUSTINE WINTER

For your inner sass. Let her out.

CHAPTER 1

INFERNUM

"*Fuck* me, you're a feisty one, aren't you? Don't you wanna play nice for Big Daddy?" I tease the bitch trying to wriggle free from my arm. She's a fighter, I'll give her that. I tighten my hold as we descend from the inky night sky, swirling like wisps of black smoke until we breach the realm boundaries to the Infernum.

"Take. Me. Back!" She huffs out every syllable, straining as she tries to halt my progress, using what strength and weight she has left to keep me from depositing her damned soul into Hell's special holding place. These buggers never think they'll be caught and end up here. It's fucking hilarious really—where else do they think their death will send them? Supernatural creatures are my worst clients, reckoning they can screw the world over and not be punished for it. Stupid bastards.

"Cut this shit out, or I'll make sure your time in the Infernum is as painful and torturous as possible."

She tuts. "You don't have that kind of power. You're just a messenger boy."

She laughs maniacally as though the fringe of the Infernum's entrance is already driving her crazy.

Screams and howls pierce the atmosphere; the walls bleed misery and torment, a promise of suffering for all trapped here. There's no escaping now.

I let her go, knowing her soul is now anchored to the Infernum's clutches.

"I may be Death's bitch," I begin, taking a cursory glance around the area. Fire and brimstone burst through cracks in this sweat box, and sulfur permeates the charred air. It's bloody offensive to my senses, like some inconsiderate arsehole's left a dead animal to rot in the scorching sun. The only thing missing here is the blowflies to gorge on these corpses. "But at least I don't have to spend an eternity listening to these acoustics and smelling shit all day. Have fun, bitch!"

I turn and walk away, releasing any hidden ties I still have on her. I meant it before—I'm not bound for an existence here. I'm an approved visitor only. These evil motherfucking souls are not bringing me down with them.

A loud whistle cuts through the oppressive air. "I see you're still making friends. You ever try bringing someone in without pissing them off, Shade?"

"What fun would that be?" I let a cheeky smile cover my face, though it's somewhat difficult to see when my face lacks flesh. Really, I'm just showing off a perfect set of teeth all denture-wearing oldies are jealous of. I'm still the sexiest skeleton around. I've got big bones, if you know what I mean. "Nobody ever wants to come down here willingly. You were the same, Sapphire. I almost broke a nail delivering you."

"You'd need nails first, Shade. Have you missed me?" The vampire sulks toward me, reaching out to touch my chest cavity.

"Babe, you might have been smokin' hot up top on Earth, but down here your skin looks like it's been ravished by moths. You're holier than all the angels." I roar with laughter, momentarily silencing the usual musical screams.

"At least I've still got skin." She pushes away from me, taking any more thoughts of seduction with her. Thank fuck. One more year down here and a human corpse will be fresher than this stubborn supernatural stiff. There's no talent for beauty contests down here.

"Sapphire, before you go, there's something you forgot," I call out, smirking to myself.

"You're not getting a kiss, Shade. Please yourself," she replies over her shoulder, not daring to look my way.

"Oh, I will, but really, you forgot something . . ." I wait until she gives in, striding with purpose to me. Her eyes widen as she catches sight of my bony hands holding something she wants back. I flex my fingers over the mass.

"What are you doing?" She seems horrified, which is quite impressive considering her home is the Infernum.

"I told you, you forgot something."

"I see that." She grits her teeth. "But what are you *doing* to it?"

"Chill, babe. I'm just squeezing a piece of your arse."

CHAPTER 2

DEATH

*F*ucking priceless.

"You finished torturing us poor souls yet?"

I stop when I hear the deep timbre of an old acquaintance. I lean against a sweat-dripping wall, crossing my skeletonized arms over my chest, my hooded black cloak flowing freely around me. I'm a handsome bastard, really.

"You ever had a woman fall apart in front of you, my friend?" I ask.

"We both know I don't do emotions, Shade." Jax, a long-serving Infernum inmate, speaks.

I shake my head. "I mean literally. That shit is hilarious." I laugh out loud all over again. The old vamp's face had been quite the picture of horror. Talk about embarrassing. "She put her arse right in my hands. Don't get more forward than that."

We giggle like a pair of schoolgirls.

"Man, this place fucks you up for good." Jax shakes his head, and I realize how tired the old bear shifter looks. Amazingly, he's endured the Infernum for a century already, and considering how slow time moves here, that's a feat in itself. Most souls crumble after five minutes because it seems like five *decades* have already passed.

"You coping? You're looking uglier these days," I quip, remembering the youthful shifter all those years ago.

"Speak for yourself, mate. Did you lose weight? You're looking gaunt."

If I had organs they'd be falling out of me with the vibrations of my laughter ripping through me.

"Dude, whatever it is you're doing to keep that humor of yours going, promise me you'll keep the secret to yourself. Otherwise, next time I drop in, I'm gonna have a riot on my hands. Anyway, gotta fly. I can hear my theme tune playing." I motion to my skull, referring to the sound of another soul that needs reaping. Death's a greedy bugger, never satisfied.

A shiver runs along my spine like fine hairs tickling my weathered bones. The air compresses around me, squeezing until I become a swirl of black mist again, my wings flapping eagerly.

I zip around the Infernum, missing walls and dodging streams of lava as I break the speed barriers whilst ascending with purpose, leaving the bleak abyss behind.

This place is no holiday destination.

A high-pitched squeal cripples my wings, and I fall, clutching the sides of my skull as pain radiates all over. I forget my flight, the urge to answer a soul's calling taking a back seat. I can't think through the agony the squeals bring. It's like my bones are being pulverized, one small section at a time as though to prolong my despair.

I'm barely aware of how fast I'm falling, how quickly fire and stone walls are now looming over me.

I pull at my skull, desperate to keep the noise from assaulting me further. My efforts bring zero comfort. It's futile, and yet, like a fucking idiot, I can't stop searching for a reprieve, like a magical mute button's going to appear on my cranium.

A sense of foreboding engulfs every inch of me, like darkness is claiming me.

"Shit!" I smack the ground with such force, it's inadvertently become my submissive. On the plus side, the pain's gone, but that's only because I've become completely numb. I'm like a Halloween pinup. Tape me to the front door, and I'll rattle the window in the wind, swinging to and fro like a puppet without strings.

"How nice it is to see you, Shade."

Shit, I inwardly groan. "Well, you know, I thought it was about time I drop in to see the big boss." I keep my distance from the tall entity in front of me.

"Don't bullshit me. Your worthiness is on the line."

I gulp, keeping my mouth shut for fear I'll say something stupid, like another pun that goes unnoticed.

"You fucked up good." Death's dark stare drives fear into my essence. I can feel terror imprinting on my bones. The otherworldly being is like a giant in size and always has his skeletal frame smartly dressed in an array of tailored suits. Besides his height, I'm sure shopping for such clothing is pretty easy. After all, he's never gonna be more than a size zero. Catwalk models would envy our figures—I hear stick-thin is in this season.

At this moment, Death's wearing his favorite onyx suit, as he likes to call it. Honestly, I don't get the bloody color names myself. I see no difference in tones. Black is black, no matter its sale-savvy description. And don't even get me started on the stupid thorned stem he's got peeking out of his pocket. There's no flower head, of course. Nothing can live with Death around. Literally. He really brings out the lack of life in the room.

Shit, he's crossed his bones over his chest, squaring shoulders he doesn't have—the suit does the work for him.

"You don't have anything to tell me? Some remorse perhaps?"

At what point am I supposed to blow his anger up by saying I don't understand to what he's referring?

Oh bollocks, I'm going to cease to exist.

"How many imbeciles do I have to employ to collect souls and get the job done? It's not fucking difficult!" Death roars, temper raging as he kicks out at the tall stands holding flames that illuminate the otherwise dark space. Fire scatters on the concrete ground, burning everything in its path, including my feet. It's a good thing I don't have any skin.

"Dude, you need to tone it down. I've been reaping souls perfectly. In fact, I just dropped another into the Infernum."

Death leans down, putting his hand in front of me. It's as large as my body. With finger and thumb he flicks me hard, sending me across the room until I hit a wall that stops me.

"Don't you fucking 'dude' me, arsehole. This is my place you're fucking with." He stomps toward me. Two steps is all it takes for him to lift me until his large skull is in front of me, mouth opening as though he's going to eat me. I don't know why—the only thing I'm good for is picking meat out of his teeth *after* dinner. "You allowed some souls to escape the goddamn Infernum!"

Death's breath wafts in my face like a gale-force wind. Shit, pass the dead guy a breath mint; he smells worse than a sewer.

"When?" I can't help the shock creeping into my voice. This is news to me. Wouldn't I know if someone left the Infernum? Despite the fact it's bloody impossible in the first place. This has to be some lame joke he's trying to pull on me—the big guy never can match my comedy.

"Not ten minutes ago. While you were busy chatting with our long-term patrons, they were distracting you from the miscreants using the portal you opened to get there. Now they're running free again. Only this time with even less of a conscience." Death's hand smacks me across the other side of the room. I struggle to stand, mostly out of fear of being flung around the room again. This shit hurts.

Did the bear shifter really sell me out? Sapphire I can understand. That bitch always has something brewing in her conniving mind. It's what sent her into the pits of the Infernum in the first place.

"I'll bring them back," I vow, slowly rising to my feet like a beaten man. When Death hits you, you know you're going down for good.

"You'd fucking better, especially the one that orchestrated this whole plan." Though he doesn't have any eyebrows, I imagine Death's scowling at me right now. The dark abyss of his eyes promises loneliness and pain if I fail to deliver.

I try straightening my cloak, brushing off the dust and flames I picked up from my acquaintance with the ground.

"Just out of curiosity, who's the evil mastermind behind all of this?"

Death smiles widely, leaning back into the throne he spends most of his time in. "Nyx, the vampire-demon hybrid. Bring them all back before they cause even more damage to the world."

I nod, knowing I have a lot of work on my hands—Nyx had been tough to capture the first time. I turn, opening up a new portal, where it will lead me to a damned soul's location. As a reaper, it's like I have my own tracking system—the souls call to me whether they know it or not.

"Oh, and Shade, one last thing. If you fuck this up even more, and fail to deliver Nyx to me personally, you're done. No more privileges. No more slack. No more wings. I'll disintegrate your existence."

I close my eyes, taking in the severity of the situation. Just as I step into the portal, I hear Death chuckle. "Good luck!"

CHAPTER 3

HAVENWOOD FALLS

I'm sucked into a whirlwind that throws me about, spinning me one way only to jolt me the other. Time disappears through this vacuum as I'm transported to my next calling. It's not easy to think in this space either, with pressure pushing in on all sides of my body, squeezing me through the fabric of two dimensions. An invisible force tugs me to the right, and I know this is my exit. It's like an instinct. A hole opens up for a split second, and I slip through with ease, popping out of the portal with a zap.

I hover in the sky, a black swirl of mist in the bright blue azure. Closing my eyes, I let the soul reach out to me, waiting for it to tug me in the right direction. With speed on my side, I descend, knowing I need to get my bearings. As a reaper, there are few places I have yet to visit. Perks of the job. Actually, its only perk really. Death isn't exactly the cheeriest guy to work for.

Thankfully, I go unnoticed once I land on my feet, due to my ability to become invisible; can't have any townies glaring at my form —they'd be screaming nonstop. I know, ladies, I'm just that sexy. Everyone wants to jump my bones.

"Hot Cocoa and Cookie Crawl! Come taste the best in the West!" A loud female voice comes from the opposite side of the road. Bodies are moving all over this small town. Surprisingly, I don't recognize it, but based on the accents alone, I know I'm in America. There's no mistaking the twang in those words.

"Come join in the fun! Hot cocoa and cookies all around town for today only! Judge them all until you can't stomach any more!"

Intrigued, I cross the road and step into the crowd. I love this part. I'm like a ninja, moving around without interference. No one sees me coming until it's too late. I'm a bad omen like that.

"You! What are you doing here? Why are you in Havenwood Falls?"

I take a step back. This girl's gotta be trippin'. There's no way she can see me. I step aside—she has to be referring to whoever's behind me.

"Reaper, I'm talking to you. Why are you here?"

Well, fuck me. How the hell can she see me? "You know, you probably look really crazy right now, talking to thin air."

"You have a British accent," she says as though this surprises her, but then she shrugs and grabs my arm. We're instantly transported to the inside of a building. It's empty, save for a reception area. There's no indication as to what kind of work place this is. Interesting. This girl's got me curious.

"What are you?" I scent the air, picking up the strength of magic exuding from the woman, but there's something else, something that matches the attitude of her attire. Ripped jeans, slogan T-shirt, leather jacket, beanie hat. What is she?

"What I am is not your concern, but why you're here is mine. Explain yourself."

Who the hell does this broad think she is, ordering me around? Angels of Death take orders from one person only, and even then that's only out of fear. The guy literally has the power to keep us in the ground for good. This girl has nothing on me.

"I'm working. I go where the souls call from. Seeing as you know what I am, I'm disappointed you didn't figure that out already." I lean against the long reception desk, commanding the space as my own. She doesn't rattle me.

"Nobody's died here. Try again."

I smirk. "I didn't know you knew everything and everyone in this town to be so clued in on who's alive." I cross my arms over my skeletal frame. I'm going to have fun messing with her.

"Actually, I do. This isn't like any other place you've visited before."

I guffaw. "Yeah, okay, princess. Who made you ruler of the land? Towns, no matter how many you visit, are all the same. The only thing that changes are the names. You still have your quirky shops, necessary businesses, park, school, church, graveyard, and emergency services. Please, stop me if I'm wrong."

She shakes her head. "No, you're just missing one crucial element, something I'm amazed you haven't figured out yet, you know, considering your *job*."

I slouch onto the desk, letting her tell me everything I need to know. "Go on then. Tell me what makes this town stand out amongst all others?"

She leans forward, whispering into my ear. "It's a supernatural town. Practically equal in the supe to human ratio."

I shrug, nonplussed. Whatever species live here, it makes no difference to my job—I take all souls, once their time has come. "Great, and how does this explain how you supposedly know whether a soul needs reaping or not? You got magic dibs on everyone?"

"Something like that. This town has its own Court and rules, something the founders set up to keep track of and protect the residents here. This place is special and a haven for many."

"Okay, princess. But you still haven't answered my question. Why does it matter if I'm here?"

She huffs loudly, as though resigning herself to a long tale. If only I had popcorn and a seat. These ol' bones are getting creaky.

"We make all supernatural creatures register with the Court. It's a way to protect them and us. And the town is warded too, so the second you step foot in our borders, we know. So, reaper, who are you here for? And don't even think about giving me vague answers. There's too much shit going on to waste time on you."

I chuckle. "Glad to know I'm of importance." This place has me even more intrigued. How did I not know of it before? In my circles, a town laden with supernatural creatures would rank high as a conversation topic. I certainly want to find out more. I consider my options and decide on absolute honesty. What's it gonna hurt? "Some souls escaped the Infernum. I'm here to collect."

"The Infernum? *Again?* Are you fucking kidding me? Who are they? It'd better not be that damn Indrori!" She narrows her eyes, and if looks could scorn, I'd be burning up right now.

Well, shit. That's it—her missing piece! "You're a hellhound."

She quickly scans the empty room. "*Half* hellhound, thank you, and I'd appreciate it if you kept that to yourself. Let's get back on track. These souls—are they going to cause a problem here? I can't have them running amok. The Court will have to intercept."

"Whoa, whoa, whoa. Hold your horses there, princess. This is my job, not this Court or special town's. I don't have names." *Except for one*, I keep to myself. There's no reason to reveal all my dirty laundry to this stranger. "You're just gonna have to let me get on with it, and then I'll happily leave this place behind."

"If you even think you're hanging around here for more than five minutes without registering and having a temporary tattoo done before walking out, then you're mistaken. You might be a reaper, and you might work for Death, but trust will have to be earned. There's too much crap going on right now as it is, especially with the Collec—"

I lean forward, goading her to say more. Unfortunately, she chooses this moment to exercise her silence. Bugger.

"Is that why you're here? You're reaping for the Collector?" She pounces on me out of the blue.

I frown. "I have no idea who you're talking about. I work for Death. All reapers work for him only. Who's this Collector?"

"If you're not working for him, then you must know something about him from all your visits to the different realms. What can you tell me?"

I stare at her, dumbfounded. "Honestly, you sound like a crazy person. What are you talking about?"

She stares hard, frowning with suspicion, but doesn't offer any insight to this madness.

I sigh, exasperated. "Look, you got shit to deal with. So have I. So let's adjourn this meeting and get back to the important stuff. Besides, I'm not sure why you think a tattoo's going to help any, especially when I have no canvas to present." I lift the cloak up my arms, showing off my bony digits, ulna, and radius. I turn to leave, but once again, the sassy hell witch grabs my arm and keeps me pinned to the wall with an invisible force field. I'll give it to her—the girl's got some balls trying to restrain a being like me. We're not exactly the cuddly-bear, forgiving kind.

"Don't make me repeat myself, reaper. I won't let you careen around without being seen. You will be tattooed until the Court decides what to do with you."

I roll my eyes. Again she bangs on about a bloody tattoo. Am I missing something here? I have nothing a needle can penetrate, let alone stain. Stupid little girl. Sodding idiots are everywhere these days.

With the magical grip she has on me, I struggle to escape, but there's a lot more strength in her than meets the eye.

"The tattoo will make you appear human, fill you out a little more." She motions to my lack of shape. "And yes, that means you'll have to wear clothes like the rest of us, eat, and sleep. And depending on your time scale, if you stick around long enough, you may even experience a few desires." She winks.

"No offense, princess. You don't do it for me, you're too . . ."

"Talented? Beautiful? Enigmatic? Doesn't matter anyway, I'm spoken for."

I grin widely, having scented the answer to this question earlier. "By a vampire, yes. Unfortunately for you, I don't do blood bag leftovers."

"Fuuuck, do you ever shut up? You must drive Death to insanity with this incessant chit-chat. Fuck knows how he puts up with you."

I shrug. She doesn't need to know of the tensions between the boss and me. She turns for the desk, leaving me to hover in the room's entryway. I watch her rummage in one of the drawers.

"Perfect. This will do. You got any picture preference or are you giving me free rein?" She lifts the gun in her hands, squeezing until the needle buzzes a few times. "Great, artist's choice it is."

As hard as I try I'm still unable to move, which works well for the witch as she lifts the cloak from my right arm and lets the needle push against the top of my right humerus. There's no pain, just an annoying itch-like scratch I can't touch. Christ, it's irritating.

"Can we hurry this along please? I've got some wall-staring to get to."

"The Court will want to have words with you."

"I thought you were the Court," I counter, watching as she puts her tattoo kit away, back in the drawer behind the reception desk.

"I'm just their business manager. I'm sure you can appreciate this town is too big for one supe to manage alone, let alone the fact it wouldn't be very democratic."

"How very civilized," I quip, having seen my fair share of savage supernaturals, and that's without them intermingling. Too many creatures consider themselves purists, and to even acknowledge another species is a big sin. These crazy motherfuckers make life interesting.

"Okay, when I let you go, the tattoo will take effect, and you'll change. No more invisibility for you until you're on a reaping hunt. Then, and only then, will you change forms while you're in Havenwood Falls, got it?"

I nod. There's not much more to say.

"Then I need to register you. A drop of blood, and your name, and you can get out of my hair for the day."

I burst into laughter, and the bubble-like barrier wrapped around my middle jiggles from the movement. "Princess, I don't have any blood to give you. I'm literally bone dry."

She stares upwards, putting hands to hips as if searching for some kind of strength. "You'll have a human form soon enough, and as that's the one meandering around town, the blood markers will do. Are you really this stupid? Do I need to explain every small thing to you? Do you know how to reap a soul or should I demonstrate the ins and outs of that too?"

This girl is no fun. She's deflated my happy buzz. "Fine, I'll give you my name if you give me yours."

"That is such a cheesy line. You want to score around here, you'll have to work harder." She clicks her fingers, and I fall, landing clumsily on my bones. "I'm Addie. You'll get used to seeing me around, and trust me when I say we'll be watching you."

"Well, Addie, I'm Shade StormIron. It's a pleasure to meet you," I say sarcastically. She grabs my hand once more and pricks my thumb —I'm no longer just bones. I didn't even feel the change. How unusual.

"Don't thank me yet, Shade. You haven't seen what you look like now."

Well, shit. I bet she's made me some old, fat bastard. Crap.

CHAPTER 4

HELLHOUNDS

"*H*ey, handsome, wanna taste my hot cocoa?"

"If it's as good as you look, then we're on to a winner." I give the woman my cheekiest smile and wink. She blushes in response. She's pretty, but there's no real interest in her brown eyes. She's just after a quick sale, and I'm almost inclined to give it to her. What the fuck is wrong with me? It has to be the human skin, right? It's making me soft. Stupid bloody rules. Of all the places the souls could've gone, why here? And how the hell have they gone unnoticed? The second my feet hit the ground here, I had Princess all over me. Something isn't right.

I make my way through the town. It looks like Santa's jizzed all over the place. There's a bloody huge tree, no doubt modelled after his own penis size, and twinkling lights everywhere. Everywhere. I'm amazed they haven't found their way into my hair. Yeah, I have bloody hair now, and it's goddamn gorgeous too, if the reflection I keep catching in shop windows is anything to go by. Never mind the stares from the thirsty locals. Yeah, baby, they want the D I'm packing. "Hey, babe, do you know what a compressed file is? You'd better unzip my pants to find out."

"Ew, gross!"

I turn away, laughing to myself. Serves her right. The ugly woman standing in front of the coffee shop window thought I was checking her out, when actually, I've just been admiring my new look. It's a lot to get used to. To begin with, I have skin. Tight skin that covers big, muscular arms and torso. I seem to be of the same six-foot-plus height, thankfully. And now I've got the perfect smolder. People can finally appreciate my charisma.

"Sir, have you tried our cookies?" A young girl comes up to me, blue eyes gazing at me through long eyelashes in the most adorable way. My heart almost skips a beat, she's that precious, holding out her hands with a cellophane bag of decorated cookies gift wrapped with a ribbon. Oh, boy, the shop owners have done well, using this bundle of innocence to coerce even the hardest of me out of my money.

Shit! Do I even have money?

My stomach starts to growl, reminding me I'm susceptible to human needs now. Fuck me, this is going to slow me down exponentially. Why this bloody town? That's it. It's decided. Death truly does hate me.

"She got you good, man. Don't break her little heart now."

I shake my head to the stranger, though I recognize him as a hellhound. Why else would you wear sunglasses when it's a dull day?

"Dude, you have no idea. I'm Shade." I hold out a hand, waiting for the fellow to introduce himself. We're of the same height and build, and I can sense the wildness in him, his second nature.

"Ace," he replies, gripping my hand firmly. It's not until he touches my skin that he realizes who I am. Although the Infernum is a massive abyss, there are times when I bump into hellhounds there. Ace isn't one of them.

"You sticking around?" He raises a brow, crossing a fully tattooed arm over the other.

I shrug. There's no real answer that offers a probable timeframe here. "Until the job is done. There's always another calling, speaking of which . . ." My spine tingles into awareness, like cold hands reaching out to me.

"Later, man. You should check out the club; you may find

someone you know." Ace tilts his head to the left, I'm assuming as a means of direction to this so-called club.

I disappear, finding my chance to escape now that the cookie-selling girl is preoccupied with conning a loved-up couple out of their money. Suckers.

My feet, now kitted out in swanky brown Timberland boots, command my body around the town, guiding me to the soul that's calling.

It's going to take me forever in this monkey suit. What the hell am I gonna do? *Oh, sorry, Death. I couldn't catch the souls in time because this fucked up mystical town made me human, stunting all efficiency. Please don't punish me further. This clearly isn't my fault. Signed, Shade.*

I snort to myself, as if that shit would ever wash.

I'm so caught up in my self-pity monologue that I don't even notice day switching to night. My stomach still grumbles, too.

"Well, what do we have here?"

I blink a few times, struggling to make sense of where I am. I'm standing in a parking lot, at the base of one of the box canyon's mountains. A big beefy bodyguard stands by what I can only describe as a gondola-shaped lift. Where the bloody hell am I? Town isn't around here, and people seem to have disappeared. Fucking excellent. This soul is leading me into some mafia's lair, I can feel it.

"What is this?" I point to the tall cave-like edifice, where the gondolas ascend. I wonder where they lead to.

"Got an invitation?" The guy huffs, ignoring my question completely. Instead, he's now preoccupied with some overly smartly dressed men and women. He checks them out, scanning the paper one member of the party hands over. What is this? Some secret club for the rich? I snort internally, having now witnessed it all.

Beefy Bodyguard sends them on their way, into the lift that takes them up and to a place I know I'm supposed to be.

"You. No invitation, no admittance. Private Christmas party tonight. It's that simple."

This guy is pissing me off. Everyone here is so sodding nosy. I don't take shit from anyone, especially not some jacked-up guy throwing his muscle around. We can all be dicks like that; some of us choose not to be. Tosser.

"I don't give a shit." I get up in his face, seeing my own reflection in the glasses he's wearing. "Fuck me, is this place riddled with hellhounds?"

Princess had me believing this is a place for species to coexist. So far, I've only met one kind—goddamn hellhounds, with their skewed self-important view of the world.

"Watch what you're talking about. You don't mess with us. Now go."

I shake my head. "Nope. Come on, big fella, aren't you even a little curious as to who I am? I mean, I totally just outed you. Care to retaliate?"

He pushes my shoulders, attempting to get me out of his face. He stops short, hands recoiling as though I've burnt him. Don't even get me started on the irony of that.

"Problem?" I smirk, knowing I've finally got his full attention.

"What are you doing here, reaper? And why the hell do you look like this?" He lifts his shades, knowing his eyes won't affect me. A hellhound's eyes are notorious for killing—look in them three times and you're frazzled. Not me, though. Death is my master.

"Witch bitch wouldn't let me walk around this place without a skin suit. Now, back to why I came. I gotta get in there." I point to the mysterious entrance above in the cave.

He shakes his head. I don't believe it. "Can't do that. Melaina will fucking kill me. There's no trouble here."

This guy is seriously testing my patience now. "You can say all you want, but when a soul calls my name, I can't walk away. You should know this." I give him my most disappointed stare. "I'm getting in there with or without your help."

"What soul?" The guy squares up to me, clearly assuming I'm telling one big lie to get involved in whatever the secret space is hiding up there. Obviously, based on the party earlier, money can get you in.

Is this some kind of cage-fighting joint? One off the books for legal reasons?

"One that escaped the fucking Infernum. Are we done, or do I have to knock you out now?"

The guy blares out with laughter. Excellent. Nice to know I've tickled his pickle. Bloody time waster.

"If there's trouble, Melaina will sort it. You won't be going up."

I pull back a fist, pushing forward for the smug grin on his face. He grabs my fist before I connect with flesh, and thrusts a punch directly at my nose, the large mass expanding to fit my forehead too. Guy's got big hands.

I stagger back, dazed and confused as the dark night swirls around me. I hit the ground and zone out, darkness taking me.

CHAPTER 5

SONG

"*J*think you broke him. He's been out too long. Doesn't look like his skin suit is strong enough to handle a reaper."

I keep my eyes closed for a few more minutes, fooling these strangers to gain the advantage. Mentally, I take note of any injuries, working from my head down. My nose is sore but other than that, I'm fine, but they don't need to know it. Winning battles always comes to whoever has the upper hand—I'm not about to reveal all my cards, especially as I don't know where I'm at, or whose company I'm now keeping.

My stomach chooses this moment to let out a wail like it's being stabbed to death; probably reckons my throat's been cut too. Stupid human needs.

"Well, shit," I exhale, sitting up. It's difficult to lie still when your belly's roar takes on a life of its own. "Don't suppose you've got some food stashed in that skinny dress?"

I forget introductions and wariness. Man can concentrate only on his gut when it demands sustenance. I'm tempted to click my fingers at the sexy brunette staring at me, just to piss her off some more, but for once, I think better of the idea and take on a polite persona. I know, it's bloody sickening behavior, but the hellhound just won't shake a leg fast enough.

How are there more hellhounds in this mysterious town than there are in the Infernum? Clearly they don't respect their roles. They're everywhere.

My neck tingles, the sensation trailing along my spine like an attack of angry birds pecking at my spinal column. It's bloody uncomfortable, to say the least. I leave the room, ignoring the protests being shouted behind me. Step by step, the pain becomes more of an irritation, reducing as a means of navigation the closer I get.

"What the hell do you think you're doing?"

Why does everyone keep asking me this?

The female hound stands in front of me as though her small frame is enough to stop me. I scowl.

"Shut up." I try halting the loud tones of her voice from spooking this soul away. "It's here." I scoot around her, peering around the corner of a room that's booming music with little care to noise levels.

True to the witch's word, my form changes of its own accord. I have no control over it. Skin disappears until I'm only bones, and I can feel my wings emerging, stretching out of my back like they've been trapped for far too long.

I take on a black mist as I swirl into the air, entering the room without being seen as I hover through the crowd undetected. I have *all* my abilities at work now.

The damned soul calls to me, like there's a bright red beacon illuminating my target. Without hesitation I speed to the mirage of a man, unwilling to let him escape my grasp. There's nothing innocent or human about this projection—it's just the form the soul wants you to see.

In an instant we slam through a portal to the Infernum, ignoring all conversations thrown my way. I'm not going to be distracted this time.

"Shit!" I snap at myself, recognizing the couch area I've just tumbled into. Of all the sodding places the portal could've opened . . .

"Back so soon, reaper? We need to set some rules." The female hellhound maneuvers around her desk at the opposite end of the room. "Now, this club is mine to protect. I can't have you waltzing your way in whenever you want. I don't give a shit if there's a soul here. If it's not causing trouble, it can party its ass off. Got it? No. Scenes. Here."

I sit back on the couch, resting my feet on the coffee table, folding arms behind my head. Yeah, she's pissed. Heels clack on the floor.

"Don't you have any fucking respect?"

"Listen, babe. We know who I work for. It's not like I can just walk away from a soul. That's not how this works. If another ends up here, I'm gonna have to come regardless of your opinion. I'm surprised, Ms. . . . ."

"Melaina Savage," she supplies.

I nod. "Shade," I point to myself. "I would've thought escapees from the Infernum would worry you."

She shrugs, relaxing enough to take one of the seats. "It does, but that's secondary to what else is going on in this town right now."

I lean forward, seeing an opportunity. "Then why don't we come to an agreement. You give me free rein in this place, and I promise to be incognito when reaping. Deal?"

She narrows her eyes. "How can you guarantee that?"

"Did anyone notice me earlier?" I raise a brow, letting the corners of my mouth lift in satisfaction. I already know the answer.

"Fine, but you don't speak of anything that happens here. Privacy is our guarantee."

I stand. "Don't worry, Melaina. I'll wear you down soon enough, and you'll start loving me." I pause, smiling. "By the way, what else has got everyone so uptight in this town? You all seem to want to deal with me, yet no one wants to spare the time." I wait, but she doesn't give in. What's going in on in this town? I sigh. "See you around, hottie. I'm being bugged again." I wink, leaving the room via the door this time.

I make my way to the lower levels, becoming more ensconced in caverns the more I descend. If I were a decent enough guy, I'd even compliment Ms. Savage on a job well done. There's certainly an allure here, whether it's the moody atmosphere produced by low lighting or the separation of rooms offering different experiences. And fuck me, some are definitely more lively than others. Lively enough I bet it's cause enough to make even Death blush.

My new, annoying stomach grumbles again, reminding me how well I've adapted to this new body. Neglect is a forte of mine. But all of that fades into the background when a song, the most enchanting piano melody, slow and seductive, calls to me in a way I've never felt before. This isn't an uncomfortable tingle along my spine where some soul is in need of direction to the right afterlife zone. This is the kind of awakening that makes me feel alive, desperate to clutch and never release. It's full of joy and promise, building excitement within me.

Listen to me babbling on like some new-age, life-is-everything guru. This body is making me soft. There's no other explanation for it.

"Can I get you a drink, handsome?"

I'm pulled from my thoughts when a blonde speaks, notepad in hand, skin more visible than clothing. Without a doubt, this party cavern is screaming sex.

"What do you recommend?" I cast it off as light flirtation, but really I have no bloody clue what tastes good. I've not had the pleasure of taste buds before, or the need to use them. It's like I'm that puppet who becomes a real boy. At least he always had wood. So far mine seems as nonexistent as it's always been. It's like a sad elephant down there.

"You know, you look to me like you're here for a surprise. Do you trust me?"

I shrug, giving the waitress the go-ahead. I'm too distracted to really care anyway. It's not a drink that's going to be wetting my whistle right now.

Who is that?

I hear the melody in my mind again, tender piano notes trickling through. If I didn't know any better, I'd say this instant reaction is the work of a mating partnering up. Too bad I know that kind of life isn't in store for me. After all, who's ever heard of a reaper getting a happily ever after? No, fairytale love doesn't exist—I'm destined for the sorrow of soul reaping only. There's no plus-one ticket where I'm heading. And this packaging I'm flaunting right now won't be around forever. I'll be back to bare bones the moment I leave this place. It's not exactly the warm and comforting body women want to snuggle up to at night. And let's face it, my figure will always be a bone of contention. Compared to me, they'll always look fat. It's not my fault God gave them organs and Death gave me a hollow shell. I'm just pointing out the facts. Anyway, who the hell has time for pointless, illogical arguments?

Fuck me. If the reaction I'm currently having is any indication, then I know what's about to happen. I'm screwed. More importantly, my cock is now pointing the way. I've suddenly become a testosterone-filled, puberty-ripe teenager. How the hell do I control this thing? Look at it—it's like a chubby baby's arm is waving around, looking for a response.

It's all *her* fault too—the woman in the center of the room, twirling her body around a long pole. Small pieces of red fabric barely cover her tits and arse, with heels that accentuate long, toned legs. I want to pin her against the bar wall, let everyone see as I claim her, running my tongue all over her body, satiating this uncontrollable thirst that's currently consuming me. I want to take her nipples into my mouth, watch as she arches her back with desire.

An unsubtle cough catches my attention. The waitress from before has impeccable timing.

"Your drink. It's a screw-me-six-ways cocktail. You look like you need it." She winks, glancing at the massive bulge I'm barely concealing in my jeans. She disappears before I have time to form a rebuke, and I'm back to fantasizing about my time with this dancer.

The club disappears as she becomes my sole focus. She pulls me in like she's got me on a leash, tugging for me to come closer. My feet move without my brain sending signals. I'm not in control of my own body. This song that still calls out to me seems to be dictating my movements.

Even from across the room, I knew this woman was beautiful, but up close, she takes my breath away. Breath I very much need to rely on in this town. She twirls some more, contorting her body around the thin metal cylinder. Beautiful long black hair cascades over her back, shining in the spotlight illuminating her. The music is coming to an end, and she slows to the rhythm, her routine over with the last note.

This is when I know I'm fucked. Her eyes meet mine, and pools of bright blue have me drowning inside them. I'm lost in their sparkling depth.

"Take a picture. It might last longer." She winks, moving to leave the elevated stage she's been dancing on.

"Wait, what's your name, beautiful?"

She hangs back, almost as though my question has startled her. "Why?"

"Because I'd like to think of the name that matches this pretty face." I cringe at the corny line coming out of my mouth. My smooth-guy ability has evacuated the building. She laughs, and I'm drawn further to her beautiful being. She's got me wrapped around her little finger.

She leans forward, her scent of flowers surrounding me.

"Thalia Prince," she whispers, then leaves, giving me the perfect view of her arse swaying with each step.

Bollocks. I want her.

CHAPTER 6

SCREWED

*H*er lips linger on mine, a taste of something sweet and spicy. Foods I've yet to try tingle my tongue like electricity sparking between us. It sends my body into overdrive, and I desperately need more.

"Thalia," I exhale, loving the way her name rolls off my tongue like it's mine to keep.

"What do you want from me, Shade?" Her lips purse, swollen from the friction of my own. Hell yeah, I like this. It raises a carnality in me.

I lean in, our faces barely a breath apart as I stare into her enchanting eyes. "I want you to bare your soul to me."

She moves swiftly, wrapping her jeans-covered legs around my waist, arms around my neck. I cup her juicy arse, gripping tightly as I claim her lips once again. Her tongue battles with mine, a duel of passion exchanging between us. I can't get enough; she doesn't feel close enough.

Her hands tangle in my hair, driving me wild. I pin her against a wall, letting her feel the length of my cock desperate to be freed.

I tear at her shirt like a savage beast, and strips of fabric are all that remain, scattered on the floor at my feet. I wait for some argument about her having some emotional attachment to the shirt, but she surprises me. My hunger's ignited her own, and now she's tearing into mine, grabbing the tight-fitting cotton stretched over my broad shoulders and chest. She huffs with aggravation, struggling to pry the top from my skin. If I wasn't so fucking horny for her right now, I'd consider the pout on her face fucking adorable. But I'm not a soppy bastard.

I stare at the sparkly black bra she's wearing, enhancing the beautiful shape of her bouncy boobs. Shit yeah, they jiggle like perfectly set jelly.

I can't wait any more. There's nothing left of my patience. I need to hear her screaming my name out, over and over like I'm the god she worships. I set her down on my bed, practically ripping the jeans hugging her arse and baring silky skin that's calling to my lips.

"What are you looking at, Shade?" Her voice comes out on a heavy breath, lust lighting up her eyes like beautiful Christmas decorations. She can be the angel on the top of my tree any time she wants, as long as she's naked.

"How much I want to make you come." I wiggle my brows, liking the pink blush that warms her cheeks. How can she look so innocent after I've seen her dance at the club?

My cock is pulsing so rapidly, it's about to take off like a rocket. Hot fluid coming at you in 3 . . . 2 . . . 1 . . .

Thalia runs her hands over my arms, my biceps flexing as I hover over her, framing her body with my own. She looks so delicate and fierce at the same time.

"Fuck me, Shade. Let me forget."

I don't need her to tell me twice. I trail my tongue along her neck, over the top of her breasts while I free them from their fabric cage. I take her perky nipple into my mouth, suckling the already hard bud. She moans in response, arching her back for more.

Her hands grip the sheets as I continue exploring her body, reaching her hips. With each new kiss to her pussy, I pull away the thong, letting her spread her legs wide, cunt completely exposed to my waiting mouth. Fuck me, even her scent has me salivating like Daffy Duck.

"Shade," she moans in anticipation; that voice almost makes me give in and shag her senseless, but I want this to last. She isn't a five minute happy for me. No, I want at least a week. I want to come all over her the way the snow lays on the ground.

I flick her clit with my tongue, letting her absorb the feeling before doing it again, but fuck me, I want to devour her already. Her pussy juices coat my tongue like the sweetest elixir.

"Oh, God, Shade. Again," she calls. Her hand fists in my hair, and I feel her legs tighten either side of my head as I swirl my tongue around her pussy, slipping in a finger, then a second as I pump my hand in and out of her, my tongue lapping at her clit. Her warmth surrounds me, building like an inferno. "Oh, Shade," she moans, breathing deeply. "Shade, I'm going to come. Oh, God . . ."

I pump my fingers harder, work my hand faster until I push her off the edge completely, screaming my name with vigor, zero boundaries between us. "Shade . . ."

I bolt upright, eyes struggling to open, confusion pressing in on me like I've been drugged. I don't understand. Where's Thalia?

"Good morning, Shade. Looks like you had a good night."

I pull the covers up over my body, a raging boner poking the duvet like an obvious beacon. The granny-like figure hovering at the foot of the bed makes zero sense. I try to speak, but between a croaky sleep-heavy voice and an inability to form a full sentence, I'm fucked from the get-go. Where the hell am I?

"Oh, dear, you look so lost. What's troubling you?"

I take a moment to gather my thoughts, sweeping a glance around the room I'm in. There's the bed I'm obviously lying in, a window ahead, though currently with plain curtains drawn. A wardrobe to my left and a desk to my right, and hopefully somewhere around the corner a bathroom, because I'm suddenly needing quite the release. How the hell do humans cope with the constant requirements a body needs? If it's not hunger, it's a drink, and if it's not a drink, it's a piss, then comes tiredness. It's like a hamster wheel of never-ending demands. How do they ever get anything done?

"Are you lost?" I ask the ghostly figure who's currently keeping my company. "Do you need me to take you to the beyond?"

She laughs. "Oh, no, dear. I'm quite all right here."

"Are you sure? I know it can get lonely. Seeing and interacting with people you know here is great, but not having any physical contact at all can leave you empty. I can offer you more than this."

"Thank you, Shade, but really, I'm needed here. I'll call on you if I change my mind."

I sigh, sadness seeping into my skin. It always pains me to see a wandering soul. "How did I get here?" I ask the woman, realizing I don't know her name, though somehow she knows mine. "Ms. . . ."

"You may call me Madame Luiza." She smiles brightly, and I can almost feel it warm the room. This lady must have been remarkable when she was alive. "You stumbled in here last night. You don't remember?"

I think hard, but it's all a blur. The only thing I remember definitively is meeting Thalia.

"You were quite inebriated, young man. Anything could have happened to you."

I laugh at her scorn, young being an adjective I wouldn't give my two hundred plus years. There's very little that can harm a reaper, even when I'm stuck in this meat suit. It may give me certain limitations, but I'm sure if it came down to it, if this body couldn't contain me, regardless of the tattoo and its restrictions, I'm sure I'd return to my usual state of skeleton and cape. Mr. Sexy in all his glory.

"But why am I here?"

"You really don't remember?"

"I think the screw-me-six-ways cocktails have something to do with that."

"Yes, you kept mentioning a beauty you found at Silk."

I can't help but pick up on the disdain in her voice. Is Silk a sore spot for some residents here?

"I'm guessing she directed you here. Not seen you around before, so I'm sure you didn't have anywhere to stay?" She continues to hover, her presence almost becoming a nuisance now. What is the deal with this bloody nightclub? Why all the secrecy and scorn?

Once again I damn the stupidity of human needs. How much precious time have I wasted being distracted by a woman and then spending hours with eyes closed? This isn't productive. Death will take me for sure.

"My niece brought you up here. This is her business. Whisper Falls Inn," Madame Luiza fills in, a wide smile plastering her translucent face as if with pride.

"Great, any souls running amok here? Besides you, of course."

"No, dear. This place is too calm for what you're searching for. You'd have better luck wandering the cemetery." She cackles, disappearing without a goodbye.

Fucking strange. Havenwood Falls is full of unusual characters.

I think about the day ahead, of the countless souls I have yet to track. Why can't I feel them all, calling me forward? I didn't expect to be spending more than one day on this mission—there's more work all around the world to be doing.

I fail to see a bathroom in my room, so I grab my jeans and head into the corridor in search of a communal one. I overhear the tail end of a conversation between two old biddies.

"Blood was pulled from her entire body. Nothing left. Bone dry."

I close my eyes, already knowing the culprit. This town might be filled with an array of supernatural creatures, but I'm certain none would be so careless as to leave a body to be found. No, this comes from someone who doesn't give a shit. And I can think of one major soul that should be calling out to me already.

"Shit," I whisper to myself. "It's Nyx," I continue to mumble to myself, thinking up my next move. A vampire-demon hybrid is bad news, even for a town like this.

CHAPTER 7

ADDICTION

I've never had to consider what it's like to be human. My verdict? It sucks. I'm standing in a long-arse queue in this coffee shop, waiting to get a taste of whatever it is that smells so bloody good in here. I don't even remember making the decision to come in here. It's like an addiction I don't even have forced me this way.

"You know, I hear the sheriff is furious, probably blaming himself if you ask me."

I stay where I am, thankful for at least one good thing about queuing: gossips.

"Why? The poor man can't stop everything going on in this town. It's not like the people expect him to know of a crime before it's committed. Our sheriff puts too much pressure on himself. Ask me, he's a fine man." This old lady winks at her friend, and the pair of them giggle like girls, sniggering at their naughty thoughts.

"It makes me wonder what kind of a monster is living among us. How can a body even be drained of all blood without a drop on the ground or an open wound?"

I have the answers they're looking for, but these humans aren't privy to this side of the Havenwood Falls they live in. If they were,

I'm sure they'd be hunting down every vampire that resides in this town, which, oddly enough, includes my current landlady, if my instincts are correct. At least there's more here than bloody hellhounds. Honestly, it's like work just follows me around wherever I end up. I wonder what Death would have to say if I asked for some time off. I inwardly snort at the ridiculous notion. What would I do with time off anyway? What I am is what I do; it's all I've been created for.

"It's lucky they even found her way out in the cemetery like that." Old Lady One finishes her sentences with a case of Tourette-like tuts whilst shaking her head. If she bobs any harder, she'll be snapping her own neck, giving me more work. Selfish cow.

I so desperately want to find out more, but how can I ask without seeming like a creep? It's not like I'm a local, with a vested interest in the people that populate this place. No, I'll only be offering myself up as a great suspect, and something tells me that if I started a conversation with these ladies, I'd never have a chance to leave. It's not that they reek of loneliness. Oh, bollocks, who am I kidding? Of course they're bloody lonely—it's the sole reason anyone gossips in the first place. Honestly, these humans think they're so infallible, when really their basic need for nurturing controls their minds and their actions, too.

"Do you know who she was?"

I lean forward automatically, praying the cashier doesn't call them up next, taking their conversation with them.

"I'm not sure. I can't remember the name now. Oh, I'm sure it'll come back to me soon; just need some java to kick-start the old brain." Old Lady One taps her noggin. "Unless it's one of the many tourists." At the same time, they both turn to look at me with knowing glances. Thankfully, the cashier's now free.

I stare at the menu board, ignoring the oldies now that I've managed to spark their interest with my presence. I read the menu again and again. Cappuccino. Latte. Flat white. Americano. What the hell is the difference anyway? I thought coffee is coffee. How can there be so many kinds? How am I supposed to know which one I'll like best?

I've heard humans talk about the drink for decades, but not once have they ever mentioned it comes in a variety! Why do they do this to themselves? Aren't their lives complicated enough without being quizzed on what type of coffee bean to milk to water ratio they want?

Wait a minute, what's this? I squint at the board some more, reading further. Christ, you have to decide what milk you want? What. The. Fuck. MILK IS MILK! What's with all these weird options? Almond, coconut, soya. I did not realize how insane the world has become. It's no wonder they're so bloody miserable most of the time. And why am I so hung up on this that I'm giving it valuable thinking time? Shit, this is it. This is how it sucks you in. *Welcome to coffee roulette. Here's your loyalty card for all offers to keep you coming back, you addict.*

What am I doing? I give up as the cashier calls me forward. I'm not here for these social pleasures. I grasp the door handle just as it's being pushed in my direction, and I freeze. Luscious black locks and bright blue eyes hold me still; sweet and spicy invade my senses, and I love it. Her scent is everything I need to bring me comfort.

"Thalia," I whisper, flashes of this morning's horny dreams filling my mind, and I'm instantly having to control my cock from making headline news.

She frowns, standing half in and half out of Coffee Haven. "Do I know you?"

Fuck me, it's like a dagger to my new heart, slashed around for extra pain.

"We met last night, at the club," I add, considering she's still staring with a blank face. My ego is not faring well here. I'm clearly not the only hunk she's crossed paths with; and here I've been thinking I'm quite the memorable guy. Shit, this interaction business is brutal. At least when I'm reaping it's all banter—what're a skeleton and a soul gonna do? Talk about bumping uglies. But this, here with Thalia, can lead to so much more, if only my cock will let me do the talking. Down, boy.

"Yes, you're the one they renamed the cocktail after."

I raise a brow. "They did?"

She nods emphatically, a smile covering her gorgeous face. "Yup, a Rookie Reaper."

If I had a drink right now, it would be pouring out of my nostrils. This cocktail name business sounds more like an insult than flattery—and if the hellhound boss had anything to do with it, I'm sure that's her intention. Savage by name *and* nature.

"Why would they do that?"

"Your drinks last night were new, so . . ."

I can tell she thinks I'm stupid. Her face says it all with the raised lip. If expressions can talk, this one is *I can't believe you're such an idiot.* I need to remedy this quickly.

"She told me it was called a screw me six ways."

Thalia bursts into laughter, struggling to compose herself. "She was messing with you. Six liquors were in it, but the rest . . . Well, let's just say she noticed you had a situation to solve." Thalia blushes, now avoiding my gaze. "They were considering calling it the British Invasion but decided against it—even though you have the weird accent, you don't actually come from there, do you?"

I shake my head. I seem to get this a lot on my travels. "When you've been to as many places as I have, there are certain phrases and pronunciations that stick." I shrug it off as though it's no big deal. I don't even pay attention to what I say anymore. It just comes naturally.

I realize we're still blocking the coffee shop's doorway, me half out, and her half in.

"Come on, let me buy you a cup of coffee, and you can tell me about the club." I grasp her shoulder gently, urging her toward me.

She slams her arm down on mine, breaking the connection. Her eyes are wide, feral, and her face has become pale.

"Don't ever touch me again!" she roars, back ramrod straight before she turns and runs away, leaving me highly perplexed.

What the hell just happened?

I take a quick glance around the coffee shop, noting a few faces

177

glaring at me, the others too engaged in their own conversations to care.

Without another thought, I chase after her, running through the town in a confused daze. I replay the moment over in my mind, wondering what I did wrong.

Did my touch really hurt her this much? I have to know why.

CHAPTER 8

PAST

*E*ven with the snow-covered ground and frigid temperatures, I'm still sweating, beads cooling instantly along my back like icy barnacles.

I see Thalia just past the water fountain, sitting in the gazebo, surrounded by the white stuff. Gone is the woman I saw dancing last night, confidence emanating from her skin. Here, I see a shy, broken lady weeping with sadness. I don't know why, but even from afar it stirs a protective hunger in me. I want to take her pain away, beat up the arsehole who did this to her.

I inch slowly, afraid she'll run away from me again. "Thalia, whatever I did, I'm sorry. I didn't mean to hurt you if I gripped too hard. You see, I'm still getting used to this—"

"It wasn't you," she interrupts, eyes glassy with tears unshed. "I overreacted."

I shake my head. I know there's more to it than that. Her reaction was too reflexive for there to not be a bigger problem behind it. Why am I so invested in her? I should be on the hunt for Nyx. Saying goodbye to this town. Returning to business. Not letting Death find new ways to kick my arse.

"Listen, I could really do with a cup of coffee, but I have no idea what I'm supposed to order. Do you think you can help me out?"

I know, it's half ruse, and certainly not a lie, but I need this to continue. For some absurd reason that I cannot figure out, I just can't walk away from her yet. There's so much more to learn, curiosities that need feeding. Why. Do. I. Care.

Urgh.

"Okay," she says, standing, "but first I want a name."

I give her my best cocky grin, seeing I'm beginning to win her over. Oh yeah, I've still got it, baby. "Shade StormIron, at your service."

"Not yet, mister. My soul's not up for grabs for a hell of a lot more decades yet. I plan on living a very full, long life."

I try not to laugh at her expense, but she's just too damn adorable. Fuck me. As if I'd take her beautiful soul before it's due. What kind of a monster would that make me?

There's something about her that's so alluring, it effervesces from her skin like a permanent glow that calls to me. I don't know if she's doing it on purpose. I have yet to figure out what creature she is. But I know she isn't human; she has this otherworldly scent about her that all supernaturals carry.

This time we enter the coffee shop together, and she orders two cappuccinos, for which I pay. As a reaper, I have no need for money. What I do under Death's rule is my purpose—not necessarily a job, but I still earn a currency. It just happens to adapt to wherever I'm based. Luckily, the princess's tattoo allowed for that, and here I am in a town, loaded with money I'm sure several would be desperate to grab. Too bad for them I'm not a big spender, flashing my worth. No one will ever know.

"Okay, tell me. How good is this?" Thalia stares at me over the top of her large mug, lips pursed in the frothy milk.

I lift my own mug, ignoring the stares of the nosy patrons nearby; our earlier display clearly hasn't been forgotten. Don't these buggers have anything more exciting to be doing?

I take a mouthful, and hot, burning liquid coats my tongue and makes its way along my esophagus, leaving a trail in its wake. My insides have never felt so on fire before.

"You do understand the term 'hot' right?" There she goes, giving me that *you're stupid* look again. "If you still don't like it, then there's something wrong with you. Coffee is the best." Tahlia's face disappears behind her large mug, dainty fingers grasping either side of the hot drink.

Against my better judgment, I try again. This time it doesn't taste as bad, but I'm still not understanding why these earthlings have an undying lust for it. "How long have you lived here?"

Thalia glances upwards, as if the answers she seeks are printed on the ceiling. "A good few years, long enough to be calling this place home. And you? Here to stay?"

"I'm only here for work. Reapers don't normally hang around one place for long. There's always a soul calling for transport."

Her smile disappears, and sadness creeps into her face again. "That's a pity. Don't you ever want to stay in one place for more than five minutes?"

I ponder. "I've never really thought about it before. I guess I've had no reason to." I don't want to think too much about this. I fear there's a black hole at the end of a realization, if I were to have it. "What's it like working at the club?"

I pick my mug up again, forgetting that I really don't want to be drinking it. This is one human experience I'd like to take back.

Thalia quiets, a blush creeping across her cheeks. "I enjoy dancing and singing. It's the only time I feel free, confident. The music helps, I think, almost like it lulls me into a trance."

Now that I have her finally talking with passion, I don't want to interrupt with the drone of my voice, but there's so much more I want to learn.

"Don't you feel free now?" It's a strange thought that singing and dancing in public with very little, if nothing, on in the form of clothes makes her more relaxed than sitting in a coffee shop during the day, all covered up. Or is it the ogling men that give her a boost of confidence at night?

She shakes her head, her shoulders bunch up around her ears, and her hands curl around the mug she pulls into her. It's as though she's trying to make herself as small as possible, perhaps even invisible. All I want to do is take her in my arms and keep the hurt away. This Thalia is a polar opposite to the one I met last night. I can only imagine how exhausting this must be for her, but why? Why is she putting herself through this?

"There's rules in the club. Laws everyone has to abide by if they want to stay and have a good night. Melaina's good to us. One rule broken and you're banned for life. But out here, in the everyday of life, there are no protective hotheads to keep the inappropriate and despicable away. There's only me, and in comparison to many, I'm not the strong type."

A heaviness settles all around me like a black, thunderous cloud. "Do you get accosted a lot? Is that what has you pulling back from life?"

I can see it clearly. She works nights surrounded by hellhounds for protection, sleeps for most of the day, and only leaves the confines of her house when it's necessary. This isn't healthy for her, and it makes me so goddamn angry, I have to internalize my rage. If only I can get hold of the culprits behind her pain, latch onto their souls and repay in kind. It's the minimum they deserve.

She puts her empty mug back on the table, and I can feel our time together is coming to an end. I can feel her withdrawing.

"Let's just say there are a lot of people in this world who find a forest nymph's attributes highly appealing in their line of work. I can get them what they want just by the way I look. It makes me superficial. A means to an end. I am not a person, someone with life and choices. No, I am an object to be used until the magic wears off."

I see it now, the real pain behind her eyes. It's buried deep, hidden beneath doors she's erected to protect herself, one day at a time. There's loneliness in her too, and I can understand why. She won't allow anyone to get close enough because she believes there's only one thing she can offer them, the only thing they'd want from her.

Her nymph abilities.

"I don't believe that. I'm certain there are others out there who are desperate to be in your world because they want you there, not because of something you can give them."

Thalia briefly, faintly smiles, as if entertaining the notion for a moment. The instant the smile is gone, it's like she's pinged back to her reality, the world she's been living in for too long. How can I make this better? I can't just walk away. Her soul is too kind to be treated so badly.

"Tell me, Shade. Why are you even bothered about me? It wasn't my personality that drew you to me last night, was it?" She snorts, clearly becoming defensive.

I shake my head. I won't be giving her the satisfaction of thinking she's right. She's heading into a downward spiral, lashing out because I dare to think the one size shoe doesn't fit all. "It wasn't your beauty, either, Thalia. It was your song."

She rolls her eyes. "Please. I wasn't even singing last night."

"That's right. It wasn't your voice belting out the music. It was every aspect of you. You shouldn't be so quick to shut people down. They might surprise you."

"Oh yeah?" She raises a brow, crossing her arms over her chest like an overly dramatic child. "Then why don't you tell me about your past, then, Shade? How does a reaper spend his centuries?"

I fail to answer, mouth agape. I think back to the last two hundred years, and all I see is a playback of reapings, day and night, forever on the death train.

"Don't tell me how to live my life, Shade, when you haven't even experienced anything. At least I have a past, no matter how awful the memories!" She storms out of the coffee shop once more, and a strong chill passes over me.

Thalia is right to be mad, but I only want to help—to help her understand it's the restrictions she's placed on herself that are keeping her from being free. But her attack on my past, or lack thereof, is hard to digest.

I need a strong drink.

CHAPTER 9

LIVING

"*A*nother of your finest, please. Just keep them coming."

The barkeep grunts at me, I'm sure because he thinks I'm being sarcastic. The Dirty Knuckle doesn't exactly sound like fine dining does it? But who am I to know any different? I'm not exactly well-educated on these kinds of experiences, as Thalia rightly, though venomously, pointed out.

"It's not like it's my fault!" I spit out between gulps of whatever beer I've been chucking down my neck all afternoon and now evening. At this point, I'm mostly talking to the air, letting out anger with bursts of conversation I've been having with myself. Replaying my coffee date with Thalia.

Everyone in here seems to keep giving me a wide berth. I don't know why. It's not like I'm crazy, just finally taking on board what I need to experience in this meat suit. Princess WitchHound gave me a gift. Why shouldn't I use it?

Clunky music blares through the bar, but nobody is dancing. I can't have that. I bring my beer with me and stomp my foot to the beat in the center of the empty floor space, sloshing more liquid on my boots than in my gullet. What a fucking waste.

I think back to the days and nights I was on a reaping hunt, and how I'd watched the people make fools of themselves on the dance floor. I try to specifically remember what they were doing with their bodies in an effort to emulate it.

I have no bloody idea how to dance, but I can't let that stop me. Fuck it. I've been a skeleton long enough. I can do the sodding robot. Move it, bitches. I got some joints to pop.

I look at my glass. It's empty of beer. How did this happen?

Oh well, time for more. Maybe I'll try this whiskey I've been hearing so much about next.

∽

"Urgh, must you really, Madame Luiza? I beg you, close the curtains, please."

"Don't you think you ought to be getting up, young man? There's no time for pity parties in this world. I didn't take you for being so weak."

I know she's trying to rile me up, but I really don't give a shit. My head pounds, and darkness is my only friend. I need sleep, not a nosy ghost nanny.

"Shade StormIron, there are souls out there that need returning to the Infernum. Now get your ass out of bed, or so help me, I will scream at the top of my lungs until you do. And trust me, I have no need for breath."

I applaud her efforts, but they're falling flat. I'm in a funk that not even the dead can bring me out of. "Go away. I'm busy being a human."

∽

I check myself in the full-length mirror, admiring the look I've got going on. Dark blue jeans. Tan Timberland boots. Tight-fitting navy tee. Black leather jacket. And the pièce de résistance? My wonderfully styled short hair.

Ladies and gentlemen, please welcome your favorite reaper in town, handsome and available, Shade StormIron!

I look at the empty bottle on the nightstand, comforted by the numbing sensation making its way into my bloodstream. It's time to get some more.

Who needs a past anyway? And so what if mine looks like a spin cycle stuck on repeat? There's nothing wrong with routine. It's dependable.

"What'cha doin', fellas? Didn't your mother tell you smoking gets you killed?" I burst out into laughter at the irony of such a notion. I'm neither alive nor dead. What the fuck is it gonna do to me? "Here, let me take these off your hands. You're far too young to have me come collecting your soul."

The few teenage kids glance at me like I'm an alien. Either that, or I've got a massive bulbous zit in the center of my forehead. Ha! Something these kids and I would have in common—greasy skin and smoke is quite the pimple attractor.

"Dude, you can't just—"

"Sure I can. Watch me. You're not even old enough for these anyway. Trust me, I'm doing you a favor."

I glare at the lit cigarette in my hand, the blurry focus making it a little challenging. "Come show grandpa how to do this. Which end am I sucking on?"

"Later, loser." The group disappear, tutting and slurring crap I care not to think about.

I take a puff, hopeful I got the right end. My tongue is still recovering from that stupid coffee. Smoke fills my mouth and instantly dries it out. I cough, and cough, and cough. Fuck me, I thought the taste is supposed to be magnificent? Why else would these humans inhale such crap? It's bloody disgusting.

I want to throw up.

My tongue is dry. Between that and the tiny blisters I've got going on, I may as well be a cat, it's so rough. Who's gonna kiss me now? I'm like sandpaper.

I try again. I must have done it wrong the first time. I hear it's something you're supposed to get used to, and with practice the technique perfects itself, right?

Right?

I touch the papery end to my lips, and that sensation alone makes my skin crawl with goose bumps. Okay, Shade. You're a badass reaper. You play with Death every day. You can inhale some dirty toxins, and not react like a sodding wimp.

Man up, loser.

I breathe it in, thankful for the blanket of night not making me so obvious. "Yup . . . No . . . Fuuuccckkkk." I cough and splutter like a choking idiot, the need for clean air highly apparent.

What the hell is wrong with people?

First coffee. Now cigarettes. So far, the only thing I can get on board with is the alcohol. Which is what I'm going to be sticking to now. I know the Dirty Knuckle is around here somewhere . . .

"Shit, yeah, that feels good. Take it all in, babe." I watch the dark-skinned beauty wrap her plump lips around my cock, sliding down my hard shaft. She's sucking and making yummy noises, but all I can concentrate on is the fucking pleasure it's giving me.

Now this is what earthlings should be doing every damn minute of every bloody day.

Her tongue swirls around my balls, and I lose all sense. The sensation is overwhelming. It takes everything I have not to blow my load right now. I think of dead bodies, of maggots and flies feeding on carcasses.

It's no good. It's too bloody amazing to hold back. I grunt and groan, feeling an explosion welling up from the pit of my stomach.

I breathe rapidly. Short, sharp bursts of air are all I'm capable of as I lose myself and come all over her face without warning. Warm, white liquid squirts out of my dick with pride and panache like a fairy elephant making its debut show.

For some reason my black beauty isn't so pleased. She stands in all her clothes, eyes half closed with my cum all over her, arms poised on her hips. She wants to shout at me, I know, but the second she pries those plump lips apart she'll be swallowing more of me. Something I'm assuming she doesn't want to do.

"This isn't a hostel, young lady. I suggest you clean up and go."

Black beauty gasps with shock at my unwelcome guest before choking on the semen sliding into her mouth. She disappears out of my room like a bolt of lightning. One flash and she's gone.

"Great timing, Madame Luiza. You saved me a lot of effort." I grab a towel and clean up my cock, ready for round two.

"When is this nonsense going to end, Shade?"

I shrug. "I don't see one. I'm here to experience everything a human does. I already have a lifetime to catch up on, if not two. Look what I've been missing out on all this time." I point to my flesh flute. Christ, that girl made it sing.

Madame Luiza guffaws, appearing even whiter. I chuckle to myself. I never knew that was a possibility.

"Shade StormIron, you're making a fool of yourself! And what for? Some little tart in town upsets you, and now you're acting like a sullen teenager. Grow up and move on. You're not even here for this. Why do you care so much what she thinks?"

White-hot anger bubbles inside me at the suggestion of Thalia being called such a slur. Not after what I learned. To be a forest nymph in this world, a creature whose powers lie in their beauty, *surely* makes you a promiscuous being. Because looks that perfect never go untouched . . .

Please. Are people really this shallow?

"Don't talk about her like that. You don't even know." The words are forced through clenched teeth, fists bunched at my side.

"Get back to your work, and I won't." She crosses her arms over her chest, hovering above me as if the elevated height gives her some kind of supreme power over me.

She thinks she has me checkmated, but I still have another move up my sleeve.

"See you later, pain. Don't miss me too much!" I shut the door behind me, walking out of the inn before she has time to manifest downstairs and berate me some more.

If there's one thing I've learned from tonight's experience, it's that nanny ghosts don't make good wingmen.

～

"COME ON, just another one. It tastes sooo good."

I like this whiskey burn in my chest; it's like a constant fire keeping me warm. Not like the hollow nothing I'm accustomed to.

"Don't stop the party now," I whine, like a little girl not getting her way. I give the barman my best puppy eyes, pouting my lip too. Hey, it works with those rich kids splashed on magazines, so why not me?

I'm just as cute and adorable as the Carwashians. My butt might be letting me down, though. It's just not big and juicy like theirs.

Sigh.

"Man, I'm thirsty. Won't you help a wanderer out?"

"Looks to me like you've had enough. Don't you agree with me, Crusher?"

I turn to see the two big, burly guys standing with arms crossed over their leather cuts. Bloody hellhounds. I just can't get rid of the buggers.

"Looks like he's ready to kiss the ground, Savage. Let's say we help him?"

I shake my head, laughing wildly at this comedic duo. "Man, you guys are hilarious. Crusher and Savage, huh? Are you guys in a rock band or something?" I chortle again, imagining their bulky frames with microphones swamped by big hands, and voices so high pitched, I wonder if their balls will ever drop. "Savage, Savage . . . Where else have I heard that name?"

I'm frowning in concentration. I can feel my forehead wrinkle. Why does the name sound so familiar? Neither one wants to answer me. They've got this stoic silence going on.

"Oh, shit, yeah. You banging that HellBitch in the club?"

Savage growls, and Crusher beams as he explains, "Well, shit, man. You dead now. Melaina's his sister."

"I know." I grin. "But we both know what hellhounds are like when you're on a rampage. You'll fuck anything in sight, you horny devils."

"What the fuck did you just say to me, pretty boy?" Savage comes up close, gripping either side of my zipped jacket. His face is right up in mine, like he wants to give me a kiss.

"Wanna dance?" I raise my brows suggestively. He replies with a fist in my gut, and I immediately bend over like a prostitute.

The bar awakens with a roar, the locals yelling profanities at me like it's all my fault. But it's okay. I know they're just biased toward the hellhounds who permanently live here. Probably out of fear than loyalty.

"Outside," I hear the barkeep grunt. Crusher nods at him. Aw, it's like love at first sight, communicating with a single look.

Bleurgh.

"Come on, fellas. Why don't you just pick your panties up off the floor and we can get back to drinking?"

"Fuck you."

"After another drink, perhaps. I'm up for new experiences." I wink, and this time I anticipate his fist coming toward my face, so I block with my left and thump with my right. Bony flesh hits muscular cheek, and like a ripple effect, his skin does a mini Mexican wave.

I burst into fits of giggles—the scene keeps replaying on slow-mo in my mind.

Sadly, Savage and Crusher can't see the funnier side of this. Like two big bullies, they push me through the bar doors, and I land on my arse, head bouncing off the snowy ground like a quick-trick gymnast.

Look at me, no hands!

"What's your problem, reaper? Don't you have work to be done?"

I roll my eyes at the pair of them. "Fuck, what is it with everyone in this town and their interest in my fucking work? You never seen a reaper before? Wanna see my magic wand?"

They growl at me again. Honestly, what am I doing wrong? I offer a drink, a dance. All the things that are supposed to come before me. Ooh la la.

I stand, brushing the icy cold snow off my arse before it has any more time to seep through my boxers. Can't have a cold pickle.

"Stay down, reaper." Crusher kicks and sweeps my legs from under me, and I go down like a hooker, all business and no grace.

Darting pain shoots through my back, ripping insides I've never had to consider before.

"And keep your distance from my sister, or this won't be our only *dance*, pretty boy." Savage's fist comes down before I can even move, pain slowing everything this meat suit is capable of. It's the last thing I see—his meaty hand coming for my perfect nose, followed by spots of darkness.

CHAPTER 10

TROUBLE

*E*verything hurts.

I can't really explain it more than that. It's just a long list of body parts that have certainly seen better days. The ground is sodding freezing, and beneath me the snow has been melting long enough that I'm all shriveled up like a prune on one side of my body. I can do a one-man act of the aging process. My right side is young. My left is old.

Yet, somehow, I just can't seem to care. I've hit rock bottom—at least, I think that's what this is.

"Shade? What are you doing?"

I'm dreaming, I'm dreaming, I'm dreaming. Don't wake up. Don't wake up. Don't wake up.

I groan as she touches my shoulder, piercing through all fantasies I have that this isn't real.

"Are you okay?" Her hand disappears quickly, and like a jerk, I remember all too late how difficult it must've been for her to reach out. It makes me feel like an absolute arsehole.

"Never better," I groan, struggling to move out of the slump my sorry arse landed in last night. I don't even want to think about how long I've been out here. The fact the sky is lightening, and Thalia's standing by my feet all glammed up like she's just finished her shift at the club, tells me more than I need to know.

What is wrong with me?

Why did I let myself get in this state?

Who am I impressing like this?

I am a bloody mess, and my head pounds so hard I'm ready to throw up food I haven't even eaten.

"I guess I'll leave you to it then." Thalia turns, and I see her feet walking away from me. Did I miss something?

"Wait, please," I call, struggling to gain breath large enough to help me on my feet. "Fuck, this is embarrassing."

"Trust me, I've seen plenty of mornings people wish they weren't awake for. The night before always seems like such a good idea. You're no different."

I can't help but bristle at that. I don't know why it bothers me so much, but I don't want her to see me as another average Joe. I want to be *different* for her.

She shouldn't be seeing me like this. What the hell is wrong with me?

I get to my feet, and everything spins. I'm like a drama queen in need of rescue. I'm pathetic. Even worse, this sorry state neglected the most important aspect of his purpose.

I've let the damned souls roam free, causing chaos and carnage I can only imagine.

How can Thalia even look at me right now?

I'm disgusted with myself. Look at me, acting out like an adolescent. Madame Luiza's admonishments were spot on.

"You need help getting back to your place?"

Shit, can this get any more depressing? "It's fine. I can hobble back to the inn. I just need the world to stop spinning for five minutes first. You should go home, get out of the cold air. You're probably exhausted after a long night working."

"Do you always behave like a martyr?" She crosses her arms over her chest, looking down on me with disdain. "Shit happens to all of us, but yours is self-inflicted. Maybe if you did your job, the rest of us wouldn't have to pick up the slack. Some company isn't worth keeping."

"I'm not a martyr." I pout like a big fat baby, and I know it. I'm not after sympathy. Shit, it's the last thing I want from her right now. "Why does my job affect you?"

I raise a brow; she has me curious. What can a nymph do with souls?

"It doesn't matter. If you don't want my help, then I'll go. There's plenty of sleep for me to catch up on." She slinks away, heels disappearing into the snow without a second glance backwards.

Why do I have a feeling something terrible has happened since I've been acting out? How much have I ignored in my drunken state?

I need to drag my stupid arse to bed and start fresh. That's the sensible thing to do, but I'm not so sure I have the ability to follow logic right now. Ideally, I want to chase Thalia down. Live in some fantasy bubble where everything is right and I'm not a reaper, and we can live some happily ever after, even for five minutes. I don't want this life anymore.

Is it even life?

These messed up human emotions are ruining everything. Is this what Princess WitchHound had in mind when she cursed my tattoo this way? Does she see my torment, taking pleasure from afar?

I'm not sure what I'm good for anymore. I just know with absolute certainty that I'm disgusted with myself for even succumbing to such lowly temptations. And why? Because some girl hurt my feelings? Feelings I don't even possess when I'm out of this bloody town!

Fuck me, I'm a little sissy.

I try to get my bearings, but with the spins upsetting my vision, it's more difficult than I care to admit. I think I'm close. At least, I'm hoping this is Main Street.

Urgh.

Christ, it's freezing today. Of course, it has nothing to do with the fact I've been passed out in the snow for hours.

I think I've finally hit the highest achievement level of being human. Mission accomplished. And am I glad I'm doing the walk of shame before anyone else is awake and able to witness my finest moments.

Except the world isn't really kind enough for that, is it?

I take in a deep breath, forcing my eyesight to keep steady. I hear a faint whimper followed by a gurgling that's unmistakable.

I have nowhere near enough physical and mental stability to deal with this now. I'm more likely to capture myself than her, but the time for excuses is over. I have to act now if I'm going to save a life. Which, oddly enough, isn't really the business I'm in.

"Didn't your mother ever tell you that playing with your food is bad for you?" Thankfully there's a handy concrete pillar I can lean against for a bit more stability. It really helps me come across all powerful and in control.

The vampire-demon hybrid glares at me through black eyes with only a hint of red. Her mouth hovers above the creamy white skin of her poor prey, bright red blood trickling from the open wounds made by fangs.

"Well, at last you found me." Nyx smiles widely, blood dripping from her mouth, coating her chin. "What took you so long, Shade?"

The girl stuck in Nyx's tight grasp whispers a plea for help. She looks like she's only in her late teens, someone who hasn't even tasted the adult life yet. It's no wonder her face is pale with fear—and blood loss of course. But I know Nyx. One acknowledgment of the girl from me, and Nyx will snap her neck whether she's finished eating or not. The bitch is that sadistic.

"Please, Nyx. I haven't even tried looking for you yet—you're not so high on my priority list these days." I shrug, realizing all too late that goading her isn't the best idea when she's holding an innocent's life in her hands. Stupid, slow brain. What a time for a hangover.

"Doesn't matter anyway, you're not going to get me. I have an Underworld to get back to and rule."

I snigger, as if she could pull that off. A woman running the Underworld? Everyone knows only the men dominate the throne down below; it's just the way it is. I try to move closer, to get the girl out of Nyx's tight vise, but the creature's too busy watching my every twitch to enable me much progress. "This is why you wanted out of the Infernum? To rule another dark, depressing place?"

She shakes her head of platinum blond hair. "Oh, you're too young to understand. There's so much more you need to learn of the worlds you frequent."

I know she's just busting my balls, but I can't help but think there's a layer of truth in what she's saying. She is, after all, eight hundred years older than my two hundred. "Then why don't you explain it to me? I've got some free time on my hands."

"And let my food spoil in the meantime? Nah, I don't think so." Her head lowers to the girl's neck, and I can't move fast enough. I can't even shift forms. It's like my inebriated and hungover state has dampened everything in me, and I'm a lazy toad.

"Don't do this, Nyx. The worse you behave out here, the more you'll endure back in the Infernum. Is that what you really want?" I inch forward, keeping an eye on the girl. She doesn't look good; if anything, she's on the brink of death. I can feel it, the subtle tingles on my spine as a soul's about to become available.

Nyx cackles, but her grip never loosens on the girl—I can see it suffocating her. "What makes you think I'm going back to the Infernum? You don't honestly believe you're going to capture me, do you? I mean, look at us. We've been doing this little chit-chat for how long now? And not once have you tried to save this girl and send me back." She pauses, raising perfectly shaped brows. "Want to know what I think? You've become impotent. Performance anxiety getting you down, Shade?"

I charge, rushing for the cocky bitch who thinks she's better than everyone else. I slam into her, the weight of my body knocking her off balance. The girl gets tossed aside—not my finest moment, but at least she's somewhat safer now.

I slam my fist into the vampire-demon, catching the side of her face as she turns. She's back up on her feet before I have time to fart, let alone move. "Nyx, you're only prolonging your pain. Give up already."

I finally have enough energy to stand, but I'm still wobbly on my feet. Though, to be fair, I couldn't stand still before anyway.

Fuck, I'm weak, and I hate it. Big baby.

"Actually, Shade, I think you're just trying to delay me so you can get your own shit together. Well, unfortunately for you, I'm not a giving person." She knocks me onto my back before I even see her coming, supernatural speed on her side.

"You know, Nyx, if circumstances were different between us," I raise my brows suggestively, lifting my hips up where she's straddling me. "We could really get kinky, especially with this outfit." I run my hands over her leather-covered legs. She dresses like a dominatrix—all black leather and heels. It's a shame I know the personality beneath the clothes.

"Please. You don't know how to satisfy me." She sinks her fangs into the crook of my neck, hands pinning mine to the ground, her feet doing the same to my legs. It's like some crazy wrestling move I can't get out of.

"Ooh, this is intimate," I joke. She sinks her fangs even deeper, and I struggle not to cry out. I won't let her know how much it actually hurts—it fucking kills. There's nothing like having a gaping hole in your neck and the life sucked out of you.

"Sh-Shade?" Thalia's voice interrupts my inner monologue, and I wonder if I'm hallucinating, wishing it were her on top of me. Ooh, bad time to display my pocket rocket.

"Get off him, you crazy bitch!" Thalia yells, and this time I know it's real.

Nyx is lifted off my body, and with a lot of effort, I'm back on my feet, blood dripping from my neck in a steady trickle. Is that good or bad? Better than a gush, right?

"Well, well, well. What do we have here? Shade's gone and gotten himself a playmate. You're a pretty thing."

I wobble over to Thalia, shielding her with my own beat-up body. What's a little more pummeling gonna do? Kill me? I'd like to see what happens then.

"You stay away from her. She's not your concern. Besides, she doesn't suit your tastes. Too much super in her natural."

I glance around, looking for the human. She's barely holding on to breath. Frankly, I'm amazed she's lasted this long. I admire her fighting to live.

I feel Thalia move behind me, coming to stand at my side. A silent conversation passes between the two females in a mighty staredown. I have no bloody idea what's going on, but Nyx is backing up. What the hell is a vampire-demon afraid of a nymph for? It's not like Thalia has any kind of advantage over Nyx—at least, not one I know of. Thalia's powers lie in beauty, not strength.

"Catch you later, Shade. I'll be back for that kiss, beautiful." Nyx winks at Thalia, and I'm thrown. I've been bashed around upside the head, which is why I'm confused. It has to be, right? Doesn't make sense otherwise. The pair don't know each other, do they? Fuck me, have I fallen for the one creature whose sexual orientation lies in women too? This can be interesting. Now how do I go about asking for a threesome? Is there some kind of manual for this stuff?

"Come on, we need to get you cleaned up. Her, too." Thalia comments on the girl groaning on the ground. How she hasn't frozen to death I'll never know.

"What did you do to Nyx, Thalia?" I'm amazed. There's no other word for it. Nyx has disappeared *and* left her snack behind. This shit never happens.

Thalia shrugs, as if it were nothing. "You saw, nothing special. Come on, she needs a doctor. Are you going to help me?"

"What's going on here?"

What is it with people popping up out of nowhere in this town? Don't they have the courtesy to at least cough to announce their presence?

"Sheriff, we need to get to the medical center. She's been attacked." Thalia kneels down by the girl. Judging by everyone's faces, no one knows her name.

"Is this your doing?" The sheriff frowns at me, fists bunched at his

sides as if he's getting ready to tackle me. It's a bad day to be Shade—
I've kissed more floors than females.

"No, it's the creature I'm hunting. Thalia can vouch for me." I
glance at the beautiful nymph who's too concerned with the girl to be
listening to what I have to say. Great.

"Don't even think about leaving town. I'll be back for questions."
The sheriff lifts the girl and takes her to his car. A scent of wolf shifter
hangs in the air.

I couldn't be more ashamed of myself if I tried. My stupidity put
this girl's life in danger. I hope there haven't been more.

"Come on, Shade. Let's stitch you up." Thalia turns, heading in
the direction she'd been walking before my drama caught up with her.

I follow, curious to see where she's taking me. I catch up, feet
slushing in a mix of day-old snow and fresh powder. The town is still
quiet—it takes on its own enchantment with all the Christmas
decorations.

"How was work?" I ask, genuinely interested in her day, or more
precisely, night.

"Busy, as always. I've been working on a new routine, but I just
can't nail this one move that ties the whole sequence together. It's
driving me insane." She grunts, rifling through the bag dangling off
her shoulder. She produces a set of keys as we near a row of houses,
and pauses a few moments as we reach a green door. Is she afraid of
inviting me in? Having second thoughts about her actions?

I don't want to make her feel uncomfortable in her own home. It
isn't right.

"Thalia, I can go . . ."

She slips the key in the lock, turns, and smiles my way. "Don't be
silly. We're here now. We just need to sort this wound before you get
an infection."

I want to laugh, but I think better of it. Knowing my luck, this
meat suit *would* contract an infection just to dampen my progress
with soul-snatching even more.

Stepping into the hallway, I take note of all the homey decorations
she has. Paintings of beautiful landscapes hang on the walls,

comforting pillows and blankets are draped on the sofa in the main room, and candle holders and vases of flowers cover every surface available. Strangely, even amongst the warmth this home brings, there's also an ominous chill in the considerable lack of pictures. There are no frames containing photos of family members, friends, even places she's visited. It's cold, as though the house is projecting the loneliness within Thalia.

"The bathroom is through there. I'd rather not get blood on the carpets in the living room." Thalia half smiles as though apologizing. "I'll just go get the bandages."

I tell myself not to follow her, willing my feet to walk toward the bathroom instead, and wait diligently like a good boy.

"Does it hurt?" Thalia catches me off guard, walking into the bathroom while I have my eyes closed.

"A little, not as much as before." I try shaking it off—can't have this gorgeous lady thinking I'm any less than the man she deserves. Christ, I want to be that guy.

"This is all new for you, huh? The coffee, the alcohol, the fights?" She raises a brow at my black eye, wetting a cotton ball before placing it on my neck to clear the blood away.

"I've never been made to feel like a human before. It's . . . different than what I assumed. Lots of emotional baggage," I sum up.

She sighs, frowning hard, pulling what looks like crossed tape off its sticky backing and putting the butterfly-like stitches on my neck, no needle necessary.

"Trust me, I know all about emotional turmoil. It's why I don't . . . Why I can't . . ." She pauses longer this time, struggling to voice what's churning in her mind. "Relationships are messy even before being accused of manipulating thoughts, making someone fall in love with you against their will."

Her eyes bore into mine, and her hands disappear from my neck. Her lips are inches from mine, and it takes every kind of patience I've ever learned to keep from closing the gap and kissing her. This has to be on her terms. I won't make her feel pressured.

"I can't really comment. I've never experienced it before."

She pulls back, eyes blinking as though clearing from a trance. "You know, you make it difficult to believe this is all new to you at times. You seem so relaxed, so at ease with who you are, despite having everything turned upside down. It makes me feel weak, makes me wish I were stronger, more capable of accepting the world as it is, instead of hiding from it."

I swallow hard. "I can help you, Thalia. Let me in, and I'll prove you have a fierce confidence within you that's desperate to be unleashed."

She slips a plaster over her handiwork on my neck, and clears everything away without saying a word. As though needing the time to digest what I've offered. It pains me she doesn't immediately agree. That she even has to think about it shows me how much she shelters herself away from life unless it revolves around dancing at the club.

This makes me sad. She's so much more than this.

"I'll see myself out," I say, realizing she isn't going to answer me, and I've made things too awkward to stay any longer.

Just as I reach the front door, I hear her small voice. "Shade, I'm not a quick fix. I won't be magically healed by morning. You won't even be here long enough to help me back on my feet the way you think I need to be."

I close the gap between us in the hallway, doing my best not to reach out and touch her. "Thalia, I don't think you're broken. You just haven't unlocked your full potential yet. I'm not even suggesting I'm the right person to do that for you either, but I'm selfish enough to tell you I want to. Spending time with you unlocks new experiences within me. I don't want to give that up yet either."

I step back toward the front door again, knowing we both need space. I open the door and step outside, holding the handle to close it behind me. "Think about it, Thalia. I already see your beautiful soul."

CHAPTER 11

BUSINESS

"Feeling better now?"

I hang my head in shame before Madame Luiza as she hovers in her favorite spot at the foot of the bed. The bed covers just about hide my drumstick, not that she hasn't seen it before, but I'm on a new road of redemption. I can't be making her blush at my wanger. It's ungentlemanly of me.

"How big of an apology do I owe you?"

"Why don't you get those pesky souls back where they belong, and we'll call it even? It's nice to see you've got your head on straight again."

I cower under the covers, feeling like a scorned boy. "I don't know what to say. Have you heard anything about the girl from yesterday?"

Madame Luiza shakes her head, moving closer to the side of the bed and perching on the edge as though she truly were sitting there. "Sheriff Kasun dropped by, gave Michaela quite the aggravation. You're lucky he didn't storm in here and wake you up himself."

Add another on my very long list of reasons to be thankful for Whisper Falls Inn and its owner.

"Is the girl still alive, did he say?"

"Yes, dear. She's holding on after a blood transfusion. Oddest thing is we still don't know where she's from. I imagine that's what the sheriff wants to know, that and how she ended up with a gaping hole in her neck, of course."

I rub my hands over my face. "I'm going to have a lot to answer for." I sigh loudly. "What about Nyx? Any gossip surrounding her whereabouts that could help me?"

"Now then, Shade. I thought you reapers were able to feel a soul when it's near. Are you suggesting you can't feel hers lurking around?"

I shake my head. "I don't know why, but I'm not the only one. Princess WitchHound hasn't said anything about the vampire-demon running around town, and she was quick to jump on my arse the second I landed in this town."

Madame Luiza frowns. "Princess WitchHound?"

"You know, light brown hair, covered in tattoos, stone in her nose, and more jewelry than body parts to wear it on?"

"You mean Adelaide? She's Michaela's best friend, I'll have you know, and a talented witch at that. You watch what you're saying, young man."

I hold up my hands. "I'm not disputing that. It just has me wondering how Nyx has gone past her detection spells and continues to fly under the radar of mine, too. It makes zero sense."

Madame Luiza seems to take what I'm saying on board, if the fierce concentration on her ghostly appearance is anything to go by. "Perhaps she has some magic working of her own. Is she known for it?"

I shake my head. "She doesn't possess those skills. The only way she'd get magic is through force or blackmailing someone who can. You know the people in this town better than I do. Hell, all I seem capable of doing is making enemies and pissing everyone off. Do you think there's anyone here that would bow down to Nyx?"

She huffs. "That's a loaded question, Shade. We all have a weakness to exploit—all it takes is the right reward."

I think it through. "Who has the most to gain? Fuck, she's a crafty bitch." I get out of the bed, needing to stretch my legs and pace the small length of the room. It's better than nothing. "So besides scorning my inability to feel her, do you have anything else that can help me?"

Madame Luiza shrugs, a cheeky smile gracing her face. "It's amazing what can be heard when you're able to walk through walls, and my oh my, do these ones talk." She winks, clearly proud of herself.

"Okay, I see what's going on here. What's it going to cost me for this information?"

"You make it sound so dirty, Shade. I'm a lady. I wouldn't infer tit for tat, you know. But if a ghost ever happens to change her mind, I want a promise and assurance that you'll be there to guide her on to the next stage."

"You have my word, Madame Luiza. Just call my name, and I'll hear your soul sing. I promise it will be painless."

She nods, a troubled expression coloring her face. I don't know what to make of it, other than the turmoil of eventually leaving living family behind for good. I have seen its effect many times—no one is ever the same again, but time will inevitably bring them together once more. It's the decades between that are the struggle.

"I don't know when," she begins, but I cut her off.

"It doesn't matter. When you're ready, I'll be around for you. It's the least I can do, all things considered."

She gives me a half smile, and I can see I'm bringing her back out of the sadness of her deep thoughts. "If what I've heard is true, then Nyx has been hanging around that motorcycle club a lot. Ask me, I'd say she fits right in there. Trouble plays well with its own kind."

I can't help but smile at her disdain. It's the same reaction she had to Silk, the nightclub. Oddly enough, both are run by hellhounds. I wonder if she has some kind of prejudice against them. That would be something, considering she herself pointed out that her niece's best friend is part hothead. Does Auntie Luiza not approve?

"What would she get from the club?" I'm thinking out loud, but Madame Luiza answers anyway.

"What could you do with a whole club of hellhounds and shifters at your disposal?"

"Shit." I grab my clothes, making the connection. "I could kiss you right now!" I head for the door, but Madame Luiza calls out, halting my progress.

"You can't just walk into the club, Shade. There are rules."

I shake my head, smiling broadly. "I know that. Look at you worrying about me. It makes me feel all warm and gooey inside."

"Don't ruin it. What are you going to do?"

"I'm going to the next best place on the list. I hear family bonds are really strong amongst hellhounds." I wink and close the door.

CHAPTER 12

ALLIES

Fuck me, I hope she's in a good mood today. The pod starts ascending through the trees, Melaina's bodyguard watching with utter hatred at my ease of access. Ahem.

Melaina steps forward as I leave the pod, already waiting for me. "Shade, I'd say it's a pleasure, but we'd both know I'd be lying. What's up? And don't tell me there's a soul here, because I know for a fact there isn't right now. Club's empty. Only my dancers are practicing their routines."

"Actually, I came to speak to you. Do you have time?"

She narrows her eyes at me. "The fact you're asking so nicely has me on edge. I don't like it. What do you want?"

"I met your brother," I begin. She rolls her eyes and immediately turns from the main entrance, heading for her office. I must have earned her seal of approval for privacy with this conversation. Family matters clearly aren't for the nosy to hear. Interesting.

"What did Tychon do that you think I'm going to help you with?" She folds her arms over her chest, one leg crossed seductively over the other as she takes one of the armchair seats. Once again she's dressed in a figure-hugging dress that accentuates her tits, and fuck-me heels that deserve to be wrapped around a man's shoulders. Hell yeah, I bet she's an animal in bed, wild with lust.

Oops. Don't get a stiffy, don't get a stiffy, don't get a stiffy.

Think floppy.

"Nothing," I begin, then catch myself. That isn't the total truth really, is it? "Well, he gave me a couple of shiners, some broken ribs, and knocked me out cold in the freezing conditions all night, but other than that, can't complain. Yet."

"Well, I'm sure you deserved it. You have a way of pissing us off. So if it's not about getting back at him, what is it you want?"

I make myself comfortable on her couch, this time leaving my feet firmly on the carpet. I've begun to understand you don't get answers in this world without a sweetener first. And respecting Melaina's furniture is step one.

I know. I'm a sodding suck-up now.

"Do you know what goes on at SIN?"

"You do realize I don't keep tabs on my brother, right? I'm not his mother, and I'm busy enough here."

I tilt my head to the side. "Still doesn't really answer my question, though, does it? Let me be a bit more precise. Have you seen, or has your brother mentioned anything about a new arrival lately? A platinum blonde, leather-loving, vampire-demon bitch to be exact."

Melaina starts to laugh. "I didn't peg you for a motorcycle groupie fucker. What's the matter, sugar? Couldn't satisfy her needs, so she hops to the first sex orgy she can find?"

Sex orgy? Is this what happens at the motorcycle club? Sounds like I need to become a member. Immediately.

"She's not my type," I answer dryly. "But I certainly do want her. You would, too, if you knew who she was. This is one soul that belongs in the Infernum indefinitely."

Melaina leans forward, legs uncrossed as if she now means business. "What makes you think she's affiliated with my brother?"

I have to appreciate her loyalty. Not once has she slipped up and revealed information *I* need. No, she's just continually pumping me for answers instead. Clever bitch.

"That's what I'm trying to find out. Are you telling me you don't know anything, or are you just trying to delay me by covering for your brother?"

Anger is bubbling within me, close to the surface. One wrong answer and I'm going to be flipping my lid. I'm sick of wasting time. I'm sick of not knowing how to control this body and its fucking emotional roller coaster.

Melaina stares, and I glare back, neither one of us blinking.

"Shit," she murmurs, getting out of her chair. "We may have a problem closer to home. This Nyx you've described, I believe I've seen her."

I stand, not sure why, but it feels like the right thing to be doing. "Where?"

"Here. In *my* club. Tell me, what's your interest in Thalia?"

I scoff, brushing her off as being ridiculous. "I don't have an interest. Reaper, remember? We don't get to embrace fantasy-like notions."

She smiles widely. Melaina moves toward me, coming up into my face as she backs me into a corner, trapping me. "I knew it. You like her more than you want to admit. But how does this end, Shade? You break her heart and return to do Death's bidding, never to reappear."

I shake my head, having already battled with this myself every time I catch a glimpse of Thalia, and I'm reminded that the stunning image I remember doesn't do her justice. She takes my breath away more than I'll ever be able to admit. I know this makes me a coward, but I'm struggling to understand it myself. This is all new territory to me.

"Hurting her is the last thing I want to do. It's why I *haven't* pursued anything more."

"I take care of my girls, Shade. And Thalia's been through enough without you adding to her pain. Do I make myself clear?"

"You know, hellhound, I like you. You don't bullshit, and I appreciate that. It's a lost quality in this day and age." I lean forward, closing any kind of space between us. "But I'm not here for Thalia. It's Nyx I want. So why did you change the subject?"

Melaina turns away, running hands through her long, luscious locks. "Before you get all hotheaded on me, I don't know all the details. Only what I've seen."

"And that is?" I struggle to hold on to my temper. Why is she dragging this out so much?

She sighs loudly, clearly having made up her mind about something. "Nyx was here, and she took a vested interest in Thalia. I don't know what was said, but I warned Thalia to be careful. Now that you're here, I can see some dots connecting. Somehow, Nyx knows about your interest in my nymph, and I can guarantee Thalia's going to pay the price for it. What the fuck is going on, Shade?"

I shake my head, pacing to and fro. "No, that can't be. There's nothing Thalia can give Nyx that works to her advantage."

Melaina comes up to me and smacks my head.

"Hey! What was that for?" I caress my temple, now pulsing from her fleshy sting.

"Are you really this dumb? Of course Nyx has something to gain from Thalia if Thalia has feelings for you, too! Fuck, why are men so clueless when it comes to love? This isn't rocket science, Shade."

I deny her observations. There's no way. "Not once has she hinted she's interested in me. You're just blowing smoke up my arse now. Why are you being so cruel?"

"Urgh!" Melaina shoves me out of her office. "Stop being an idiot, or I *will* let my rage out on you. Don't you see what advantage Nyx has to gain in this?"

I stare blankly, which isn't the right answer if the despair on Melaina's face is anything to go by. In fact, she's so tightly wound, it's like she's constipated right now.

"Fuck me, do I have to spell it out for you? She'll use Thalia to get to you, and once she has you . . ."

I shrug. "Nyx doesn't want me taking her back to the Infernum, so she'll try to get rid of me."

This isn't really a marvelous revelation. In fact, it's bloody obvious. For the vampire-demon, I'm what stands between her and freedom to rule the Underworld. Ha! It still makes me chuckle every time I try to imagine a female on the throne. Christ, even the lowly creatures would ridicule her rule. Can't be a leader without a following.

"Why aren't you panicking about this?" Melaina frowns, hands on hips.

"Because I'm not the only reaper in Death's arsenal. If I don't get the job done, he'll send another, and another, and another until it is. You can't tell me Nyx hasn't thought of that."

"Yes, but you're her immediate threat. There's nothing more to it than that."

It can't really be that simple, can it? But how can Melaina be so sure when I haven't even explained Nyx's motive behind it all? How would she know I'm Nyx's temporary problem, standing between her and the Underworld? But then, how is she taking over the Underworld without an army behind her? This is what I was hoping to find out from Melaina. I'm sure Nyx has some dastardly plan to use SIN's club members to act on her behalf. Are they even aware of what's in store for them?

I feel so bloody clueless.

"What are you gonna do, Shade? Because I'm not losing any of my girls to this crazy soul you let escape."

"I didn't let them escape, dammit. It's not like I stood by the portal and said, 'Hey, guys, fancy a free ride back to earth to wreak some havoc?' Clearly Nyx has been planning this for a long time. And I'm the sucker that got stuck with cleanup. So before you go around pointing the finger, I'd reevaluate your own mistakes."

I make haste. This stupid back and forth conversation isn't getting me anywhere, and I'm clearly wasting precious energy on this. "Call me when you have something of use to give me," I shout, walking down the hallway, turning a corner and entering the maze of corridors that lead to rooms I have yet to explore—though that's for when I have the time.

"I don't know if I can do this," a male whisper carries through the hallway.

I stop. I'm not sure why, but I have this strange suspicion that I'm meant to listen.

"Don't even think about chickening out on me."

I freeze. The female voice is unmistakable. How long has she been here?

"You're bringing me the nymph whether you want to or not. I have your life in my hands, remember? You do what I say or your precious future in the club is gone. I don't think the president will take too kindly to a weakling such as you."

I peek around the corner wall, hoping to see who Nyx is trying to coerce, but really I'm lucky enough that she hasn't noticed me so far. Her instincts are always too perfect to sneak up on.

I take it slowly, making sure to keep my breathing even and quiet.

"When? When do you want this done?" There's an unmistakable quiver in the male's voice, but I still can't see. All I can catch a glimpse of is a leather cut. It isn't much to go on, considering I've already heard about an affiliation to the club. Proof that Nyx has been running amok there.

"When do you think, you babbling buffoon? Immediately. Get it done. I'll be waiting."

Footsteps come my way. I do the only thing I can. I turn and run away.

Fuck me. I need to save Thalia.

CHAPTER 13

DAMSELS

She's mesmerizing. Not an ounce of care mars her beautiful features. She's calm, happy, enjoying the music as she dances to the upbeat tempo. It's like the first night I saw her all over again. Limbs contort around the metal pole; she's a professional gymnast with complete control over her strength. I can't imagine the hours of training it takes for such discipline.

She catches my eye, her step falters, and she misses the beat. She tries to pick it up again, but I've clearly distracted her too much. I wonder why.

"Looks like you're back to your normal self," she calls, moving to sit on the edge of the small square stage.

"Yup, I'm all healed. Turns out this meat suit likes to take on some of my reaper abilities when it wants to. Too bad it hasn't helped much before now."

"So what are you doing here? Come to give me a hard time for working at the club?"

I frown, taken aback. "Why would I do that?"

She waves her hand, as if passing it off. "Plenty of people have strong opinions about what we do here. I guess I've just been waiting for you to express yours."

"You've been getting a hard time for dancing?" I raise a brow, intrigued. Who'd dare question the use of such talent? "Want me to kick some asses?"

She laughs, a sound I've rarely heard but will do anything to bring out of her again. She's got me hooked. At this rate, she can ask me to do anything, and I'll gladly do it, no matter the price.

"Listen, I need you to come with me." I hold out my hand.

"Why? I'm working. I can't just leave."

I shake my head. How much do I tell her? Do I scare her, use fear to get her to do what I want so that I can protect her?

Honesty has always been my motto; I won't change now. "Your life is in danger, Thalia. Please, trust me."

She recoils from my touch, a reaction that stings even more every time it happens. Hadn't we gotten over this hurdle yet?

She stands, towering above me as she's on the raised platform. "Are you threatening me, Shade? Is this because I haven't given you an answer about helping me yet? You're making up trouble to get me to agree?"

Where the hell does that notion come from? "No, I'm offering you my protection, Thalia. I need to keep you safe from what's coming."

She thrusts her left hip out, hands firmly placed on her sides. "You mean you need to keep me for yourself to help you feel human or whatever? Well, no thank you. I'd rather take my chances here with the protection we've already got against this so-called danger I'm in."

I shake my head. She doesn't understand. "Why won't you trust me?" I lean on the edge of the platform, looking up in earnest. "I'm trying to save your life."

She takes the steps down from the stage, turning toward me. "You've given me no reason to trust you, Shade. If anything, you make me question things even more. I don't need your help. I've been saving myself for years, despite your assumptions about me." She walks away, heading to an area clearly designated as off-limits to non-personnel. Changing rooms, I think.

I can't force Thalia to take me up on my offer, but I also can't sit back and watch the inevitable. Nyx has someone coming for Thalia.

She might not comprehend the true danger she's in, but no way in hell am I going to let them take her.

I'm no white knight, but for Thalia, I'll be the hero she deserves, one incognito move at a time. Starting with Nyx.

~

My spine tingles, running a current from my neck to my coccyx and back again. It's an unmistakable feeling, and one I'm more than thankful for at this moment. I need a distraction. A win in the Shade box for a change.

I follow the sensation, the pin pricks increasing the closer I come. I move through the town, darkness having cloaked the sky, making the Christmas lights illuminate like colorful stars. I consider the holiday decorations for a brief moment, the town busy with late-night shoppers preparing for the big day in a few days. If I could live in this dimension, I could easily see myself being sucked into the festive spirit. The smiles and cheer are practically contagious. I've never known anything like it.

What would it be like to wake up on Christmas morning in a house fully decorated with Thalia at my side? Does she like this season? I can imagine the glow on her face as she sees the presents under the tree, her name plastered all over them. I would spoil her rotten, a small example of my growing love for her.

"Yeah, right. As if that's ever going to happen," I mumble to myself, sadness threatening to send me into a deep depression. Not now. I'm not falling back into the trap of moping around again.

I square my shoulders and get back on track, dodging shoppers left and right as the soul calls me on until I reach the place it's hiding. There's no mistaking this is it. My spine is going into meltdown mode with pain.

Havenwood Falls High.

What the hell is a soul doing at a bloody school, for god's sake? Suddenly feeling the need to get smart?

I shake my head, laughing at my own joke. Where's an audience when you need one?

The tattoo on my arm vibrates. I can feel the change coming on, allowing me to return to my natural state. Skin, muscles, blood, and organs disappear as though being ripped away from me. Oddly enough, it's painless, probably because they were never mine to begin with.

I feel my wings desperate to be stretched, begging for freedom. I flex the beauties, stretching wide until they're pulled taut. I hover above the ground, a black mist that enables me to become invisible except to the soul that's calling.

I slip through the school doors, instincts taking over as I zoom through the corridors, working my way around the building as though it's a place I've frequented many a time before.

"Well, well, well. Bingo," I call, seeing the soul in the middle of a classroom, book upon book spread across the table in front of it. "You escape torture and your ideal haven is a school? What's wrong with you?" I laugh out loud, gaining the soul's attention. It was so immersed in the textbooks, it had no idea I slipped in. This doesn't make a lick of sense.

"I like to read. What's wrong with that?"

I shake my head. "Nothing, but the last time I checked you're a monster, not a student. Are you trying to atone for your sins?"

"It's none of your business, reaper. Get out of here. You don't own me."

I tut loudly, snatching the soul tight before it has time to register my intentions. "That's where you're wrong, mate." I speed through the corridors, calling upon a portal to open up for us to slip through.

The soul struggles, trying to wrangle free from my grasp. I hold on tighter, flapping my wings faster.

"There's no other choice for you, mate. This is where you belong."

The Infernum opens up, loud screeches, roars, and yells playing out—the place's own theme song. The temperatures climb to a mighty swelter in here. I see the way it affects the creatures, wearing them down, bodies decaying in record time.

I find an empty cell along my assigned cages, this length of the Infernum reserved for my captures. The Infernum only lets them out to wander the abyss when it deems them ready. Until then, they remain bound to chains I've pinned them into. This soul is no different.

I shackle the soul and disappear, scrambling out of this place before any more mishaps can happen. I make sure the portal closes behind me, no unwanted hitchhikers trying to sneak out, and pop back into the waiting portal at the high school in this weird and wonderfully charming town.

The large bubble of opalescent energy shifts and reduces in size until finally it disappears, sealing completely. My wings fold into my spine, and I'm once more shifting forms, this evil tattoo at work already. Honestly, it's like I have to beg for it to get me out of this skin suit, but the second I'm back in this world, BAM! Instant dressing.

"You're in my town, and you've got my people in a spell. You'd better start talking, and fast, or there will be hell to pay."

What's going on? I recognize that voice, coming from one of the rooms. I take myself and my big nosy nose around the building until I find the source of the voice. It's the sheriff, with a group of people I haven't seen in a long time.

I slip into the back of the room and watch the scene unfold, trying not to get too involved. I make some quick jibes about Hell. How can I not, when they're cursing the place? Then I disappear out of the room before the sheriff has time to chase me down and question me over the girl Nyx took a healthy dose from.

Oh, sodding Nyx. What am I gonna do about her?

HOLY SHIT. I'm in heaven.

There's no other word for the deliciousness in front of me. A juicy burger stuffed with bacon and melted cheese, a basket of fries, and a chocolate milkshake so big, it's like swimming in dessert.

I'm never leaving this place again. Screw my responsibilities. The gods of food have taken me in; I'm no longer fit for purpose.

Please?

Everything in this Burger Bar is perfect, from the appreciative and happy servers to the pretty holiday decorations that just want to banish every Grinch-like personality. Actually, the only thing that's letting this place down is its taste in music. I'm just not a fan of the Beatles. However, if Thalia managed to find a way to dance to this crap, I may just change my mind. Mostly because the music would disappear as I lose myself in her. Fuck me, I need to see her. Keeping my distance is turning me inside out. I want to shag her senseless and knock the idiocy out of her at the same time. It's a confusing time for me.

Thankfully, I at least have food to comfort me, and I'm instantly berating myself for not coming here sooner. I've been neglecting a lot of my human needs. It's not until my meat suit practically screams at me to go to the bathroom or find some sustenance that I even remember I need those things to make it through the day. I should probably get it stamped on my hand or something as a reminder.

I take a big bite out of my burger, chewing slowly to savor the experience. I want to remember this place when I'm back to my skeleton ways.

"No, no, no. Not now." I want to cry. I'm not ready to say goodbye to my food. There's a special bond between a man and his grub, and I'm just beginning to understand it, but my spine tingles again. I'm just about ready to curse these souls to hell for bloody interrupting the one good thing I've finally got going on. Couldn't it have waited just another thirty minutes?

Reluctantly, I leave the restaurant, giving my food moon eyes for the last time. I step outside, the drive-in surprisingly empty of the town's teenagers. Apparently, it's a known hotspot for the curious adolescents.

"Oh, and this will be why," I mumble to myself, coming up to my destination. It seems a large percentage of the town's population has gathered in one place. "What is this?" I see a sign with large script written in blue ink. "Cold Moon Ball." I scratch my chin. "I guess my invite got lost in the post."

I keep getting stared at, and I'm not sure if it's because I'm talking out loud to myself or because my attire doesn't correlate with the fancy pants festivities. Jeans and boots aren't welcome among the black tie suits and ball gowns parading around like kings and queens. Uppity fuckers. If only they knew I get to decide where their souls end up in the afterlife. Mwahahaha.

I pause. The call for a reaping has suddenly disappeared; the soul's been saved. Christ, I can't catch a break. This town is proving to be one big bloody nemesis! I could've finished my food after all. I am *not* happy.

"Where the fuck have you been?"

I'm stopped in my tracks by a beautiful babe demanding my attention. I'd almost consider myself lucky, except for who it is.

"Working. You? Shot any more guys through the heart with your big mama bear speeches?"

She frowns, grabbing my arm, burning my skin. "Stop being so pathetic. Is she with you?"

I shake my head, confused. "What the fuck are you talking about, Melaina? Is who with me?"

"Thalia, of course! Who else? She's not been at the club all day, and when her shift started two hours ago, she still didn't show. I thought you finally decided to sweep her off her feet and screw me over."

My eyes widen with fear. "You mean she's missing? She's not just taking a day off sick or something?"

Melaina laughs. "You're so naïve. Thalia's never taken a day off from the moment she started working for me. My girl doesn't get sick either."

I rub my hands over my face, feeling a chill run through my bones that isn't only created by the freezing temperatures.

"Nyx took her," I whisper, not wanting to admit the truth. I left her to fend for herself, sure it's what she wanted, but I shouldn't have listened. I should've done the man thing I've seen so often and forced my protection on her. This is what I get for allowing her the freedom of making choices for herself. "I'm an idiot."

"Why are you saying this? Where would Nyx take her? This has the Collector written all over it." Melaina's standing strong, hands on hips. All business. She's certainly projecting an attitude that's keeping onlookers away.

I shake my head. Again with the bloody Collector. Who is this douche? "At Silk, I overheard Nyx trying to coerce someone from SIN into taking Thalia. I tried to get Thalia to come with me then, but she insisted she had all the protection she needed. She blew me off."

"And you took her word for it? You *are* a fucking idiot. I thought *you* were taking care of her after our chat! What the fuck have you been doing?"

"I was, until she rejected me! I was pissed. It's not like I put myself out there for everyone, you know. I needed to cool off, then I got distracted with reaping. Nyx is now the last soul I need to return before I can get back to regular scheduling."

"And you didn't think that happened to be a ploy to keep you distracted, better still in another dimension? Come on, Shade. Use your head. Nyx played you, again."

I shrug. Whether she's right or not doesn't make much difference now. "It doesn't matter, Melaina. When a soul calls, I have no choice but to go to it. That's how I've been made."

"Which she exploited. You ever wonder why she wasn't the only soul that escaped that day? I bet this has been her plan all along, using the other souls to keep you distracted long enough to meet her end goal. I'm assuming she has one, besides fucking everyone else's lives up."

"She wants the Underworld, and if you're right, then I guess this means she's got her army ready to back her up. But why Thalia?"

Melaina gives me one of her famous head smacks. It makes my ears ring like Santa's sleigh bells. "To finish you off, dummy. Where would she take her?"

"You're not gonna like the answer." I sigh, my shoulders aching with tension. "There's only one place I know she's been using to hide, if my sources are right."

Melaina groans, catching on. "This is why you wanted to know about my brother and SIN, isn't it?"

"Ding, ding, ding. We have a winner."

"Fuck you, reaper."

"All in good time, baby. One damsel at a time, please."

CHAPTER 14

CHALLENGES

I snoop around the outskirts of the SIN building, grateful for the night's blanket of darkness. Parked Harleys are lined up like soldiers on parade. Under any other circumstances, I'd take a moment to appreciate the glorious machines. Fear for Thalia's life has me distracted enough. Where is she? She has to be close.

I slip into the MC, the back entrance left wide open and unoccupied. I don't like this. It smells like a trap.

"She's not here, reaper. You can stop hiding."

I walk into the main room. When did I lose my stealth? Standing in the center of the room, I see my two buddies, Savage and Crusher.

"I just got off the phone with my sister. Interesting chat. You think a vampire-demon's been sniffing around here without me knowing?"

In for a penny, in for a pound, right? I'm already in the shit by the looks of it. "What better place to get an army of rebels than here?"

Savage roars, coming toward me. It's like a repeat of that night at the bar all over again.

"Listen, I don't know for sure who she has or hasn't corrupted. I just know creatures who aren't too fussy about what side of the law they sit on appeal to her nature. And she's good at manipulating everything she wants. She's got my girl, and I'm getting her back, one way or another. You gonna help?"

Savage cracks his knuckles, glancing at Crusher. "How can you be so sure this isn't the Collector's gig?"

I grit my teeth. "I don't know who this bloody Collector is! My battle is with Nyx. I see no other logical reason for anyone else to be involved."

Savage grunts after a momentary pause. "We've got members hunting the town already. When they find Nyx, we'll know."

I shake my head. I can't stay here, being still. I have to be doing *something*. "She wouldn't take Thalia someplace open for anyone to walk in on. Not unless she wants to be found," I begin, confusing my own thoughts as I think out loud. What did Nyx do?

"Where?"

I lift my head, noticing the phone Savage has pinned to his ear. I didn't even hear it ring.

"On it." He pockets the device, striding for the door. "She's in the cemetery."

I rush ahead. "Meet you there."

I call on my reaper form, begging for my tattoo to let me roam free. Now more than ever I need my abilities at full strength.

My wings pop open, and I'm almost giddy with appreciation. I ascend to the sky in a quick burst of energy, zooming through the air until I see the cemetery below. It's taken less than twenty seconds. And in the background I hear the roar of motorcycles approaching at speed too.

I take a sweep of the grounds, surprised to find Melaina and Princess WitchHound are already here. Sneaky bitch. No wonder she didn't follow me to her brother's club; she had her own agenda.

I land on my feet beside the two of them, skelly and cape back in action. Princess doesn't seem so upset to see me like this, not like I expected.

"She's in there. Hasn't come out yet."

"Why? What is this place?" I point to the large boulder fused with trees. It doesn't look like much to me.

Princess shakes her head. "It's just an empty cave. One way in, one way out. Not quite sure what she expects to achieve here." The rock-chic beauty frowns, which has me concerned, considering the amount of power she wields.

"So, let's storm right in and get this over with, shall we?"

Behind me, I hear Savage and Crusher join us on foot, their bikes obviously parked up.

"Face it, Nyx. This is over," I yell into the cavern. I see her platinum blond hair, illuminating the way before the rest of her comes into view.

"You're right, Shade. It's finally time to get it all done with."

Overhead, a scream echoes as two females jump from the tree above. Their faces are wildly feral, fangs stood proud from their mouths, bright red eyes from the demon who sired them.

I now know the fate of Nyx's mealtime victims.

"You went back to finish her off?" I point to the girl on the right, the teenager who I thought was safe in the hospital.

Nyx laughs, clearly happy. "Why wouldn't I? They're not the only ones either." She winks, and suddenly the cemetery is filled with an army of poor, helpless victims who know no better than the savageness of their first month as vampire-demons. "Aren't you going to congratulate me, Shade? I have a big family."

They all come, crowding around us all at once, blocking us into a tight circle.

"Any brilliant plans, Shade?" Melaina asks, stance ready to fight.

"Fuck if I know. I thought she was turning the club against us, not literally turning an army. Where the fuck have all these people come from anyway?"

Princess WitchHound stiffens beside me. "This is going to take some serious explanation with the Court and coven. How have we missed all these dead bodies?"

I can hear Nyx giggling away, clearly enjoying this scene and our ignorance. "Fools. You didn't think I only stayed in this town, did you? What fun would that have been?"

I shake my head. Of course. That's why I couldn't feel her soul in the vicinity. The other souls in the town were masking hers. She wasn't around but they were—there's only so many I can answer at the same time.

Bollocks, she played me way too good. Death's gonna have my arse for this.

"Melaina, you're on Thalia. Savage, Crusher, you're on the baby brats. Princess, you're with me. I'm gonna need that power of yours."

Without another word, we disperse into the foray, wild screams and the sounds of ripping flesh bathing the night air. Nyx backs up, seeing me coming for her. I look to Princess. "You got something to hold her still in that arsenal of yours? Anything that blocks her from running away?"

She nods once, and I see the fissures of magic spark between her hands like bolts of electricity. Nyx panics, head turning from side to side, and she figures out which route to take. Clearly, she hadn't made the time to take note of the creatures that already lived here. This is her rookie mistake.

I let my wings out, getting ready to pin the bitch back in the Infernum for good.

"Now!" Princess calls out. I see a momentary blip in energy that flattens Nyx to the earth, almost as though she is paralyzed. I don't waste time.

I scoop the vampire-demon up, chaining her body to mine. Above us a portal opens before I even have time to summon one, and I see Princess manipulating the elements for me. I give her a nod, and disappear as Nyx and I are sucked into the vacuum, tossed and turned and spat back out into her place of torment.

She slams her body into me over and over as she tries to escape the bindings wrapped around her.

"It's over, Nyx. I told you this is where you're meant to be." I untether myself from her and offer the Infernum walls her arms. It reaches out and pulls her in, sucking her into the framework, until only her face is visible.

"What are you doing to me?" she screams, utter fear cloaking her face.

I shake my head. "This is your own doing. The Infernum's reacting to the punishment level you deserve. I warned you, you were making it much worse for yourself. So long, bitch! I look forward to seeing you in the next millennium!"

I zap back out of the place, only to have my being pushed and pulled in a new direction. I thump onto hard rock—red, fiery, noisy Hell replaced with dark, quiet, and somber.

"Well, you're not such a fuckup after all, Shade."

I stand, taking a second to get my bearings. There's nothing like a good brain shake to get you all confused.

"Do I get a raise?" I joke, enjoying Death's cheerier side. He's even wearing a bright blue suit. Guess I did something right for a change.

"I thought you would've asked for something much different. Something to do with a certain supernatural town."

I quirk an eyebrow, wondering what he's getting at. "What would I want with that place?"

Death chuckles. It's a throaty laugh I've not heard before. I wonder how often he does it. "You can't fool me, Shade. I made you, and that town gave you a glimpse of a different life. One with a certain nymph-like damsel."

I try not to blush, but even in this skelly form, it's a little difficult not to when your creator, otherwise known as Dad, starts talking to you about the motions of human interaction. "It would've been nice to see where that life could've taken me. But it's not for me. We both know that."

Death shrugs as though it doesn't matter. "You'll always have the ability to go back there. Especially with that tattoo imprinted on your arm. That'll never change. See you around, Shade."

I'm falling, the ground disappearing, and I'm popping back out of a portal.

"Well, that was weird," I comment to myself, noting the ground I've landed on. What did Death mean?

"Oh, so you're not just fucking off then? I thought you'd gone back to that cold heartedness I first met. You can thank me now."

I smile at Melaina, at the hard time she's giving me. I knew it. I've won her over. Back in the cemetery, I'm surrounded by the bodies of Nyx's victims, and on their feet are Savage, Crusher, Princess WitchHound, and most important of all, Thalia.

I walk up to her, reaching for her hands, which she's already presenting me. "I'm so sorry. Are you all right? Did she hurt you?"

Thalia shakes her head, tears welling up in her eyes. "I'm okay." Her throat catches on a sob, and it makes me mad to see her so sad. This is all my doing.

"You're safe now, I promise."

She lunges at me, throwing her arms around my neck, burying her head in my chest. I don't know how to react; she's surprised me. Is she finally accepting me? I fold my arms around her tiny waist, pulling her in tight. Over her shoulder, I see Melaina motion to the guys to scramble out of there, but Princess stops her from giving me this moment of bliss. I don't blame her. This night is barely over.

"We've got quite the mess to clean up, which you're definitely sticking around for, reaper. And you can answer to the Court. I'm not taking the fall for this."

I shake my head, a smile gracing my face. "I didn't expect you to. I'm looking forward to finally meeting this Court you keep threatening me with. But first I have one more important matter to attend to."

"Oh no, you—" Princess begins, but luckily Melaina covers her mouth, stopping the little witch from her tirade.

I look at Thalia, her beautiful blue eyes beaming up at me like I've suddenly become her white knight. It's not an attribute I even deserve, not after everything I've put her through. But it's this look in her eyes that makes me selfish enough to ask the unthinkable.

"Thalia, I know I've made a lot of mistakes. And I know I've got a lot to learn. Hell, I don't even know what's going on anymore—Death left me with quite the mixed message. But there's one thing I know for certain, and I don't want to fuck it up any more than I have done."

"Oh, just spit it out already, Shade!" Melaina yells, and I can imagine her rolling her eyes behind my back.

"Thalia, will you help me do this the right way and let me take you out on a date?"

"Finally!" I hear Melaina call in the background, but I'm too hung up on the beauty in front of me to give it much attention. Thalia stares, searching my face, for what I don't know. The silence stretches on forever, and I don't know what to make of it.

Fuck me, I've pushed too far. Took her outreach and pressed too hard. Fuck it. Fuck.

She reaches up on tiptoes and presses a quick kiss to my cheek.

Oh, crap. Here comes the disappointment. Okay, I can do this. I can act graciously. Don't be a big baby.

"Yes, Shade. I would love that."

FUCK YEAH!

EPILOGUE

HORIZONS

THREE MONTHS LATER

"*S*hade, I'm ready."

I glance up from the newspaper I've been reading and see Thalia standing in nothing but bright pink lacy lingerie that grips onto her curves. I'm instantly hard and having to adjust myself for a more comfortable position on the seat.

"You are beautiful." I can't take my eyes off her. I'm sure they're bulging out of their sockets like I'm a cartoon character. "You can't wear that at the club tonight." The thought of another man enjoying this view right now kills me.

She saunters over to me, straddling my lap, her core teasingly placed over my cock. "I'm not working tonight," she whispers in my ear, teeth grazing my lobe and down my neck. "I'm ready for you."

She kisses me hard, moaning deeply as our tongues fuse together. It's like fireworks of passion exploding in my mind.

"Are you sure?" I gently pull her away, checking her eyes for honesty.

"Never been more positive in my life. I trust you, Shade."

I scoop her up in my arms and carry her to the bedroom,

knocking over vases in my haste. I lose myself in her lips again as I lay her on the bed, hovering over her curvaceous body. I have to control my excitement, or I'll be ejaculating before I even enter her.

"Make love to me."

I'm lost in her doe eyes as she rips my clothing to pieces and leaves them to scatter on the floor. It's here I see she's been holding back on me, as she gets on top, losing the seductive underwear she used to lure me here.

She kisses me wildly, eyes feral with lust, and lowers herself onto my cock, her pussy taking all of me in. She moans wildly, and I'm surrounded in pleasure as she rocks back and forth, my cock slipping in and out of her, each time filling her up even more.

I have to squeeze my bloody toes to keep from coming already. I flip her onto her back, leaving kisses from her neck to her navel. I flick my tongue over her clit and listen to her moan, hips bucking against my face.

She's so fucking sexy.

I slip a finger inside her, setting a slow rhythm as I circle my tongue on her swollen clit. She pants loudly, hips matching my movements.

She reaches for my head, tugging me upward until we're face to face.

"Together," she says, and I need no extra explanation from her. She wants our first orgasm together, as though it means something more.

I take her lips again, greedy for every sensation she gives me, and I feel her impatience clawing at me as she flattens me on my back again. My girl likes to take control.

She slams her pussy onto my cock and rides me hard, giving me zero time to savor the pleasure. There's no mercy here.

I suck her left nipple whilst rubbing the right, and she pounds harder, clenching my shaft tightly. "That's it, baby. You feel so fucking good."

She bites her lip as she swirls her hips, and I struggle to contain myself.

I lick my thumb and reach for her clit, watching her head tilt back with pleasure as she moans louder. It turns me on as she calls my name, reaching toward an orgasm.

"Oh, Shade. I'm gonna, I'm gonna . . ." She cries out. I feel her pussy tightening even more, and it sends me over the edge, shooting my cum deep inside her whilst hers drips down my balls.

She collapses on top of me, her heavy breathing in synchronization with mine. I kiss her tenderly, savoring the moment.

"Don't crash on me yet, Shade. The night's only just begun."

I smile, hopeful with the promise. "I love you, Thalia."

She pauses, eyes wide as though I've shocked her. I begin to retract, not wanting to ruin this perfect moment now that she's completely let me in.

She smiles. "Got ya!" She giggles. "I love you too, Shade."

ABOUT THE AUTHOR

Justine Winter is the author of the bestselling paranormal romance series Nature's Destiny. She is the proud owner of an MA degree in Creative Writing, and currently divides her time between living in South West Wales and London. Justine loves food, hates coffee, and gobbles up books like they're oxygen. She's often geeky, always funny, and claims her dad jokes will go down in history.

You can stay up to date and in touch with her pretty much on all social media platforms; she's everywhere!

Sign up to her newsletter
   Facebook
   Twitter
   Instagram

ACKNOWLEDGMENTS

Firstly, I'd like to thank Kristie for creating the Havenwood Falls world and opening it up for other authors to collaborate. I am honored to be involved in this amazing universe. I had such fun creating Shade the reaper. He's almost a paranormal version of my character Grayson in Wicked Sunshine. They share a likeness for humor and banter. And both guys have exceptional taste in women.

Thank you to the authors whose characters I've used to help push Shade along in his quest—I couldn't have done it without them.

A big thanks to my readers; I hope I brought you some laughter and that you enjoyed this book. Thank you for your support.

Now I'm heading back to the Winterverse: there's lots of writing to be done in the Winter Cave.

Speak soon, Wolves.
Alpha J - XO

SAVAGE SALVATION

KRISTIE COOK

~ A Havenwood Falls Sin & Silk Novella ~

HAVENWOOD FALLS
sin & silk

Savage Salvation

KRISTIE COOK

To the one who inspired Savage
First you made me see stars at the Stargate, next we rode hard across the
Dothraki Sea, and then you took me to deep, dark, and very wet
places . . . all the way to Atlantis . . .
Because you make a lady think all the naughty things, this book is
dedicated to you, my fictional husband, Jason Momoa

CHAPTER 1

The service came to a close, and everyone stood, the metal chairs creaking almost as loudly as all the leather in the room. I stared at the focal point of the space—the gleaming wooden box dressed in flowers flowing over its edges—as several pairs of heavy boots thudded toward it. At the direction of some guy I'd spoken with only briefly, the six men gathered around the box and lifted.

I stood, turned, and hurried down the aisle, out the other way, my heels clicking in loud echoes on the tile floor as I crossed the lobby. The door nearly knocked over a group of girls when I threw it open, and they yelped as they jumped out of the way. They bitched and moaned, straightening their skin-tight dresses that barely covered the goods. The skanks had no respect. This was a funeral, for mother's sake, and they were dressed like they were auditioning for their next role in a porn.

"Rey." The deep, familiar voice called after me, but I ignored him, heading for my car. I slid into the two-seater Benz, but didn't quite get the door closed before Niall grabbed it. "Reyna. Don' be like this." His Scottish accent came thickly when he was mad.

"Go to hell."

"C'mon, sis."

My jaw clenched. "Don't call me that. You're not my brother."

"For all intents and purposes—"

"What do you want?" I pressed the Start button, and the engine purred to life.

"You're coming to the cemetery, right?"

"Of course I am," I muttered.

My gaze stayed forward, but in my periphery, I saw his thick beard bob as he nodded, then he closed the door. I inhaled deeply and blew the air out slowly, refusing to shed a tear. Unable to, if I was honest. I hadn't yet been able to cry for the man who'd been like an uncle to me, who'd taken a sort of fatherly role when my own had passed. After another deep breath, I followed the procession to the cemetery, also known as the city of the dead. The above-ground tombs and mausoleums lined the pathways like buildings lined the city streets.

Pops didn't get a traditional New Orleans funeral. No jazz music and parading through the streets. Besides all the other reasons, the club wouldn't allow it. Like they should have any say. The New Orleans chapter of the Swords of the Infernal Night motorcycle club, SIN or SIN-NO for short, shouldn't have a say at all in our lives, as far as I was concerned. In fact, if it were up to me, this would be the last time I'd see any of them. Pops trusted them all with our lives, and he lost his for it. I would never trust any of them again.

Not that I ever did in the first place.

I liked to think Niall, who had been like a brother to me, looked out for us, but the rest of them? To hell with them all. They didn't do their job.

I went for a drive once I made sure Pops was in his final resting place, two Harleys rumbling loudly behind me the whole time. Supposedly the two members of SIN were there to guard me, but I couldn't fathom what they thought they could do from back there if I were attacked. It wasn't like the people after me could be taken down with a bullet. If that were the case, Pops would still be alive.

My phone rang, and I ignored it. It persisted until I finally hit the answer button on the steering wheel.

"Reyna," Niall's Scottish lilt came over the car speakers. "Come on home, lass."

"That's not my home." I hadn't been to my home in months.

"Well then, come to *my* home."

"Why? So you can make me a prisoner?"

"We need to talk. Plans have been made."

"Screw you and your plans, Niall. Look where it got us. Pops is —" I hiccupped before continuing— "dead, and I—"

"You're goin' to be okay. It's been arranged. Just come to the club house. You know I hate talking on these things. Especially about this."

He had a point there. We were practically screaming "here I am" at all those who wanted to find me.

"Don't make us force you," he added.

I blew out a sigh. "Fine. I'm on my way. But one thing, Niall."

"What?"

"I'm nobody's bitch. Not yours. Not anyone's. And I'm certainly not an old lady or anybody's property. So stop treating me like I am."

"I'm not. I'm treating you with concern for your safety, which is my job, my qu—"

"Don't you fucking say it." I disconnected the call before he said the word that made me want to hurl every time I heard it. Gah! A shudder ran through me. I'd rather he call me sis or anything else than the word he'd been about to say.

The two bikers followed me like puppy dogs through the streets into an industrial area a few blocks from the French Quarter. As soon as I turned in to the driveway, the gate across it started rolling to the side, and I pulled in. The compound was lit up in more ways than one. The club was obviously having some kind of celebration of life ceremony—just another excuse for everyone to drink until they passed out. I knew this was supposed to be a big honor, since Pops had been a friend of the club but never an actual member, but it felt like salt followed by tequila in my wounds. And not in the good way. Drunk members, friends of the club, hangers-on, and groupies whooped and hollered from inside the brightly lit main building, and the moans and grunts of people fornicating were scattered across the grounds outside. It had only just grown dark. It was going to be a long night.

Niall opened my door for me before I even cut the engine. He stood there in loose jeans, motorcycle boots, a black T-shirt, and his leather vest, called a cut in MC terms, covered in patches. One of them said "Torq," his road name—what everyone here called him. He angled his dark head toward a smaller building to the right of the main one before turning, the large patch of a skull with its head impaled by a rose-wrapped sword staring back at me.

I followed silently, surprised to be heading toward the small structure. The big house was where some of the members lived and where Pops and I had been staying the last several months. It also housed the party area, with a long bar, a couple of pool tables, and a few threadbare couches stained with substances I didn't want to think too hard about or I'd need to bleach my brain. It stunk, pun intended, having supernatural senses when you lived where there was practically an orgy every other night. This small building, though, served as the club's church—where they held their meetings and did their business.

I didn't like the idea of being a piece of their business, but at least they had the decency to invite me in on the subject this time around. Well, not really invite. It'd still been more like an order, even if it had been delivered by my so-called brother. And I was only assuming that was what was going on—that this was about me. Pops may have been a friend of the club, but I'd never been all that friendly with them. In fact, I'd always made my disdain quite clear. And now Pops was dead, and they needed to figure out what to do with me. Throwing me out would be disrespectful to Pops's memory. And while I thought of them as no more than criminal scum, I couldn't deny that the club did have a code, and respect was important to them.

And it wasn't just about Pops.

They'd have to deal with kelpies worldwide—some of whom were already in town for the funeral—if the club tried anything stupid with me. Considering the number of kelpies in the various chapters of the club, that'd create a lot of extra tension for the SIN president to deal with. Of course, he was known for doing such things when he was bored, and I was pretty sure he'd grown bored of me a long time ago when I refused to screw him.

"Reyna, come in and have a seat," Prez said when Niall and I entered the building. I paid him little notice, but I could feel his gaze undressing me as he motioned toward a room with a large conference table surrounded by a dozen or more chairs. The dim lighting from a table lamp in the corner created shadows, the far end of the room doused in obsidian darkness—but I could sense the people there. Or beings, anyway. As I entered, a hint of sulfur burned my nose, but then it was followed by a scent that was musky, warm, and mouth-watering, making my belly tighten and my thighs squeeze together. *What the hell?* Whoever was back there, they definitely weren't human and not kelpie, either—not my kind here to protect me.

Not that my people were a huge threat to most of the SIN members in any chapter, including those here. They were all supernaturals, many of whom were a lot more badass than people who shifted into horses. Unless there was a body of water around and the other supe couldn't swim, kelpies were mostly dangerous only to humans.

Except me.

I was the first in many generations of our kind to grow a horn. One single horn, right out of the top of my forehead. Yep, I was a damn unicorn. The silver horn had first broken through when I was twelve, only a few months after my first shift. It'd hurt like a bitch, and even in my human form, I still had a scar at my hairline, barely visible under all my curls. I'd only been able to shift a few times in the thirteen years since then, because as soon as word got out, my life was endangered. From my horn to my tears to the hairs in my mane and tail, I had way too many valuable parts. Parts that some would love to harvest.

Hunters came for me almost right away, in my home country of Brazil, and killed my parents. Pops, who wasn't really related but had been like an uncle to me, escaped with Niall and me, whisking us off to America. Niall had always been like an adopted brother, coming to us as an orphan when I was nine and he was supposedly fifteen. I didn't learn until we were found again a year ago that he was much, much older—kelpies, like all fae, lived very long lives while retaining youthful appearances, especially when we used glamour—and that he'd been groomed all his life to be a warrior to protect the future queen. He'd been sent to Brazil when a fae Seer prophesized that the next kelpie queen would come from our small South American town. We hadn't known then, before I'd ever even shifted, that this queen was me. Because for some reason in kelpie law, the one with the horn ruled.

I really did not want to rule.

At least, I didn't want to rule a smattering of supernaturals that hadn't been a true herd in generations. The kelpies had escaped to the earthly realm during a devastating war in our Faerie homeland many centuries ago. They stayed together in Scotland for a while, but rifts over time sent more and more away, and after the last unicorn queen died, what remained of the herd scattered. If the need arose, they'd be compelled to come together once again for me, but could they ever be a herd again? Especially since so many had joined a different kind of herd—the SIN MC? Whom would they truly be loyal to if it came down to it? Me and each other or their patch?

Hopefully, the need would never arise.

As I walked farther into the room as though drawn to the far end by that delicious smell, annoyance doused the desire when I noticed my designer luggage piled by the doorway. I turned on Niall, Prez, and Chintz, the VP, while trying to tamper my anger—not because they were kicking me out, but because they'd dared to touch my personal property.

"Not wasting any time, I see." I gave them a saccharine smile. "No worries, though. I wasn't planning on staying anyway."

Niall reached out, cupping my elbow and leading me toward a chair. "Sit, Rey."

"I'm not a dog." My patience was waning. Someone at the far end of the room snickered.

Niall sighed. "Sit down and listen. Like I said, we have a plan. It's all taken care of."

None of the bikers sat, so neither did I. "I don't need your plan."

"Ya do," Niall insisted.

"He's right," Prez said, his voice deep and full of promise of dark, ugly things. His beady eyes were barely visible behind all his dark facial hair, but I felt them on me, the sensation like cold slime. He crossed his log-thick arms over his barrel chest. "The hunters know you're here this very second. Our guys followed two of them who were following you."

"They're dead," Chintz said flatly. He leaned his thin yet sinewy arms on the back of one of the chairs, also appraising me as I let that sink in. My insides felt sick, but I refused to squirm in their presence.

"You're willing to go to war over me, yet you're kicking me out?" I asked.

Chintz shrugged. "We've gone to war for lesser reasons."

"We swore an oath to Pops," Prez said as a better explanation. "We don't go back on our word."

"Yet you're kicking me out," I repeated, my hand gesturing toward my suitcases.

"We're sendin' you to a safe place," Niall said.

Every muscle in my body tensed up. "You're *sending* me to a safe place? What does that mean? You're not sending me anywhere! Who do you think you are?"

"Reyna!" Niall barked, and I'd never heard him say my name so sharply. "You need to listen. It's for your own god damn safety."

My ample chest heaved as I tried to regain control of my anger. My inner beast had awakened. I'd learned long ago how to contain her, but she always showed interest when my emotions rose, hoping I'd finally let her break free. This would be the absolute worst time to indulge her, especially with strangers in the room, so I forced her to settle down and go back to sleep. Crossing my arms over my breasts, I cocked my head, my only indication that I was listening.

"A SIN chapter in Colorado has agreed to provide you protection," Prez said.

My jaw dropped. "*Colorado?* No way in hell!"

"They'll take you in, under the wards of their town," Prez continued gruffly, ignoring my outburst.

"It's a small town in the mountains," Niall added. "I bet you'll love it."

I'll bet I won't.

Someone on the far end emerged from the darkness—over six feet tall, sandy brown hair, wearing sunglasses—at night, inside, in the dark—and a leather cut with a small patch that said Pirate and another under it that said President. That vague hint of sulfur wafted to my nose. Demon, perhaps?

"Our town isn't like anyplace else," he said, his voice deep and raspy. "There's no safer place."

"No offense, Mr. . . ."

"Pirate," he said.

"Mr. Pirate."

"Just. *Pirate*," the stranger growled.

I blinked, suppressing the urge to roll my eyes. "Okay, no offense, *Pirate*, but these assholes here couldn't protect us, so what makes you think you can?"

That snicker sounded again from the dark end of the room.

"And I can't go all the way to Colorado," I hurried on, because my question had been rhetorical and I didn't want them thinking they needed to answer it. "I have a business to run, which these dumb shits seem to have forgotten."

I turned back to Niall and Prez with a raised brow.

No, I didn't want to rule a kingdom. But I did want to rule an empire.

And I'd already been on my way to building it with my plus-size fashion and lifestyle blog and specialty lingerie designs when the hunters discovered our location and we had to go into hiding a year ago. That made running a business a little difficult, and I knew my clients were almost out of patience. Good thing for me that they loved my designs too much to completely give up on me.

But disappearing to a small mountain town in Colorado where they probably didn't even have indoor plumbing, let alone internet service? That would be a career killer.

"Your laptop's packed," Niall said. "All your business stuff is. You've already been running it remotely for a year. You haven't lost any business yet, have you?"

"I haven't gained any, either," I sniped back. My brain knew it wasn't Niall's or anyone else's fault that the hunters were after me. Somewhere deep down I also knew it wasn't his or the MC's fault that I'd been found. But damn it, it was their fault that Pops was dead and we were even having this discussion.

All I wanted was to be in my own bed in my own home, preparing for tomorrow's work day like any normal person. Just like I had been before the hunters had discovered my general location, and now they'd come way too close. If Niall and the MC had done their jobs properly, I could have at least had some semblance of my old life. We definitely wouldn't be discussing some trip to Colorado or the future of my business that wasn't looking so promising anymore. So repressing my anger wasn't easy.

Besides, if I didn't stay angry, the grief would kick in.

"Don' be difficult, Rey," Niall practically begged, his accent thicker than usual. He knew I had a soft spot for it. "Yeh know yeh can't stay here, love. Yeh can't leave this compound and expect to live. And how many people here are you goin' to let die for yeh?"

I scowled. He knew exactly what buttons to push.

"Yer life, yer people's lives, these people's lives—no matter how much yeh don't like 'em—they're more importan' than anythin', aren't they?" he continued, tilting his head as he stared me down with piercing sapphire eyes, challenging me to argue further.

I opened my mouth to do just that, because I was stubborn like that. There had to be another way. No, I wouldn't let anyone here die while protecting me. Niall was the only one who had any kind of place in my heart, but just because I didn't like the MC and their crowd didn't mean I wanted them dead. Especially not for me.

But Colorado couldn't possibly be our only choice.

Those words were on the tip of my tongue when the other figure stepped out of the shadows at the far end of the room, that delicious scent wafting toward me again.

And if my body's reaction meant anything, any other options had just been wiped off the table.

CHAPTER 2

"*P*rez, time's about up." His voice was deep, gravelly, rough —the sound guttural, feral, like an orgasmic groan that made my belly drop and flip.

He spoke to Pirate, stepping up next to the other chapter's president, but I somehow knew that behind the mirrored sunglasses, his focus was completely on me. And I felt it in every cell of my body that lit up like a flipping Christmas tree.

He was possibly the tallest, broadest man I'd ever seen. I'd been around supernaturals all my life. An outlaw one-percenter club full of them for half my life. I was used to extra-large males, but this one made everyone else in the room look average. Made me feel small. He stood nearly a foot taller than me, and I was five foot ten. His shoulders and arms were perfectly proportional to his height—in other words, massive. Muscular. But not competitive bodybuilder type. More like bodyguard type. Much more intimidating than a gym rat.

His hair hung loosely, waving down past his shoulders, dark on top and growing lighter toward the ends. Dark brows arched sharply upward at the outsides, giving him a naturally mean look. He wore a closely cropped beard, yet his full lips were still quite noticeable. At least, I was noticing them and thinking way too much about what they might taste like . . . feel like.

I forced my gaze downward, trying to break contact, but then I wondered just how close to perfect his chest and abs were . . . and if his dick was like the rest of him—big and full of promised poundings. *Reyna!* Even as I mentally scolded myself for such uncharacteristic, wayward thoughts, my thighs clenched and my panties dampened.

His nostrils flared. He growled quietly.

"Let's get the package and go," he snarled at Pirate.

And then he had to open that perfect mouth and remind me what he was.

The focus of my gaze widened outward, taking in the black T-shirt and leather cut. A damn biker. To him and everyone else here, I was nothing more than property and a job—not a woman or sentient being with a brain and heart and soul, but a thing to possess and control. How could I have forgotten? I'd nearly been willing to do anything and go anywhere with this beautiful lowlife before me. Pheromones. It had to be the pheromones clouding my judgment. I'd do well to never forget again exactly what he was.

His name patch said Savage and his title was VP.

Savage.

I bet he's a savage in bed.

My mind drifted again to more naughty thoughts. My panties were no longer damp. They were soaked.

Damn it. Stop it, Rey!

Disgust filled me—disgust with myself. I'd never had thoughts like this for anyone, especially not a biker. My fantasies centered on boardroom executives dressed in suits, whisking me off on private jets to Milan for dinner and London for a show. And my reality—well, we'll just say it lacked any of the above. There was little reality in that area of my life, a couple of boyfriends here and there, each quickly scared away by Niall, if not my body type.

"If we're doing this, we gotta do it now, Torq," Pirate said.

"We're definitely doing this," Niall replied.

"The hell we are," I said, although I could hear the conviction in my voice wasn't as strong as it had been two minutes ago. Savage had awoken my inner beast in a way she'd never been woken before. Curiosity aroused us—in more ways than one.

Biker, Rey. You. Don't. Do. Bikers. Another voice, this one dripping with sarcasm, piped up, *You don't do anyone.*

"Brothers, we need the room for a minute," Niall said as he glared at me.

The bikers shuffled out of the door with a gruff "hurry up" growled by one of them.

Niall stepped in front of me, lifting my chin with his finger as he angled his head to look me in the eye with his blue ones, extra bright among all the dark hair on his head and face. "The club went out of their way for us, Rey. These guys from Colorado don't have to do shite for you or me. They owe us nothin'. But when there are supernatural beings to hide and protect, they're the ones who can do it like no one else."

"Then why didn't Pops go to them?" I asked, one side of my mouth curling back with skepticism.

"Because he didn't know them, and he did know this chapter. We've known SIN-NO as long as we've been in the States, Rey. You know that. The Colorado chapter is different, though. Nobody knows why. But when you're in trouble and they offer to take you in, that's something you don't turn your nose up at. Not even you, lass. You can't afford to. Our people need you to remain alive and well. And you can't build your empire if you're dead."

I turned my head, just enough to free myself from his grip. "Maybe I just need to sneak off by myself and find a way to lay low. The hunters won't expect me to be on my own. They'll be looking for an entourage."

"First of all, over my dead fookin' body. You daft? Second, there won't be an entourage out of here. Third, if the guys couldn't protect Pops, what makes you think you can protect your own arse? And last but not least, if something happened to you, Pops woulda died in vain. Your parents, too. Is that what you want, lass?" He lifted a single eyebrow.

I scowled in return. "Of course not."

"Then let's go skiing, love," he said with a half-smile, before signaling for the others.

They filed in, their boots scuffing heavily along the floor.

"Are we doing this?" Pirate asked, and Niall nodded. He looked over at Savage. "Let 'em know."

The big guy's big fingers tapped on a phone that looked like a toy in his oversized hand. For the next several minutes, it became quickly obvious that they'd carefully crafted some complicated strategy to extricate me from the MC's compound without being seen. While they put it in action, I changed out of my funeral clothes, into black jeans and a black hoodie that Niall handed me. Lovely. Then they took my phone with the promise to get me a burner down the road and said my computer and tablet had already been scanned and double-checked for bugs and tracking devices.

"We're not fookin' around this time," Niall said when I balked at handing my phone over. "We messed up once and look what hap'n."

The hunters had first discovered us because someone had sensed me at an industry show, and a photographer for a fashion magazine had caught my face on camera just right, able to confirm what they sensed. After that, it was just a matter of following the paper trail— well, electronic trail, consisting of my blog, business contacts, and eventually my ISP and phone. I hadn't been to a show since, which wasn't helping my career at all.

I reluctantly fished my phone out of my purse, glad that everything I needed on it was safely stored in the cloud. Prez took it and pocketed it.

"Let's ride," Pirate said, once they ensured everything was in place.

"I'm going with Prez and Chintz on a decoy run," Niall explained to me, and when I opened my mouth to argue, he added, "But I'll catch up. I'm not sending you out there alone. You can't get rid of my arse that easily."

I'd never felt like a piece of property more than when I was hidden in the back of a cargo truck with a bunch of boxes, and I swore when this was over, I'd never have anything to do with these assholes again. As I crouched in the dark corner of the metal box, I lumped Niall in as one of those assholes. What the hell had he been thinking?

We drove for what felt like hours, but I couldn't be sure from my corner of the truck. My butt was numb, and I had to pee, so it'd been a while. Finally, the truck stopped, and the back door rolled up. Pirate climbed in and picked his way back to me, holding out a coat, a hat, and sunglasses.

"Right over here," he said once I was disguised, leading me out of the U-Haul truck and to an older RV.

We were behind a row of semis in the dark corner of a truck stop. I hesitated at the step leading to the door of the RV. I didn't know this guy from anyone. How did I know he wasn't one of the hunters or about to turn me in to them?

"We gotta ride," Pirate said, urging me upward.

While he was a biker—president of his club, no less—there was something calming about him. Authoritative, rough, and pushy, but I sensed something else that made me think he might have been a father. For some reason, believing that brought a bit of ease, but I still remained apprehensive, my foot on the step and my hand reaching for the door handle, but unable to move. Pirate sighed behind me, then held a phone up to my ear.

"It's okay." Niall's voice came through the earpiece. "I can see you on the step—I'm that close. We thought you'd be more comfortable in the rig."

Swallowing the small lump in my throat, I went up and inside, relieved to find a working toilet.

As I came out of the bathroom, that mouthwatering scent hit my nose. Savage had just come in, his large body filling the space at the front of the RV.

"I'm driving," he growled, grabbing the kid in the driver's seat by the collar and yanking him out.

"You?" the kid said with a laugh, grabbing his cut from the passenger seat and slipping it on. His patch read *Prospect*. "You're gonna drive and not ride?"

Savage only grunted as he draped his cut over the seat back before sliding in behind the wheel.

"What about your bike?" the kid asked.

"You ride it."

The kid's jaw dropped. Mine nearly did, too. For a biker, that was like saying, "Here, have a go with my old lady."

"Don't make me regret it," Savage snarled.

"But . . . I was supposed to drive her." He jerked his head toward me.

"No. Fucking. Way."

The kid paused for another moment, then hurried out the door. I remained frozen for at least a minute, then figured I'd better sit down. I'd just started to move when Pirate came stomping up the steps and through the door.

"This wasn't the plan," he barked at Savage.

"It is now." He didn't even look up at his president.

Pirate glanced at me, then turned back to Savage. "You can protect her out there just as well. Probably better."

"Nope."

A silent beat passed and then another before Pirate sighed loudly. "What the fuck ever." He jogged down the steps and banged on the side of the rig. "Let's ride."

The door closed at the same time the engine turned over.

"Sit down and buckle up," Savage said, the sound low and rumbly. The man had permanent bedroom voice. Unfortunately, his tone seemed to be permanent asshole tone.

I hurried into the passenger seat and pulled on my seat belt. He seemed to be staring straight forward, but I was sure behind those sunglasses—yeah, he still wore them, even at night and inside the rig —he was peering over at me. I could *feel* it. The sensation dissipated when we began rolling forward, toward the truck stop's exit. Motorcycles rumbled in the distance. I watched as four turned onto the main road a hundred yards ahead of us, but there were more, somewhere behind us.

"You gave up your bike," I said, the curiosity killing me. Savage replied with some kind of confirming noise. "Why?"

"Doin' my job."

I turned in my seat to look at him. "Being my chauffeur is your job? Wasn't that the other guy's job?"

"I don't trust him to do it right."

"You don't trust him to drive this grandpa-mobile, but you trust him with your *bike*?"

He turned to look at me—I knew for sure he was now—and it was more than a stolen glance. He was staring at me, as though appraising me. The weight of his gaze was warm . . . and tingly. His nostrils flared before he turned back toward the road, shifting in his seat.

"I don't trust him to protect you. Not like I can." The way he said those last four words made me feel like protecting me was somehow more than a job for him. I sensed ownership in his voice, but not in a me-biker-you-old-lady-grunt-grunt Neanderthal kind of way. More like in a you're-important-to-me-and-I-will-die-for-you kind of way. Which was absolutely ridiculous. I nearly snorted at myself for even having the thought.

Even if he didn't feel that, I could tell he felt something. This sexual tension in the air couldn't have been completely one-sided. Could it?

"I still don't get it," I pressed, trying to feel him out. When he didn't encourage me to continue, I did anyway. "Your president said this wasn't the plan. That you could protect me better out there. Yet you changed the plan." I paused, but he still didn't say anything. "And gave up your bike." I waited again. "For me."

He blew out a harsh breath. "She's not my bike," he snapped.

"Oh." That was unexpected.

"I just bought her on the way to get you. *My* bike's at home."

"So this is a backup?"

"A new project. And you—" He looked over at me again and slid his sunglasses down his nose. I couldn't tell the color of his eyes in the glow of the dash lights, but I could see a very prominent reddish-orange glow before he quickly pushed the glasses back up. And suddenly so much made sense.

"You're a hellhound," I said with understanding. The sunglasses were a protective measure—if a human and even some supes looked into his eyes three times, they could die. Sooner, if he wanted. I'd just been given time number one.

"And you're my charge."

Hellhounds were extremely protective of those put in their care. That must have been what I'd sensed from him, and nothing else. The sexual tension really was one-sided.

I turned to stare out the side window, into the inky night.

"There's a bed in back," Savage growled after a while. "Go sleep."

Don't tell me what to do. Instinct made me want to argue, but the more I thought about it, the more a bed sounded nice. After another hour or so of riding in silence, I made my way to the back, where I could breathe more normally without his scent invading my senses. The tightness between my legs loosened, and it didn't take long for the motion of the RV and the sound of the road to lull me to sleep.

I awoke to the sound of a quiet song and rolled over, getting my bearings. Savage still drove, though the sky had lightened quite a bit outside. It was his voice singing, and it was mesmerizing.

After stopping to pee in the tiny bathroom, I stumbled up to the front seat. Desert spread out before us.

"Where are we?" I asked as I glanced at my watch. 6:30 a.m. We'd been driving for nearly twelve hours.

"Texas panhandle." Savage glanced over at me. "What the fuck is that?" I looked around, my eyes still bleary and not seeing what he was. "On your wrist."

I held it up, confused. "My FitBit."

"God damn it," he growled, and somehow, in one quick motion, he managed to jerk it off my wrist, roll down the window, and throw it out in the road.

"Hey, asshole! What the hell did you do that for?" I yelled.

"Tracking—" He never finished his statement.

Something slammed into the side of the RV, and we went rolling.

CHAPTER 3

 he vehicle rolled twice before coming to rest on its side—
on my side. I landed smooshed up against the window,
something extremely heavy weighing me down. I wiggled just enough
to see what I was dealing with, perhaps a seat and hopefully not the
engine.

Nope.

A hard-lined, rugged, sexy as hell face hovered only inches from
mine, his hair curtaining the space between us. We stared at each
other for a long moment, both of our chests heaving against the other.
The weight of his body on mine suddenly felt completely different,
and my own began to respond. Swallowing, I forced myself to break
the hold, cutting my eyes to the side to see the cracked windshield.

"You hurt?" Savage asked, his breath warm and smoky on my face,
but his tone harsh as usual.

I took a quick mental inventory of all my parts. I had no sharp
pains anywhere, and anything less, such as bruising, I didn't think I'd
notice at the moment. My body was too busy feeling other things.
Stupid body.

"I'm fine. You?"

I swore the corner of his lip began to curl the slightest bit before
he went stoic again. "Fine."

He maneuvered his way off of me, and my body immediately missed his. *Stop it, Rey! More important things to worry about.*

With one thrust of both feet, Savage shoved the windshield out. He climbed outside, then turned back toward me. "Glamour yourself."

I blinked. "What?"

"You're fae. Do I need to spell it out?"

"I . . . uh . . ." I stammered. Kelpie were from Faerie, which technically made us a type of fae, but we weren't like faeries or elves. Did he not know what I was or just not know the difference? I had some glamouring abilities, but nothing like theirs. I did the best I could, lightening my tan skin and dark hair, straightening the kinks into waves.

"You can't do better than that?" he grumbled, and I shook my head as he reached his hand in and grabbed my wrist, pulling me out of the wreckage.

I jumped down from the prone RV onto the asphalt of a barren stretch of highway in the middle of the desert. There wasn't much there to hide behind besides cacti and some low brush, but I could smell the attackers—dark fae. Possibly Unseelie, but I couldn't be sure. Faerie was home to many dark kinds. Were these the same hunters who had killed Pops? Nobody had said anything about dark fae before. If they weren't the same, then the word of my whereabouts had spread. I was in more danger than I realized.

A figure streaked from the shoulder toward us. Savage jumped in its way, tackling it to the ground. They rolled around the road, all snarls and growls, snapping teeth and fists on flesh. They quickly came to a stop, Savage jumping to his feet and bringing the attacker with him. His large hands, now clawed, were gripped around the fae's head, squeezing it like a melon, the man's eyes bulging from their sockets. Savage's shades had come off in the tussle, and he stared directly in the fae's face, dark gray smoke swirling into the air from his skin. Savage's growl turned into a howl. My head felt like it was about to explode from the deadly sound that could only come from Hell, and I clamped my hands over my ears. The fae had no way to defend himself, and he crumpled, held up only by the hellhound's partially shifted hands.

"Savage!" I screamed, my heart pounding from the scene unfolding before me.

His howl fell silent.

"We could use him," another voice rumbled, and Savage let the fae drop to the ground, his chest barely moving with shallow breaths.

In all the commotion, I hadn't noticed the others' arrival. Several motorcycles circled us, their riders already standing in defensive positions, guns out.

"Get her out of here, Savage," Pirate growled. He'd been the one to stop his VP from killing the fae. Smoke rose from his skin, too, smelling of brimstone. Pirate was also a hellhound.

Savage stomped toward me and, taking my wrist again, tugged me toward the kid from the RV and the massive bike next to him.

"No bitch seat," the kid pointed out.

Savage growled, while I suppressed my own. Why did they have to call the back seat that?

"Take mine," Niall called from the other side of the circle as a jolt of energy slammed into the RV, missing me by less than a yard.

Guns started firing into the desert, as if they could hurt the fae. Although, if they used iron bullets, maybe they could at least slow the hunters down. We ran for Niall and his bike. Savage swung his leg over the motorcycle.

"If anything happens to her—" Niall began.

"I got her," Savage barked.

"Niall?" I turned toward him. As mad as I'd been, I couldn't bear for anything to happen to him. "What about you?"

"We'll be right behind you, lass. Now go!" He practically shoved me onto the bike, which was already rumbling under Savage.

I hesitated, unsure of the mental stability of the man whose hands I was about to put my life in. He'd just nearly killed a man! Not even a man—a fae. They weren't exactly easy to kill. When another blast of fae magic soared right by us, I hurriedly climbed on and wrapped my arms around the large body in front of me. I held on for dear life as Savage twisted the gas, and we practically flew out of there.

We rode for hours, far above the speed limit, until we had to stop for gas at some hole-in-the-wall place near Albuquerque. My ears rang from the wind, and I could barely move my legs to climb off the bike. They wobbled under my weight when I finally managed to stand. It'd been years since I'd been on a motorcycle, at least for any length of time. As soon as I was old enough, I'd distanced myself as much as possible from the MC, not wanting any part of that lifestyle. When Niall and I did anything together, I always drove. So I wasn't exactly used to the constant vibration between my legs. With that and the man I'd had no choice but to hold on to with my breasts pressed against his back, inhaling his scent with each breath, my thighs had stayed clenched the whole time.

"We gotta ride before someone finds you again," Savage said, joining me in front of the shelves of chips inside the shabby store. "Hungry?"

I wasn't sure if I was, my gut all twisted up after everything that had happened, but it had been close to twenty-four hours since I'd eaten before the funeral. Gods. Was that really just yesterday?

Savage must have been starving because he loaded up on beef jerky, chips, and drinks. As soon as he opened the first package of jerky once we were back outside, my stomach rumbled loudly. He handed it over to me, and together we devoured the craptastic junk food. I'd have to eat salads for the next week to make up for it. And then I silently laughed at how unlikely that was.

We rode for a few more hours, and at the next stop, Savage removed his leather jacket and handed it to me.

"Shifter here. I run warm," I reminded him.

"It's dark, we're headed into the mountains, and it's January."

"And what about you?" I eyed his massive body, now clad in only a long-sleeved black shirt and whatever he might have worn underneath it.

"Hellhound here. I self-generate heat."

"Oh. Good point." I took the coat. As soon as I put it on, I wondered if it was a big mistake, because now I would not only be inhaling his scent with every breath, but I was totally enveloped in it.

"Just hope the roads are clear," Savage said before firing up the bike once more.

"Are we almost there yet?" I asked, my body protesting at the thought of getting back on. He looked at me with one of those sharply arched brows raised even higher. "Yes, I'm feeling childish."

"No, we're not." He said no more.

With a resigned sigh, I climbed on.

Savage sped us up the mountains, down the ridges, and up some more. My ears popped at some point. The scenery streaked by us, and even with my supernatural vision, I could only see blurred trees and snow glowing in the darkness. The temperature continued to drop the farther up we climbed, but Savage's body remained toasty warm. I couldn't stop myself from pressing harder against him.

I was comfortable enough—and exhausted enough—that I was about to doze off when something zinged through my body.

"What was that?" I yelped, completely alert now.

"Town's wards," Savage yelled back, the wind devouring his words. He slowed some. "You're safe now."

We rode for another fifteen minutes or so before any kind of town came into sight when we crested a ridge. It was late, but many lights sparkled in the village spread out below us. We were only partly down the ridge, though, when we turned off the road and began to climb again. This road was rougher, but Savage expertly maneuvered the bike around snow and ice patches. We turned off that road onto a gravel driveway that ran through the trees. It opened up, and we came to a stop in front of a log cabin that was way too big to call quaint or cozy. Not a mansion, by any means, but not a one-room rustic shack, either. Savage cut the engine and heaved out a loud grunt as he stood up, signaling for me to climb off before he set the bike on the kickstand.

"Where are we?" I asked as I dismounted.

"Home." He swung his leg over the bike and walked toward the front door.

I hurried after him, but stopped short and gasped when I entered. "Whose home?"

He paused and turned to look at me with the beginnings of a smirk. "Whose the fuck do you think?"

"This is *yours?*"

"Anyone ever tell you not to judge a book by its cover?" He bent over to untie his motorcycle boots.

I gaped, first at him, and then at the house.

The interior was cozier than I thought it would be from the outside, but still open and beautiful. Although the large leather sectional facing the wide, two-story stone fireplace, and the rest of the décor were all very manly, it definitely was not biker bachelor pad style. Still standing in front of the door, I faced a wall of windows looking out on trees and snow, some of the town lights below visible. I couldn't wait to see that view in the morning.

"We're staying here?" I asked.

"Yes." He said it so fast and so firmly, there was obviously no room for argument. Not that I wanted to. But someone did, because when his phone rang on his hip, he answered it with, "I brought her to my place." Pause. "The fuck she's staying at the clubhouse." Another pause as he kicked off his boots, then he turned to glare at me. His voice changed to something almost unrecognizable, almost sweet and way too formal, as he forced a smile. "Ms. Moreno, would you prefer to stay here or at the clubhouse?"

I didn't like it. His tone—it was unnatural and just didn't fit him —or the question.

My nose wrinkled of its own accord. "The clubhouse?"

"She's staying here, Peters," Savage growled, the sound more normal for him, and he ended the call. He leaned against the counter of the island that separated the kitchen from the living room, folded his arms over his chest, and surveyed me. Excitement rippled through my body, but he remained still and quiet, long enough that I began to question everything.

"Um . . . unless it's a bother for me to be here?" I asked, suddenly nervous. He was probably used to having his own space. Or, I considered for the first time, maybe he had an old lady, and I was an unwanted guest. I didn't see any evidence of a woman living here, but maybe she had a more masculine style. Or, with how the whole biker and old lady thing worked, maybe she didn't have a say in the décor at all. "I don't want to intrude."

"I wouldn't have brought you here if I didn't want you here."

"And your . . ." My question lingered on my tongue, because I didn't want to ask—to know. While my brain screamed reminders that he was a biker and I could never be with him, just the thought of him with someone else made me feel sick to my stomach with jealousy. "Uh . . . your old lady?"

He let out the closest thing to a laugh I'd heard from him yet. "No old lady."

I thought I saw another ghost of a smile before he quickly turned and headed for the fridge. He began pulling out the makings of a breakfast. The clock on the stove read 3:06. The witching hour.

"What did you mean by wards?" I asked, while watching him make breakfast.

"What?"

"You said something about the town's wards."

He grunted in acknowledgment. "The town's heavily warded, twenty-five miles out."

When he didn't continue, I had to push for more. "What does that mean?"

He glanced over his shoulder at me, then went back to placing bacon in a pan. "This place is different. It's magically protected by some powerful mages and other supes. You'll see soon enough. Just know you're safe."

I smiled. "Wow. Did you just say more than three sentences in a row? I wasn't sure you were capable."

He snorted. "I'm capable of many things, you'll soon learn."

And the tone in his voice, full of underlying promises, made my already sore thighs squeeze again.

I wasn't sure if he was a really good cook or if I was just that hungry for food that didn't come from a gas station, but I devoured the Southwestern-style breakfast he served. As soon as I swiped the last bit on my plate with a final bite of soft tortilla, exhaustion set in. My belly was full, and my eyelids felt just as heavy.

"I need a shower and a bed," I said on a contented sigh as I leaned back in the barstool.

Just finishing his own meal, Savage looked up at me, still wearing his sunglasses. I wondered if his gaze would hurt me. Usually only immortals and those extremely difficult to kill could tolerate looking into a hellhound's eyes more than two times. Kelpies weren't that strong—but I wasn't a typical kelpie. I wasn't sure how to test it, though, and I'd already been given my first look.

He cleared his throat as he stood, but he still sounded grumbly when he said, "Follow me."

We crossed the living room to a door near the back wall of windows. Through it was a short hallway that opened up to what must have been the master suite, with a bed that appeared larger than a king-size facing another wall of windows. There was a cold stone fireplace in the opposite corner and then more windows that stopped at another doorway. We rounded the bed and entered an impressive bathroom, with a huge bathtub in front of a large picture window. The décor was mostly wood and stone, the flooring a dark gray slate.

Savage threw open a door on the tower of cabinets that reached from floor to ceiling.

"Towels," he grunted, then he pointed at the stone and glass structure in the corner. "Shower."

"I think I figured that one out on my own," I joked. He didn't laugh.

"You're good then?" he asked as he headed back out the door.

I glanced around, about to nod, then something occurred to me.

"Wait." He turned back toward me, cocking his head expectantly. The direct attention caught me a little off guard. "Uh . . . I don't have any, uh, clothes. They were in the RV . . ." I let my voice trail off.

He frowned, then heaved out a breath before heading through another doorway off the bathroom, which appeared to be a closet.

"Here." He left two pieces of fabric on the vanity before striding out.

After closing the door, I leaned against it, closed my eyes, and blew out a breath. The effects of the long ride still hadn't worn off, which was a little disorienting—I was standing still, but felt like the world was still whizzing by. I forced myself to straighten up and peel off my clothes.

The shower was amazing—almost as good as my own at home. Well, my old place that I hadn't been able to live in for nearly a year. So this one felt like heaven, three different heads streaming water on me—one from the front, one from the back, and a rain head from above. Without my own toiletries, I had no choice but to use Savage's. I smiled when I noticed he had both shampoo and conditioner. The man liked to take care of those long, beautiful locks of his. Unfortunately, they weren't Curly Girl–approved, and they'd probably wreak havoc on my hair. I'd have to deal with that tomorrow. There was no way I was sleeping with road-greasy hair.

Once the shower washed away the dirt and grime and the heat relaxed my muscles, I stepped out, dried off, and lifted the two items of clothing he'd left for me. A rather large Metallica T-shirt and a pair of boxer shorts.

"You've got to be kidding me." Holding them out at arm's length, I inspected them carefully. I couldn't exactly go commando, but I wasn't about to wear a man's dirty underwear, either. Peering at them and sniffing from a distance, I realized they were brand new, right out of the package. They had that industrial smell to them, and the inspection sticker was still stuck to the waistband.

With a sigh, I pulled them on, and then the T-shirt. While the underwear smelled new, the shirt most definitely did not. It was clean, but Savage's scent clung to it. I hated how much I liked it. The hem brushed against my mid-thigh, making me feel small, something I rarely ever enjoyed.

I walked into the bedroom to find a fire crackling in the fireplace and Savage on the far side of the bed in nothing but boxers and those sunglasses. We both froze, staring at each other. His body was just as magnificent as I expected it to be. Godlike. Chiseled pecs, a mountain range of ab muscles, massive arms and shoulders, much of his tanned skin covered in ink . . . I swallowed as I broke the eye contact to avert my stare, heat creeping up my neck and cheeks.

As always, I could feel his gaze as a tangible caress even when I couldn't see it. His nostrils flared as it traveled down to my legs, lingering for a moment at the hem of the shirt before coming back up. He grabbed a pillow from the bed, holding it in front of him— but not quick enough for me to miss how the fabric at his crotch had begun to tent.

"I changed—" Savage cleared his throat, but the huskiness didn't leave his voice. "I changed the sheets for you. Just needed to grab a pillow."

My brows pinched together. "Isn't this your bed?"

"Not tonight, it isn't."

"I can take the guest room. I am the guest, after all."

"Don't have one."

I glanced around, bemused. "This big house doesn't have an extra room?"

"That's not what I said. I never have guests, so I don't have a guest room. I'll be on the couch." He turned for the short hallway and strode toward the door.

The bed looked so inviting to my weary body, I could cry. But . . . "You drove for more than twenty-four hours straight while I slept for some of that. This is your house. You take the bed. I can sleep on the couch," I called after him.

"Get in the fucking bed," he snarled before shutting the door behind him, hard enough to make me jump.

As exhausted as I was, sleep evaded me, and not for lack of comfort. The bed was perfectly firm, my head sunk into the mounds of pillows, and the sheets' thread count must have rivaled any luxury hotel, because they felt like silk against my skin. But even though they were clean, they still smelled like Savage, so much that I could taste him in the back of my throat. And that made my breasts tighten and my nipples harden, and every time I shifted to try to get comfortable enough to silence the need, the fabric of his shirt only aroused me more.

I couldn't stop thinking about what it would be like to be with him. He was all man. Big. Rugged. Dangerous. Completely opposite my type, which made him all the more intriguing. Was he into handcuffs, whips, and chains? I imagined his voice and his body were enough to make a girl comply, and imagining that led to envisioning his spectacular naked body towering over mine, his large hands assaulting me in all the right ways as he laid out one-word orders. Just how rough would he be? How badly would it hurt, and how much would I like it?

Though not my usual thing, I gave in to the surprising fantasy and my growing need, slipping my hand under the waistband of his boxers and sliding my finger through my wet folds. I gasped at the sensation and stroked again before finding my clit, circling and rubbing it until it swelled and throbbed. Sliding a finger inside, I brought myself to a quick but silent climax. Unfortunately, it felt hollow, doing little to satisfy the need throbbing through my body—need for something more than I could provide for myself. The need for him.

"Fuck," I heard Savage growl from the living room, and I wondered if he knew what I'd just done. In his bed. In his clothes.

He must have, probably picking up the scent, based on the tone of frustration that filled that one word. I rolled over and smiled as I closed my eyes. My life had spun out of control, but that single groan had sent a surge of power through me, making me feel like I could bring an outlaw named Savage to his knees—in front of my naked body. And that was more satisfying than my self-induced orgasm.

The feeling didn't last long, though. I was just drifting off into dreamland when reality crashed down on me all over again.

What the hell was I doing here? What was happening with my life? And why the hell did Pops have to die?

CHAPTER 4

$\mathcal{I}$ awoke to muted light filtering through the floor-to-ceiling windows and someone coming into the room. I quickly ensured all body parts were sufficiently covered before rolling over.

"It's me, love," came Niall's voice before his disfigured frame came into the shadowy room. "Thought you might like your things." He carried in all of my luggage, creating the lumpy silhouette.

"You're okay," I said. The last I'd seen or heard from him was when we left the wreck scene on his bike.

"I am. Not that you seemed too worried—haven't lost any sleep by it, anyway, considering it's two in the afternoon."

My gaze went to the windows, framing the snow-covered trees and gray sky beyond, all I could see from here without sitting up. "I'll have you know that it wasn't any darker than this when I finally fell asleep."

He came closer to the bed, inspecting me, it seemed, as his sapphire gaze roved over me, and his mustache lifted as he smiled. "I figured as much. You got your goods now. You all right, then?"

I pushed myself to sit up against the pillows. "Yeah, I suppose. What happened after we left? Is everyone okay? Were they the same ones who killed Pops?"

He sat on the edge of the bed and frowned as he rubbed and

pulled at his beard. "I'm afraid not, from what we could get out of the one faerie, anyway. The one Savage caught. He wasn't very forthcomin', but I'm thinkin' someone back in NOLA tipped 'em off. Only a few knew where we would be, too."

I sucked in a breath. He seemed to be implying that someone in the club gave us up. That was a serious violation of code.

"Pirate and Savage asked me to come to church this afternoon. We got a lot of shit to work out. You okay here?"

Glancing around, I easily nodded.

"Savage okay?"

I shrugged. "He's no Mr. Congeniality, but more of a gentleman than I expected." I lifted my hands and spread them to indicate the bed I sat in. "Case in point."

He patted my leg. "Good, because it's either here or the clubhouse for a while, until we're sure you're indeed safe in this town."

"You know my answer to that. If it's okay with my warden, of course."

He gave a lopsided smile. "This isn't a prison, love. His hellhound's protective instincts have kicked in. If you go to the clubhouse, I'm sure he'd stay there with you. Pirate had to give him a hell of a talkin' to just to get him to leave and come to church."

"Like I said, my warden." I returned his half grin. "I guess we'll both be more comfortable here."

Niall stood. "Just for a few days. When everything settles down and we know for sure their special wards are protecting you, he'll chill, and we can move you to the inn. Nice place, from what I hear."

"And how soon before I can leave? As in, go home?"

He blew out a breath as he stared out the window for a moment, then turned and left without answering me, except to say, "You'll be gettin' a visitor in about an hour for a tattoo. It's her wards protectin' the house and property, so if her arse makes it to the door, you'll know it's her."

"A tattoo?" I called out, but he'd already closed the door.

After hearing him and Savage leave the house, I swung my legs from under the covers and immediately wanted to crawl back into bed. *Good gods, it's cold here!* But the beautiful view drew me to the windows, and I nearly gasped as I looked out. No matter where I gazed, left to right and straight across, were mountains rising high above, their peaks and trees blanketed in snow. I couldn't remember the last time I'd even seen snow. It was a rare occurrence in New Orleans. I'd always wondered what it would be like to be in a winter wonderland, and it looked like I'd be finding out.

A deck ran along the back of Savage's log house, and beyond it was a small lawn that quickly gave way to forest and a sharp descent. In the distance below, the town spread out, some of it visible between the trees. Closer in was a creek and a cemetery—two actually, with a road dividing them. A human probably wouldn't be able to make out the creek, since it was mostly frozen over and covered in fresh snow, or the markers in the cemeteries, but I could. The closer one appeared to be more chaotic, more natural than the other on the far side of the road. This seemed to be the perfect view for a hellhound, protector of not just the living, but also the dead.

A shiver yanked me out of my reverie, and I hurried over to my suitcases to find some warm clothes. I didn't own any winter wear for the mountains, so a soft pink pair of jeans, a camel-colored cashmere sweater, and tan booties with a wedge heel would have to suffice. Just as I'd finished putting on makeup and doing my best to manage my dark curls, feeling more like myself than I had since before Pops died, the doorbell rang—at least, that's what I finally discovered was the cause for what sounded like hounds howling and baying.

A young woman about my age with long light-brown hair trailing out from a slouchy beanie hat, glasses, and a crystal piercing in her nose stood on the other side of the door, a messenger bag slung over her black puffy coat.

"Reyna?" she asked before jutting out her hand. "Addie Beaumont. I've come to register you and ink you up."

I stared at her without extending my own hand, and her brows pinched together.

"They warned you that I was coming, right? I know you're in danger and all, from what I've been told, but I put up the protective wards on this house myself. Trust me—they work. Only certain people can pass through." She tilted her head. "Of course, I guess someone nefarious would make sure they could pass through, huh? Well, I guess you'll just have to trust me." She smiled, still holding her hand out.

I didn't know her from a faerie queen, but she gave off a positive —and powerful—energy. So after another moment's hesitation, I reached out and shook her hand. As soon as we touched, Addie's brown eyes grew wide behind her glasses, and she audibly gasped.

"Whoa," she breathed, still holding on to my hand. "I didn't realize just *how* dangerous of a situation this is. Savage didn't tell me everything. Does he know?"

"Know what?" I asked as I withdrew my hand from hers.

"What you are." She pushed by me, closing the door behind her, but still, her voice dropped to a whisper. "You're a unicorn."

I stepped back. "How did you know?"

She lifted a shoulder in a shrug. "That's my thing, but when I register you, your blood will verify it. Won't it?"

She entered the home as if she was familiar with it and went over to the kitchen island. Shrugging out of her puffy coat, she revealed a hoodie that said *Coexist* but not with the normal religious symbols I'd seen in other, similar designs. The letters seemed to be created by different types of supernatural creatures. Her sleeves were partially pushed up by all the bracelets she wore, and as they swayed with her movement, colorful ink was revealed on her skin underneath.

"Savage said you were a kelpie," she continued as she unloaded some items from her bag onto the granite counter. "I wonder why he lied to me."

"It's not a lie," I said. "I am kelpie."

Her eyes narrowed at me. She didn't believe me.

"I'll find out soon enough." She gestured at one of the barstools. "Have a seat."

"What exactly are we doing?"

Looking up at me, she paused, took a deep breath, and unloaded as though she'd said it a thousand times before. "Our town was specifically founded as a safe haven for the supernatural. A place where all species, including humans, can reside together under secrecy and protection from those who'd like to exploit us. We're able to do this by special protective wards around the town and its outlying areas. We register all supernaturals, residents and visitors alike, so we know who's coming and going—and who's creating problems, especially with the humans. We have two main rules: protect the secret of the supernatural and don't kill humans. Do you have a problem with that?"

I shook my head as I eyed the gun and ink she placed on the counter. "No, but what do tattoos have to do with it?"

"We learned nearly a century ago that it's the best way to ensure we can track the supernaturals, since our ink is impossible to remove. Not even traditional methods of tattoo removal work. Of course, if you leave town, it becomes invisible, and you forget about it, along with everything you know about the town and the people here."

"I'm sorry. I'm still stuck on the 'tracking' part." I really had come to another prison, hadn't I? How long until I could escape?

Addie let out a small laugh. "Yeah, a lot of people get hung up on that part, but it's not what it sounds like. The ink in the tats works with the wards. We only pay attention if there's trouble. If a supernatural energy passes through the wards, everyone in my coven feels a blip. Usually, we ignore it. If it's a threatening energy or trouble ensues after its arrival, though, we know the first place to start looking. Unless you plan on creating problems for us, you have nothing to worry about. We won't even notice you're here."

I gnawed on my lip. "But you would know if someone else, especially the nefarious, as you say, passed through the wards?"

She nodded and smiled. "Sure would. I'm surprised they didn't tell you all this already. I thought it was why they brought you to Havenwood Falls—for the protection we can provide that nobody else can. Especially now that I know what you are."

"They didn't give such a detailed explanation. So the tattoo isn't optional?" It wasn't as though I had anything against ink—in fact, I thought many tattoos were downright beautiful pieces of art—but I'd yet to get one on myself.

"I can make the ink invisible, but no, it's not optional. That's how the magic is infused."

I blew out a breath before finally taking the seat she'd gestured at minutes ago.

"You think about what you want and where, while I do the registry part." She picked up my hand, and with no warning, pricked my finger with a tiny pin. I hadn't even seen her remove it from the package now lying on the countertop. She pressed my finger to a parchment page in a leather-bound book, and writing began to appear. She closed the book before I could read it, and looked at me with a knowing grin. "I was right, of course. About what you are. But so are you. You're a crossbreed?"

"I don't know the history well enough," I admitted. "I'm the only unicorn of our kind—of the kelpie. Every several generations, one of us grows a horn, but whatever the reason for it, it must have been lost somewhere along the way. I happen to be the one this time around."

She studied me, as though trying to ascertain the story from somewhere on my face, then she shrugged. "It just doesn't make sense that Savage didn't say anything about the unicorn part. It's not like I wouldn't find out, and I could have come better prepared."

"Honestly, I'm not sure he knows. I'm just a job—a thing to protect under orders of his president and as a favor to my brother. And, well, now because his instincts have kicked in, and I'm his charge. Nothing more, though. I don't think he really cares what, exactly, I am."

She rolled her eyes. "Hmph, sounds like him. So what do you want and where? Something with a unicorn?" She laughed when I wrinkled my nose and shook my head. "It wouldn't have to be too girly."

"I think Niall would kill me. Even if nobody saw it, it'd still feel like a billboard of what I am."

Her head tilted slightly to the side. "You don't like being a unicorn."

It wasn't a question, and her directness made me squirm.

"I don't like what it means. How it's affected my life," I murmured.

"I can imagine it hasn't been easy. Good thing you're here now. Do you have family?"

My throat tightened, and I stared at my hands, breathing deeply as I suffocated the desire to cry. "Just Niall now."

Her hand landed on mine and squeezed. A warm energy passed from her to me. "At least you have him, though, right?"

I lifted my eyes and forced a small smile. "Yeah, thank gods. But he's not blood. My parents, my only blood, sacrificed themselves for me years ago. Pops, who finished raising me, died last week, but his killers had been after me." Blinking rapidly, I sniffed and took another calming breath. "And now . . . I've lost my independence and any kind of freedom to live my life on my terms."

Realizing I'd shared entirely too much, I smacked my mouth closed and looked away.

"So, Niall's the one with the sexy accent?" Addie asked, her tone teasing and lifting the mood. Relief flooded through me. I knew she'd heard the rest, but she'd chosen to focus on the least uncomfortable part of my diatribe. Well, she probably thought it was the least.

My nose wrinkled. "He's like a brother to me. But yes, the one with the Scottish accent. And I guess if he was anyone else, it'd be sexy."

She smiled, and I knew we'd moved past that dark, awkward moment. "Okay, back to business. What tattoo do you want? Maybe a lotus to honor your kelpie?"

My breath catching, I returned her grin with one of my own. The answer came quickly, but not easily or lightly. In fact, I'd been considering a tattoo for a long time. I'd refused for years, because I'd been stubborn and stupid in believing it'd make me too much like the skanks who hung around the MC, screwing whichever brother happened to show interest that day—or could offer the best high. After seeing some incredible artwork on beautiful and professional women, though, including some of the models of my lingerie, I'd started fantasizing about a couple of designs and styles I really liked. I'd just never wanted it badly enough to force myself to choose which one and actually get it done.

"Hold on." I hopped off the stool and rushed for the bedroom. Fishing my laptop out of a suitcase, I opened it as I walked back into the great room, glad to see that the outside, at least, had survived the crash and the trip here. Pressing the power button, I said a prayer to the gods that the inside survived, as well. Thankfully, it had, and within a few moments, I was able to show Addie some of the pictures I'd saved. "Would you be willing to do one of those?"

"Wow, they're amazing. I have a garter one kind of like that." She pointed to the image of a woman's leg with a tattoo of a lacy garter wrapping around her upper thigh, just under her butt, ribbons hanging down the side and front. "Mine has a wand in it, though, like it's a holster." She gave me a toothy grin. "So which one do you want? Here's your lotus." She tapped on the screen.

The water flower really was perfect for my kelpie and my heritage. I described to her the extras I wanted, to honor my parents and Pops —and, in a way, my people. She drew it out on a sketch pad, making adjustments as I talked. When she added in a little extra touch, I realized that it, too, honored those who had sacrificed their lives for me. A little acknowledgment to show that they hadn't died in vain.

"It's unbelievably perfect. You're sure you don't mind?" I asked.

She waved her hand, dismissing my concern. "I've done tattoos on pretty much all body parts, both male and female. This is nothing. Just be ready, because the next day or so is going to be fucking miserable."

"I hadn't thought of that." I shrugged. "Well, it's not like I can go anywhere in public anyway for a while. I'll just be hanging out at the house, and if Savage sees . . . well, I'm not sure if I'd mind that anyway." I clapped my hand over my mouth, wishing I could take that back. Now it was Addie's turn to wrinkle her nose. "You don't like him?"

Her face took on a greenish tint, and she looked like she was trying to suppress a shudder. "Not in that way. But hey, each to her own. I like you, and maybe you'd be good for him. I'm just not sure I can picture you two together."

"Honestly, neither can I."

"But?" This girl was way too intuitive. That's a witch for you.

"But . . . I can't *stop* picturing it either." *Damn it, Rey. Shut the hell up already.* I covered my mouth again, unsure of where all this candidness was coming from. It so wasn't like me. I blamed the witch. She was too easy to talk to.

Once again showing that she could easily read me—or maybe for her own reasons—she quickly changed the subject. "We should probably go somewhere more private than out here. In case he comes home—and possibly not alone."

I glanced around, unfamiliar with most of the house. "Will the bed be okay?"

"Not ideal, but it'll work." She gathered her tools and followed me into Savage's bedroom. "Or that chaise longue would be better."

She pointed across the room. I hadn't even noticed it in the corner, wedged between the fireplace and the windows. I'd been too enamored with the view outside, I supposed.

While Addie hunted for outlets and moved the long chair for better lighting and accessibility, I turned my back and removed the necessary clothing before lying on the chaise, shyly covering myself with my hands as much as I could.

Addie lifted a brow when she saw me. "Please don't feel like you need to be modest for my sake. Like I said, I've seen a lot—and rarely as nice as this."

Heat crept up my neck and cheeks, and I held my position for a while as she began, but at some point, the discomfort of my arms and the increased ease of being with this woman I'd just met an hour ago won out. My hands fell away, and I sighed as blood flowed back into them.

"You know, you can have that freedom and independence you want here in Havenwood Falls," Addie said as she worked.

I stared outside at the scene of snow and evergreens, catching the pounce of a small fox hunting for food, the snow spraying up around him as his face plunged into the white stuff. "Here? In the middle of nowhere?"

"Well, there are benefits to being in the middle of nowhere, especially this place." She continued on for a while, selling her little town as the best town anywhere on earth, as though she hoped I'd buy a house tomorrow and bring all my tax dollars. I could hear the sincerity in her tone, though—she really believed this *was* the best town.

"I don't think this place is exactly my style. I'm a city girl. But even if you're right, I doubt Niall and the hellhounds will let me out of this prison for a while."

"I think you'll be surprised. They called me over here immediately for a reason, and not only because it's town law for you to be registered in the first forty-eight hours. The MC isn't exactly known for abiding by the law, you know, but Savage and Liam know what I can do for you, and they'll convince Niall."

"Liam?"

"The other hellhound. President of SIN?"

"You mean Pirate?"

"Ah." She nodded. "I guess that's how you'd know him, by his road name. He's always been Liam Peters to me."

"So what *are* you doing for me, Addie?" I asked.

She paused and looked up at me with that winning smile. "Like I said, giving you your freedom."

Another hour passed before Addie started doing the cleanup work, gingerly wiping at me with a cloth. I could see pink tinge her cheeks while heat flooded mine at her touch. Then she placed her hand over the artwork and closed her eyes. Her lips moved with some kind of utterance, and at the same time, a warm energy flowed into me, twisting and curling through the fresh ink.

"Done," she announced. "You are not only registered with the wards, but I gave it a little something extra to help keep you protected. Your freedom, so to speak. As well as something for you and Savage. It could make life easier if you'll be staying here at his house." She explained further as she stood and arched her back in a stretch. "Well, are you going to go check it out?"

Forgetting all modesty, I scrambled to my feet and hurried to the bathroom. My jaw dropped when I saw myself in the mirror. I was so impressed with the artwork and the overall effect, I didn't even cover myself when Addie came in.

"Do you like it?" she asked.

"I, uh, flipping *love* it!"

She laughed. "You really have a great rack, you know, but now it's just sexy as fuck. And I don't even like girls."

My turn to laugh as I twisted and turned to study the design from all angles. A large lotus covered my sternum, the tip of the top petal twisting into a unicorn horn that rose up between my breasts and ended with a fleur de lis. Scalloped lace and chains with dangling charms arced underneath each breast, framing them perfectly, the longest piece hanging down the center to end a couple of inches above my navel. I couldn't stop staring at it, which wasn't really like me. And I couldn't stop thinking about Savage staring at it—and tracing the lines with his fingers . . . his tongue—which seriously wasn't like me.

What the hell was going on with me? Was it this place—or that man—making me so crazy?

At least there was one thought to hang on to: I didn't plan for either to be lasting in my life.

CHAPTER 5

*N*ot that Addie hadn't done a terrific job of selling Havenwood Falls to me. And the scene from Savage's windows was picture-postcard perfect. It just wasn't New Orleans. It wasn't home.

I loved to travel, though I rarely ever got to. This was the kind of place I'd love to visit and spend a little time exploring. And that's all I'd be doing—visiting, exploring, then leaving.

If Niall and the hellhound ever let me.

Speaking of, they walked in just as Addie was leaving. Niall handed me a box with a new phone in it.

"Accounts have already been set up so they can't be traced, so don't go connecting to your old ones," he warned. "My number is in there, and so is Savage's. Both on autodial. Now, you wanna go shopping?"

"Shopping?" I echoed with surprise.

"You need some winter clothes, love. At least boots and a coat, because what you have on—you'll freeze your arse off here." He eyed my outfit. "Unless you plan on staying in the house all the time?"

I blinked, still in shock. I actually had planned on staying in the house because I didn't think they'd let me go anywhere. "It's safe?"

"Addie inked you, eh?" Niall scanned me again, looking for my tattoo. "You're not goin' to show me?"

"Uh, that's a big negative," I said, a little too quickly. He picked up on my meaning, and so, apparently, did Savage, because he suddenly looked up from the mail in his hand with interest. Why did that cause tingles to run along my skin?

"My little Rey got a little crazy, eh?" Niall grinned, and I denied him an answer.

We piled into the only vehicle in the garage that wasn't a motorcycle—a shiny black Cadillac SUV. The rough biker continued to surprise me. He drove us into town with Niall in the front passenger seat. I looked out the back window as we descended the mountain and turned onto a main road that took us right into downtown Havenwood Falls. We passed a high school on the left, and on the right, a burger joint with a neon sign reading *Burger Bar* that looked like it was stuck in the fifties. A shopping plaza sprawled behind it. Looking down the side streets as we passed, the residences appeared to be an eclectic mixture of everything from old Victorians to modern cement-and-glass structures, with plenty of bungalows and log cabins sprinkled in. Ski lifts climbed up the mountain to our right with several cleared trails and slopes coming back down.

Cute town, just as Addie had made it out to be.

When we rolled in to what was obviously the town's central business district, I sat up a little straighter. As though giving a grand, though silent, tour, Savage drove all the way around the square, past quaint little stores and coffee shops. The area reminded me of a small version of Jackson Square Park back home, except where St. Louis Cathedral sat in New Orleans was a building with a clock tower and *City Hall* embossed into one of the stones. The center square was a park-like setting with a fountain in the center and even a gazebo decorated with twinkle lights. Twilight was quickly descending, so everything was lit up, and talk about picture-postcard perfect. It was like a town straight out of the movies—one of those cheesy Hallmark holiday ones, considering everything was blanketed in fresh snow. Those movies may or may not have been a guilty pleasure over the holidays.

Savage parked in front of a place called Backwoods Sport & Ski.

Seriously? Did I look like the type for this place? When we walked in, the guys flanking me, everyone turned to look at us, then scattered. Except for a young girl who stayed at the cash register, eyeing us. Her nametag said Willa. She smelled like a wolf.

"Let me guess, you need bike gear?" she asked as she came out from behind the counter, her gaze bouncing to the bikers right behind me before landing back on my face.

"Um, no." I glanced over at their women's clothing section, which was definitely not what I was accustomed to—the small selection or the styles. "I guess just a coat and boots."

"Cross country or downhill?" she asked.

"Not ski boots," Savage rumbled. "Walking."

She seemed to shrink a little at his gruff voice, and I wished I could elbow him in the ribs. Up until that moment, she'd given off a more confident air than normal for her age—the air of a leader. He didn't need to be knocking her down. Being a teenage girl was hard enough, especially in the supe world.

"Well, we have, uh, some good hiking boots." She led me over to the shoe section, and eventually I found a pair of boots that would keep my feet warm and weren't completely hideous. In fact, they were somewhat fashionable—if this look was your thing. It wasn't mine.

We then looked at coats, hoodies, pants, and socks. Niall and Savage never strayed more than five feet from me, scaring off anyone who tried to come close simply by their overbearing presence. Except for Willa, bless her heart. She hung right in there, helping me find the cutest things they had to offer. I left with a bag of clothes I'd never be seen in again once I left town, but I threw the coat on right away and sighed from its warmth.

"Did you lose your love for shopping?" asked Niall, who was used to me leaving stores with multiple bags.

"Not exactly my kind of place."

"Ah. Well, you can do your online thing then. You'll need more than what you have there."

I nodded, but wasn't too worried about it. I had enough to get by for a few days of lounging around the house and maybe taking a walk in the woods. And surely they had washing machines in this town.

"Try Callie's," Savage said, lifting his bearded chin toward the line of buildings perpendicular from the one where we were parked. "Looks like she's still open. Might not be much longer."

Niall put my bag in the SUV, then we made our way over there, passing by a jewelry store on the corner before crossing the street diagonally. Then we passed a bar with old-fashioned swinging doors marked *Haven Saloon*, a bookstore called Shelf Indulgence with an elaborate wintry display in the window, and a coffee shop with a sign that said *Coffee Haven*, which was closed for the day.

"You got five minutes, and then I'm closing," a voice called out when we entered the store marked *Callie's Consignments*.

It was an eclectic sort of place, expansive and filled with a variety of vintage-looking clothes. Still not my style, but I was drawn in anyway by all the colors and textures. Someone here had an obvious talent for merchandising and an eye for design. I looked up a staircase to a second floor, catching glimpses of old but stylish furniture beyond the railings.

"I'm serious. I'm already here later than I'd planned." The owner of the sassy voice appeared from behind a display of dresses, her hazel eyes going wide when she looked over my shoulder, where the two burly men in their leather cuts stood. "Oh, uh, well." She broke her gaze from them to land on me and stuck out a hand while plastering on a fake smile. "Callie Montgomery. Sorry. I, uh, just wasn't expecting . . . customers."

She meant customers like us. Well, like the two outlaws who refused to leave my side.

I shook her hand, showing that I was civil, even if they weren't. "Reyna. And we won't stay. I love your store, so I had to sneak a peek, but I can come back another time."

She waved an arm, her many bracelets clinking together as she did, reminding me of Addie. While both gave off a hippie-like aura, the witchy tattooist's style was a little different than this girl's. Although I'd only met her once, I sensed that Addie's all-black wardrobe was common for her, dressed up only with jewelry, all of the metaphysical kind. This woman was more colorful and feminine, dressed in a gauzy top and long skirt, decorated with colorful scarves and jewelry.

She flipped her hand in the air. "You're here. I'm here. You may as well look around. Anything you're looking for in particular?" Her gaze scanned over my puffy ski jacket and the rest of my much nicer outfit. "Maybe a coat?"

I chuckled. "It's not that ugly, is it?"

Callie cringed. "Well . . . it just doesn't seem like you. Come. Follow me."

I didn't have the heart to tell her that there was probably nothing here that was me, either. Instead, I followed her toward the back of the store, Savage and Niall on my heels, to a rack of leather coats. She flipped through them, then pulled a dark brown one off and displayed it with a swoosh of her hand. I stared, no words forming.

"Right?" she said with a twinkle in her eyes. "Feel it."

As though compelled, my hand reached out and petted the soft leather. "Wow."

"Go on. Try it on." She thrust it into my hand.

The skin under my breasts was already sore, but I gritted my teeth as I shrugged off the ski jacket and pulled this one on. Callie led me over to a three-way mirror.

"It's meant to be yours!" she declared. "I don't think it would fit anyone more perfectly."

I glanced at her reflection, but didn't see a hint of cruelty or teasing in her expression or hear it in her voice. I didn't exactly have an off-the-rack body type. Rarely did anything fit me perfectly unless it had been custom made for me—the whole reason I went into clothing design myself. But this wasn't off the rack. It was vintage and unique, the cut just right to emphasize my breasts and diminish my waist while flaring out over my round hips and ass. The hem hit my knees, giving me plenty of butt protection from the cold.

"I have some boots that came in with it. They're not exactly for hiking or anything, but a little more practical than those heels, when it gets icy." She took my hand and pulled me over to the shoe section, picking out a pair of knee-high, low-heeled boots. "Size ten?"

My size, but again, I hesitated, knowing my calves were usually too large for standard-sized tall boots. But again, I was surprised. They fit just as well as the coat did, like they were made for me. Shrugging off the coat, I gave myself another look in the mirror for a better look and caught Savage's reflection. Though his eyes were forever hidden by the shades, I again felt the weight of his gaze on me. I felt my eyes lock with his, holding for a long moment as his tongue swiped over his lips. I mirrored the gesture, and he made that growly rumbling sound before turning away. There was something feral yet empowering about his response. I smiled to myself, butterflies taking off in my belly.

"Feel free to look around," Callie offered. "Between us, I wasn't really in a huge hurry to leave anyway, now that I know you're not one of the broke-ass teens who only come to try on every item on the rack while giggling over boys, only to leave empty-handed."

She left me alone. Well, not really alone. I tried to browse the shop—there was so much to see, a surprise around every corner—but the guys continued hovering, making it difficult to relax. One other woman entered the store, looked at the three of us, and turned right back around before Callie could even welcome her. Between that and my clothing rubbing against my freshly inked skin, I'd had enough. I was already headed for the counter when the door chimed again.

"Savage!" a familiar voice barked out. We all looked at Addie standing there, her brow raised high into her beanie hat and her hands on her hips. "Outside. Now."

"Oh, shit," Callie muttered with a chuckle.

To my surprise, Savage gave a soundless nod to Niall, then obediently strode outside, his booted steps heavy on the carpeted floor.

"She's about the only person who could get away with that," Callie whispered as I placed my items on the counter to make my purchase.

"Are they . . . ?" I didn't know how to finish my thought, not sure what I was asking or what I wanted to know.

"Their history is . . . weird. But that's all I'm saying." Callie quickly busied herself by ringing up my two items.

Niall came up next to me, pulling his wallet out, since I couldn't use any of my cards. While he and Callie handled the transaction, I watched out the window as Addie seemed to be giving Savage a piece of her mind. She did all the talking, throwing her arms up animatedly, gesturing toward the store—toward me, no doubt—more than once. What the hell? She'd acted like she wanted nothing to do with him, but now seemed to be . . . jealous? I wasn't sure if that was the right word, but she was definitely angry about something. Even with my supernatural hearing, I couldn't catch any of their words, and I wondered if she'd used a muffling spell. After another moment, she stomped off, leaving Savage outside, standing in front of the door. His back was to us, so I couldn't read his expression.

"You didn't need to rush for me," he said gruffly when we exited the store.

"Uh, I was done in there," I said, confused by his tone and meaning.

"Where now, then? All the shops will be closing soon."

"Actually, I'm good." My stomach rumbled at that moment. "Well, I'm starving. I haven't eaten all day. But I've had enough shopping."

I wasn't sure there were too many more places to go anyway, and what was the fun in discovering the whole town within a couple of hours?

"We'll take Napoli's home," Savage said, then waved me in the direction of the car. "This way."

This time, as we walked toward the vehicle, Savage seemed to be keeping a lot more space between us. He wasn't breathing down my back like he had been earlier. I hadn't minded too much, because he was warm, and I wasn't used to these freezing temperatures that were plummeting even more now that night had fallen. Addie must have really gotten to him. I liked her and didn't want to create an enemy—

especially after seeing the man named Savage, the man I'd witnessed nearly kill a fae without a bat of an eye, submit to her so easily. So I'd keep my distance, too.

Savage must have remotely started the car, because it was nice and toasty when I slid into the back seat. He and Niall exchanged a few words before he sauntered off farther down the block and rounded the corner. After taking off his cut, Niall climbed into the front seat.

"You sure you'll be all right with him tonight?" he asked, turning in his seat to face me. "I need to get back to the clubhouse and see if they were able to find out anything. They got this guy, Axle, who's magic on the dark web. Should be able to find any intel on our attackers."

I shrugged. "I have a feeling I'll be entertaining myself, but I'm sure I'll be fine."

"Good. I'll be able to breathe easier once I know we can take care of those guys. With your trail cold, you should be good for a while."

"And when can I go home?"

Niall didn't answer, his gaze dropping.

"Niall?" I pressed.

He sighed and looked out the window, toward the lit-up ski slopes. "Why don't you just enjoy yourself, love? This place has a lot to offer."

I snorted. "You've been here one day, and you already sound like Addie."

"Turns out, I've been here before. I'd forgotten about it, after I left, but my memories are coming back now. That's how their wards work. I'd been trying to get Pops to move you here a while ago, but you refused to leave New Orleans." He stopped there, but I inferred the rest. Staying in NOLA had gotten Pops killed.

I turned to look out the window myself, not wanting to think about that, and was glad to see Savage striding down the sidewalk with two big bags in his hands. When he opened the back door and set them on the floor, my mouth immediately watered at the fragrances of cheese, tomatoes, and garlic.

We left the town square area by a different street than we'd entered, passing by a majestic Victorian structure with a wooden sign in the lawn that said Whisper Falls Inn. A couple of blocks down, we entered a sort of industrial area with warehouses. We pulled into a parking lot between one such warehouse and a brick building with the SIN logo over the door. Niall said his goodbyes and slid out, leaving me in the back seat and Savage in the front.

"Hey! What the hell are you doing?" Savage growled when I opened my door. He jumped out of the car as I slid out and rushed over to my side.

"You don't exactly have the right demeanor to be a chauffeur," I said as I reached for the handle of the front passenger door. With a harsh exhale that bloomed out in a fog, he grabbed it first and opened the door for me.

We rode in silence for several minutes, leaving the main part of town behind and passing by the high school again, this time on the right.

"How does it all work—the wards and everything?" I asked, trying to strike up a conversation. "I understand that the magic-infused ink works with them, but Niall said he's been here before but had forgotten about it because of the wards."

"Visitors lose their memories as soon as they pass through them. Remember when you felt us enter the wards?"

I nodded. "So what? Your memories get wiped when you leave?"

"Right away for visitors. Residents get a lunar cycle, but we can't talk about Havenwood Falls or the people here. The magic fucks with us, tying up our tongues or making us forget what we were saying if we try to share too much."

I watched the snowy night pass by. "So as soon as I leave, I'll forget all about this place and everyone I've met."

He was quiet for a long moment. "Yeah, you will."

We drove the rest of the way in more silence. Not until we were seated at the kitchen island with a spread of pasta and bread did we talk again.

"I wasn't sure what you like," Savage said, "so I got a variety. Assuming you're not one of those salad-only girls."

I gave him a sideways glance. Did I look like a salads-only girl? Not that it mattered. Even if I was, I was just big-boned and would never be considered petite. Perhaps because I was part horse.

"I think I need to try everything." Smiling, I doled out a spoonful of chicken alfredo, another of lasagna, and grabbed one each of garlic knots and fried mozzarella. "So I'm still trying to understand. How do you get supplies and inventory for the stores if nobody knows where this town is to deliver to?"

He swallowed the big bite of pasta he'd already taken. "CDI takes care of all the deliveries in and shipments out. Cerberus Delivery, Inc. —my and Liam's business. Our guys drive and escort the trucks. It's the legit side of the club."

"Legit?" I asked with a raised brow and a smirk.

He shrugged. "As close to legit as we get."

"So there's no smuggling or anything going on . . ."

"You're here, aren't you?" And though I could barely see his eyes behind the darkly tinted glasses, I swore he winked at me.

"What else do you smuggle? What other kinds of jobs do you take?"

He stood and carried his plate to the sink. "Sweetheart, you're much more than a job."

He said no more, avoiding my question as he dropped his plate and fork into the dishwasher.

"I'm going out to get some wood," were his only other words before he disappeared down the hall that led to the part of the house I hadn't been shown yet.

I cleaned my own dishes and put the leftovers in the refrigerator, but Savage hadn't returned, so I slipped into the bedroom, planning to retire for the night. I needed to remove my bra, the friction against my tattoo driving me insane. Shutting the door behind me, I stripped off my top and bra, dropping them on my suitcase and sighing with relief as I walked into the bathroom. My own image in the mirror stopped me, the dark ink on my golden brown skin looking even prettier than it had earlier, now that it was no longer red and raised. I could see where my bra had been bothering it, but my own healing properties had taken away the worst of the sting already. Opening the little jar of salve Addie had left on the bathroom counter for me, I rubbed it on.

"Oh, gods . . . yes," I moaned, the ointment immediately relieving the irritation—and realizing a moment too late that the little sound I'd heard was a soft knock on the bedroom door. Ointment in one palm and my other hand cupping under my bare breast, I turned at the movement in the corner of my eye to find Savage standing in the bedroom staring at me, the logs in his arms rolling to the floor with a loud clatter.

We both stood frozen, just staring at each other for a long moment. Long enough for my boobs to tighten and my nipples to harden—and for him to shift his hips as a very noticeable bulge twitched in his jeans.

"I thought you meant yes as in *enter*," he accused, his voice thick and his gaze still weighing heavy on my chest.

Coming to my senses, I spun around and grabbed a towel to cover myself since my shirt was on the other side of the bed—past Savage.

"Uh, yeah, um, completely my fault," I stammered. Sufficiently covered, I turned back around to find him picking up the wood.

"I thought you'd want a fire. And I need workout clothes."

"Okay." I still stood just inside the bathroom like a deer in headlights. My breasts swelled painfully under my arm as he quickly built the fire, an obvious expert at it. Then he stood and moved to the bathroom door. "What are you doing?" I squeaked.

"My closet is through there." He gestured, though I already knew that.

"Oh, uh, right." My brain focused on trying to escape the bathroom and nothing else, I moved forward instead of backward and out of his way, and at the same time, he stepped in. We bumped into each other, and my towel shifted. His arm brushed across my exposed breast, and we both froze again. That one soft touch sent my heart racing even faster than it had been and made my stomach flip over. Wet need pooled between my legs at the same time he inhaled deeply.

"Fuck, woman, you're going to kill me," he growled without

looking over at me. Then he murmured so quietly, he probably didn't think I'd hear, "The things I want to do to you . . ."

My breath caught.

"Are you able to?" I asked, sudden boldness coming from somewhere unknown.

He looked over his shoulder, his brows drawn together. "What the fuck does that mean?"

"Well, are you . . . free?"

"I don't have a woman, if that's what you mean."

I nodded, and we continued to stare at each other.

"So . . . how about we just get the fuck part over with?" I blurted, my brain apparently having gone into shutdown mode.

A low rumble sounded deep in his throat, before he turned his whole body toward me and advanced until I was pressed up against the door jamb. His hands cupped the sides of my face as he came in even closer, my arm between us, trying to hold the towel somewhat in place. I could feel his eyes piercing into mine.

"Is that what you really want?" he growled.

I stared up at him. "Don't you?"

He shifted his hips forward, offering me his answer by grinding his erection against my belly. I let go of the towel to give him mine.

CHAPTER 6

$\mathcal{H}$e leaned in, his lips parting, but first, I stopped him by reaching up for the sunglasses.

"You can't," he snarled.

"It's okay. I'm safe from your death glare."

I slid the sunglasses off and stared up into beautiful hazel eyes framed with long dark lashes. They were filled with apprehension at first, but then a hunger I'd never seen in a man's eyes before—at least, not while looking at me. He wanted me at least as badly as I wanted him. In fact, maybe even more, the way his whole body vibrated as we looked into each other's eyes, a soft orange glowing in the depths of his. Okay, safe might not have been the best word, but his gaze wasn't going to actually kill me. Send me into cardiac arrest, maybe, from that lascivious way he watched me, but not make me drop dead.

"Fuck," he muttered, his lids dropping. "This is a bad idea."

"It is."

He nodded, opening his eyes again, staring right into mine. "I don't think I can stop, though."

"Then don't." I grasped his face like he had mine and pulled him to me, our mouths crashing together.

Our lips moved as though we'd both been starving for this, our tongues immediately finding each other as if they were long lost

295

mates. He tasted like he smelled—of oak and fire and whiskey. His beard rubbed roughly against my skin, the abrasion turning me on even more. His hands slid down my shoulders, finding my breasts and squeezing. I groaned, and then gasped when he pinched and rolled my nipples. Then he palmed his way down my sides, his fingers lightly brushing over my ribs, careful to avoid the tattoo. Sliding his hands to my ass, he lifted me up, and I wrapped my legs around him, grinding against his bulge as he carried me into the bedroom. He groaned into my mouth before dropping me to the bed.

Standing over me, he pulled his shirt off, exposing the perfection of his torso I'd seen last night. The man could seriously play a god in a movie —Adonis had nothing on him, was barely more than a boy compared to Savage. His gaze traveled to my breasts as his hands undid his buckle. Watching him, I played with my nipples as my tongue darted over my lips.

He groaned and then commanded, "Take your fucking clothes off, woman."

"You take them off," I countered.

He lifted one of those sharp brows, and I wondered if anyone had ever challenged him in this way before. Part of me wanted to obey everything he said as long as it meant his cock would be inside me soon, but another part couldn't help but do the opposite.

In one quick motion, he grabbed me at the waist and lifted me to stand on the bed in front of him. Even as tall as I was, I still barely looked down at him.

"I said to take your fucking clothes off." His hand jerked at my waistband, somehow undoing the button and the zipper without ripping a single thread.

I grabbed his hands and placed them on my hips, sliding them underneath the straps of my panties. "And I said for you to do it."

Together we pushed my jeans and panties down at once, and I stepped out of them at the same time he stepped out of his. I kicked mine off to the side, off the bed. His gaze raked over me, a certain carnality in it that made my legs weak. Well, that and his enormous cock standing tall and thick.

"God damn, you're fucking gorgeous."

"So are you," I breathed as his mouth clamped onto one of my breasts, drawing it in as his hand played with the other. My fingers slid into his long locks, grasping his head as my back arched, thrusting my breast farther into his mouth. His tongue circled the hard pebble of my nipple, then his teeth grazed over it, biting just hard enough to feel good.

He pulled away too soon, panting, his breath hot on my already burning skin.

"Turn around," he ordered.

I cocked a brow, but then made the decision to obey, if for no other reason, to see where it would go. Besides, I was too wet and needy to argue. I turned on the bed and looked over my shoulder. His hand lifted, sweeping my curls to the side. He grasped my shoulder while his other hand lightly brushed down my spine, sending chills over my skin. As his fingers reached the small of my back, the hand on my shoulder pushed me forward.

"On your hands and knees," he said, his voice mesmerizing, authoritative, giving me no choice but to obey.

I knew exactly the view in front of him now, and just the thought of it made my core clench. I should have felt embarrassed, my ass and pussy on full display for him, but I didn't. All of my inhibitions I'd always carried into my few previous sexual encounters suddenly fell away. He did that to me. I'd known him for two whole days, but he already made me feel safer and more comfortable than anyone I'd ever dated.

"Fucking gorgeous," he muttered again, and maybe that was why. He appreciated my body, soft, luscious curves and all, where most men were intimidated or worse—rudely critical.

He leaned over, hovering over me so his cock rubbed against my ass as his lips landed lightly on the nape of my neck. One hand slid around, cupping my breast, his mouth slowly making its way down my spine. His tongue swirled along my skin. His fingers squeezed and tweaked. Goose bumps rose over my flesh. He took his time, as though appraising with his lips and tongue every inch of my back. My inner beast awakened inside me.

Releasing my shoulder, he grabbed my ass cheek as his mouth lowered. His tongue circled over a dimple before moving to my other cheek. His hand abandoned my breast, traveling down until his finger slid between my folds, quickly finding my already swollen clit. He kissed and sucked at the flesh of my ass as he worked my clit, stroking and rolling, building me quickly to an orgasm.

Then he bit my ass. Hard.

I cried out, not in pain but in ecstasy. His tongue swirled over it, as though to soothe the pain, taking me even closer to the edge. His fingers still stroking, circling, and pinching my clit, his other hand pushed my shoulders down so my breasts pressed into the bed and my ass lifted higher in the air. Then his fingers left me, and I whimpered as he knelt behind me. His hands slid between my legs, pushing them further apart, then grabbed my ass again, separating my cheeks. He groaned, and I looked over my shoulder to see him appraising me once again. My kelpie shuddered and my thighs trembled as his tongue slid out, over his lips. Then he finally leaned forward, his mouth taking over where his fingers had left off.

He was an expert, his tongue flattening into my folds and licking once . . . twice . . . three times. His thumbs opened me wider, and his tongue circled and pressed against my clit, teasing it until I was whimpering and moaning. Then it dove inside my opening, making me cry out as I rocked against him. One thumb brushed over my puckered hole, then gave a slight pressure, almost entering.

"Oh, fuck," I screamed, bucking against his face.

"Come for me," he ordered, his breath hot on my sensitive sex, but he didn't have to. I was already there, crying out his name as his tongue swept in again.

Just as I peaked, he smacked my ass right where he'd bitten it before, and I came completely unglued. The world shattered around me, everything diminishing to only the physical sensations of my orgasm. It came in wave after wave, my stomach dropping like it does on a roller coaster, time after time after time. And I realized I'd never truly orgasmed before—not like this anyway.

At some point while I was falling apart, he'd managed to put on a condom, because I'd barely finished when his cock was pressed against my opening.

"Hang on, sweetheart." He grabbed my hips and thrust inside me, making me scream again. He stretched me wide, then filled me thoroughly and perfectly. My core clenched around him.

I expected sex to be rough with him. That might have been what had me so intrigued, because I'd never experienced what I'd imagined it would be like with him. And he didn't disappoint. Far from it. His cock was huge, proportionate to his body, and my pussy loved every swollen, hard inch of it. My ass loved how he slammed against it with each thrust in, and how his thumb again pressed against the most sacred area that I'd never understood as an erogenous zone until now as it barely stretched in a slightly painful but tantalizing way. My muscles squeezed around him as he pulled outward, only to drive into me again. I rocked fast and hard against him, fucking him as fiercely as he fucked me. Like I'd never fucked before.

He broke me apart nine ways to Sunday, feeding the need that had been building in me for months. No, years. Since the first time sex had even been a thought for me. This was what I'd been starving for all this time.

He made me feel like his Athena—like his goddess. A sex goddess who knew how to give and receive pleasure that went way beyond this world. I felt powerful . . . empowered. Especially as his rhythm increased, and I felt him losing control.

"Fuck, *yes*," he groaned as he pounded into me. I could feel him on the verge of climaxing, bringing me to yet another one myself, squeezing and thrusting my ass against him, twisting and rolling my hips until he shouted with his release at the same time mine came. We froze, every single muscle clenched as we rode the waves of ecstasy out together.

Then we both collapsed on the bed, me face down, him on top of me, our breaths coming fast and hard. I was sore all over, but never ever had I been so sated as I was at that moment.

Once our bodies stopped quaking with aftershocks, he rolled off me and got up to clean off. On legs like jelly, I managed to follow him into the bathroom to do the same, and when he turned to look at me, his gaze traveling up and down my body, I suddenly felt very shy and wished I had something to cover up with. My arms moved in, kind of doing the best they could. He frowned.

"That might have been the best bad idea I've ever had," he said, turning around. He walked over to the shower, his back muscles rippling and his perfectly round ass looking as though it were made of steel.

"I think that was my bad idea," I corrected.

"Well, I have another one." He tilted his head, inviting me in.

We fucked again in the shower, my back against the wall and my legs around his hips. I'd never been able to do that with a man before —none had been able to hold me up in that position, but Savage acted as though I weighed no more than a buck at the most. This time was slower and gentler, not as rough as before, but I'd been right when I saw him for the first time: He was a savage in bed. And my body— and my inner beast—couldn't get enough.

"This is sexy as fuck." Savage's finger trailed over my tattoo the next morning as we lay in bed—well, afternoon. Our hours were all messed up after that long drive, and we'd been up until sunrise again, though this time tossing and turning in a completely different way.

"That's what Addie said." Regret filled me as soon as the words popped out of my mouth.

Savage groaned and rolled onto his back. "Why the fuck did you have to say her name? You ruined my moment."

I grimaced. "Sorry. I, uh, well . . . I don't exactly know what the deal is with you two, but there's something. Just know that I don't plan on coming in between you and anyone. This . . . this was just two consenting adults having fun. Right?"

He continued staring at the ceiling, his only response a grunt.

"I mean, we're complete opposites. Last night was amazing, and I wouldn't mind doing it again. But you're you and I'm me, and I will never be anyone's old lady. And I know that's your life and your thing. So this is just what it is—a good time." I didn't know what was wrong with me. I couldn't shut the hell up. The thoughts had been going through my head since the moment I'd woken up—probably even while I'd slept. I had this desperate need for him to know that I didn't expect anything from him—and that I didn't want him to expect anything from me.

"Do you even know what it means to be an old lady?" he asked.

"I practically grew up in the club life. Yes, I know. You give up your life for the club. You become a possession, and will never be a partner. Everything is about the club, and you come after that."

He rolled onto his side to look at me, his gaze traveling over my naked body. Feeling incredibly self-conscious, I pulled the sheet up over my breasts.

"Don't fucking do that," he snarled, yanking it back down.

"See? You're already ordering me around."

He scowled. "I just want to look at you. You're too fucking beautiful to cover up." My whole body might have flushed, and it took everything I had not to cover it up again as his eyes again raked over me. "Being an old lady means you're protected for your whole life, even if your old man dies. It means nobody in the club can fuck with you, and anybody outside of the club who fucks with you fucks with the whole club. You will always have what you need and be taken care of. You're not a possession. You're family."

"But the club always comes first," I countered.

"You're part of the club."

"Not really."

"Well, you don't get to vote," he conceded.

"You don't get to go to church at all," I pointed out. "You know nothing about the club's business—your old man can't share anything with you—but you must abide by all the rules anyway and accept their decisions, regardless of how they affect you. You have no say, but you must meet their demands. That sounds like they own you. That makes you a possession."

"Family," he repeated.

"Which is still secondary to the club. If you had to choose between your old lady and your club, you'd have to choose the club."

He frowned again. "It's not like that."

"It's not?" I lifted a brow.

"No. It doesn't have to be an either-or."

I studied him like he'd been studying me. "Do you want an old lady, Savage? Have you ever had one?"

He stared at me for a long moment, our gazes locked. "How can you look in my eyes? You should be dead by now."

I laughed at his pathetic change of subject. "The witch who shall not be named thought it would help if she gave my ink a little extra magic. She said it wouldn't work on just anyone, not even most supes. But I'm not just anyone and not like most supes, and apparently it worked. Since, you know, I'm not dead by now. Do you have a problem with it?"

He broke our hold and rolled away, getting out of bed. "It's a little unnerving. I'm not used to it."

I smiled to myself. Big badass biker boy felt vulnerable.

AFTER EATING leftover pasta for lunch, I settled down on the sofa with my laptop, knowing I had at least a few hundred emails waiting for me. I learned that someone had gone through all my settings, and that everything was now encrypted so nobody could trace anything I did online to my whereabouts. Considering that was how my location was discovered before, that was nice, and I wondered why nobody had thought of it sooner. I couldn't even say anything in my own messages about where I was—nothing more specific than the Colorado mountains—or the message would turn to technical gobbledygook, and the receiver wouldn't be able to read it. Apparently, the leaders of Havenwood Falls thought of everything to protect their little town and their big secret.

I spent the afternoon responding to emails and checking out and approving a prototype of a design I'd submitted to a client a couple of weeks ago. I loved seeing my lingerie designs come to life on the kind of models they were created for. Sure, I could sew my own, but I wanted to be sure my lingerie looked good on a variety of big girls, not just those with my body type.

Savage never went far—the farthest being outside for wood. He spent most of his time working out, though. He showed me the extra bedroom he'd converted into a home gym, the reason he didn't have a guest room. After dinner, I did my own workout, but when he came in to join me, it turned into something much more fun that ended in the bedroom.

After, he pulled out an acoustic guitar and played for me by the fire as I sat naked in his bed, sipping wine and watching the snow fall outside.

"I'm not used to an audience," he said almost as an apology, when I clapped after he'd ended a particularly moving rendition of "The Sound of Silence."

"Will you ever cease to surprise me?" I wondered out loud.

"I told you—I have a lot of talents. But stick around long enough, and maybe one day I will."

I stared out the window, not acknowledging that statement. I didn't look over at him until I felt it was safe, and I found him watching the floor, seemingly in deep thought as his fingers strummed of their own accord. Thankfully, they found a familiar tune, and we were both whisked away on the sounds again.

Our days and evenings played out quite similarly for the following week. Niall stopped in regularly to check on me and keep me updated. They'd located the one behind the dark fae attack and were "handling it." I knew what that meant in outlaw-speak, so I asked for no further details. I was just glad that Savage stayed with me and wasn't a part of it.

Of course, I knew he'd killed plenty before. I wasn't an idiot. But I didn't want to be the reason. I'd seen a different side of him that I didn't think too many people knew, and that's *all* I wanted to know. I wouldn't remember him when I left, but for now, I only wanted to think of him as the good guy who kept me safe, fed me, and taught me how to be strong and confident in my most vulnerable state —naked.

I'd been in Havenwood Falls for over a week when Savage went out for much-needed groceries and to run other errands, so I did my laundry while he was away. As I was putting my clean clothes back in my suitcase, I came across the last project I'd been working on when I'd received the call that Pops had been killed. I'd spent my New Year's Day hand-stitching it. I'd forgotten all about it until now, but whoever had packed my bags while I'd been at the funeral must have deemed it worthy of saving. Pulling the slinky black material out, I decided to try it on for the first time.

Studying myself in the mirror, I noticed how the angle of one of the few seams needed to be adjusted and envisioned the effect of moving the cinched ribbon up a couple of inches, to fall right below the breasts, emphasizing them. Perhaps both designs would work. Some bigger women tended to prefer showing off our boobs over drawing attention to our waists, while others tried everything they could to downplay their overly large chests, and then some had little to worry about in that area. That's what so many designers got wrong —big, beautiful women did not fall into one specific shape. We ran the gamut, just like smaller women did. Only recently had the industry started accepting this fact, but there was a long road to travel before it actually embraced our differences.

Lost in my own head and visions, as I tended to get when creating, I never heard the door or the footsteps. I didn't realize I was no longer alone until the voice came into the bedroom and had practically reached the bathroom.

"Tychon Savage, where the hell are you?"

A stunning woman, curvy but much more petite than me, wearing a blue tight-fitting dress that barely covered her bits and four-inch heels, stopped short in front of me as I stood in the bathroom doorway. The fact that the situation was similar to the first night Savage and I hooked up wasn't lost on me. And there was something about this woman that had me imagining doing with her what Savage had done with me that night.

I blinked away the startling thoughts.

"That is fucking gorgeous," she said, staring at me.

"Who the hell are you?" I asked at the same time.

"Melaina Savage," she said as she strutted into the bathroom, checking me out. And for some reason, I let her. Even though— another woman? With his last name? What the hell? "And you must be what's got my brother all jacked up. You wouldn't happen to be a dancer, would you? Because damn, you, wearing that—oh, holy shit. That tattoo! Yeah." She nodded her head as she continued to assess me. "You'd be a knockout on stage."

"*Me?*" Was this woman insane?

She nodded again. "Oh, yeah. Your tits are fabulous. And those curves . . . I have a niche clientele who'd pay out the snout for you."

Her odd choice of words brought me back into focus. "I'm sorry." My hand went to my temple. "Would you mind if I got dressed, and then maybe we could start over?"

"Oh, darlin', don't mind me. I own Silk, the nightclub. And gentlemen's club, and ladies' club, and home of special rooms for the supes, and even more special rooms for the VIPs, if you catch my drift. Trust me—I've seen it all. So go on and get dressed. I just came to grab something out of Tychon's closet. But I really would love to know the name of the designer of the piece you're wearing," she called over her shoulder as she disappeared into his closet.

I was too hung up on her use of Savage's first name to answer her. It'd been the first time I'd heard it. It was a strong name, and quite unusual. Not at all what I expected. Yet another surprise.

Although . . . I couldn't imagine him being a Bob or a Kevin. I internally snickered at the thought.

I'd just gone back into the bedroom to retrieve my clothes when Melaina popped back out. Somehow in the last twelve days, I'd lost much of my modesty. Not only did I not mind that she stood there, all of my bits on full display, but I was kind of turned on by it. What the hell was happening to me? What kind of monster had Savage unleashed in me?

I pulled my clothes on over the lingerie, afraid if I took it off, she'd notice how much she was affecting me.

"Well, at least now I understand why I haven't seen my brother in nearly two weeks," she said as she sauntered for the bedroom door, motioning for me to follow. Her ass swayed beautifully in her skimpy dress, and a part of me hoped the material would ride up just a little more to bare the curve of her cheek.

I shook my head, hard. *Shit.* I'd become a sex-crazed idiot. That's what he'd done to me!

"I can't blame him, though." She went to the kitchen and found our unfinished bottle of wine in the fridge and two glasses. "If I had you in my bed, I wouldn't want to leave, either."

Fortunately, I hadn't taken a sip yet, because I would have blown it out of my nose like the mature lady I was. "Um . . . excuse me?"

She paused as she was about to pour the second glass and looked up at me. "Beauty is beauty—in many shapes and forms, and I, for one, have a true appreciation of it all, regardless of form. And darlin', you're a damn goddess. He'd better be treating you like one."

Heat flushed my face as she passed me a glass. I lifted it to my lips, trying not to down it all in one swallow.

"What do you mean, he's all jacked up?" I asked.

She took her own drink as she studied me with hazel eyes much like his. If she was his sister, which meant she was a hellhound, I wondered why she didn't feel the need to keep her eyes covered. Then

I noticed the telltale sign of contacts. Were contacts enough, or were hers a special kind?

"What's your name?" she asked.

"Reyna."

"Well, Reyna, it's not unlike my brother to disappear for a while. We don't exactly keep daily tabs on each other. But he does usually drop into the club on a regular basis, if for no other reason than to check on his boys who work there. Liam's been doing that, though. And he was the one who told me Tychon's been a little . . . not himself. Delegating all his club and business duties. He's even missed church twice this week. And that definitely is not like him. But now I see why."

"Well . . . he's protecting me."

She smiled, her eyes sparkling with a knowing gleam. "He's been doing a lot more than that. I can smell it."

Oh, gods. My face heated again. Hellhounds and their damn sense of smell.

She shook her head. "You really are something else. What's your heritage? Your skin is beautiful."

"I'm from Brazil."

She nodded. "That explains the exotic look. The skin, the dark, almond eyes. I can't blame him one bit. You have that look of being a queen on the streets and a wench in the sheets."

Now I did spit out my wine. "*What?*"

"No judgments here, darlin'. The naughtier the better is my personal belief." She gave me another smile, this one coy as she winked. Then she leaned over the edge of the island, closer to me, her face growing serious. "Just . . . be careful with him, okay? Tychon's been through a lot lately. I don't know if he's okay. And if someone—anyone—fucks him over, they will have to deal with this bitch." Her eyes glowed an orangish red. "And I'm literally a bitch."

Her threat was clear, but I refused to show any fear. Rather, I seized the opportunity to interrogate the one person who might know what he never wanted to talk about. After all, the only way to know how to handle the situation when I left was to know more about it. I sat up straighter and squared my shoulders.

"You mean Addie?" I asked, pinning her with my stare. "He's been through a lot with her?"

She nodded. "Addie. Rachelle . . . that Zandra bitch. It's been a messed up few months around here, and I don't know if he's dealt with it all in a healthy way."

All these women . . . and in a few months?

"How long since he was with her?"

Confusion flickered through her eyes. "He and Lyra? They haven't been together in over a quarter century. They have other issues."

"Lyra?" I had meant Addie, as she seemed to be a recent thing, but now I was curious about yet another name. "Was that his old lady?"

She laughed. "Lyra Beaumont could never be an old lady. That was their problem. But now, I don't think he'll ever have an old lady. Not after he saw what Liam went through with his." She paused, her eyes glazing over. "That loss was unbearable for all of us. And, of course, the mess with Lyra . . ." She focused on me again. "We hellhounds shouldn't breed. Tychon and I are both staunch believers in that."

"What do you mean?"

Her finger traced the edge of her wine glass. "Most females don't survive giving birth, and to be honest, I think that scares the life out of Tychon. Lyra barely made it and only because of magic and taking some seriously drastic measures. Tychon just can't put anyone through that again, and won't put himself through the loss."

"Again?" I asked.

"Addie? Rachelle?"

I shrugged.

"He hasn't told you about them?"

I bit my lip, shaking my head. "He hasn't told me anything. Only that he doesn't currently have a woman. I kind of figured there was something with Addie, although with the way she acts with him, I'm not sure it's healthy."

"No, not at all. They don't exactly have a close relationship. I mean, she just found out he was her father about a year ago. Up until then, they knew *of* each other, names and such, but not even really acquaintances."

I managed to swallow my wine this time before I gave her another shower. "Her *father*? Addie's his *daughter*?"

She nodded. "Rachelle, too. Addie didn't know about Rachelle, either, and she'd run away years ago. None of them were ever close." She sighed. "Like I said, it's been a big complicated mess. And with Rachelle's death last month . . . I'm just not sure how he's dealing with it all."

Holy. Shit. Savage had lost his daughter not too long before I'd lost my Pops. And he hadn't said anything. Hadn't even mentioned he had daughters, even after I'd met one of them. An array of emotions swept through me, most of them sadness for the man they called Savage.

Melaina watched as I blinked away tears of sorrow. I turned my head to swipe at my eyes and draw in a steadying breath. When I turned back, Melaina was pouring herself more wine.

"Look. He probably hasn't told you any of this because he didn't want you to know," she said. "And he might kill me, but I think you should. You need to know what you're getting into. And he needs someone who can be there for him as he puts his pieces back together, not break him all over again. Because I'm afraid of what he'll become otherwise. I never thought I'd say this, but Tychon Savage needs salvation. He needs to know love again."

I stared at the counter, letting this sink in, then I grabbed for the bottle and drank straight from it. I finally looked up at her, into her hazel eyes with that orange glow still in the depths of them.

"I can't be his salvation. My own situation is way too messed up. But I don't think you have to worry about me breaking him. We're not like that."

"Are you sure about that?"

"Positive."

She studied me for a long moment, then shrugged. "Too bad. I think I could really like you. But I'm well versed in the need for a little fun in the sack as a distraction. If you're ever interested in something different . . ."

Her voice trailed off right before the door opened, and Savage and Niall strode in, each carrying several sacks of groceries.

"Get your own," Savage growled at his sister, and Melaina laughed before taking in Niall.

As her eyes roved over him, the sexual energy she'd already been exuding intensified exponentially, doing strange and not entirely unwelcome things to my body.

"Mmm . . . maybe I will." She winked at Niall before sauntering through the door they'd left open, swinging those shapely hips of hers. "Thanks for the key, brother," she called out before closing the door behind her.

Niall watched through the side window. "Bloody hell. Wouldn't mind a taste of that arse."

"That's my sister," Savage rumbled.

Niall turned and glanced at me, then at Savage with an arched brow. "And payback's a bitch, brutha."

I TRIED NOT to let Melaina's words affect me, but I couldn't completely erase them from my mind, either. Savage hadn't shared that personal information with me for a reason—he knew there was no need for me to know. We'd both agreed that we had no intentions of anything beyond the short term happening between us, and that wasn't the kind of shit you shared with a fling. And laying such heavy stuff on someone you might never see again wasn't fair to either of you or the fun and distraction you were trying to create. So acting any differently, treating him any differently wouldn't have been right to him or what we had.

But when the stray thoughts made their way in, my heart hurt. I'd seen enough past the savage beast to the man inside to understand what Melaina meant. A part of me wished I could be the woman he needed, but I knew myself too well. Our worlds were too different, and I could never fit in his.

"Nice blog post today," he said a couple of nights later as we hung out on the sofa, me working on my laptop and him tossing his tablet onto the coffee table. His hair was pulled back in a man bun—a style I normally despised, but he made it work extremely well—and he wore nothing but sweat pants as he lounged on the other part of the L-shaped sectional, looking more like a model than a biker.

"You read my blog?" I asked with surprise.

"Every post you've ever made. It's changed a lot over the years. Evolved."

I stared at him with a slack jaw. He looked over at me and smiled. "I shocked you again, didn't I?"

"Um . . . yeah. Why the hell did you do that? I mean, unless you have some secret cross-dressing life or something?"

He shrugged. "I like lingerie."

"Oh. So it was for the pictures." That at least made sense.

"And I like your words."

I rolled my eyes, but smiled on the inside. "I'd love to do a write-up about Callie's shop, but that's probably not allowed."

"That's something the Court would decide."

Right. The Court of the Sun and the Moon—the decision makers Addie had told me about when she'd been dragging tiny needles over my skin. The ones who kept the registry and made sure everyone stayed in line.

"They have ways to draw the tourists in without giving us away. But you'd have to get on their good side first."

I didn't foresee that happening. I imagined that took time, to build their trust, and I didn't plan on spending much time here. Although, I really hadn't had a chance to explore yet.

"You should go back into town," Savage said, as though he'd read my mind. "Get to know it better."

"I've been busy with work. Besides, I didn't think it was allowed."

"Mmm . . . well . . ." His mouth pulled to the side. "Would you be mad if I just really didn't want to share you?" He winked at me before I could respond, softening the blow. "I'll take you tomorrow," he added quickly.

"So you can stalk me around the shops and breathe down my neck again, scaring everyone away?"

The corner of his lips curled upward in a smirk. "I thought you liked me breathing down your neck . . . and other places."

A chill ran up my spine. "You know what I mean."

He sat up, turning to set his feet on the ground. "No worries. I don't want the wrath of Addie again."

"The wrath of Addie?"

"You didn't see that fit she threw that night? Chewed me a new asshole about how Torq and me were scaring off everyone's customers and then went on about how you needed 'space and independence.'" He dropped those last three words with quotes, although he didn't do the air quote thing. I could hear them. "So I'll take you into town tomorrow, and you can have your space and independence."

"It's safe?" I asked.

"As long as you stay within the wards, yeah."

I leaned back. "So you let Addie chew you a new asshole, huh?"

And for some reason—maybe he was just in a talkative mood that night—he spilled everything Melaina had told me and more. He gave more details about Addie and Rachelle that sounded more like a soap opera than real life. He told me about his agreement with Lyra to never tell Addie until the appropriate time came, and how he could watch over her from a distance, but couldn't be a part of her life as she grew up. He talked little of Rachelle, only explaining how a friend of the family had raised her in another town, that he could have been a part of her life, but she wanted little to do with him and then ran away. Amends had never been made between them before they lost her again. He told me about Liam and his wife, and how she'd died after their third son was born. How badly it had wrecked Liam.

"Wow," I breathed. "I've never loved anyone like that." I didn't know if I ever could, either. Not with my . . . situation. I peered over at him. "Have you?"

He pondered his feet propped up on the coffee table. "Like Liam and Savannah? No. I might have come close twice. Once with Lyra and once in the 1700s."

"1700s?" I murmured. I hadn't realized how old he was. Supes were so weird in that way. Pops and Niall were way older than they looked, so I was kind of used to it, but still, I now felt like an infant.

Savage's lids lifted, his eyes raising to me. "You remind me of them, in certain ways."

"I do? How?" *Gods, please don't say anything that's going to make me cave.*

"You're an old soul, like both of them. Intelligent. Witty. Sassy. Wise beyond your years. Born to be leaders." He stood and walked over to the window, placing his hands on his hips. His voice came out low, still rumbly but the edge softened. "Another fascinating female too good for me. I always want what I can't have."

Oh, fookin' hell.

As usual, we couldn't keep our hands off each other when we crawled into bed. The mind-blowing sex had remained just that—mind-blowing. Over the past two weeks, we'd done things I'd never done before. We experimented. We had fun. My inner beast pushed at the surface, making me wild.

But tonight . . . tonight was different. Not in a bad way. Not. At. All. In fact, it might have been the most amazing time yet. When I yelled out "Tychon" instead of "Savage" on my climax, he froze for a moment as our eyes locked, and when he continued, something was different. I couldn't put my finger on it, but something was changing. Something between us.

CHAPTER 8

Savage was gone when I awoke the next morning, having left a note by the coffee maker saying that he had to go on a CDI run. I had to wonder if that was the full truth or if he'd euphemized a club job because he knew my feelings about it. Niall texted me, saying he was also going on the run, but as long as I stayed within the town's wards I'd be safe—though he preferred if I just stayed home. By mid-afternoon, though, I hadn't heard from either of them, and I was tired of working on Savage's couch . . . or at the kitchen island . . . or on the chaise longue by the fireplace in the bedroom. My creativity for drawing had dried up, none of the designs in my head translating well to the sketchbook. I was also bored with the home gym equipment and longed for fresh air.

I replaced my black dress pants and silk blouse with fleece-lined leggings, a hoodie, thick socks and hiking boots, and the ugly but warm puffy ski jacket. A quick search in Savage's coat closet led me to an extra beanie hat—a Harley-Davidson one, of course, but it would have to do. I was going hiking.

I didn't plan to go too far. I wasn't stupid. It was the middle of winter, the mountains were treacherous, and the woods vast. I understood it could be easy to get lost. But that was the benefit of having an inner animal with extraordinary senses and a sharpened instinct. Besides, I was only going to go down to the creek by the cemetery that I could see from the house and come right back up. I figured that would be a decent enough workout.

As I picked my way down the slope, slipping and sliding in some places, that inner beast begged for release. Once I made it to the creek, my kelpie, a water creature, reared its head with intensified interest. Inhaling deeply, I caught an intriguing scent that made my nostrils flare and my heart pick up speed. It was crisp and sweet at the same time, calling to me like a frozen drink on the beach. The intriguing smell came from nearly straight north from where I stood, if I had my directions right, which I was pretty sure I did—the scent of frozen water with a hint of something else. Something that made my senses tingle with exalted anticipation, that pulled me toward it like a magnet.

I couldn't say how long I hiked—an hour, maybe less, maybe much more—until my feet landed on a path that took me straight to where my soul pulled. As I rounded a copse of evergreens and stepped into the clearing, I gasped at the sight before me. She looked like a bride rising hundreds of feet up the cliff, her dress a frozen mass cascading down into a pool of ice. There was only a slight trickle along the massive icicles that created a small hole in the frozen pond at the bottom of the falls. This must have been the great falls that gave the town its name.

The sight was probably beautiful in warmer weather, but it was breathtaking almost completely frozen over—what one might call a once-in-a-lifetime view, although, I supposed, not for the people who called this town home. I wondered how many actually came out to appreciate its beauty. I was glad nobody did now.

Because it wasn't the beauty that had drawn me here. How could it have been, since I hadn't seen it yet? It was something in that water. Something that called to me. A source of magic that had my kelpie bucking inside me, demanding to be freed. Something I didn't want to share with a single soul.

I slowly stepped toward the edge of the pond, scanning the area to double-check for other life. Boulders bordered the water and beyond them were woods of evergreens and thin white aspen trunks. The mountain climbed up sharply from here. The sky above was already turning from blue to a light shade of purple, the sun already behind the mountains to the west. I sniffed, but that intoxicating scent was all I could pick up—no trace of anyone nearby.

Climbing up to sit on one of the boulders, I swung my legs around and gingerly tested the ice with one foot, pressing on it to see if it was as solid as it looked. Deciding it could hold my weight, I carefully walked toward the hole, but the closer I came, the less I worried. Why was I even concerned? I was a creature of the water. If I fell in, I wouldn't drown. Once I was close, I dropped to my knees and pulled off my mittens. Reaching forward, I scooped my hand into the hole.

Magic zinged up my arm and throughout my body.

The ice around me cracked and fell away.

I plunged into the freezing water, my arms and legs flailing as I gasped for air before submersing completely.

But then, I was no longer me.

Not human me.

Kelpie me.

Unicorn me.

Something had caused me to lose all control. I didn't even have a chance to calm her and try to keep her contained. One moment I was human, and the next I was not.

With powerful muscles, I sprang out of the water and onto the ice, galloping across it to the boulders. Once on land, I shook myself out, spraying the nearby tree trunks with water that quickly became ice crystals.

Free! I was fucking *free*!

I wanted to shout it—whinny it—whatever. I'd never felt such elation in my life. I'd kept her trapped inside for entirely too long, and this week, when my animalism had been at its most basic, she'd been kicking and thrashing to be released. It had been years, and now, finally, she was out. I'd thought it'd been my time with Savage that

317

was calling so loudly to her, but maybe it had been this place all along —these falls, this water.

I bucked and reared and pranced in and around the trees. I desperately wanted to run and run and *run*. Maybe never come back.

But the water still drew me to it. I moseyed back over to the pond and stood on a boulder, gazing down at my reflection—an all-black hide with a silver mane and tail and a silvery, glimmering horn spiraling out of my head. I was magnificent. Nothing this beautiful should have to be imprisoned.

Sadly, that was my lot in life, though. And I knew I needed to rein her back in, pull her into me, and return to my human form. I didn't know what to do about my clothes that appeared to be floating in the freezing water on the far side of the pond, but if I were ever seen like this—

As though on cue, a gasp sounded from behind me.

"Are you real?" the male voice whispered, and I turned around to find a man peeking out from behind a tree, his eyes large as plates as he stared at me with fascination.

Shit. Fuck. Damn. And every other word in the book.

I should have run. Or I should have charged after him, hoping to scare him off and make him wonder if he'd really seen what he thought he had.

But I didn't.

I stood frozen, staring at him as he stared at me. Then that animal intuition picked up on something about him. Something not right. In fact, something very wrong. My kelpie instinct kicked in, and there was nothing I could do to stop myself. As much as I tried to turn the other way, my legs carried me forward to him, and as I approached, he stepped out from behind the tree, just as drawn to me as I was to him. His hand reached out. His fingers brushed over the fringes of my mane, and then his palm settled on my side. And that was all it took.

Nothing but instinct—my prime purpose as a kelpie—controlled me, turning me toward the pond, pulling the guy with me.

"Hey! What the hell?" He yelled and thrashed, but once he'd touched me, he'd signed his own death warrant. The water in my fur became like super-glue, of the supernatural kind. Nothing he nor I did could free him. I would haul him into the water, take him down into its depths, and not release him until he drowned. It was the terrible and terrifying side of my nature.

My hooves lugged us over the boulders, and I tried to force myself to stop, but I couldn't. My kelpie had taken over. She was in complete control. We dragged him over the ice as he continued to fight me and I tried to fight myself.

No! I silently screamed. *We won't kill him! We don't kill!*

I threw myself at my kelpie, and her body bucked, but she continued on. I cried out, a whinny in the night, tossing my head side to side. But she continued on. As hard as I tried to pull her back into me and become human again, she fought me even harder. This was what my kind was meant to do, and there was no way to stop her. Even as our hooves dragged across the ice, she continued on.

The man shouted for help, twisting and turning, and begging for release. Then I felt a sharp pain in my flank. His free arm swung outward, and in my peripheral vision, I saw a dagger in his hand. The dumb ass had stabbed me! He shouldn't have been able to, though. That was no ordinary blade. It had to have been infused with magic to pierce my hide.

I reared back, tossing him in the air, but never losing my hold on him. His free hand arced down again for another slice, across my hindquarter this time, and I jumped and bucked.

Even as we fought, though, she continued on.

When agony screamed from my withers and up my neck from another carving through my flesh, this one much deeper, I threw my head back with a cry. And I no longer cared if we drowned him, because if he plunged the blade into my throat next time, we would both die. So I twisted my neck backward, trying to catch the right angle to spear him with my horn.

But my front hooves had hit the edge of the ice, and it cracked behind us. The piece we were on teetered forward, rocking down into the water. No matter what, he was going to die. I'd known it from the

319

moment I'd sensed that darkness in him, whether I wanted him to or not. But now I did.

As I was about to plunge us downward, a huge fireball streaked toward us, slamming into my accidental rider. His agonizing scream indicated much more than the pain I'd felt, and his body went limp. I turned just in time to see the fiery blaze, nearly as big as me, fly at us again. I whinnied loudly, throwing myself sideways, but the fire slammed into the man, and this time carried him off.

And I knew what that meant.

My kelpie couldn't release him until—unless—he was dead.

I galloped across the pond to the bank where the fireball had stopped. And I realized it wasn't a fireball at all, but a hound almost the size of my kelpie form, flames shining out of its eyes, nose, and mouth. Its skin contained an orange glow that defined its thick muscles, as though the fire burnt within rather than on the surface. It stared at me with those orangish-red eyes, smoke rising from its body and billowing out of its mouth between six-inch fangs as it panted.

My attacker lay on the ground in a pool of blood flowing from his ravaged throat, shredded skin and tendons all that remained of it, the hound hovering over him.

We regarded each other in a standoff. I wondered if that was Savage in there—or somebody else. I'd never seen a hellhound before, but this looked like it could definitely be one, and the rotten-egg smell of sulfur and brimstone wafted on the air. I'd nearly taken a life. Was this beast here to escort my soul to Hell?

If I shifted now, I'd surely die. I looked from side to side, wondering if I could make a break for it—and if that would be any better. Running would improve my chance of someone else seeing me, and either they'd take me or I'd kill them. Staying, though, would improve my chance of dying.

The hellhound moved.

Dropping my head, I pawed at the ground and snorted, my breath big plumes not unlike the smoke from the hound.

Then its shape twisted and morphed . . . and a moment later, Savage knelt close to the ground.

He rose to his large, gloriously naked body's full height and took a step forward. I exhaled again. He lifted his hands, slowly, palms out. To show he meant no harm, to calm me. His gaze roved over me.

"Reyna?" he asked, his raspy tone genuinely curious—a mix of uncertainty that it was actually me with wonder at what he was seeing. He must not have known what I really was, after all. He took another step closer, and I stepped back. "Mother fucker. You're hurt."

I was, but I was healing. The longer I stayed in this form, the less I'd suffer when I took my human shape.

A neigh from the woods had my head jerking in that direction. A black horse trotted into the clearing, and I recognized the kelpie. Niall.

"*Reyna, my queen,*" he said into my mind. "*You're okay.*"

I tilted my head toward the hellhound.

"*It's okay. It's over. Savage saved you.*"

"*No! He killed for me. Someone else died because of me!*"

"*He would have died because of you anyway.*"

"Niall, get her to fucking shift," Savage ordered. "You need to take her home before the rest find us."

"*You heard him, Rey. You can't be seen.*"

My kelpie balked, not wanting to lose herself again, not knowing the next time she could be released. She reared and bucked as I struggled to pull her back in, but footsteps in the distance, the snapping of twigs under heavy boots, and the odor of more brimstone sent us into a panic—fear of being seen but also of being tempted to kill—and she finally submitted. My muscles and bones screamed in pain as they shrunk and reformed themselves. My insides felt like they were shredded as my organs reshaped and rearranged. It shouldn't be this painful, the result of not shifting often enough. I was left shivering and panting in a tight ball on the ground.

Something heavy draped over me. I dared to lift my head, my still-healing skin searing with the movement, to find Savage standing over me, covering me with clothes. His clothes. I had no idea where they came from, but I noticed he stood between Niall and me, blocking me from Niall's view. If I wasn't such a physical and emotional mess, I would have laughed at his chivalry.

"Let Niall take you home," he said quietly as he leaned down to pull the shirt on the rest of the way and help me stand. He gripped my face with both hands, his eyes searching mine as though hunting for some kind of answer, but I didn't know the question. There was something in his I couldn't quite decipher. Something I'd never seen before. "Hurry. Get the fuck out of here. Others are coming fast."

With that, he lifted me up by the waist and placed me on Niall's back, slapping the kelpie's hindquarters. Good thing hellhounds were immune to the kelpie's kill instinct, or we would have had more problems. Instead, Niall shot his hind leg out and kicked Savage as we took off, not appreciating the smack on the ass.

Gods. I didn't know who would be more humiliated when this was over—me for riding Niall or Niall for having been ridden.

"*I would do anything for you,*" Niall said as he trotted through the woods. At least if he were seen, people would only see a woman on a horse—a half-naked woman in the dead of winter, but that was much less worrisome than their sighting of a unicorn. "*There's only one other ass I'd allow on my back, but for you, my queen, anything.*"

I tried to tell him to stop calling me that, but the skin of my neck pulled too much when I opened my mouth.

"*I can still hear your thoughts,*" he informed me.

Oh. "*Well, then, stop calling me queen.*"

"*Did you see yourself, love? You're majestic. Everyone should call you that.*"

"*If you do, I'll shank you.*"

He snorted.

A shiver racked through my body, and Niall picked up the pace. His body was warm, but not like Savage's. I pushed aside thoughts of him. Thoughts I didn't want Niall eavesdropping on.

Once we were back at Savage's cabin, I hurried inside even before Niall shifted. A hot shower was all I could think about, at least until Niall could no longer hear my thoughts. I felt it in my consciousness when his mind disconnected from mine, and I sighed with relief as I turned the water on, letting my thoughts run. As the water heated, I gave myself a quick once-over in the mirror. The wound on my butt was now only a red welt. The one on my side, just above my hip, a small scar. The gash on my neck had been the worst, and it was already mostly healed, the skin still tight and somewhat sore, but the wound closed and scabbed over. Only a centimeter or two over or deeper, and he would have hit my jugular, killing me. My muscles, joints, and bones hurt more from the transformation than any of my injuries. I gingerly stepped under the hot water, but it felt too good to notice the burn on my wounds.

No matter how long I stood under its warmth, though, I couldn't stop shaking. No longer from the cold, but from the thoughts running amok in my mind and the emotional upheaval they brought.

I didn't know if I was more sickened by what I'd almost done or that Savage had finished the job for me. I feared what would happen next. What the repercussions would be for us. Addie had made it clear that humans couldn't know about the supes, and I'd let one see me. And he'd died because of it. Now Savage would have to suffer whatever punishment their Court gave. I could handle banishment. It wasn't like I'd planned to stay anyway. But this was his home, his family, his life. If he didn't hate me for it, I'd hate myself enough for the both of us.

All because I'd decided to go for a fucking hike.

"Reyna?" Savage's gravelly voice jolted me out my mind.

Without waiting for me to respond, he stepped into the shower with me. His eyes traveled from my head to my toes, lingering on what was left of my wounds. Relief filled his features as his arms snaked around my back, and he pulled me up against his body, enveloping me with all that was Savage. He felt strong, protective, and comforting, and I leaned into him, a sob escaping. He held me tighter as I cried into his chest.

He stepped back when the sobs finally stopped and lifted my chin to look up at him. "Better?"

"Why did you do it?" I asked, more tears forming in my eyes. "Why did you kill him?"

"Because you were about to."

"I didn't want to!"

"I know."

My brows squeezed together, my head shaking. "I don't understand. What? Are you so okay with killing that you just had to do it instead? Kill an innocent?"

Now his brows dropped low. "First of all, he wasn't an innocent. He was wanted by the Court for rape and murder. And no, I'm not that okay with killing, regardless of what others say and think. But I do what I have to do."

"But you didn't have to! If he had it coming anyway, you should have just let me do it."

His warm breath fanned over me with a heavy sigh. "Honestly, I hadn't intended to kill him. The Court wanted him dead. That's why they keep us around—to serve as their bounty hunters and executioners. And I'm usually the one to do the takedown. Something kept going through my mind as we hunted for him, though." His eyes bounced between mine. "You, Reyna—thinking you'd be waiting for me at home. And I decided I wasn't going to be the one this time. I couldn't see myself being able to look into your eyes afterward."

"Then *why*? Why did you? And so . . . so *gruesomely*. So—"

"Savagely?" he offered, and I gulped, nodding. "Because any of my other ways would have killed you, too. And when I saw that beautiful creature, I just knew it was you, injured and bleeding but about to serve him justice. And I just couldn't let you do that."

I jutted my chin out. "Well, you should have."

"Don't you get it?" he growled, his hands grasping the sides of my face, holding me still as his gaze pierced into mine. "That's *why* I had to. You're not a killer, Reyna. I couldn't let that one moment in time forever change who you are. I couldn't let it darken your pristine soul."

I blinked away the forming tears and water pouring down my face, my anger sluicing down to the drain with it.

"And what about yours?" I murmured. "I'm supposed to accept that I let yours grow even darker with yet another kill?"

A smirk curled his lips as he blew out a breath. "Sweetheart, I'm a creature of Hell. My soul can't get any blacker than it was the day I was born." He dropped one palm from my face to land on my chest. "But yours . . . it's beautiful and pure."

I shook my head. "You don't know that."

"Hellhound here. I see souls." He leaned in, his rock-hard cock pressing into my belly as his mouth dropped near my ear. "And you are fucking glorious, inside and out."

His lips and hot breath on my ear sent a shiver down my spine. The hand on my chest slid to my breast, cupping it, my nipple immediately pebbling against his palm. The other went behind my head, twisting into my hair and pulling, tilting my face up to him.

"I need to fuck you now, Reyna," he said, leaving no room for argument.

CHAPTER 9

*N*ot that I wanted to argue. I was completely defenseless as his mouth crashed on mine, his tongue thrusting between my lips, parting them. I matched his need, his intensity. After everything that happened, I understood the desperation for human contact, for some kind of release of the buildup and tension of the day. My hands latched on to his thick shoulders, pulling him closer for more skin-to-skin contact. His hand between us squeezed my breast almost too hard . . . almost. I tasted him as he tasted me. Bit his lip as he bit mine. When he began to pull away for a breath, I pressed harder into him, my tongue sweeping over his full lips, my mouth sucking the water that dripped over them.

His cock was like a steel rod between us, and I slipped my hand over it, curling my fingers around the head, then sliding down the thick shaft. A low growl rumbled deep in his throat. It turned me the hell on. I needed to hear it again. Still stroking him, I slowly lowered myself before him, my mouth skimming over his wet beard, his neck, his ridiculously sculpted chest and abs, until I was on my knees before him. My other hand slid over his sack, cupping his balls, as I took his head in my mouth.

"Fuck, Reyna," he growled, making my core clench.

I took him in farther, my tongue swirling and stroking as my hands also worked him until he gripped my head, and he was thrusting into my mouth. I matched his rhythm, tasting him as he was about to come, sucking hard so he would, but then he jerked away. He suddenly stood on the other side of the large shower, out of my reach.

"As much as I like fucking your mouth, I need to fuck *you*."

Good gods, that was hot.

With a small nod and knowing what he liked, I turned around on my knees, and bracing my forearms on the built-in bench, I rose onto my feet, lifting my ass high in the air for him. He didn't hesitate. He palmed it with both hands, squeezing and kneading my flesh as he moved closer behind me. One thumb slid between my crack and over my hole, pausing to press against it, making my hips buck up toward him. He always teased me there, but never entered. I never asked him to—even being touched there was new to me—but each time, my curiosity grew as I fantasized about what it would feel like to have him inside what I'd always thought to be my Do Not Enter Zone.

He moved on before I could decide whether to say anything this time, his fingers coasting through my wet folds, circling around my entry before continuing on to tease and taunt the already swollen bundle of nerves. I whimpered and moaned, my legs trembling and jerking. Then two fingers entered, and my pelvis jerked. They curled and hit the G-spot perfectly, making me cry out and thrust backward.

"Fuck me, Savage," I begged. "Please . . . fuck me. Everywhere."

"Everywhere?" he rumbled as his hand moved faster, stroking in and out, one finger still working my clit furiously.

"Gods, yes! Everywhere!"

His other hand skated over my ass, moving to tease my puckered hole. "Here?"

My core clenched around his fingers inside me just at the thought of it. I'd done so much with him. Things I never imagined doing before. Why not this, too? Why not go all out? It was so dirty. So naughty. So taboo, in my head. And at this moment, so necessary.

"Please!" I shouted.

He growled, low and sexy as hell, the sound of a virile beast, making my breasts swell tightly against my skin. Then he gave a slight push, and I cried out as I was stretched and full in all the places. The sensations—the pressure on my clit, his fingers stroking my pussy, the fullness and tightness in my ass, even my nipples sliding over my forearm—were overwhelming. I lost it. My body moved of its own accord, because my mind was gone. Completely fucking gone. My hands grasped my breasts, pinching and rolling my nipples, as my legs rocked and bounced, increasing the friction inside me. It was all so sensuous . . . so erotic . . . so . . . so . . . oh, *gods*, so explosive. He made my body shatter around him and beg for more at the same time, until all I could do was scream his name over and over as I soared away on the final wave of ecstasy.

My trembling legs gave way, but Savage caught me before I hit the ground. His arms scooped under my knees and around my shoulders, and he carried me out of the shower, our wet bodies dripping a trail over the floor as he crossed the bathroom and went to the bed. He gently lowered me in the center and crawled over me. His long wet locks fell forward as he closed his mouth over mine. But not for nearly long enough. I wanted to taste him more, devour him even, but he moved down.

His sodden beard and warm tongue skated over my neck and collarbone. He took precious time on each breast, and my body quaked, whether still with aftershocks or with renewed need, I didn't know. One was flowing into the other, especially as his mouth lowered, his tongue swirling around my belly button before moving on to the crease between my pelvis and leg, then he sucked the inside of one thigh and the other before pushing my legs wide. Then, oh, gods, his mouth closed over my already pulsing sex and sucked, and I lifted myself against his face, about to lose it again.

Before I did, my fingers entangled in his hair and pulled him up. "I need your cock."

He smirked before flattening his tongue and swiping it up my folds, twirling it around my hole, making me gasp. "And I needed to taste you."

He took another long, languid taste before rising on his hands and moving back upward. He held himself over me on his hands and knees, his gaze a weighty caress up my body, full of such promises that could never be spoken aloud. When his eyes came back to mine, we locked onto each other. His became unreadable as he moved his knees between mine. He straightened his legs behind him, lowering his hips, our gazes still holding as his cock pressed into my opening. Then his eyes fell shut as he gradually slid inside me.

So thick.

So long.

So perfect.

So excruciatingly slow.

He'd said he needed to fuck me before, but this . . . this was not fucking. Not like we had every other time, not even last night. This was . . . so different. Something had definitely changed. He drew out his strokes, taking his time filling me up again and then withdrawing just as slowly. My heart raced from the massive orgasm he'd already given me, but my body easily fell into the more leisurely pace, rocking with him, each torturously slow movement in and out increasing the sensation exponentially, causing waves of chills to run over my flesh.

His arms slid under me, gathering me into his chest, my breasts pressed between us, his face nuzzling into my neck and shoulder, his mouth wet against my skin. My arms curled under his and up around his back. Somehow, without releasing or losing any contact, we shifted to sit up, me on top, my legs wrapped around him. We continued moving together, my nipples rubbing deliciously against his chest, his hands stroking up and down my back. One slid up and wrapped around my hair, pulling. My head fell, and my back arched, giving his mouth access to my breasts. He didn't disappoint, his tongue swirling over my nipple, his teeth grazing over it, then his mouth pulling it within. My hips rocked harder, trying to pick up the pace as my need continued building.

He shifted us again, starting the build all over.

My inexperienced self thought we'd done pretty well in trying out all the different positions during our time together, but tonight we explored even more. More intimate than ever. More pleasurable than ever. Still luxuriously slow. Still somehow different.

At some point, I ended up on my back again, in the only position I'd ever personally experienced before Savage. Back to the basics. But it was far from basic with him. With us. As my hips lifted to meet his, he gazed at me with hooded lids. Our eyes locked again, something passed between us, and he began to quicken the pace. His weight on his elbows, his hands cupped my face.

"Reyna," he moaned as he thrust inside me before pulling out. "My Reyna." He drove in hard again and then wrenched out. Our eyes held as our breaths came faster, my hips rolling up with each of his strokes inward, pulling back when he did. Our movements quickly escalated, reaching an urgent pace, our pelvises slamming together. "My unicorn," he groaned as he rammed into me, my core squeezing around him. And then as we climbed to our climax, he growled with each hard thrust, "Mine. Mine. Mine."

And as everything within me came apart again, I got caught up in the wondrous moment, and my mind already far over the edge, I shouted as I came, "Yours. Yours. *Yours.*"

I climaxed first, but he was right after me, closing his eyes and still moaning *mine*. We floated down, and he collapsed on top of me, his body trembling. Rolling off to my side, he wrapped his arms around me and pulled me close, whispering my name as we both drifted off.

MY EYES POPPED open as the realization hit me. I'd been sound asleep one moment and wide awake the next when it came to me—why sex with Savage had felt different tonight. I'd chalked up the "mine" possessive bullshit to the heat of the moment, but even now as I realized the truth, that claim of ownership explained the change. He'd said he needed to fuck me when we were in the shower, but that's not what we did. We hadn't been two people just having a good time, scratching an itch, meeting a need. Not tonight.

We'd languished in it. We'd explored every inch of each other not only in an erotic way but with care and adoration. We drew it out, relishing how the other felt against us, around us, within us. And not just physically. The connection was deeper this time. More real. We were using our bodies to express how we felt . . . emotionally.

We were making love.

Oh, gods. Did Tychon Savage love me? Did I love him?

The thoughts had me squirming, and I tried to sneak out of bed, but Savage's arms wrapped tighter around me, his face nuzzling into the back of my neck. I froze. Was he awake? His breathing remained steady. I relaxed, but I couldn't go back to sleep, my mind reeling.

Did he possibly love me? Was he even capable of it anymore? He'd sounded like he'd given up on the emotion and all that it entailed ever since Addie's mother, Lyra. He'd been with other women since then, of course, but none that captured him beyond the physical. So why me? There was nothing extraordinary about me . . . except that I was a unicorn. And he'd called me *his* unicorn. Had seeing me in my other form changed the way he felt about me? Or was it a ploy, now that he knew what I was and therefore my street value, so that I *would* be his unicorn?

I mentally shook that thought away. It wasn't a fair accusation to harp on, for him or for me, because my self-esteem didn't need that kind of negative self-talk.

And there was a very good chance everything had been one-sided. Maybe only I had felt the difference because the change had only been in me. I didn't know if I loved him—it was too soon and the thought too terrifying to dwell on—but I did know I'd developed some kind of feelings for him, and that just couldn't possibly happen. We couldn't be together. There were too many things against us. For one, I was not old lady material, no matter how good he'd tried to make it sound, and he wasn't going to give up his life as a biker for me. I wouldn't want him to. That was too much a part of who he was—it was one half of the dichotomy of Tychon Savage that I liked so much. The man I was . . . falling for.

And for two, I was not staying here in Havenwood Falls. Tonight was proof that not even this place was safe for me—and definitely not for anyone else. This had never been a long-term solution for me. New Orleans was my home—the sultry South, the bayou, the accents, the music, the Garden District, the French Quarter, the beignets and seafood and red beans and rice and gumbo . . . I could go on and on just about the food. That was my home. Not this remote town in the mountains.

Then why haven't you so much as given it a second thought for over a week now?

I ignored that voice. Staying was not something I should be trying to talk myself into. No. I needed to make plans to go home, and I spent the rest of the night formulating a mental checklist until I finally drifted off again, not to wake until after noon.

"You good?" Savage asked as I sat at the kitchen island with my coffee. "You've been quiet today."

I looked up at him and smiled. "Just tired. Still a little sore."

His lips turned up in a smirk, and he winked at me. Yeah, he was part of the reason for being sore, the part I didn't mind. Regardless of my epiphany in the middle of the night, I didn't regret one moment I'd spent with Savage. He'd done so much for me, more than he would ever know or even understand. He would be a good memory to hold on to—the man who turned this near-virgin queen on the streets into an uninhibited wench in the sheets.

"Take a nap. Or go to bed early. I don't know how long I'll be. We have church, and then Liam and I gotta meet with the Court tonight, give them the story about what happened last night."

"They're going to want to meet with me, too, aren't they?" Part of me kind of hoped they would banish me, because that would make this whole thing a lot easier.

"Not if I can help it. They got what they wanted. I did it. They won't even know you were involved." He came around the island and kissed my temple before going over to grab his leather coat. "Your secret is safe."

I sucked in my bottom lip, biting the flesh to keep it from trembling as emotion swept through me. Blinking, I looked away, toward the windows, but my gaze stopped as I noticed a dresser sitting in the living room near the bedroom door. It hadn't been there before.

"Where did that come from and why is it there?" It was a beautiful piece—a lot like the furniture I'd had in my own apartment, but the style didn't fit in here, especially not where it stood now.

Savage followed my gaze and turned back to give me another wink. "Brought it back from yesterday's CDI run. I thought you might be tired of living out of suitcases."

Oh, damn. The tears rose, and I blinked rapidly to keep them away.

"Hey." He moved back over to me and lifted my chin with his finger. "We'll talk about it later. No assumptions. Just know you're welcome here. Always. For as long as you like."

I nodded, unable to speak. Well, that answered that question— the feelings weren't one-sided, and his weren't because he'd discovered what I was. He'd bought the dresser, thinking of me, before he'd known.

He shoved his arms through his coat sleeves, studying me the whole time. "Reyna, seriously. Don't fucking worry about it. I'll take care of it when I get home." He leaned over and kissed me on the mouth this time. "I promise not to wake you if you're sleeping." His lips turned up. "Unless you want me to, then leave me a note."

He bent down for another kiss, and I leaned up into it, savoring it, committing to memory his taste, his scent, his touch, the way his tongue felt against mine, how his fingers pressed into my hips, tightening his hold.

And as I watched him stride out the door, I recalled sadly that I wouldn't remember him when I left. I wouldn't remember any of this.

CHAPTER 10

When I was sure he was gone, I let the dam burst and cried into my coffee. Then I renewed my resolve and sent a text to Niall.

Me: What are you doing? I need a ride.

Niall: about to go into church

Me: How long?

Niall: no idea but gotta go to court with them too since I was there

Me: Shit. Does this place have Uber? Or can you get me a taxi?

Niall: where you going

Me: Is it safe to leave town yet?

Niall: fuck no need another week or two

Niall: why you talking about leaving anyway?

Me: I need to get out of here

Niall: outta the house?

Me: for good

My phone went silent for a while, and I wondered if he'd gone into the club's meeting. Or worse, if he was asking Savage what happened to make me want to leave.

Niall: rey, you fuckin ghosting him?

Now I hesitated with a reply. Part of me wanted to, but I'd hate myself for it. Once I had some space and could gather my thoughts to share them properly, I'd let Savage know and give us a clean break. Deep down, he had to know it was coming.

Me: I'll talk to him later, after I'm out. I need space first.

Niall: They have luber here

Me: Uber? Can you get one for me? I can't get the app on my phone

Niall: No, luber not uber

Me: Luber? Ew!

Niall: yeah as bad as you're imagining, they said

Me: Who? You didn't say anything to him, did you?

Niall: course not

Niall: gotta go church starting I'll ask about a truck

Damn. I didn't know how long they'd be meeting, and then they had the Court thing. Niall could be out of pocket for hours, and when he was done, that meant Savage would be, too, and on his way home. That could make things ugly. I needed to get my stuff out of here, and then meet with him on neutral ground, maybe in town somewhere. But how was I going to get into town?

I considered the Cadillac in the garage, but how shitty would that be? Leave him without a word *and* steal his car? Both would be temporary, but I didn't want to deal with that, either. I had two other people's numbers available to me on business cards. Melaina wasn't an option, though, not after her not-so-subtle threat about breaking her brother's heart. I didn't think Savage and I were close enough for it to be that bad, but any bit of hurt would have been enough for the female hellhound. The other card belonged to Addie. She was definitely my safest bet.

"Thanks for coming," I said as we loaded my suitcases into the back of her Jeep.

She shrugged. "No problem. And don't worry, I won't ask any questions."

My heart ached as we pulled away from Savage's cabin, but it was a pain I would have to endure. Before Addie had arrived, while I searched to make sure I had all of my belongings, nostalgia had already set in—and a longing for something I could never have. He and I could never have. It's strange how much we can grieve for something that never was more than a figment of our imagination—an unfulfilled wish, a dashed dream, a desire for what could have been but never was.

"Okay, I lied," Addie said as we came to the end of the road at the bottom of the mountain, about to turn onto a main street into town. "I have one question, but it's not about him. It's about you, and I'm dying to know—how was it to shift again?"

My head swiveled toward her in surprise. "How—?"

"Witchy senses." She laughed at my expression as she made the turn. "I felt it last night."

"You *felt* my shift? Wait. I thought you don't pay attention to anyone unless there's trouble." It was a good thing she'd brought this up, because if she—or anyone else—knew what happened last night, Savage, Niall, and whoever else were about to get into a lot of trouble if they lied to the Court.

She shrugged. "We don't. But I was kind of hoping you would shift while you were here. I could tell from your energy that it'd been a long time, and this is a safe place—as long as there are no humans around. So I guess subconsciously, I was feeling for it. And honestly, it was kind of a big fucking energy jolt and no doubt you."

I turned to look back out the window. Shit. "Did anyone else notice?"

"Not that I know of. Nobody's said anything. No alert went out or anything. I think your secret's still safe."

That was the second time I'd been told that today. But I had a lot of experience with secrets not being kept that way.

"So how was it?"

I couldn't help my smile, even with everything else that had happened. "It was kind of nice."

"Kind of nice?" she echoed. Stopped at a light, she peered over at me with a brow raised above her black-framed glasses.

"Okay, okay. It was unbelievable. She was happy to be free.

Unfortunately, I was afraid of being seen, so she didn't get to be out for long."

The light changed, and we moved on, heading into the town square area.

"You could do it again. You could do it a lot here," she said as we passed by the coffee shop and bookstore.

I sighed. "I don't think so. I'm not like other shifters. Not even like other kelpie. I can't be seen by anyone—not humans or anyone else. In fact, the supes are more dangerous for me. Besides, I'm not staying long."

She turned and pulled into the parking lot for Whisper Falls Inn, a large and beautiful Victorian manor that sat catawampus on the corner, facing town square, a line of cottages behind it. She pushed the gear into park and turned in her seat to look at me.

"Like I said, I'm not going to pry. Any more than I already have. But don't leave because of him. I know he can be an asshole. Trust me. I fucking *know*. But you can still be here. I lived here my whole life and barely knew of him until recently. There's a lot this town has to offer, especially for someone like you. *Haven* is in the name for a reason."

I blew out another sigh. "My life is at home. I need to get back to it."

Needing to stop the conversation there, I opened the door and slid out.

Addie met me at the back of the Jeep. "Michaela's my BFF, and she owns the inn. I'll make sure she gives you a good deal."

Fifteen minutes later, Addie and her vampire best friend had me settled into a nice suite on the second floor. The inn was beautifully decorated, boasting a perfect combination of modern amenities while honoring its historical roots—the plaque by the front door said it was built in 1854, and that was a lot of history for this part of the country. My room contained a queen-sized sleigh bed, an armoire with a television inside, and a small writing desk in front of the window that looked out at the town square. It was feminine and beautiful, and more my style, but I already missed the masculinity of Savage's cabin.

Sighing and blinking back tears, I pulled out my sketch pad and sat on the bed. I'd intended to work on a new one-piece design, but without realizing it, I'd sketched an image of Savage. Damn it. Getting over him was going to be impossible. At least, until I left town and forgot him completely. That couldn't come soon enough.

Another vampire, a sassy redhead named Sindi, brought my dinner to my room, and I ate while writing a blog post, trying to keep my mind distracted. Later, my phone rang, showing Savage's number. I pressed the Ignore button. A couple of minutes later, it rang again: Niall.

"Where the fuck are you? Are you okay?" he demanded angrily as soon as I picked up. I could hear Savage yelling in the background.

"I'm fine. I'm at the inn."

Niall blew a harsh breath into the phone. "God damn it, Reyna. You had everyone in a fucking panic."

"Sorry. I thought you'd know."

He said something to Savage about calming down, then I heard footsteps followed by a door opening and closing and wind in the background. When he spoke to me again, he'd calmed down. "I came to get you, Rey. You couldn't wait a few hours?"

"For Savage to get there first?"

"You need to tell him. He was worried as fuck. Possibly more than I was. And now he's goin' to be fookin' mad."

"I will. Tell him that I'm okay. That I needed space, but I'll see him soon."

"Lie?" he asked.

"Unless you're ready to leave town right now, it's not a lie."

"Ach. We can't go, love. It's not safe for you out there."

"It's not safe here. You saw what happened last night."

He made a dismissive grunt. "That was a fluke."

"Yeah, well, I almost killed someone because of a fluke."

"You almost killed someone because he deserved it."

"I didn't know that, though!"

"Your kelpie did. I can see it clearly," he said. "As soon as you saw him, your kelpie knew something wasn't right about him, yeah? She knew he needed to die. Otherwise, she would have turned and run. She definitely wouldn't have let him get close enough to touch her, unless his arse deserved the outcome. *You* wouldn't have let him, Rey."

My mouth opened and closed, and I pressed my fingers to my forehead. "Our instinct is to kill."

"Our instinct is to draw out the evil and then kill, love. Only then. And I imagine yours is even more fine-tuned, considering what you are. The only other time the kelpie *has* to kill is in self-defense."

I rubbed my scar at the hairline in the center of my forehead. "Then why did Pops say I'd want to kill anyone I saw?"

"To scare you off from shifting. He knew you wouldn't want that guilt, so it was a way to force you to learn control."

The line fell silent for a moment as I let that sink in.

"Listen, love, I gotta talk to Savage before he destroys his own house. You're safe here. Relax. SIN-NO is dealing with some internal shit, and we're still tracking others who know about you. It's going to be a while before we can leave. Plus, I gotta do my part for the Havenwood Falls club. Getting them to protect you didn't come free, you know. At least, not at first." There was a loud crashing sound from his end of the line. "Gotta go!"

The call ended. I stared at the phone in my hand for a long while, still wrapping my mind around what he'd said about my kelpie's instincts and Pops lying about it. Guilt pricked my heart for being so mad at him when he died. He'd really done everything he could to keep me safe, even if his trust had been in the wrong place. Tears stung my eyes, and for the first time, I cried for him—ugly, loud sobs —missing him more than ever.

Then I cried for Savage.

My phone blew up with calls from him, but I ignored them. The next morning I awoke with puffy, swollen eyes to one message from him:

Just need to know you're ok. Tell me that and I'll leave you alone

I texted him back that I was and tossed my phone on the bed. Blowing out a heavy breath, I swung my legs out of bed to shower and dress. I had one night to feel sorry for myself, and it was over. Time to move on. He obviously was.

Knowing I had a lot to do for my business, I focused on work for the next two days, barely leaving my room except to grab something to eat in the inn's restaurant. My ears perked up every time I heard a motorcycle, and I found myself glancing out the window to see if it was him. His size alone would make him easy to pick out from most people, but I never saw him.

On the third day, there was a knock on my door.

"According to a little birdie, you've barely left your room. I thought you were on vacation," Addie said when I opened the door. "Instead, you're cooping yourself up in here and *working*."

I snorted. "I assume your birdie drinks blood."

"Among other things. Like coffee. But she's ditching our standing date today, so come join me for a cuppa joe. And a scone. Have you tried Coffee Haven's blueberry scones yet?" She licked her lips as though tasting them. "I won't take no for an answer."

I sighed. "Fine."

Grabbing my jacket and purse, I followed her downstairs, and we walked down the street to Coffee Haven.

"Oh, good. Willow's here. She has special blends for us special people, if you know what I mean."

A petite woman with silvery-blond hair turned from the espresso machine, her turquoise gaze falling on us. She smiled and came over to the long marble counter that looked like it belonged in an old-fashioned soda shop. "Hey, Addie. The usual?"

"Witch's Brew, yes, please."

"And for you?" The woman turned to me, her eyes narrowing. I sensed that she was fae—the light kind, possibly Seelie. Could she sense me, too? "I bet you'd like a Unicorn Fart."

I spluttered. "*Excuse me?*"

She and Addie both laughed.

"Their reactions get me every time," Willow guffawed, and Addie nodded, holding her belly from laughing so hard. The fae's expression eventually sobered. "Sorry. It's a special drink we recently started

340

offering." She leaned in and whispered, "It's magical." She wiggled her fingers and winked before straightening up. "It's colorful, too. My 14-year-old cousin Dalton named it. It's really good, though, if you like vanilla and a bit of mocha." She leaned in again, once more whispering, "And a little extra energy boost."

"Oh, um, I think I'll just have a grande vanilla latte."

Willow laughed and pointed at the menu board. "Try again."

Her subtle reminder we weren't at Starbucks. Her drinks' names and flavors were much more interesting, and I took my time studying them.

"Oh, for fu—" Addie started before Willow cut her off.

"Language," Willow warned.

Addie sighed. "For *goddess's* sake, just get the Unicorn Fart. You know you want it. It's really good, especially with the scones."

I sighed. "Okay, fine." I smiled at Willow, but she stared at me expectantly. "You're going to make me say it, aren't you?"

"Where's the fun if you don't?"

I laughed, shaking my head. "I'll have the Unicorn Fart, please."

Willow gave a warm smile. "Now that wasn't so bad, was it? We women need to ask for what we want more often, no matter how ridiculous it sounds, you know?"

She winked again before turning away to make our drinks.

The next day, Addie stopped by to invite me to lunch at Napoli's. Afterward, she showed me the ice skating rink at the park and offered to teach me to ski or snowboard, my choice. The following day, she and Michaela asked me to join them for drinks.

"We usually go to the Dirty Knuckle," Michaela explained as Addie drove us. She was turned in her seat to look back at me, trying to keep my attention on her. That usually wasn't hard because she had the most amazing grayish-green eyes that pulled you in, but I had a hard time because we were headed in the direction of Savage's cabin. My heart had picked up speed. "But uh, SIN's usually at the Knuckle."

Now she had my attention. Biting my lip, I nodded in appreciation.

"I also wanted to show you something," Addie said as we made a turn that took us away from Savage's road. My relief was short-lived. As we ascended the side of the mountain, the road twisting and turning its way up, I felt the magical pull of the other night. We were near the falls.

"I'm not sure about this," I said, apprehensively. What if I lost control again?

Addie caught my gaze in the rear view mirror. "I am."

We turned into a parking lot of a large log cabin with a sign that said *Fallview Tavern & Grille.* The inside was cavernous, with an almost dungeon-like vibe, but in a comfortable and nice way. Not formal, but far above a hole-in-the-wall biker bar. There was a lot of wood and ironwork, which I found interesting, considering the fae population. Although I barely felt it, a benefit of the tattoo's magic, according to Addie. But that's not what had my attention. The view of the falls right beyond the outside patio had me mesmerized, my veins thrumming.

"Can you feel it?" Addie whispered from behind me, her head so close to mine, her mouth was nearly on my ear. I nodded. "I figured you could. There's aether in the water—an ancient kind of magic. It calls to you, doesn't it?"

"Like no other water does," I admitted. "Which is saying a lot."

"But you're stronger than it. You're stronger than anything that tries to control you." Her fingers twitched in front of us as her lips moved silently, and she must have done a muffling spell, because now she rocked back, her voice nearly normal. "When I was little, I was taught how magic can try to control us witches, if we let it, but that we have to be stronger and learn to control it instead. Because once we can, the power works *for* and *with* us—we use it, rather than the other way around. So I sat by the falls for hours every day until I learned how to control their effect on me. Until I learned how to absorb that power and make it mine." She leaned forward again, twisting her head to look at me intently. "That's how you gain your freedom and independence, Reyna. Empower yourself, and then use that power to make the choices *you* want. It doesn't matter where you are or who you're with. You're free as long as you have that power within."

I looked over my shoulder at her, dazed by her words of wisdom.

Her brows jumped, as a small smile curved her lips. She whispered again, "You didn't hear that from me. If you try to say otherwise, I will vehemently deny that there's any magic in those waters until my dying day. It's not meant for everyone to know. You won't find anything like these falls anywhere else, though. I *can* guarantee you that."

I was lost in thought the rest of the evening, barely paying attention as Addie and Michaela introduced me to some of the locals whose names I'd never remember, and checked out some of the tourists. When their conversation turned to weddings and fiancés, I completely tuned out, because my heart couldn't take it. I focused on what Addie had said instead, concentrating on the buzz of the magic in my veins and taking control.

The next day, I was happy to see her when she knocked on my door.

"I need a favor," I said, motioning her into my room.

"What's up?" She glanced around before settling her gaze on me.

"You gave me special protection in my tattoo, right?" I waited for her to nod. "Can you make it work outside the wards? So that I can leave and still be safe?"

She frowned. "I don't know . . ."

"Please, Addie. I know you've been trying to get me to stay, but I can't. I need to go home, and the sooner the better, but Niall won't let me. I can't be here any longer, though. It hurts too much. And you were right last night—about taking control. This is what I want. I want to go home."

She gnawed on her lip. "I'm really not supposed to, but there might be something I can do. But first, I need to show you something."

I groaned. "You've shown me so much, and I really appreciate it, but you're not going to convince me to stay. Why do you care so much?"

She shrugged. "I like you. I like your aura and your energy. And I want you to be safe. It's not perfect here. Trust me, I know. But this place is specially made for people like you." I began to shake my head, but she held up a hand. "Just let me take you one more place. It's a beautiful day for January, I have to go out there anyway, and I think you'll like it. And then, you do what you need to do. What you think is best for you, and I'll help however you need me to."

"One more place on the grand tour of Havenwood Falls?"

"Just one more. I promise. And you probably shouldn't wear those shoes."

I changed into my hiking boots, which Savage had rescued from the pond, grabbed what I needed, and headed out with her. I'd already learned that she preferred to walk everywhere around town, so when she led me to the Jeep, I knew we'd be going beyond the town proper. We drove for a while, turning off the main road and pulling up to what looked like commercial horse stables. A man stood by one of the fences, watching a teenager walk her horse around a large pen. He was tall, with midnight skin, short-cropped black hair, and muscles bigger than tree trunks. He might have possibly been bigger than Savage.

"Avalar," Addie called out as we walked toward him. She was right —it was a pretty nice day for January, causing the ground to squish in a muddy, slushy mess. The unseasonable temperatures wouldn't last long, though, according to the weather reports calling for plenty more snow.

The man she'd called Avalar turned. "Addie Beaumont. Thanks for coming."

"I hear you have someone in need of some ink."

His eyes cut over to me, black and cold. "And you are—" He paused, his nostrils flaring as he turned completely toward me. His head cocked to the side. "I know exactly who you are."

I glared at Addie. She threw her hands up, palms out. "Don't worry. It's okay. He's . . . like you."

I shook my head. "Can't be."

"Not quite," he said at the same time. "But she's right. I won't hurt you—unless you give me reason to." He looked back at Addie. "You said you were bringing someone I could trust."

She lifted her chin, not missing the accusation in his tone. "You can. I guarantee she'll bring neither you nor the others any harm. She's no threat. She only needs to see."

He considered me again, his gaze studying me from head to toe. His nostrils flared. Finally, he lifted his chin and bit out, "Fine. But don't make me regret this, Addie Beaumont."

He called out to someone to come keep an eye on the girl walking the horse, then he led us through the horse barn. When we came out on the other side, magic zapped through me—the zing felt like that of the town's protection wards when Savage and I had crossed over on the motorcycle.

My breath caught at the sight before us—on this side of the magic, unicorns galloped around the field.

CHAPTER 11

"*I* thought I was the only one," I said with wonder.

They were breathtaking—three horses colored periwinkle, magenta, and mint green with long horns and flowing manes and tails. They appeared to be racing each other around the field.

"You're the only one like you," Avalar said from my side. "Unless I'm completely wrong, you're a kelpie, too, aren't you?"

I peeked over at him. "Yeah. How did you know?"

"I sense my kind in you, but your kelpie side is stronger. Our kingdoms in Faerie neighbor each other. My great-grandmother told stories about one of our kind leaving the herd to go live with the kelpie and how ever since, there was a black unicorn that roamed the worlds—Faerie and now this one—every few hundred years. Black is the only color we don't see in our herd. Like ours, your kingdom was decimated by war, and those who were left came to this realm. Also like us, I believe your herd has scattered to all parts of this world?"

My hand pressing to my chest, I nodded. "Many of the stories had been lost among our kind. So that's how I have a horn? I'm a crossbreed?"

"There must have been a certain amount of magic involved, too.

Our kinds can't normally reproduce together. I'd heard tell of one like you long ago. I didn't realize there was another."

Staring at the unicorns in the field, I frowned. "We can't reproduce. That's why we never know who will be the next one, not even in which family."

"That must be part of the magic. I don't know much about it. Just the stories that were passed down."

"So these unicorns . . ." I gestured toward the field.

"I'm the leader of the herd. I'm trying to collect them in one place again. Here, by Havenwood Falls. It's the safest place I've found on this earth for us. You surely understand the dangers for our kind in this world. And if the Seelie-Unseelie War in Faerie spills over into our kingdom, or gods forbid, into this world, we should all be together. With some help from the Luna Coven, we have this cloaked field, private and secure, where we can shift and stretch our muscles, so to speak."

I watched them run, their heads thrown back as they whinnied—the sound of joy. Of security. Of freedom.

"That was a dirty trick," I grumbled to Addie on our way back to town, after she'd given Avalar's most recent arrival a registry tattoo.

She shrugged. "Well, you weren't getting it through your stubborn head that you belong here. I have no idea if you belong with Savage or not, Reyna, but I feel it in my gut that you do belong in this town. And you know what they say about a witch's instinct."

"What?"

She looked over at me, square in the eye. "Never question it."

As we closed in on Havenwood Falls, the rumble of motorcycles came from behind us.

"Maybe it's coincidence that they've been following us for several miles, or maybe you're being tailed," Addie said, after glancing up at the mirror.

I turned around to look out the back window. Two motorcycles followed us, the riders clad in black. I didn't recognize the front one, but the second guy was definitely Niall, his beard blowing in the wind.

"Yeah, probably being tailed." I turned back around, a lump in my throat.

"That looks like Liam out front."

Liam and Niall. Not Savage. Of course. I turned around to verify, and the man in front surely wasn't big enough to be Savage. The lump dissolved, but my heart hurt that he hadn't wanted to be part of my security detail. I had to admit, if only to myself, I missed his inherent need to protect me.

"Well, if you still want my help, you know how to reach me," Addie said as she pulled in front of the inn. "But you do what you know is right for you."

Climbing out of her Jeep, I nodded and gave her a wave just as the two bikes pulled up, rumbling loudly. Addie took off, and the engines cut, the sudden silence nearly deafening for a moment. Both guys swung off the bikes, Niall removing his helmet and sunglasses before opening his arms for me.

"You remember Pirate," he said as he hugged me.

I nodded, but said nothing. Liam stood there for a moment, his hands on his hips, his face downward, but his eyes still covered, so I wasn't sure where he looked. When he lifted his head, I assumed he was looking at me, but I couldn't feel his gaze—not like I could Savage's.

"Look," he started, his voice raspy. "You got our protection no matter what, and this normally isn't my thing, but I gotta say it. Savage is my brother, in all the ways. Maybe not blood, but we've spilled plenty of it together to count." He scratched his head as it turned away for a moment. "I've never seen him like he is now. Last week, he reminded me of a Tychon I knew long ago, but hadn't seen in centuries. Not since Anna. He changed after her—not for the better, mind you—then got worse after Lyra. But now . . ." He rubbed his head again, and then his neck, his mouth twisting. "Look, I need our guys ready to do what needs to be done, and Savage always has been. But I don't need any loose cannons. Especially not him. I don't like him like this, Reyna. Last week, he was my old friend. Now, he's fucking lethal. And I don't want to have to escort his ass back to Hell and have to leave him there, if you catch what I mean."

I crossed my arms, tilting my head. "It can't be about me, though. I don't think he cares. Not that much."

Liam peered at me through his glasses, focused enough that I could now feel it. "Trust me. He fucking cares. More than I've ever seen him care about anything or anyone in over three hundred years of knowing him."

With that, he swung his leg back over his bike and fired up the engine. Not knowing what to say, I just stood there and watched as he took off again.

"We need to talk," Niall said, his arm still over my shoulders as he steered me toward the inn's entrance.

"What is this? An intervention?" I muttered.

He didn't answer, didn't say anything at all until we were up in my room. Even then, he only looked around at first, picking things up to inspect, brushing his fingers over the décor. He finally turned around and nodded.

"This place suits you."

I shrugged. Savage's place, masculine yet warm and comforting, like him, had grown on me—like he had.

My throat felt thick at the thought, and I swallowed. "So what do we need to talk about? Are we able to finally leave?"

Leaning against the wall, he crossed his arms over his chest. He looked so out of place, all leather and chains and heavy boots in my lovely little room. Staring at me, he frowned.

"Is that what you really want?" he asked.

"I want to go home."

He sighed. "New Orleans isn't safe, love. SIN-NO is fucked up. One of the pledges gave you up, and they're findin' other arseholes who have snaked their way in. I really don't want to go back there, meself. And honestly, we don't think it'll ever be safe for you again."

I sucked my lips between my teeth to keep from scowling and lifted my chin. "It's my home, Niall. I hear what everyone's saying. And a part of me would love to stay. But I miss home. I miss my life."

One of his dark brows arched upward. "And what's there now to make it home, lass? What's left? *Who's* left?"

I sucked in a breath, clapping my hand over my heart. "Ouch!"

He stood up and strode over to me, picking up my hands. "I'm sorry, love, but it's the truth. Pops is gone. What else is there?"

I looked around the room, as though the walls here would give me answers. "I don't know. My apartment. My friends. Everything I know and love. You—right?"

He rolled his eyes. "Of course. I go where you go. But your apartment is gone. Went up in flames right after we left. You knew you couldn't go back there, anyway. Your friends? Axle's been watching your old account records. Nobody's called you, Rey. And are you sure *everything* you love is there?"

Pulling my hands from his grip, I turned my back to him.

"Reyna, it's not safe. If you really want to leave, we can go anywhere but there."

I spun back around. "I don't want to go anywhere else! Nowhere is going to be safe for long, Niall. I don't even know if this place will be. But I'm done living out of fear! They're not going to scare me away from my home, god damn it!"

"Well, good then, lass. Don't live in fear." Niall ducked his head to look me in the eyes with his piercing sapphire ones. "But you'd better think real hard about what truly scares you. Are you goin' home to face one fear—only 'cause you're runnin' from a bigger one?"

He left me gaping at him, but as soon as the door closed, I sank onto the bed and dropped my head into my hands. Then after a while, I lay back and stared at the ceiling. And then I decided to fuck my rule of one night to grieve and let myself cry again. But this time was all for Pops and the life he'd tried to give me. The life we could no longer have, ever again.

He was really gone. He wasn't going to show up in a bar in the Quarter or come knocking on my apartment door. But if he did, or if he showed up here right this very moment, I knew what he would tell me. What he would want me to do. Hell, he and Niall had already tried to get me to come out here once.

I didn't know what time it was or how long I'd been sobbing before my eyes dried and I blinked up at the ceiling. My room was dark, and so was the window. Night had fallen, but how long ago remained a mystery. I rolled over and searched blindly for my phone.

It was nearly midnight. I blew out a sigh and pulled up the text app. If I was going to stay here, make this town my home, I had to overcome my real fear. Damn Niall for being so astute.

Me: Are you busy?

It took a moment for his reply to come, long enough to have me panicking that he wouldn't talk to me anymore.

S: On a job

Me: Liam told me to call you

S: Liam needs to mind his fucking business

Me: Was he wrong then?

S: Probably

My heart sank.

S: What did he say?

I hesitated, then swallowed my fear, empowered myself, as Addie had said, and charged forward.

Me: That you care

Me: About me

S: . . .

S: . . .

Me: If he's right, why did you let me go so easily?

S: . . .

S: . . .

S: Are we really talking about this over text?

Me: Well, I was going to go to your place but I don't have a car

S: Be there in a minute

Me: What about your job?

S: She just said she wanted to go home

Exactly a minute later, there was banging on my door, making me jump. I opened it, and Savage advanced on me, driving me into my room. He shut the door, hard enough to make the pictures on the wall rattle, without stopping until he had me up against the wall.

351

"I'm your job?" I asked breathlessly.

"I already told you—you're more than a fucking job." He looked down at me, then yanked his sunglasses off and really scrutinized me, his gaze tangible as it roved over my face, the carnal look in his eyes sending a shiver down my spine. "You're my everything, Reyna."

My heart skipped, and I blinked up at him. "Then why did you let me go so easily?"

"Why did you?" he growled back.

I cringed, then looked over his shoulder, unable to look at him, knowing the question was completely fair. "I . . . I was confused and . . . scared."

He gave a sharp nod. "Exactly. And you want your freedom and independence, so I was giving you that. I will give you anything you fucking want, even if it's not me."

My gaze flew back to his face. "I can't be your old lady, Savage. I can't be a possession that you own. Does it have to be an all or nothing deal?"

He leaned in, pressing his thick forearms against the wall, caging me in as he lowered his forehead to mine. "I need to fucking own you, Reyna. I need you to be *mine*. But not how you're thinking. I need to fucking own you the way you already own me—mind, body, heart, and soul. *All* of me is already yours. So yeah, it's all or nothing."

My heart raced as I stared up at him. His breaths came quickly, warm on my face, that oaky, smoky scent of his flooding over me. I could barely breathe myself, my head spinning with dizziness. My hands shook at my sides, and I pressed them against my thighs.

He waited patiently, lifting his head only enough to watch me. Could he see all the emotions rushing through me? He could surely hear my pounding heart. The vampires downstairs probably could. Because the strongest emotion of all was fear—and not of some unknown hunters who might be out there searching for me, not for what they would do to me if they ever caught me.

No, my biggest fear was of this man in front of me, of what *he* would do to me . . . to my heart.

I will not live in fear. I will trust in me, in him, in us. This is what I want.

My trembling hand lifted slowly and cupped the side of his face. His eyes falling shut, he leaned into it.

"If you intend to say goodbye, don't," he said. "Just tell me to leave."

I watched him, noticing how his body stiffened, bracing for the blow. "Tychon."

He didn't open his eyes, but exhaled a long, slow breath.

"Don't leave me," I whispered.

His lids flew open, his eyes bright as he looked at me for assurance. I nodded.

"Never," he growled, turning his face in my hand to kiss my palm. "You are mine."

Swallowing, I nodded. "I am yours."

Leaning up and into him, I tilted my head back. His lips crashed onto mine, his hands gripping my hips and pulling me closer, his fingers digging into my flesh. The way he kissed me, the way he held me, I thought he may never let go. I wasn't sure I wanted him to. Ever.

But the kiss slowed, then he broke it, but without letting go of his hold on me.

"I can't give you kids," he said roughly. "I won't do that to you."

I shrugged. "I can't have kids. But there are other ways to have a family . . . if we want one. That's probably a conversation for later, though. Much later."

He shook his head and chuffed. "My fucking unicorn."

I frowned. "You can't be calling me that. But why do you?"

One side of his mouth curled up. "You wrote in one of your blog posts about your dream mentor. That designer who's too close to perfect and you admire so much and wish you could meet just once because you know it will change your life. I'm pretty sure those were your exact words. But you wrote that you probably never will because the opportunities are so rare. You called her your unicorn."

I nodded, remembering the piece. Niall and Pops had been pissed, afraid it would give me away. That was years ago, long before I ever was discovered.

"So . . . you like my designs?" I asked, confused.

He rolled his eyes, then leaned in closely. "No, sweetheart, you're *my* unicorn. The one woman who's perfect for me, a once-in-a-lifetime experience. And I knew the moment I saw you in that dark room back in NOLA that you would forever change my life."

Oh, gods. My knees went weak.

"Tychon Savage," I breathed, "I am most definitely your fucking unicorn."

He studied me for a moment, his nostrils flaring, probably scenting the dampness between my legs. Then, breaking our embrace, he turned and threw open the closet, tossing my suitcases on the bed. With both hands, he yanked all my clothes out of the closet and threw them in one of the bags. I was too bewildered to protest at the way he treated my precious clothes. He emptied my drawers next, stuffing everything into the rest of my bags. When he was done only a few minutes later, he sent a text, stacked up all the suitcases by the door, and finally looked at me.

"We're going home," he rumbled, grabbing my hand and pulling me out the door.

"But my stuff . . ." I looked over my shoulder at my suitcases, but he was already closing the door.

"A prospect will bring them out." He hurried down the stairs, so fast I could barely keep up with him.

He said nothing more as we climbed on the motorcycle and he turned the engine over. His body heated, keeping me warm for the ride. The unusually nice weather had already turned, and I could smell snow on the air. When we arrived at the cabin and climbed off the bike, he grabbed my hand and led me inside. Once the door was closed, his body visibly relaxed, and he turned around to face me. Still he seemed surprised to see me standing there, in his house again. I heard the lock click into place behind him, before he strode toward me.

"Am I your prisoner again?" I asked, my voice lilting in a tease.

"No, I am yours," he rumbled before curling his large arms around me and pulling me into him.

My hands pressed against his hard chest, feeling the planes.

"Is this mine?" I asked.

"Yours," he rumbled.

Sliding my arms around him to move closer, I dropped one hand down to his ass, hard as a rock as I tried to give it a squeeze.

"And this?" I asked, leaning back to look up at him with a small smile.

He smirked and nodded. Then he grabbed my other hand, pulling it in between us and pressing onto the bulge in his jeans, nearly as hard as his ass.

I stroked my hand up and down.

"Oh, this is definitely mine," I declared as I gave a gentle squeeze. "All. Mine."

He growled. "Fuck yeah, it is."

And the next thing I knew, I was in his arms, and he was striding for the bedroom. I was naked by the time he dropped me to the bed. I lay back on my elbows, lifting my breasts and spreading my legs wide.

Looking up at him through my lashes, I purred demurely, "Now take what's yours, my savage beast."

And he did. He took, but he also gave. And gave, and gave, and gave. Until neither of us could give any more.

As we lay in his bed, thick flakes of snow drifting down beyond the window, I settled into his big, strong, secure, and comfortable arms, resting my head next to his. And I finally admitted it—*this* was home.

EPILOGUE

*D*eath is a part of life, and so is saying goodbye. For nothing is permanent in this world, and the only guarantee in life is that someday death will come, and so will the goodbyes. But they're the two things that make you feel most alive because they make you *feel*.

Two months ago, we buried Pops. I hadn't allowed myself to feel right away, and I hadn't allowed myself to say goodbye.

Two months ago, I met Tychon Savage. And he made me feel again. Because of him, I was able to say goodbye to Pops. Because of him, I was able to learn to live.

I'd been living a life of fear since I was twelve years old, and that wasn't truly living. It'd been so long, though, I hadn't known better.

Until I met Savage.

And now, as I watched him and my brother come through the door, laughing and carrying two cases of beer and a bottle of whiskey, my heart filled to bursting. A life of love—I knew it now. I understood it. I lived it.

"So?" Melaina asked from her seat on the sofa next to me as she eyed the guys.

We'd just been going over plans for a lingerie fashion show at Silk, her nightclub. She'd introduced me to Izzie Itzae, who owned

Pleasurez, an adult toy store in town, which would be handling sales at the show. Izzie and I were already in talks about partnering together in an online retail store for my lingerie and other designs.

"It's done." Niall turned, showing us his new patch on the back of his cut. The bottom rocker that had said New Orleans was gone, replaced with a bright white one with *Colorado* on it. "My arse is officially in SIN-CO."

Melaina and I cheered half-heartedly while Savage poured him a drink. She didn't like the club much more than I did, but we'd both accepted it as a part of our lives. And we were both glad that the club had voted for Niall to patch into it.

"So, now that you know we're definitely staying, are you two . . . ?" I nudged my shoulder against hers as she eyed Niall like she wanted to devour him.

She stood up and smiled down at me. "I don't know if he can handle this."

We laughed as she walked away. Niall plopped down in her place.

"She might be right," he muttered. "That lass is fookin' somethin' else. Or I should say, *someones* else."

This surprised me. "Really? I honestly thought she wanted—"

"Oh, she wants me. How could she not want a fine Scotsman like me?" He winked, then slouched down closer to me and lowered his voice to a soft murmur, his beard tickling my ear. "She's not like any woman I've ever met, Rey. Bloody amazin', she is. But she has lovers. Plural. And she wants more."

"That's right," Melaina called from the kitchen. He should have known she'd hear. "I don't know that there's ever enough for me."

Niall lifted his chin and grabbed his crotch. "You just need a bit of this, sugartits, and that'll be more than plenty."

A pillow flew across the room and slammed into Niall's head.

"Can you fucking not?" Savage growled.

"Yeah, let's not," I quickly agreed, needing to know no more. I changed the subject, turning to Niall. "So . . . the kelpies?"

"You really want to do this?" he asked.

I nodded. "I've thought long and hard about it, especially about what that Avalar guy said. He's right—the war in Faerie could spill into our realm. And if that happens, all hell could break loose. I want as much of my herd together as we can get."

"They'll expect you to be their queen."

"I know." I looked at Savage, and he nodded in support. "I can do this. I want to do this. Even if there is no war, our people deserve what we have here—a life where we can be who and what we're meant to be. What we want to be."

"Get it approved by that damn Court first," Niall said, "then I'll start reachin' out."

We didn't know how many would come, and because of the Court and the rules, it might not even happen at all. But I had to at least try. I owed it to my people.

After Niall and Melaina left, Savage pulled me into his arms and nuzzled his face into the crook of my neck. "You're already my queen. And my goddess. And my . . ." He seemed to falter as he searched for another word.

"Your unicorn," I supplied.

He nodded against my skin. "My fucking unicorn."

Yes, this was living. And I knew Pops and my parents were smiling at me from another plane, happy I'd finally found home.

We hope you enjoyed this story in the Havenwood Falls world featuring a variety of supernatural creatures. If you want to read more about Addie, she's in *Forget You Not* and *Lose You Not*, and she stars in *Break Me Not* and *The Collector: Awakening*, all in the main Havenwood Falls series. Read Melaina and Niall's story coming to Havenwood Falls Sin & Silk in Fall 2019.

Havenwood Falls is a collaborative effort by multiple authors.

Books in the Havenwood Falls Sin & Silk series:

Taming the Beast by Nadirah Foxx
Plans Laid Bare by J.D. Nelson
Shift of Fate by Victoria Escobar
Stolen Wishes by Victoria Flynn
Damned Allure by Justine Winter
Savage Salvation by Kristie Cook
Dark Seduction by Michele G. Miller & R.K. Ryals
Soul Laid Bare by J.D. Nelson
Stray With Me by E.J. Fechenda
Chase the Flames by Desiree Lafawn
Prison of Asria by Randi Cooley Wilson

More books releasing on a monthly basis

Also try the signature line, Havenwood Falls, and the historical paranormal line, Legends of Havenwood Falls

Stay up to date at www.HavenwoodFalls.com

Subscribe to our reader group and receive free stories and more!

ABOUT THE AUTHOR

Kristie Cook is a lifelong, award-winning writer in various genres, primarily New Adult paranormal romance and contemporary fantasy. Her internationally bestselling, award-winning Soul Savers Series includes seven books, as well as several companion novellas and short stories. Over 1.2 million Soul Savers books have been downloaded. She has also written The Book of Phoenix trilogy, a New Adult paranormal romance series. Her books have been featured in *USA Today's* HEA section, on Good Morning America, and in the Emmy's Gifting Suite.

Kristie also created, writes in, and publishes the award-winning Havenwood Falls shared world, a collaborative project with multiple series, dozens of authors, and countless stories.

Besides writing, Kristie enjoys reading, cooking, traveling, getting her hippie on, and feeding her addictions to coffee, chocolate, cheese, The Walking Dead, Game of Thrones, and Supernatural. She has lived in eleven states, but currently calls Florida home.

Email: kristie@kristiecook.com
Author's Website & Blog: http://www.KristieCook.com
Amazon: https://www.amazon.com/Kristie-Cook/e/B0046KG8R4?
tag=kriscook-20
BookBub: https://www.bookbub.com/authors/kristie-cook
Facebook: http://www.facebook.com/AuthorKristieCook

ACKNOWLEDGMENTS

Much appreciation goes to my parents, for supporting this crazy dream of mine and really being there when things get so hard, it seems impossible to go on. Thank you, thank you, thank you. But I really hope you never read this one.

So much gratitude to the Havenwood Falls Collective—our little family of authors, editors, and designers. I'm so glad you've joined me on this adventure and grateful for all you've done in growing, shaping, and molding this world. Sometimes I'm just overwhelmed and completely humbled that you've put your trust, time, and energy into me and this project. It's been so much work and so much fun so far. I hope you'll stick around!

Special thanks to R.K. Ryals, who helped create the hellhound lore and the SIN MC, and for allowing me to use Liam "Pirate" Peters. To Kallie Ross for the use of Willa, to Randi Cooley Wilson for Callie, to E.J. Fechenda for Willow, and to Megan Linski for Avalar. I know I dropped some other names and places that our authors created, so thank you all. Oh, and to Melissa Wright, for creating the SIN logo.

And last but far from least, thank you, dear reader, for giving me a few hours of your time for this book. I hope it was worth it. I'm always stunned that you love Havenwood Falls and the characters as much as we do. There's still much more to come so don't be a stranger. In fact, Addie's waiting for you to give you your tattoo.

AN EXCERPT

~ A Havenwood Falls Sin & Silk Novella ~

Havenwood Falls

sin & silk

Dark Seduction

MICHELE G. MILLER
R.K. RYALS

Dark Seduction (A Havenwood Falls Sin & Silk Novella) by Michele G. Miller & R.K. Ryals

He is tormented by the past. She is traumatized by her present.

Tied since birth to a darkness that longs to break free, spiritual psychic Harper Sinclair fights a never-ending battle with demonic spirits. Her only relief comes from the fallen angel whom she's long ignored deeper feelings for. Physically scarred and emotionally wounded from a year of fights and revelations, Harper is losing herself to the one thing she's always been afraid of: herself. And in the process, she's changing her relationship with the one friend she trusts the most.

Elias Jamison is a fallen angel. He lost his place in Heaven when he chose his friends over his creator. He fell, but he is not lost. For centuries, Elias maintained his innate goodness, fought against evil, and protected those in need—except for one. Grief-stricken, Elias pushed his loss aside for over one hundred years as he watched over the Freeman bloodline from afar, but the deeper his feelings grow for Harper Sinclair, the deeper old guilt digs in. Regret is a powerful tool when wielded against us, and vanquishing Harper's demons means confronting his own.

There's a little darkness in all of us. Are you ready to embrace it?

DARK SEDUCTION

BY MICHELE G. MILLER & R.K. RYALS

"Oscar Wilde," I whispered, the author's name rolling off my tongue, merely a breath in the middle of the night. The name was an odd thing to think aloud, but I'd been listening to an audiobook recently and, after the dream I'd just had, it was a Wilde quote I thought of as I locked gazes with myself in the mirror.

A dreamer is one who can only find his way by moonlight, and his punishment is that he sees the dawn before the rest of the world, I mouthed.

I thrived during the night, but I felt lost after the dawn. The darkness was my friend, the day my punishment for paying too much attention to the night. Hell, the darkness was my family, in the form of shadow demons and spirits. My constant companions.

My face was pale, my long brown hair a chaotic nest around my head, my eyes home to dark circles put there by too little sleep.

The bathroom mirror was too honest, telling me things I didn't want to know about myself.

As a spiritual writer who'd been brought into this world after my pregnant mother was stabbed by a necromancer's athame, I'd always been tied to darkness in one form or another. It was this gift that introduced me to the fallen angel who helped me understand myself and subsequently, the other fallen angel who became my closest friend.

It was Elias Jamison—my best friend—I thought of now, my gaze on my reflection. My breathing was too rapid, my heart pounding, beads of sweat clinging to my brow. All because I'd had a scorching hot, completely inappropriate dream about the man who'd slowly worked his way past my wall of defenses over the last year. I trusted him more than I did anyone else.

He'd helped save my life twice.

I wasn't an easy person to befriend. I was reclusive, but Elias didn't seem to mind. The way he checked in with me—the texts he often sent—was important to me. Which was why when he left recently, his absence affected me more than I thought it would.

Because you're angry, the spirits around me said bluntly.

"No," I argued. "It was good he left."

When Elias had disappeared on angel business, I honestly thought the distance would be good. I'd become too dependent on having him near. I needed to be more open with the friends I'd made recently, but while I'd become closer to the others in town the last year, especially after our recent alliance to battle against the one known as the Collector, it was still Elias I felt most comfortable with.

Until now. Until this dream. This was why I shouldn't sleep.

"Is this going to become a habit?" a snide voice asked. The bronze-barbed mace—he was basically a baseball bat on steroids—who lived with me bounced near the doorway, impatient and agitated. Desi—short for Destroyer—was a sentient weapon that shape-shifted into a huge lion with wings. He'd been a gift from the first and only lover I'd ever had. I didn't quite know what finally losing my virginity to a high-ranking fallen angel at twenty-three and being rewarded with a weapon said about me, but I was all about collecting odd experiences and memories.

Desi was annoying as hell, but I couldn't live without him. Some people spoiled their cats and dogs. I spoiled my ancient shape-shifting pet weapon. Go figure. He needed lots of love, attention, and validation.

"What woke you up this time?" Desi asked.

It wasn't a nightmare that had me this restless.

A red blush bloomed across my skin, and I turned on the sink to splash cold water on my face. Images of flesh on flesh, Elias's hands and lips in places I'd never imagined his hands and lips being before, burned into my subconscious. Elias was a big man, brawny and broad, a beard covering a handsomely rugged face. His voice was raspy, deep, and sexy in a rock star kind of way.

He'd called my name in the dream. Over and over again.

I stared at the running water, watching as it circled the drain and disappeared, the dream replaying in my head.

"Harper."

Elias breathed my name into my ear, surprising me, because I'd been asleep when he slid into bed behind me. His voice and the warm feel of his body woke me. I should have pushed him away, the shock of him being there bringing me to my senses, but all I felt was excitement and contentment.

"Finally," I whispered, because I wanted this. Really wanted this.

"Harper," he repeated, his arms pulling me into his embrace.

He was naked and hard. As was I—the naked part anyway— which was strange, because I didn't sleep naked. Tonight, however, there was only desire and need between us, his hand sweeping over the smooth contours of my stomach before slipping between my legs to caress me.

"You're wet," Elias said, satisfied.

His fingers slid through the moist heat to my clit, the sensation he caused with his touch so painfully pleasant that I almost lost it. My whimpers filled the room.

What was I doing? What were we doing?

"Elias—"

He stopped me with a kiss, rolling me over so quickly, I had no time to think before his lips crashed down onto mine, his tongue invading my mouth. His hand gripped my ass, our bodies pressed so closely together there was no space between us, the hard length of him hot against my belly.

"Tell me you're ready for me," he told me, pulling back to rest his forehead against mine, his breath fanning my lips.

"I'm ready."

He had me on my back in seconds, entering me quickly, as if he were afraid I'd change my mind. He filled me up completely.

"So tight," he growled.

His hips moved, and I lost the ability to think.

"Eli—"

I had woken on the verge of saying his name. My hand drifted to my stomach, the sudden tickle in my gut new and fresh and different.

"I want Elias," I heard myself say, my voice huskier and sexier than usual.

My eyes shot to the mirror, to the gaze staring back at me.

"What'd you say?" I asked myself. My free hand found my lips, my fingers tracing my mouth.

Desi snorted from his spot by the door. "Look what you've done to her. She's finally gone crazy," he said, his words directed at the dark spirits.

Shadow figures ducked in and out of the bathroom, ghostly images that played with my shower curtains and hissed at Desi.

Despite the chaos and their presence, the hand I had on my stomach drifted lower, and I jerked, forcing it up and away from my body.

"Out!" I yelled suddenly, my voice too rough. "All of you!" Embarrassment turned my skin hot, and I shooed the mace and ghostly shadows out the door before slamming it shut and turning to slide down to the floor. "Holy shit!"

I wasn't sure what bothered me more. The fact that I had been about to pleasure myself in front of a group of demonic spirits and a sentient weapon or the fact that I was about to masturbate while thinking about my best friend.

"What's going on with you, Harper?" I asked aloud.

The freaky thing wasn't me talking to myself or having sexy dreams about Elias. It's not like dreams could be controlled, and I talked to myself all the time.

It was the fact that I *answered* myself, my voice seductive when I said, "Being horny isn't bad. Not doing something about it is completely terrible for a person's health."

I knew what this was. This was me fighting with myself because part of me wanted what another part of me wasn't sure of, but fear and confusion shot down my spine nonetheless, immobilizing me. The last time I'd fought with myself like this, the last time I'd been this conflicted, was when I was taken captive by an evil doll—long story—and held in a creepy dollhouse for weeks in a nightmare that had ended with me physically wounded and emotionally bruised.

"No one understands you, Harper." The shadows returned, thick, dark, and seductive, their voices strong and powerful in my head. Their voices didn't sound like mine. I was used to their voices.

"But we *understand you. We understand you like no one else ever will. We understand your desire and your needs."*

Trembling, I slid back up the door and turned cautiously toward my mirror.

It was just me. The same plain Jane I'd always been—messy brown hair, scared green eyes, and a plaid pajama set that was two sizes too big.

This was the Harper I knew. Only there were dark forms crowded behind me, shadow people, their wispy, sinister arms outstretched as if to hug me.

"We are everything you will ever need and more."

Desi pounded on the bathroom door. "At least use the air freshener when you're done."

His light joke broke the tension, and the shadows scattered. A small, nervous laugh escaped me, my wide eyes dropping to my hands where they gripped the bathroom sink so tightly, the knuckles were white.

I felt like I was torn in two, completely divided between who I used to be and who I was tempted to be. I'd even started talking to myself in my sleep, getting up at night to leave written messages I found later. I'd once written a message in red lipstick on my mirror. It was hell to clean off.

Releasing the sink, I walked on unsteady, light feet from the bathroom, into the bedroom, and out into the kitchen. My hands were swifter than my brain, quick to make a cup of hot cocoa that I cradled in my palms, the warmth comforting.

Desi followed, quieter than he'd been before. It was hard reading him in weapon form. He didn't have eyes or lips. When he communicated, words were just *heard*. I didn't question how it worked. I was just glad he could speak, sarcasm and all, because he kept me from feeling lonely.

My mouth was full of hot chocolate when Desi murmured, "You feel different, and I don't think it's because you had a sex dream."

Holy hell!

Cocoa spewed everywhere. "You didn't just say that!"

"What did I say then?" he asked sweetly. "It's—"

"There are certain pet privileges you don't have."

"I'm not a pet," he spat.

Arguing was normal for Desi and me, but tonight it cloaked an entirely different problem. And it had nothing to do with dreams. I felt different. Antsy and impatient. As if my body was telling me I needed to *do* something.

My phone, which I rarely used because the signal tended to be bad in Havenwood Falls, lay on the kitchen counter, and I touched it lightly.

The urge to text Elias was strong, but I'd promised myself I wouldn't reach out to him until he returned. Elias had an entire life and problems of his own outside of me. Besides, it would be a little weird to text him after having an erotic dream about him, right? More so since it was the middle of the night.

I tapped the phone's screen and touched the messenger icon to scroll through our old texts. I was one of those people who never deleted anything.

Sweet memories surfaced, the messages a reminder of the first time I'd met Elias outside Coffee Haven. The day I realized he was open to befriending a naïve, shy girl who'd just experienced her first heartbreak and learned exactly how deep her ties to Hell and the spirit world went. Christmas in Havenwood Falls a year ago. Back when all I'd cared about was tackling a list of firsts.

A lot had happened in a year.

"You've got too much drama for being a loner. You need a fuck buddy." The moment the words left my mouth, my hands flew to my lips, my eyes widening.

Desi bounced up onto the counter, leaving scratches on the surface. He was going to ruin my house.

"Was that you?" he asked, incredulous.

It *was* me, but I was behaving differently than usual.

Me and *not* me.

"Because you have different needs now," the shadows revealed. *"Let go, Harper. Let go and be everything you were born to be. Listen to yourself."*

"Your eyes," Desi breathed.

Grabbing my phone, I clicked the camera icon and put it on selfie mode. My eyes were dilated, the black pupils completely overtaking the green.

"I'm pretty, aren't I?" I asked myself, a small smile lifting the corner of my lips.

Me and *not* me.

This me liked the way she looked in oversized plaid pajamas. She oozed a confidence about her messy hair and startled eyes that I lacked.

This me had a thing for fallen angel Elias Jamison, and she wasn't the kind to sit back and let him slide through her fingers.

"We know each other so well," I said aloud, my gaze on the camera. My finger pressed the picture key, my brows arched as it captured my image. "I should send this to him. I look good."

Was I possessed? All because of a sex dream? Did demons possess you if you had dreams about sex? Because if they did, the entire population was a walking exorcism project.

"Wow." Desi whistled. "You've officially lost your mind."

I didn't answer him because I was sending a picture text I wasn't sure I wanted to send.

Purchase **Dark Seduction** where books are sold.